FATAL FELONS

SAINT VIEW PRISON, #3

ELLE THORPE

WWW.ELLETHORPE.COM

Editing: Emmy from STUDIO ENP

Proofreading: Karen from BARREN ACRES EDITING

Cover design: Elle Thorpe at IMAGES FOR AUTHORS

Photographer: Wander Aguiar

Model: Jeff Burton

For Emmy.
I don't know what I'd do without your rainbow edits. Thank you
for all the years of making my books better.
Love, Elle x

1

HEATH

"Don't make this all be in vain. Take it! Escape."

I stared at Mae, then at her fingers, clutched in the shirt of Rowe's uniform. They didn't tremble. There was no sign of the chaos that pinged around my body, riling up adrenaline until my heart beat so fast I was sure it was going to pound right out of my chest and take off down the empty prison hallways without me.

If Mae was nervous, she didn't let on. All that showed in her beautiful eyes was a steely determination that I would not walk death row.

She was insane. They all were.

Rowe coughed, wincing as he straightened. He tried to hide the flash of pain, but I felt it like it was mine. The brown skin of his muscled torso was mottled with angry red marks from Liam's fists. They'd turn the ugly purple of bruises by morning.

I offered to help him up, but he pinned me with a glare that said if I touched him, he'd throw a punch of his own in my direction.

My hand dropped limply by my side.

Liam would be sporting matching bruises across his knuckles. He breathed heavy, his gaze pinned on Rowe, too.

Rowe undid the buckle of his belt and then the button on his pants. They fell around his black boots, which he pulled off with a groan of pain.

I clenched my fingers into fists. I fucking hated this. I wasn't worth his pain. I may have been sentenced to death for a crime I didn't commit, but I wasn't an innocent man either. I'd done things in my past. Horrible, unspeakable things that had finally come around to claim their penance.

He kicked his boots in my direction and then did the same with his pants.

I wasn't doing this. I'd go down, but I wouldn't drag any of them with me.

Anger flashed in his eyes, no less potent because he stood in nothing but black boxer briefs. Like he hadn't just taken several slugs of Liam's fists to his face and ribs, he stalked across the tiny cell, so we were eye to eye.

Electricity crackled between us.

He was pissed. More pissed than I'd ever seen him. His hot breath mingled with mine. "Put. Them. On," he growled.

I didn't move.

The palms of his hands hit my chest, delivering a bruising shove that sent my back into the cinderblock wall. And then he was yanking at the prison-issue clothes I wore, yanking my shirt up, his fingers grazing my abs, while I fought him off, grabbing his wrists.

Frustration poured off him in waves. He stepped back, snatching his arms out of my grasp and turned to Liam. "Hit me again."

Liam didn't hesitate. He threw his fist into Rowe's midsection.

It was a hard punch, landing solidly with a smack of skin against skin, but if Rowe felt it, he didn't show it.

It was me who cracked under the pain. It ripped through my midsection, churning my stomach until I was sure I was going to vomit.

"Again," he demanded. He turned to me, though his words were still directed at Liam. "Don't stop. Don't stop until he's gone."

Liam landed another blow that I felt just as heavily. My hold on my patience disintegrated. Not caring if I hurt him, because he was already hurting himself, I shoved Rowe up against the wall. "Stop this," I hissed at him. "I'm not gonna fucking watch him beat you to death!"

His gaze strayed to my mouth for half a second, and dammit if I didn't want to lean in and kiss him.

I didn't dare. He inched closer so his mouth grazed mine, not in a kiss, but the touch still lit me up inside. His lips trailed along the stubble of my jaw to my ear. "Well, now you know how we feel. Either you watch me die right here, right now. Or I watch you die with a lethal injection hanging out of your arm."

I blanched.

He pulled back, glaring at me once more. "I'm not doing it, you hear me?" He snatched the shirt from Mae's hand and slammed it against my chest. "Put the fucking clothes on, Heath."

Something flickered inside me.

Nobody had ever cared about me the way these three did. Not my father. Not my mother, who had laughed when I told her I was in prison. Not even Jayela, who had claimed to love me but could never truly commit.

I didn't want this to be over. A full life played out before me, taunting and teasing images of being surrounded by people who cared about me as much as I did for them. Family in the true sense of the word. The one thing I'd always craved more than anything. I'd found it here, with three people who were determined to give up everything for me.

A tear dripped down Mae's cheek. Liam stood behind Rowe, gaze trained on me, waiting for me to make a decision.

This wasn't over.

I grabbed the back of my shirt with one hand and yanked it over my head.

Mae let out a tiny cry, but it was one filled with relief. Then there was a flurry of movement as Rowe and I swapped clothes, right down to our socks. His boots were a size too small, but the pinch around my toes was nothing compared to the beating he'd taken for me, so I didn't say a word.

"What's the plan?" Mae crouched on the floor with me, both of us tying my shoelaces. "Where's he going to go?"

Liam folded his arms across his chest. "You can't go home. Or anywhere you would have gone before. Not to any of our places either. All of us could be investigated."

I eyed him. "So what? I just wander around Saint View until the dog squad catches up with me?"

"Rowe's cabin," Mae interrupted.

Liam shook his head. "We're making it look like Heath jumped him, but there's a good chance they'll have Rowe as the first suspect in aiding Heath's escape."

Rowe struggled into my prison uniform. "Yeah, but my registered address is still the house next to Norma's. They'll go there first if they do suspect me of being involved. It'll buy us time. And if I do a good enough acting job, they'll cross me off the list before they look any further than that.

You know how to get through Saint View to Old South Road? It's by the Mountainside turnoff."

I tied the final knot on my shoelaces and stood. "I know it. I go fishing around there in the summertime."

"You need my ID pass and the codes. Two-five-four-six to get through the solitary doors. Eight-five-four-five to get out the main ones. Repeat them."

I mumbled the numbers a few times until Rowe was satisfied, and then the four of us stood staring at each other, inching in so we formed a tight circle.

Liam eyed me. "You can't take any of our cars without drawing huge suspicion. Stay off the main roads." He cracked the tiniest of grins. "If you have to, dredge up those old high school memories and hot-wire a car."

"What makes you think I ever hot-wired a car?"

All three of them stared at me with disbelieving expressions.

"Fine. I might have stolen a car or two, but I didn't make a habit of it. I doubt I could still do it, even if I could find a car old enough. But I won't have to. I know Saint View. I know the backstreets and alleys. I'll get myself to the cabin." I filled my voice with a confidence I didn't feel. Because I knew, deep down, that this wasn't going to be even half as simple as I was making it out.

I picked up Mae's hand and squeezed her fingers between mine. She looked up at me, her nerves finally showing through beneath her bravado.

"Be careful," she whispered.

"Always." I leaned down and placed confident lips against hers.

She pressed up onto her toes immediately, wrapping herself around my body and clinging like it was the last time she was going to see me.

I clung to her right back, because there was every chance this would be the last time. I was well aware that the guards in the towers surrounding the perimeter weren't shooting blanks. Rowe's guard uniform was still only cotton and polyester.

It wasn't going to protect me from a bullet in my back.

I breathed in the scent of her hair and the taste of her lips. Nerves kept me from deepening the kiss the way I wanted to, but it was enough to just hold her.

Liam and Rowe watched, but there was nothing sexual in it this time.

When I pulled away, I turned to the two of them. "See you on the outside?"

They nodded.

I swallowed hard, then drew them both in, hugging them both quickly and a little awkwardly before stepping back. I couldn't look at Mae again.

With my gaze to the floor, I slipped out the cell door to escape.

2

ROWE

*T*he moment Heath walked out the door, relief cascaded over me. We still had a long way to go, but getting him to actually agree to try had been half the battle.

When the doors closed behind him, I had no regrets. I hadn't been lying when I said I wasn't going to stand by and just watch somebody else I cared about die. Not if there was anything I could do about it.

Steeling myself for what I knew had to happen, I turned to Liam. I sucked in a deep breath, letting it fill my lungs beneath the ugly prison-issue clothes. I closed my eyes. "Do it."

Liam hesitated.

"Do what?" Mae asked.

Neither of us could face her. It was one thing for me to take punches from Liam, but both he and I knew that a few bruises across my ribs and a black eye wasn't gonna cut it when the cops interviewed me.

We had to go all out.

Liam grimaced at me. "Fuck man, I don't want to but..."

"I know. Just do it. If you do it well, I won't feel it for hours."

"Mae, don't watch."

Her eyes went wide. "Wait, Rowe—"

Liam's fist connected with the side of my head, and the world spun around me. I stumbled forward, vaguely aware of him catching me, before the darkness took hold completely.

3

HEATH

*I*t killed me to walk away from Solitary and leave Mae and the others behind. I didn't want to do this alone, and yet I didn't want them with me either. If they got caught, there'd be no explaining it. With every step toward the main exit, I clutched Rowe's employee ID card and chanted the codes beneath my breath. I wouldn't pause when I got there. I wouldn't rush and give away the nerves that coursed through my body. At this time of night, there was nobody around, and most of the cameras in this shoddy prison had either never worked or hadn't been replaced after the riot. But if there was a working camera? It would highly likely be the one on the main entrance and exit.

I made it there without incident, keeping my eyes down. Rowe wasn't much shorter than me, and from behind, with his cap pulled low on my head, we could probably be confused for each other. But if they got one glimpse at my face, I'd be recognized instantly. I hadn't exactly managed to keep the low profile I'd wanted while I was in here.

I swiped Rowe's card and then punched in the memorized code. I don't know why I was surprised when the lock popped. Maybe there was still a tiny part of me that suspected Rowe was setting me up.

That door swinging open put all doubts to rest. We might have started on opposite sides, but that line had blurred somewhere along the way, and now, as I walked out into the main waiting room, I realized there was no longer a line at all. Rowe had my back.

Just like I'd had his.

I still hadn't come across another soul. I crossed the dingy reception area, taking a quick peek over at the visiting rooms, visible through clear plexiglass. I was never going to sit at those tables again, wishing I could reach across them to hold Mae. Either this insane plan would work, and I'd get to hold her as much as I liked, all day, every day. Or any minute now, sirens would blare, metal doors would slam down, and I'd be dragged off back to solitary where a lethal injection would be waiting for me at the first available opportunity.

It wasn't going to be the latter.

At the main exit, cool night air kissed my skin, and despite still being within the confines of the prison gates, it felt like freedom. Trying to keep my posture as casual as possible, I headed for the gate, praying the guard on duty would be asleep. My mind raced with ways to explain why I was leaving on foot when Rowe's car was sitting in the parking lot.

"Shit," I muttered to myself. "Think, dumbass. Think."

I didn't focus well under pressure. It had never been my forte. It was why my father had always called me brick head. I was big and broad and dumb. Only useful on a football field, but I hadn't even been good enough at that to please him. He'd reminded me of it every time he got drunk and came home wanting a fight.

"Good thing you're big, because you sure ain't smart."

"Obviously no brains in that thick head of yours. You take after your mama."

The words might have been uttered twenty years ago, but they were always there in the back of my mind. They never went away, just like the memories of him. Time hadn't diminished them one iota.

I hit the final gate separating the prison and the outside world. I swiped Rowe's card and punched in the code for the last time. To my right, the cement box of the guards' hut sat silently. If there was anyone inside, I couldn't see them through the dark glass. I didn't dare look for long. I simply pulled the pedestrian gate shut behind me and kept walking. One foot in front of the other, head held high, shoulders pulled back. Twenty yards and I'd be in the clear.

"Hey."

I didn't stop. But inside, everything shriveled at the sound of the guard's voice.

"Hey! Stop for a second."

I had no idea what to do. I wished I were Liam. He would have known instantly. Or Mae. They were both so smart, they probably would have come up with a believable excuse in seconds, but they'd left it to me. All I had was a head full of my father's voice telling me I was too dumb to breathe.

I couldn't run. I was fast, despite my size, but nobody was faster than a bullet.

I spun on my heel, facing off with the guard in the darkness. I peered at him from beneath the brim of Rowe's hat. He wasn't familiar.

"What are you doing?"

I filled my voice with a confidence I didn't feel. "Going home."

"Shift doesn't change for another hour."

"Got let off early."

The man stepped out of his booth and walked toward me, his heavy boots, identical to the ones I wore, crunching over the dry summer grass. "I'm Maynard. I don't think we've met yet, right? I only started after the riot. Got brought in by Tabor after he fired half the staff. I worked with him at his last prison. Good guy."

"Yeah, the best." I barely managed to stifle my sarcasm. Tabor was a walking, talking sadist.

The guard kept coming, his hand held out for me to shake.

Panic speared through me. I couldn't get that close to him. It was one thing to talk to a guard in the dim light at the edge of the floodlights illuminating the prison, but another thing entirely for him to be close enough to identify me. Just because I didn't know him, didn't mean he didn't know me.

I held my hand up in a stop motion. "Ah... Might not want to come any closer. I'd shake your hand, but truth is, you hear about that stomach bug going around Gen Pop?"

The man made a face, dropping his hand to his side and wiping it on his pants, as if he'd caught my fake germs from a distance. "Shit. That why you're going home early?"

I eyed the gun holstered at his side before forcing my attention back to his face. "Yeah. I've got a bit of a walk, too, and I'm kind of living on borrowed time here, if you know what I mean."

That was actually true, just not in the way I was implying.

His hand rubbed across his stomach, like he was

suddenly feeling a little bit sick himself. "Yeah, right. I gotcha. Go. See you around."

With a half-hearted wave, I turned and hurried into the darkness. By the time I got around the corner, out of sight of the prison, I realized I truly did feel sick. But there was no time to stop and heave like my body wanted to. Hell, if I could have, I probably would have curled up in the fetal position right there on the side of the road.

But this wasn't all going to be in vain. I was out. I moved through Saint View stealthily, sticking to the shadows, turning down backstreets and alleys and for a while, everything around me was quiet. For a big guy, I could move silently when I needed to. It came from years of avoiding my father. If he couldn't find me, he couldn't beat the shit out of me.

For the first time in months, a tiny bit of the weight lifted from my shoulders. I didn't deserve that death sentence. Not back then. Not now. If I went down for Jayela's murder, then the person who did kill her walked free. I could practically feel Jayela on my shoulder, urging me on, demanding that the true murderer be found. As much as she was a stickler for the rules, she was also a stickler for justice. She wouldn't want me dying for a crime I didn't commit, while the real murderer was free to take another life. Jayela's blessing was a whisper beneath my father's taunts, but it grew louder with every step I took away from the prison until hers was the voice I heard loudest.

It whispered other things, too.

Look after my sister. She needs you. Be happy.

Happiness. I couldn't remember the last time I'd truly experienced that, but an inkling told me it might have been those nights on the couch with Mae, back when we were just friends, when we would talk for hours about nothing and everything. I wanted more of that. I wanted a life.

A siren pierced the air, as loud and obnoxious as a tornado warning. Except the sky was filled with a fat full moon and a galaxy of stars.

The only tornado in sight was the one I'd created.

They knew. And they were coming.

4

MAE

*D*espite attempts to catch him, Rowe fell to the cell floor with a sickening thud, taking Liam down with him. Liam's head cracked off the wall, but it was Rowe's lifeless body on the floor that terrified me.

I dropped to my knees beside him, pressing my fingers to his neck, checking his pulse. "My God, Liam! What the hell?"

Liam disentangled himself from Rowe's deadweight. "He's fine. I just knocked him out. He knew it was coming." He shook his hand. His knuckles were bruised, bleeding, and rapidly swelling. "Fuck. That really hurts. He's got a hard head."

I stared at him with big eyes. It would have almost been laughable except that none of this was funny.

Liam sobered. "How's his pulse?"

"Fine, I think. My first-aid knowledge is pretty basic, though."

Liam eyed him for a moment. "If he ever played high school football, he's probably had worse." He held a hand out to me. "We've gotta go."

I knew he was right, but walking away from Rowe when he was unconscious didn't feel right.

"Mae, come on. This was his idea. Don't let your feelings ruin it now. We need to get to Heath. It won't be long before they find Rowe, and then they'll call the cops, and then they'll bring the dogs. Heath can't be wandering around Saint View on foot when that happens."

I knew he was right. Part of my heart was already out on the street, searching for safety, but another part of it was right here and hurt. I was torn right into pieces. The third grabbed my hands and dragged me from the room. I let him, because of the two of us, he was the one thinking more clearly.

We beelined straight for the parking lot without coming across anybody else and got in Liam's car. I flashed my access card at the bored-looking guard, and he opened the boom gates to wave us through.

Both of us heaved a huge sigh of relief as the prison disappeared behind us in the darkness. But it was short-lived. I glanced over at Liam who was staring out the driver's-side window, scanning the shadows instead of paying attention to the road.

I nibbled on a fingernail. "We should have left together. What if we can't find him?"

"You know we couldn't. Even if none of the cameras work, the guard on the gates would have been an eyewitness. Then we'd have been on the run, too."

He was right, but we hadn't even thought to make a meeting place. It had all happened too quickly. "How do you know we're going the right way?

He shook his head. "I don't. But I do know Saint View. I know the way I would have gone. And this is it. So keep an eye out."

I stared through the windows as we drove around the streets, but there was nothing out of the ordinary. It was just house after house, some more run-down than others. There were people out on the streets, but not many, and the ones who were looked mostly up to no good. They congregated on street corners in groups of three or four with seemingly no purpose to being out at this hour. That worried me, too. But I was also well aware that Heath could hold his own. At least against a couple of thugs hanging around after dark.

Against an entire police force all searching for him? That was a different story.

"Are we crazy?" I asked Liam.

He choked on a laugh. "I think you already know the answer to that one. We're driving around Saint View in the middle of the night, searching for the convicted murderer and death row prisoner we just helped escape."

"Well, when you put it like that..."

Liam and I looked at each other, and both of us burst into laughter. It wasn't the good kind, though. It was the kind that nervous energy escaped through when there was no other option for release. It died off quickly, and both of us went back to searching the streets for Heath.

When the siren started up from the prison, it was barely a surprise. Liam glanced at the clock on the dashboard. "A fifteen-minute head start. Twenty-five max by the time they call the police and assemble the dogs."

"That's not much time, is it?"

Liam pressed his lips together. "No. It's not. We need to find him. And now."

5

ROWE

"Stand back! Give him some room, Goddamn it!"

The headache was so instant and severe that I immediately wished I could pass out again. A siren wailed in the background, doing nothing to help the spearing pain. The groan that seeped out between my lips wasn't put on. It really did hurt that bad. I would need to ask Liam where he'd learned to punch like that because fucking hell.

A bright light flashed in my eyes. "Rowe? Can you hear me?" Perry screeched in my face.

I winced again and waved her torture device away. "Yes. Pretty sure they could hear you on Mars, you're so loud."

She frowned but lowered her voice. "Sorry. Was just making sure you weren't dead."

"Not dead." I tried to sit, but the world spun around me again, and Perry pinned me to the floor by my shoulders.

"Don't move," she demanded. "There's an ambulance on the way."

I shook my head, but that was a huge mistake. "What happened?"

It was only partially a lie. I knew exactly how I'd come to be lying on the floor in a solitary cell, but nothing after that.

"Heath Michaelson attacked you and escaped. Do you remember any of it?"

I twisted slightly, making sure Mae and Liam were nowhere to be seen, but the only people I saw were Perry, two new guards I didn't recognize, and the scowling face of the new warden, Steven Tabor.

My gaze met his, and it burned through me like a wildfire, searching out every scrap of fuel, every dry leaf, anything so it could build into something deadly.

It was a stare that said he knew what I'd done, even if he couldn't prove it. It was a stare meant to intimidate. Meant to force a confession from my lips.

But it had the opposite effect on me.

I smiled at him.

"I don't know," I said, answering Perry's question. My voice came out a little slurred, which I probably could have corrected, but I let my tongue move lazily, drawing it out. My brain was fuzzy, and moving hurt, but there was a clear voice in my head that told me to stay alert, to watch what I said, because giving anything away now would not only be a disaster for Heath, but also for me. Probably better I just closed my eyes and said nothing at all.

I didn't mean to drift off.

Perry's voice grew frantic, and I was vaguely aware of her fingers pressing into my shoulders and her fight to keep me awake, but her voice grew dimmer and dimmer until I couldn't hear her at all.

I slunk into the blissful darkness once more.

6

HEATH

*R*owe's shirt clung to my biceps, digging into the skin. Sweat dripped down my back, plastering the thin material to me uncomfortably as I ran through the backstreets of Saint View. The siren never let up. It wailed through the quiet night, drawing people from their homes and forcing me to hide in alleys until they lost interest and went back inside. I couldn't risk any of them seeing me. How long would it be before my face was all over the news? Not long, I imagined. I'd probably be the most wanted man in America if I managed to last the week, and the safety of the woods was still too far away. Though I knew Saint View from my years of living here, it was also a highly populated area, with too many eyes just waiting and watching, ready to turn me in at just the sniff of a reward.

I craved the solitude of the woods, but getting there on foot was no longer an option. I needed to move, and move fast. From my hiding spot behind a rusted refrigerator in a vacant lot, I eyed a van parked beneath a broken streetlight. It was old, but if it ran, it was probably my best bet at hot-wiring a car to use as an escape vehicle. I didn't want to do it.

Even as an irresponsible teen, stealing other people's possessions had never sat well with me. I'd gone along with my friends because that's what dumb teenage boys did, and I'd been desperate to fit in, but all I could think about, then and now, was how hard people had it around here. Banks didn't give people in Saint View loans. So if you owned a car, you'd probably scrimped and saved every cent to buy it. It was likely your pride and joy. It also probably didn't have insurance.

In the distance, dogs barked. I froze. I had no way of knowing if it was a dog squad or just somebody's backyard pet. But a pounding urgency filled my muscles, telling me I'd left it as long as I possibly could and that if I didn't get my ass into a vehicle, a dog would track me down in a matter of minutes.

I waited for the elderly man standing on the porch to lose interest in the sirens and go back inside his house. "Sorry, Mister." I crept from my hiding spot and rounded the car, keeping to the shadows. "I swear I'll bring it back in one piece." I lifted the handle and screwed up my face in frustration when the door was locked. I tried the one at the back, but that didn't budge either. "Fuck."

Breaking the window would be noisy and draw attention, but if I was lucky, maybe the wailing siren would cover it. In the darkness, I pulled off my shirt, wrapping it around my fist, and threw back my arm, readying to plunge my hand through the glass.

Headlights lit me up like I was a freaking Christmas tree. I froze, arm in mid-swing and knowing full well that whoever was driving had caught me red-handed.

I covered my eyes with one hand when the lights blinded me. It was all over. By now, they'd have cops all over the neighborhood. More dogs barked, probably only one street away, following the trail I'd unintentionally left for them.

"Need a ride?"

I dropped my hand. Liam's face poked out the driver's side window.

I gaped at him. And then ran for the back door, yanking it open and throwing myself across the back seat. "Took your sweet-ass time, Banks."

Liam grinned back at me. "Nah, we've been hanging around just waiting for you to take your shirt off."

I shook my head because there was really little else to do. Liam could find a smart-ass comment in any situation, it seemed.

My gaze drifted to Mae as Liam put his foot down on the accelerator. "How you doing? Having some serious second thoughts right now?"

To my surprise, she shook her head no.

I raised one eyebrow as we whizzed through the streets of Saint View. "No? Because I sure am."

She twisted in her seat, the belt stretching with her. She reached into the back and picked up my hand, threading her fingers between mine. "You don't belong in there. You belong here. With me."

Nobody had ever made me feel the way Mae did. I didn't know how I'd missed it all those years ago, when I'd been dating her sister. I should have seen the amazing woman she was. How kind and caring, always making you feel like whatever you brought to the table was enough. I'd never felt more important than in that moment. I couldn't help myself. I grasped her face between my hands and put my lips softly to hers.

She trembled beneath my touch, despite her brave words.

I dug my fingers into the muscles at the back of her neck, kneading out the hard rocks of tense muscle beneath her skin. "It's gonna be okay," I assured her. "We just gotta get to Rowe's cabin so we can regroup and work out a plan. A proper one, not something thought up on the spur of the moment when emotions are riding high."

She pressed her forehead to mine and nodded.

I closed my eyes, just drinking in the touch of her. "I'm a lucky son of a bitch."

Liam swore low under his breath. "Maybe just a son of a bitch. Because I think our luck just ran out. There's a police blockade ahead."

Mae whipped around, facing the front.

I ducked instinctively, flattening myself out against the back seat. But not being able to see what was happening was terrifying. "Talk, guys. What's going on out there?"

"There's three police cars blocking the road."

The instinct to stick my head up and have a look was strong, but I was smart enough to stay down.

Mae glanced over her shoulder. "Can you crawl through to the trunk, maybe? Do one of the seats fold down?"

"Even if they did, I'm six-foot-four. Unless Liam's BMW turns into a four-wheel drive, I'm probably not going to fit."

"No need for that," Liam piped up. "We're not going through the checkpoint."

Mae's panic was palpable. "We're not? That's the only way to Rowe's cabin. Where else are we going to go? If they've got this road blocked, they've probably got every road out of Saint View cut off."

Liam nodded grimly and swung the wheel down a tiny side street.

I groaned. "They would have seen you turn off. They'll send someone after us."

Liam put his foot down on the accelerator right as the police sirens started up, confirming my theory.

I closed my eyes, shaking my head a little bit. "Well, it was nice while it lasted."

"Defeatist, much?" Liam bit out, eyes on the road.

He made another turn, and Mae let out a squeal, slamming into the passenger side window. I let out a grunt as I half fell off the seat.

He put his foot down harder, and the car lurched forward. When I snuck a look at Liam, his grin was ear to ear. "Are you seriously grinning that were in a police chase right now? What are you, some closet adrenaline junkie?"

Liam laughed. "What do you think court is? It's an adrenaline high all in itself. Does it really surprise you that I like fast cars? And don't be insulting. It's not a police chase if they can't find me. It's hide-and-seek." He spun the wheel again, taking us down another unfamiliar street.

But Mae seem to recognize it. "Liam, isn't this your..."

Liam nodded and turned into a driveway. He steered off the crumbling cement, bouncing his car over the grass and pulling it around at the back of the house. "Yeah. It's my mom's place. Let's go see if she'll let a couple of fugitives hang out with her for the night."

7

MAE

*A*s quietly as I could, I closed the door to Liam's car, my palms damp with sweat. Even still, Heath jumped at the noise. I put a steadying hand to his arm.

"We need to get inside," he murmured.

He was right. There were no fences around Liam's mom's place, which had made it easy for us to just drive around the back. But it also meant we were very exposed. All the neighbors could see everything we were doing.

All three of us tensed as the wail of a police siren flew past the front of the house without slowing, its blue and red lights reflecting off the windows of the house next door.

I held my breath, waiting for them to turn around and come back. At any minute, they'd realize we were here and come storming in, guns drawn, shouting about putting our hands in the air, cuffs flashing.

It didn't happen, but it didn't help my nerves any. Neither did the jarring ring of my phone. It split the quiet air around us, and I dove on it, desperate to silence it before it drew any further attention.

I was just about to press my thumb to the cancel call

button when I noticed the name on the display. I flashed it to the guys while silencing the ringer. "It's Perry."

Heath's eyebrows knit together, while Liam found an old silver key on his keyring and fit it to the back door.

The lock clicked, and Liam blinked. "Can't believe she hasn't changed the locks in all the years since I lived here."

He stuck his head inside to call out to his mom, but when nobody answered, he nodded at me.

"We've already made that much noise. I don't think anyone is here. Answer it. Put her on speaker so we can hear what's going on."

I nodded, trying to pull myself together. I liked Perry a lot, but I couldn't tell her what we'd done. I couldn't tell anyone. It was a relief to find Liam's mother wasn't home. Although we did need somewhere to stay, I didn't want to involve anyone else in this.

I took a deep breath and lowered my voice, trying to emulate the scratch I'd have if I'd been woken up. At 1 a.m., I should have been sleeping. "Perry?" I asked. "What's wrong?"

She cleared her throat. "Mae. Listen, I'm sorry to wake you, but something's happened. Heath—"

"Is he okay?" I closed my eyes, hating that I had to lie to her. But I couldn't tell her the truth. I had to play along.

"Honestly, I don't know. He escaped."

My acting performance was Oscar worthy. "How?"

"He beat the shit out of Rowe." There was an anger in Perry's voice I'd never heard before.

I glanced over at Heath, who had absolutely not done any such thing, and then at the bruising and dried blood across Liam's knuckles. Quickly, he tucked them into his pockets and walked stiffly from the room.

I bit my lip. Until that moment, it hadn't even occurred

to me that he might have been upset about what he'd done to Rowe. It had been for a good reason, and yet, Liam had hurt one of his best friends. That couldn't feel good. "Is Rowe okay?" I asked. "Where is he? In the infirmary with you?"

"No. I called an ambulance and had him taken to the hospital. He's still unconscious as far as I know."

"What?"

He shouldn't still be unconscious, should he?

Liam reappeared, eyes wide. He obviously thought the same thing.

"I'll go down there," I told Perry. "He needs someone with him. He doesn't have family."

"Unless you're listed as his next of kin, they're not going to let you in until morning. Sit tight. If I hear anything, I'll let you know, okay?"

I sank down on one of Liam's mom's couches, barely feeling the softness of the old, worn fabric. "Okay, thank you."

"Mae..."

"Yeah?" I asked distractedly.

"If Heath comes to you, you have to turn him in. You know that, right?"

I swallowed hard, my gaze meeting Heath's across the room. "I know," I lied. One day, when all of this was cleared up, the first thing I'd do would be apologize to Perry for lying to her. But right now, I had to protect the people I loved. Heath was one of those people.

He seemed to sense the shift in my mood and came to sit beside me as I hung up.

"I'm sorry," he whispered. "I hate that you had to lie to her for me."

It didn't matter. What mattered was that he was here,

and safe. But Rowe wasn't, and that ate at me. Worry gnawed away at my insides like a rat, but then I noticed Liam watching me from the tiny kitchen, and my heart broke in two.

He was barely holding it together.

I rushed to his side, wrapping my arms around him.

He folded in on me, engulfing me in his embrace, tucking his face into my hair and inhaling deep breaths. "What if he dies? What if I hit him too hard and caused a brain bleed or something?"

I shook my head, but I couldn't offer any condolences because I was terrified of the same thing.

But Heath could. He stood from his spot on the couch and inched aside the curtain, peering out into the street. His face was a grimace when he turned back. "You did what he asked. If this is anyone's fault, it's mine and Rowe's."

But nobody could take away the literal blood on Liam's hands. It was there as a reminder until the cuts and bruises healed at least.

Not only that, but being in this house again had to be hard for him. I knew he hadn't been here since he was a teen, and there were reminders of his childhood all over the place. Photos of him and his brother hung proudly on the walls, yellowing slightly with age and sun exposure. It was a double whammy of epic proportions, coupled with a day and night none of us would ever forget. "I think we should go to bed," I suggested, running a soothing hand down Liam's arm. "Today has been...a lot. There's cops everywhere, so we aren't getting any farther tonight."

Heath nodded quickly, and Liam let me lead him down a short hallway. There were only three doors, all of them closed. I looked back over my shoulder at Liam for guidance, and he pointed to the door straight ahead. "That was mine and Hayden's room when we were kids." He opened the door to his left. "Bathroom, if anyone needs it."

He didn't need to point out that the other room was his mother's. There was no need to open it and intrude on her privacy any more than we already were.

I moved ahead and twisted the handle on Liam's child-hood bedroom door. I couldn't help the smile as I walked inside. It was like stepping into a time warp. The bedroom was barely big enough for two single beds and a chest of drawers. But the beds were neatly made with matching bedspreads, and baseball posters still stuck on the walls.

Liam gazed around the room. "It's almost the same as the day I left." He ran his hand over one of the bedspreads, smoothing out a nonexistent wrinkle. "I don't know why she kept two beds. She could have gotten rid of one so Hayden had more room after I went to live with my grandparents."

I stepped in and wrapped my arms around him from behind. "She kept it there for you. In case you ever needed to come back. That's probably why there's still two beds in here, even though you and Hayden are both grown men. Just in case you ever need her."

Liam hung his head. His hand covered mine, holding them tight to his chest. "She ran away from us at the shelter that day..."

I nodded into his back, remembering the way she'd taken one look at Liam and bolted. "And that's something you two can discuss...but this..." The room had a fresh, clean scent to it, like it was dusted and cleaned regularly, and the linens changed, even if nobody slept in them. "I think this proves your mother doesn't hate you. I think it proves she always hoped you'd come back to her."

Heath had gone silent at my back, but now he sat on Hayden's old bed. The frame squeaked, and I was sure

Heath's feet would hang out the edge, but it was a hell of a lot comfier than his bed in solitary. "I'll take this one. You two can share that one, if you don't mind snuggling. But Liam seems like he needs it."

I didn't want to be apart from either of them, and the small gap between the beds felt like a chasm. I needed to be touched. Held. I needed that reconnection with both of them.

But it was nearing two in the morning, Heath barely fit on the bed alone, and Liam did look drained. Rowe's condition weighed heavily on my mind, so I simply nodded, stripping down to my underwear before pulling back the blankets on the bed to slip beneath them. The sheets were old and worn, but clean and smelling of lavender. From my spot beneath the covers, I watched Liam and Heath both take off their clothes until all they wore were boxer briefs. Liam crawled in beside me. Heath switched off the light and got into his bed on the other side of the room.

As soon as Liam pulled the covers over us, I sought him out, desperate to feel the warmth of his skin against mine. He was just as eager. We met in the middle of the narrow bed, chest to chest, our legs entangled around each other. Instantly, his cock thickened between us, and he sighed before pressing his lips to my bare shoulder.

"Sorry," he whispered. "Ignore that. Sleep."

I bit my lip, sure that wasn't what I wanted, but trying to respect his boundaries and the fact Heath was in the room as well. Now wasn't the time or place for any sort of dirty sexy fun, so I nodded and shifted onto my back. I entwined my fingers between his, though, and he mirrored my position. A quick glance at Heath showed he stared at the ceiling, too.

I closed my eyes and tried to sleep, but the minutes

ticked by. Outside, the occasional car passed, the engine distracting me from the distant wail of the prison siren. When blue and red lights flashed on the street, I tensed, ready to leap out of bed and run, but each time they eventually passed, and I went back to staring at the ceiling, exhausted but unable to switch off. The longer I lay there, the worse it got. I twisted and turned, wrestling with my thoughts, and a growing anxiety that refused to ease up, no matter how much I told myself to just go to sleep.

Eventually, Liam got up on one elbow, peering at me in the darkness. "Are you okay?"

I forced a nod. "I'm fine." But on the inside, I was hysterical. What the hell had we done? I glanced between the two men, eyes wide, and then clapped a hand over my mouth as the emotion tried to burst its way free. I didn't want to let it, because I wasn't sure if it was going to come out in tears or laughter.

"Fucking hell, Mae. No, you're not!"

Heath instantly sat up, too, and switched on an old bedside lamp that was shaped like a baseball. It let off a dull white light, but it was enough to see each other by.

I knew what they were seeing when they looked at me. Eyes wide, chest heaving. The beginnings of a full-blown panic attack bearing down on me until my chest was so constricted I was convinced I couldn't breathe. There were so many things I was scared of I could barely keep count anymore.

Liam pulled me into his arms, but it wasn't enough to keep the shakes at bay. Heath watched the two of us for a long moment, then he swore softly beneath his breath and pushed to his feet. I had my back to him, but it was clear from the dragging and squeaking noises that he was rearranging the furniture, bringing his bed closer to the one I shared with Liam. When the two beds were lined up perfectly, he climbed beneath the sheets once more and fitted himself to my back. Sandwiched between the two big men, their skin warm against mine and their breaths regulating my own, I finally found the off button to my brain. Their touch shut me down hard, each muscle relaxing beneath nonsexual, featherlight strokes of their fingertips and mumbled nonsensical words from their lips.

I practically purred between them, more content than I'd felt all day, but the urge to sleep was still missing. I watched Liam in the dim light of the baseball lamp, and he watched me. It was a soul-deep connection that had gone missing for a little bit, only to be found once more. He lowered his head, brushing his lips over mine, and I returned the kiss, needing it more than he did.

His mouth opened, and I explored him with my tongue, meeting him stroke for stroke and refamiliarizing myself with his taste.

God, that taste was good. My lips fell off his, kissing my way along his jaw, darting my tongue out to take little licks of his skin. He moved his head slightly, giving me better access and letting me kiss a path to his ear. I bit softly at the lobe because I knew it turned him on.

He groaned quietly. "Mae...stop."

It was the most lackluster stop I'd ever heard. But I paused anyway.

His eyelids fluttered open. "Yeah, okay. Don't stop. That felt great."

Heath chuckled from behind, the deep rumbling sound vibrating through me. I went back to kissing and sucking Liam's ear and neck while Heath's arm, banded around my middle, tightened in a possessive grip. His erection pressed to my ass, his knees tucked to the back of mine, spooning me.

I ghosted fingertips along the ridged bumps of Liam's ab muscles, delighting in the goosebumps I elicited in their wake. The pure raw pain in his expression was still burned in my memory, and I was reminded of it again when I grazed the cuts on his knuckles and he quickly pulled away.

"Did I hurt you?" I whispered.

"No. Never."

Liam's pain was on the inside, in places I couldn't see to heal. But I was going to try anyway. I kissed him over and over, each lick of my tongue, each press of my lips, reminding him I was here. "I love you. Today didn't change that."

He stilled and then let out a shuddering breath filled with relief. "I...I needed that."

"I still love you, too, Liam," Heath spoke up from behind me. "Even though you got me death row..."

I elbowed him sharply to the midsection, and he grunted.

But Liam let out a snigger, the mood lightening. "If you're just saying that so I'll give you a handy while Mae's are otherwise occupied, you wasted your compliment."

Heat burned behind my cheeks, but Heath laughed. "Duly noted. You're not really my type either."

"What's Rowe got that I don't?" Liam asked, mock insulted.

"A ten-inch cock?"

Liam laughed. "Fair call. I've seen that thing. It is stupidly sized."

"Try having it in your mouth."

Liam pushed up on one elbow to look over me at Heath. "You went there?"

Heath shrugged, and Liam lay back down, a small smile playing around his lips. It was Heath's turn to push up to stare at him. "What's the smug look for?"

I knew. "Liam's a perv." A smile played around my lips. "He likes to watch."

"No shit?"

"No shit. Her more than you two. But in a pinch, I ain't picky." He winked at me.

Heath settled back in behind me, pressing his lips to the back of my neck once more. I sighed in contentment, wriggling back against him. His fingers splayed out across my belly, dancing dangerously close to the elastic of my panties. I wriggled a little more, trying to nudge his fingers in the right direction.

Heath nuzzled into my hair and whispered in my ear, his warm breath lifting the long blonde strands. "I want to give him something to watch."

The heat from my cheeks rushed lower, beading my nipples and pooling at my core.

Liam groaned, because the three of us were so close, there were no secrets. Heath's whispers in my ear had been easily picked up by him.

"You give him something to watch. I'll give him something to feel." I snaked my hand over the trail of hair that dipped below Liam's underwear and circled my fingers around the base of his erection.

He hissed when I made contact, gripping his thick cock tight and rolling my hand slowly up his length. He shoved the sheets down, and I tugged at his underwear, freeing him to give me better access.

Liam didn't want to watch me work his dick, though. His gaze trained on Heath's fingers working their way down the soft curves of my stomach, the tips sneaking lower into my panties.

"Take them off," Liam murmured, to me or to Heath I wasn't sure, but both of us were quick to do it.

Liam tucked his fingers into the straps of my bra, yanking them down my shoulders and flipping my breasts out of the cups. He didn't bother trying to undo my bra, he went straight for two handfuls, artfully squeezing the tips and rubbing them between his fingers. I pumped his cock and pressed my ass back against Heath's dick, now fully erect behind me. There was no doubt what I wanted. There was an aching void inside me that begged to throw a leg over one of them, sink down and ride until I found my bliss.

Anything to avoid thinking about the desperateness of our situation.

But the two of them kept me pinned. Liam touching my breasts, Heath's fingers dipping lower to roll my clit. The bundle of nerves between my legs sent shooting spurts of excitement through my body, deepening the ache until my breaths became ragged. Precum beaded at the tip of Liam's cock, and I desperately wanted to taste him. Heath's fingers moved low into my core, coming out shining with my arousal. He stopped to bring them to his mouth, sucking my juices from his fingers.

My core gave a little clench of need. I couldn't wait anymore. "Somebody needs to put their dick in me." I didn't even care that it was well out of the realm of things I normally said. Liam had broken me in that regard, teaching me that I didn't need to be some timid, quiet mouse in bed. I could be a wildcat if I wanted to be, or anything in between.

Tonight I just needed touch. Closeness. And if I was being completely basic, I wanted dick in pussy.

"How about we both do?" Liam murmured, thrusting his hips slightly into my grasp.

"Yes," I moaned, not exactly sure if it was because Heath was fucking his fingers into me at a deliciously punishing tempo, or if I was agreeing to Liam's suggestion of both of them. I didn't know what he meant by that. One at a time? Both together? Where? But I let my brain blank out, because one thing I did know was that I was safe with these men. They would never hurt me. They would never do anything without making sure it blew my mind in sixty-nine different ways.

Heath lifted my leg, draping it over Liam's muscular thigh. Liam didn't hesitate, taking the invite, nudging in closer until his dick prodded at my entrance. Heath kept his arm draped over my hip, his fingers pressed between me and Liam, rolling my clit while Liam slid inside me.

I groaned at the way he stretched me wide, while my clit throbbed in her pleasure at being so thoroughly worked during sex. I hooked my leg right around Liam's waist, opening myself up to him fully and writhing on the mattress, arcing my body to meet his thrusts.

My orgasm built quickly, so quickly I barely got out a warning before I was clamping down around Liam's dick, muscles spasming and sending him into an orgasm as well. We bucked and writhed together, our timing getting sloppy but Heath never letting up on my clit.

Liam withdrew from my body, flopping back on the mattress, breathing rapidly, with one arm slung over his eyes.

"You're gonna want to watch, Banks," Heath warned.

He rolled me onto my stomach and spread my legs wide so I was star-fished across the bed. I was so lost to the sensation of my orgasm I was as pliable as a rag doll, Heath's to control.

Liam leaned in to kiss me, his tongue meeting mine, slow and leisurely. My core gave a delayed thump of pleasure at kissing him after just having him inside me. His cum coated my pussy, but Heath didn't care. He gripped my hips, lifting my ass up in the air. He plunged deep inside me, riding me doggy style while I closed my eyes in ecstasy. Liam found my clit this time, tapping it slowly, in time to Heath's thrusts. His eyes were lit up like a kid on Christmas morning, watching Heath take me.

My second orgasm was building when Heath pulled from my body. I whined, needing to fall over the edge again.

"Not yet, sweetheart," Heath soothed. He put two fingers deep inside me, coating his fingers before dragging them back to my ass.

I didn't care that I sounded like a bad porn star. I moaned my encouragement, pressing back against his waiting fingers. "Yes!"

His dick plunged inside my pussy again, grinding slowly against my G-spot, while he fingered my ass. I already knew by now, through practice with Rowe and Liam, that nothing turned me on more. I was heady with everything that had happened today, high on having Heath here with me, and I wanted my mind blown. One finger became two until I was wild, taking more of him there than I ever thought I could.

It still wasn't enough.

My clit throbbed, and my pussy ached. I was so turned on, so desperate. I looked over my shoulder at my man.

He kneeled strong behind me, his biceps bulging, abs flexing. His tattoos even darker and more pronounced in the dim light.

God, he was beautiful.

With his gaze pinned on mine, his cock took the place of his fingers. He pushed inside my ass so slowly it did nothing more than fulfill the need he'd created inside me. He was gentle, giving me time to adjust until I was so crazy with want that it was me who hurried the process along, grinding back, taking as much of him as I could.

"You're so fucking tight," he whispered. "I want to make you come."

There was going to be no problem there. Liam's lips found my neck, and he brushed aside my hair, licking and sucking his way across my skin to my ear. His lips brushed over my cheek. "Watching you take his dick there...fuck, Mae. I'm so hard." He grasped my chin, tilting it to face him, and kissed me. His tongue plunged inside my mouth, a branding kiss that seared my soul even with another man inside me.

Heath rocked in and out of my body gently, building an orgasm that felt entirely different to every other one I'd ever had. New nerve endings came alive and mixed with the ones Liam worked. I lost control of my body. My pussy clenched, and I was almost surprised to find Liam's fingers there, giving me something to clamp down on. His thumb stroked my clit, exploding light and fireworks behind my eyes, but it was Heath's deep-throated growl of approval that sent me to the edge. He picked up the pace, driving home with each thrust, his groan making me feel so sexy and wanted. His fingertips dug into the flesh of my hips, slamming my body tight to his, riding me until I couldn't do anything but turn my face into the pillow and scream his name. Heath came with a shout of his own, his hips pounding against my ass. Liam picked up a punishing pace with his fingers inside my pussy, and I yelped against the soft fabric as a third orgasm came out of nowhere.

"Oh my God," I yelled, though it came out as nothing more than a muffled jumble of sounds.

Heath pulled from my body, flopping back on the mattress, completely spent, and letting Liam take over once more.

He rolled me to my back, and my fuzzy gaze cleared for him.

"I love you," he murmured.

"I love you, too."

I spread my legs for him once more, and he settled on top of me, sliding inside me easily. We kissed, deep and powerful, and he came quickly, too turned on from watching to hold out, but I wanted it. I held him tight to me, his body shaking on top of mine. I trailed one hand up and down his back, while the other groped around, looking for Heath.

Heath caught my searching hand and brought my fingers to his mouth, kissing each of them while Liam settled.

Distant sirens still pierced the silent room, but I was right where I wanted to be.

Everything was clear once more. All the reasons why we'd done what we had. All the reasons we'd keep fighting. They were right here with me, and I was never letting them go. None of them.

8

LIAM

My mother's house was exactly as I remembered it. Nothing had changed, though the years had ticked on since the last time I'd been here. It was a shrine to my childhood, a rusted set of swings in the corner of the large yard, and an upturned wading pool nearly grown over with weeds. Coming here had been instinct. The one place I'd always felt safe.

It had just been just me, Mom, and Hayden when I'd lived here, though sometimes I'd sat out on those swings and wondered what it would be like if my father had stuck around to be involved in our lives. My mom had done an amazing job of being both mother and father, always putting herself last, so we wouldn't go without. But I was aware how hard she'd had it.

We could have had a whole different life if my father hadn't flat-out refused to admit we existed. I'd gotten a taste of his lifestyle when my grandfather had plucked me from poverty and taken me to live with him in his sprawling mansion in Providence. But that had cost me this home and a close relationship with Mom and Hayden.

At fifteen, all I'd cared about was the money, and the flashy car and the expensive private school. But I wasn't even twenty by the time the novelty wore off and I realized how those things truly meant nothing. I'd felt that wound more and more as I got older. It joined the loss of the father I'd never even met.

I turned away from the back windows as Mae wandered into the room wearing the shirt from my suit. It hung around her bare thighs, and I couldn't help but lift the tail to check out what she had beneath.

Nothing.

I groaned and busied myself making coffee.

She laughed and pressed a kiss to my bare back. "How did you sleep?"

"After getting off twice in a row? Like a freaking baby."

She smiled. "Me, too."

I brushed a kiss over her lips. "Heath still out?"

She nodded. She opened a few cupboards and eventually found the one that held faded coffee mugs. Her fingers hovered over an ancient-looking one that said, 'World's Best Mom' in faded print. "A present from you?"

I wasn't sure. "Or Hayden. I don't remember who bought it for her, but I remember her drinking from it every morning."

"It's right at the front, perhaps she still does."

I shrugged one shoulder. It was hard to reconcile that notion with the fact she'd completely dismissed me the last time I'd seen her. "I wish I knew where she was. Where does a middle-aged woman go on a Thursday night?"

"A bar?" Mae asked.

"At her age? I don't think so."

"She's mid-fifties at worst, Liam. That's hardly dead."

"Hardly prime clubbing age, though, either," I returned.

"What sort of bars are open all night anyway? It's eight in the morning."

"Strip club," Heath offered, appearing behind Mae, rubbing a hand through his sleep-tousled hair.

"My mother was not at a strip club."

"You don't know that." Heath grinned.

"Remind me never to help you escape from prison again," I huffed. I poured boiling water into the instant coffee and waited for the granules to dissolve.

Mae passed me a carton of milk from the refrigerator, her fingers brushing mine. The polish on her nails that had been immaculate yesterday for Heath's trial was now chipped at the edges. "I don't feel right about breaking into your mother's house."

Heath and I both glanced at her.

"Really?" I asked. "That's what you don't feel right about in the scheme of everything we did yesterday?"

The tiniest of smiles tilted the corner of her mouth. "Well, I suppose when you put it that way…"

I passed her a mug of coffee. She took it, slipping her fingers around the handle while she wandered around the living room. "Aww!" She stopped in front of a framed portrait on the wall. It had yellowed with age, and unsurprisingly, since the two-year-old boy in the photo was now a twenty-seven-year-old man. "This is you, right? Or Hayden?"

Hayden was a couple of years younger than me, so he likely hadn't been born when the photo had been taken. "It's me," I confirmed, joining her.

"You've got some fossil-aged artwork on the refrigerator, too," Heath called from the kitchen. He came back, munching on an apple. "Sorry, I'm starving."

I gave him a wry glance. "We already did a lot worse in that bedroom, so I think eating the food is okay."

He sniggered. But at the mention of what we'd done, his gaze drew back to Mae. Mine followed. She had such great legs. She wandered the wall of photos, checking out each one, completely oblivious that both Heath and I were watching her every movement. When she lifted onto her toes, reaching up to straighten a frame while unknowingly flashing us the curve of her ass cheek, both Heath and I groaned in unison.

She turned with a confused look on her face. "What?"

"You..." Heath started, his interest in his apple forgotten. He stared at me helplessly, like he couldn't find the words.

"He's trying to say that you, in that shirt, with nothing beneath it, is hella distracting."

Heath nodded. "What he said."

She smiled softly. "We should probably come up with some sort of plan, but I don't think we can go anywhere in broad daylight... We've got some time to kill."

Heath crossed the room to trail his fingertips over her bare thigh. "You want to watch TV, sweetheart?"

She shook her head. "Not exactly what I had in mind."

My dick twitched, already up for whatever was on her mind. I knew what I wanted. I'd watched Heath take her perfect ass last night, and I wanted to do the same, if she wasn't too sore.

I boxed her between us again. She undid the top button, giving us a hint of her cleavage, and I pulled aside the collar to kiss her neck.

She let out a happy little noise of pleasure, one that I was suddenly desperate to hear more of.

Heath seemed ready to pick her up and throw her over his shoulder. "Those noises, Mae..."

She closed her eyes and undid another button.

A key being inserted into the front door lock froze us all

to the spot. Mae barely had time to clutch her open shirt around her breasts before the door swung open.

I pushed Mae behind me. "Mom, I—"

A man stood in the doorway.

Most definitely not my mother.

"Who the hell are you?" I asked.

At the same time, he said, "What going on here?" His gaze fell on Heath, and his eyes widened in instant recognition. "Holy shit. You're the guy from the news. The prisoner who escaped last night!"

His panic clear on his face, he reached behind him, pulling a gun from the waistband of his jeans.

Mae screamed. Heath dove at her, while I spread my arms, keeping them both behind me.

"I'm Liam Banks. I'm a lawyer," I said in a rush, keeping my gaze pinned on the man's gun. "This is my mother's house, and I assure you, nobody here is armed or wants to hurt anyone. Want to tell me who you are?"

A small figure pushed the big man aside. My mother's eyes went wide as she took me in, disheveled and clad in nothing but the suit pants I'd worn yesterday. Her gaze strayed to Heath and Mae behind me but bounced straight back to me. "Liam? What on earth?"

"Surprise?"

She stared at me blankly.

I dropped my arms, eyeing the man behind her. He'd lowered his gun, but it was still clutched between his fingers like he might change his mind at any time.

I ran a hand through my hair. "Okay, bad surprise."

She stepped inside the house properly. "You broke in?"

I pointed at my keys sitting on the kitchen countertop. "You haven't changed the locks in a long time."

"I suppose I haven't. But..."

I could see the questions tumbling over themselves in her mind, fighting for the top place to come blurting out of her mouth. I knew I owed her an explanation. But there was something I'd been wanting to do for such a long time. And today, after all that had happened the day before, I wanted it more than ever.

I stepped toward her, closing the distance between us. I towered over her, I had even at twelve when I'd gone to live with my grandparents. That was the last time I remembered hugging her.

It had been too long. We had so many wasted years. All of them my fault.

I put my arms around her and squeezed her tight.

She was stiff in my arms for a long moment, and I eyed the man behind her, wondering who he was, and a little wary about whether he might think about shooting me again. But then my mother relaxed in my arms and wrapped her own around my waist. She became all I could think about. Her face, pressed to my chest, grew damp with tears, and I had to blink back a sudden moisture as well. She trembled, clutching me tighter with every passing moment, and I did the same to her. Emotion clogged my throat, making it impossible to explain why I was here, but I felt the acceptance in her embrace.

I felt the safety. And I knew this was the whole reason I'd come here.

For everything I'd done to her over the years, all the rejection and pain I'd caused her, she was still my mother. The mug in her cupboard, my photos on the walls, all the mementos of a long-ago childhood... They were all proof she didn't hate me as much as I'd feared.

"I'm sorry," she whispered against my chest.

I blinked at her. "For what? You've done nothing wrong. It was all me."

She pulled back, gazing at me with watery eyes.

I took her by the shoulders. "I'm the one who's sorry. I wasn't here when you needed me. I've been a terrible son." The words hurt to say, but they were the truth.

She squeezed my fingers. "I think there are things we need to talk about." She darted a look at Mae and Heath again. "Maybe a lot of things? Starting with what on earth the three of you are doing in my house in your underwear."

I glanced over at the man, now leaning against the doorframe. "And maybe who your bodyguard is?"

She glanced over at him, and when she turned back, she was smiling, though there was a nervous edge to it. "Yes. That, too."

We all disappeared into our bedrooms, me and Mae dressing properly in our clothes from yesterday, but Heath stared at Rowe's guard uniform lying crumpled on the floor. "I can't wear that again."

He was right, he couldn't.

At a soft knock, we all paused. I crossed the room and opened the door. My mother stood there with a pile of clean folded clothes in her hands. She looked past me to Heath. "I wondered if perhaps you might be in need of these... I don't imagine someone in...your position...would have had time to pack a bag..."

I stared at her and then choked on a laugh. Mae and Heath laughed as well, and my mother's thin lips turned up at the edges.

She passed the clothes to Heath. "QB isn't quite as big as you, but he likes his clothes baggy, so hopefully they fit. It's supposed to be warm today, but if you get cold and want a sweatshirt, just say the word."

QB was more than a friend then, if he had clothes here.

Heath stared down at her, gaze full of gratitude. "Thank you, ma'am." He took the clothes from her carefully, and she left the room so he could dress.

"I like your mom, Banks," Heath gruffed out, pulling on the clothes she'd given him.

"I do, too, but we can't stay here. We're putting them in danger. We've already made them accessories."

Mae nodded. "We'll leave for Rowe's cabin as soon as it's clear. But Liam? Take the time to sort things out with her while we're here. This might not be the way you wanted to do it, but it's the opportunity that's presented itself."

I nodded, and the three of us straightened up the little room. Mae and Heath went to the living room, while I gathered the bedsheets and put them in the washing machine.

Eventually, there was nothing else for me to do except join them.

Mom lifted her head when I entered the room, and her gaze hung on me. "Mae and Heath have explained everything. I've just told them you're all welcome to stay here as long as you need. We don't have much..."

"We?" I asked her, glancing between her and the man she'd called QB earlier.

She bit her lip, looking nervously between me and him. He sat in a recliner, but he didn't appear relaxed. He watched me carefully, and a flicker of recognition flashed somewhere deep in my mind, but I couldn't place it.

"You two didn't officially meet... Liam, this is QB. Or... Jacob, I guess. We called him QB in high school, and I haven't been able to switch ever since he came back."

She wrung her fingers nervously, glancing between the two of us. I frowned at her, but in a split second, it dawned on me why she was so nervous.

I jolted up off my chair and stumbled back like she'd electrocuted me. I stared at QB...Jacob, with a lightbulb going off in my head.

He pushed to his feet and crossed the room, holding his hand out to me. "Jacob Banks. Seems we have something in common."

Anger replaced the shock as I stared at the man who'd knocked my mother up and run. "Like DNA?" I spat at him.

I turned and glared at Mom. "What the hell is this? Dear old dad comes back after nearly thirty years of doing his own thing, denying you and I ever existed, and you just take him back to play house?"

Jacob sighed and sat back down. "Oh boy."

I could barely keep myself in check. I wanted to launch across the room and throw a punch at the man who'd been nothing more than my sperm donor. "No, you don't get to act like I'm the one being dramatic. Fuck you, *Dad*."

My mother's fingers trembled. "Liam, there are things—"

I cut her off. "I don't want to hear his excuses. And I don't know how you do either. Does he know how hard you've had it all these years? All the things you sacrificed to have a baby at sixteen? I'm his kid, too, but he got to go off and have a life, where you were stuck with me."

Mom's mouth dropped open. "I was never stuck with you!"

QB sighed. "And I was never your father."

All heads in the room whipped to face him.

"QB!"

He sighed and reached a hand out to my mother. "Sorry, love. I know this wasn't the way we discussed telling him, but—"

I rolled my eyes. "Telling me you're not my dad? Yeah, been there, heard that."

"Liam. He's not." My mother's bottom lip trembled. "He's your half brother."

Shock punched through me.

The world around me spun. I'd always prided myself on being a smart man, but right now, I couldn't make the pieces fit together. I kept trying to shove them in, but they just kept ramming against each other, each piece getting dog-eared and tattered the more I tried.

Much like my heart, that already knew before my brain did.

Mae got up from her seat and put her arms around me. I didn't push her away, but I didn't feel her embrace either. I was too numb to feel anything.

I stared at my mother. "My grandfather..."

"Is your biological father, yes. So Jacob is your half brother."

"How?" I choked on the word. But I already knew. My mother had been sixteen. My grandfather in his forties when I'd been born. Bile rose in my throat, choking and thick.

There was no such thing as consensual sex between a grown man and a teenage girl. A grown, *married* man. I turned to Jacob. "He blamed it on you to avoid the scandal."

He nodded. "I was seventeen. He shipped me off to a boarding school in the UK. I tried keeping in contact with your mother, but..." Guilt played out all over his face.

She picked up his hand. "It wasn't his fault. After everything that happened, I couldn't even look him in the face, knowing the lies spreading about him were my fault. It was my choice to end our friendship."

But none of that mattered to me. All I could hear and think now was that every day, every moment of my life had been a lie. One that was born of an unspeakable evil. It echoed around my ears like a storm, building strength with every ticking second until I was sure I was going to explode.

I needed to leave. I needed to get the hell out of this house and away from everything and everyone.

I strode stiffly to the counter and picked up my car keys. I turned apologetic eyes on Heath and Mae. "I can't be here," I choked out.

Mae grabbed my hand. "You can. Talk to them."

But she had a false sense of who I really was. She knew the Liam Banks outer shell. The one who laughed and joked to avoid showing something real. It had been chipped away by my mistakes with Heath's trial. By what I'd done to Rowe.

But this? There was no coming back from it. The shell around me exploded, leaving me raw and vulnerable in a way I couldn't stand.

I clutched my keys in my hand, but there was one thing I had to do before I left. My mother stood, tears rolling down her face, watching me move around her living room like the walking dead. I wouldn't have that. I swept her into my arms and hugged her again. "This isn't your fault."

Her knees gave way, and the floodgates opened, her tears wetting my shirt as she cried.

QB stood and was there to put his arms around her when I transferred her to him. Something passed between us, a moment of understanding. "I got her, don't worry."

Mae and Heath watched on, their faces etched with worry and indecision.

Mae rubbed her palms over her thighs. "We can't just drive out of here with Heath. Not in broad daylight."

"We can't stay here, either." We'd already put my mom in enough danger.

QB glanced toward the front door. "There's cops every-where. All the airports would have been notified by now, and I'm betting the entire town is roadblocked." He scratched at his beard. "You might get out of town through Johnson Lane, if there's still no house on that vacant lot that backs onto the woods. You could hunker down there for a while until the heat dies off. You might have to walk because it's pretty overgrown this time of year, but we used to have parties out there back when we were in school."

I still couldn't quite believe this man was my brother. He looked a lot like my grandfather, their eyes a similar color, their cheekbones high and regal.

I nodded my thanks and made for the door, my strides robot stiff. There'd been too many bombs dropped here.

The biggest one plummeted straight into the very core of who I was.

I left my mother's house feeling absolutely nothing.

iam drove to the edge of Saint View. I sat in the passenger side again, Heath in the back, with a baseball cap pulled low on his head, Rowe's guard uniform left for QB to burn. I shot glances at Liam, more and more worried by what I saw in his expression. Even last night, when everything had been scary and going to shit, there'd been traces of Liam's natural good humor. But right now, there was nothing. A complete and total blankness. He drove on autopilot, oblivious to anything going on around him.

Including the cop car coasting down the hill in the opposite direction.

I gasped, and behind me, Heath let out a guttural swear.

I was sure neither of us breathed.

But the cop was in a hurry to get somewhere else and passed us by without stopping. Liam blinked as it drove by but didn't utter a word. He made the relevant turns, getting us to the vacant lot that bordered the woods.

I glanced at the GPS on my phone. Rowe's cabin was

only a five-mile walk, but I doubted there would be a well-worn path that led straight to his door.

"Just drop me here," Heath said. "It's too far for Mae to walk in those shoes."

I shook my head. "I'm not leaving you again. Trying to find you on the streets last night nearly sent me gray. I'm coming with you."

He raised an eyebrow. "You're gonna walk five miles in heels and a business skirt?"

"I'm counting on you piggybacking me after two."

He shook his head with a smile on his lips, but he didn't argue any further.

Liam got us as close to the woods as he could, but he didn't make a move to turn off the car.

"You aren't coming?" I asked.

"I'll meet you at the cabin later. Can't leave my car here. It'll stick out like a sore thumb and draw unwanted attention."

Liam's hundred-thousand-dollar car had no business being in a Saint View neighborhood. Especially if its owner was nowhere to be seen.

But I hesitated over the dead nothing behind his eyes. He glanced over when I didn't shut the door.

"Go, Mae," he snapped. "The longer you hang around, the more likely it is for someone to see us."

I blinked at his tone. He'd never spoken to me like that before. I knew where it came from, and I hated it, but he was right. I stepped back and shut the door.

He took off without waiting to see if we made it into the woods. He didn't look back.

Hurt curdled deep inside me at his rejection, but Heath hustled me into the privacy of the trees. It was only once we were a hundred yards in that he stopped. "He didn't mean it, you know that, right? He's hurting."

I nodded. "I know."

"His whole life just imploded. That's gonna take him some time."

"I just don't like seeing him in pain. I want to fix it."

Heath sighed. "I don't think this is one any of us can fix for him."

I hated feeling helpless. But at least Heath and I had other things to focus on. I checked the GPS on my phone. "It's a pretty straight walk to Rowe's cabin from here."

"Let's just hope the terrain stays like this. Neither of us are dressed for hiking, but the undergrowth is pretty sparse right now, maybe we'll get lucky."

We set off again, and despite my worries over all three men, the warm sunlight filtering through the trees was bliss. Birds sang, and occasionally some small animal scuttled in the bushes trying to get away from us. The walk remained easy, the two of us picking our way around trees and shrubs with no difficulty until I found myself actually enjoying it.

"What are you smiling at?" Heath asked, a small grin of his own plastered to his lips.

I shrugged. "Simple pleasures, I guess. You're not in a jail cell."

He slung his arm around my shoulders and tugged me into his side. "No, I am not. You know the best part about that?"

"Seeing the sky? Not having a toilet by your bed?" I wrinkled my nose at the memory of the tiny solitary cell. We'd stolen moments there, because it was all we'd had, but in hindsight, it had been very bleak.

"Seeing you whenever I want to. When I woke up this

morning and you weren't there beside me, I thought for a second I'd dreamt it all."

I wrapped my arm around his lower back, clutching the fabric of his borrowed T-shirt. "It's not a dream."

He pressed his lips to my hair. "I just want you to know that for however long this lasts…"

I pulled away to stare up at him. "You're not going back."

He diverted his gaze, looking over to his right and into the trees. "I'll be glad for whatever time I get with you."

I didn't want to think like that. "Can I take you on a date?"

He chuckled at my attempt to change the subject. "A date, huh? Like, we both get dressed up real fancy and go out for cocktails and an expensive dinner before a stroll along the beach?"

"Is that your idea of a perfect date?"

"No," he admitted. "This is." He spread his free arm out, gesturing around us.

"Tramping through the woods in inappropriate footwear?"

"Being in nature with a beautiful woman beside me. Finding some special spot where we could put down a blanket and just watch the water trickle down a stream."

"That does sound nice." I could imagine it. Another time, another place, where he wasn't being hunted. We hiked along in silence for a while until the rushing sound of water filled the air around us. "The lake," I told him. "We mustn't be far from Rowe's place then."

I fished out my phone and checked the map. "Only a mile to go, and we're pretty close to on track, too." I raised my hand to slap his palm in a high five. "Told you my shoes would make it."

I didn't mention that my feet were killing me and I had a blister the size of the sun.

The last mile felt like it took forever, and it did take a little longer because we stumbled across one of Rowe's neighbors, though I used the term loosely, because the house was surrounded by woods and still quite a hike away. But we stopped and took the long way around when we heard voices and country music coming from a speaker.

The music faded, and I followed my phone's directions until we found ourselves in the clearing surrounding Rowe's cabin. "Well," I said. "This is it. What do you think?"

Heath stared up at the log walls and the wide wrap-around porch before taking in the yard with its firepit and shed. "It's perfect. And so are you."

He leaned down and kissed me, tasting slightly of sweat and dirt, but it was an earthy taste that I lapped up because it was him.

"If you two are done making out, you want to tell me where you've been all night?"

I pulled away and stared up at Rowe, standing on the front porch. It took a moment for my feet to catch up, but then I was running for the stairs, kicking off my heels to thunder up to the porch, and then launching myself into his arms.

"Oof," he said quietly, wincing as he caught me. "Go easy."

I jerked away. "Oh my God, I'm sorry. Did I hurt you? Show me." I yanked up his shirt.

He batted my hands away, trying to pull it back down, but not before I'd taken in the full extent of his purple ribs.

Evidently, Heath had seen the extent of it from his spot across the yard. He came storming up the stairs behind me and yanked Rowe's shirt up once more.

Heath and I both stared at the damage across his torso. It matched the bruises beneath his eye and cheekbone that I'd barely even noticed in my haste to get to him.

"How bad does it hurt?" Heath gritted out.

"Not much," Rowe lied. "The concussion was the bigger problem. They only just let me out of the hospital. The ribs aren't even cracked. Just bruised. I'll be fine."

I was suddenly glad Liam wasn't here to see the extent of Rowe's injuries. He already felt bad enough for what he'd done.

Heath's and Rowe's gazes collided, and like always, something hot and heady passed between them. But when Heath put his arms around Rowe and hauled him in for a hug, it was with nothing but tenderness. "I can't believe you did that for me. You're a fucking idiot."

"Yeah, well, I can't believe you went and got yourself death row. You didn't give me much choice, did you?"

"I'm tempted to punch you in the ribs right now."

"Please don't."

All three of us chuckled, then froze at a buzzing noise.

"Is that a drone?" Heath asked, ducking beneath the porch roof.

My heart picked up a rapid beat as the three of us scanned the blue sky. There was nothing but the odd cloud and birds coasting leisurely on wind currents, and yet the noise kept coming, getting louder and louder with every moment.

"Fuck, it's not a drone, it's a helicopter." The noise of the engine and the whip of the blades doubled in intensity when the huge mechanical beast with POLICE in huge letters on the side flew into view. I looked around wildly for Heath, but he'd completely disappeared, the bang of the screen door the only indication of where he'd gone.

Rowe and I watched the helicopter fly over without pausing, and both of us let out wobbly breaths when it disappeared and the silence of the woods engulfed us once more.

"Coast is clear," I called to Heath.

But he didn't reappear. Rowe shot me a worried glance, and wordlessly, we both went inside.

We found Heath in the small living room, staring out the window.

"They're gone," I said again, in case he hadn't heard. I tried to keep my voice peppy and upbeat, like I was talking about an annoying houseguest.

But Heath didn't smile. "Is this what it's going to be like now? Even out here in the middle of nowhere, I have to hide every time a helicopter flies over?"

"That doesn't happen very often," Rowe offered.

"What about when the mailman comes? What about when you want to invite a friend from work over for dinner? What do I do then? Hide in my bedroom? Leave the house and hide in the woods and watch through the window like a creeper?"

Neither of us had an answer for that.

"And what about going out in public? Am I ever going to do that again? I can't. Not here. Maybe not anywhere."

"It's better than being dead," I said quietly.

Heath looked up at me with big eyes. "Is it? Or is it just a different sort of dead?"

I didn't want him to think like that. None of us had thought this through. We'd acted in the heat of the moment, but I refused to consider we might have made the wrong choice. "I wasn't going to just sit there and watch you die."

Heath didn't say anything. He got up to walk away, but Rowe wouldn't let him.

He blocked him in. "No. Stop it. You're not walking away. Is this ideal? No, it's fucking not. But this is temporary."

Heath seemed like he wanted to argue, and I knew exactly how quickly things between the two of them could blow up.

I stepped between them. "We keep going to work. Rowe, me, and Liam. We cooperate with the police as much as we can."

Rowe was insistent. "And we find who really murdered Jayela. That's your ticket to freedom, Heath. We find them someone to take your spot on death row, and everything else gets downgraded to a misdemeanor."

Heath's voice was quiet when he finally answered. "We've been trying to work out who killed Jayela for months. What makes you think we can do it now?

Rowe pulled his mouth into a tight line and shoved his hands into his pockets. "Because there's more on the line now than there ever has been. Failure isn't an option." He sucked in a sharp breath. "You get caught, you're right back where we started, only we're there next to you."

*I*t took two days for all of us to settle down and stop flinching at every little noise. But when no police showed up, eventually, we all began to relax. And it wasn't long after that boredom started setting in.

Heath wandered the interior of the cabin for the hundredth time, though it didn't take him long because there wasn't much to see. When he returned, he sat uncomfortably in the camping chairs we'd brought in from the shed. His big body really didn't fit well in them, his legs too long, his shoulders too wide. "Your interior designs skills, suck, Pritchard. Jail cells have more pizazz than your place does. You couldn't have sprung for a couch?"

Rowe narrowed his eyes at Heath from his perch on an identical chair in the middle of the living room. "Really? I take a beating for you. Spring you from jail. Lie to the cops. And let you crash at my place, but you want to whine about my lack of furniture? How do you spell ungrateful prick again?"

Heath shrugged, the insult not bothering him at all. "Just sayin', a rug wouldn't go astray."

I fought back a laugh. They'd been like this the entire time. They were two grumpy old men, trading barbs with each other, but there was a fondness beneath it that I didn't miss even if they were pretending it wasn't there.

Rowe glared at him. "What the fuck would I do with a rug?"

Heath threw his hands up in the air. "I don't know, perhaps it would give you a place to sit beside these two-dollar Walmart chairs you seem so fond of? Put a coffee table on it so you've got somewhere to eat a fucking meal?" He shot a frustrated hand toward the fireplace. "Light a fire in the winter and have somewhere to get our girl naked?"

They both looked over at me, and I flushed hot at the thought of being their girl.

I cleared my throat. "I vote for that last option."

Rowe smirked at me. "Do you now?" He got up and sauntered over to me. "I got other places to get you naked, Mae. Don't need a rug for that."

I swallowed hard. Rowe's injuries had prevented anything from happening for the last two days, but he was walking better today, his ribs not causing him as much pain, and he'd had no lasting effects from his concussion. Before the trial, I'd put in to have some time off work, expecting to be celebrating Heath's freedom, and Rowe had been given some sick leave, so neither of us had been back to the prison, but there'd be no avoiding it come Monday.

I really needed to go home and get ready for the week ahead. "As much as I'd like that...I've been here for ages. I should get back to my apartment."

Heath pouted, wrapping his arms around me. "I hate it when you leave."

I did, too, but I couldn't stay here all the time. The police hadn't spoken to me yet. If they sent someone to my house a few times, they'd realize pretty quick that I wasn't living there. I wanted to be there when they came to question me. I was still surprised I hadn't even had a phone call from them. All I could assume was that they didn't think a convicted murderer would run to the sister of the woman he'd supposedly killed.

"You've got Rowe to keep you company," I told Heath.

"He doesn't smell good like you do." He nosed his way up my throat, and I couldn't resist the urge to tilt my head to give him better access.

Rowe snorted. "You don't exactly smell like roses either, brother."

I thought they both smelled amazing. I'd spent an hour today, watching Heath work out in the yard. He'd come inside dripping with sweat, and it had been all I could do not to throw myself at him and dry hump his leg. I hadn't missed Rowe looking at him in a very similar manner.

I disentangled myself from Heath's embrace, kissing him on the cheek before picking up Rowe's keys. "I need to go get us some food."

"There's food here," Rowe complained. "Stay."

"There's other things I need to do, too."

A silence fell over us, and Heath rubbed at the back of his neck. "You going to try Liam again?"

I nodded. He hadn't come out to the cabin at all. He'd sent a text saying he had to work and that the police were on his ass, so he was keeping a low profile, but I wasn't buying it. "I need to check in on him."

"He shouldn't be alone right now." Heath gave my backside a pat, pushing me gently toward the door. "Go. Bring a rug with you. Maybe we'll show Rowe how to use it." He winked at me, and I shook my head as Rowe threw a shoe across the room at Heath. I left them to their squabbling and got in Rowe's car.

I drove back into town, stopping at my place to shower and change. I checked the mail, watered my plant, and then, curiosity getting the better of me, I knocked on my elderly neighbor's door and asked if the police had been by to see me.

She frowned at me, her light eyebrows drawing together. "Don't tell me you've got yourself in more trouble? Haven't we had enough of the police around here after what happened to your sister?"

She wasn't wrong, but her tone irked me anyway. I hadn't asked for any of this. I didn't want the police sniffing around any more than she did, but I thanked her politely, because it wasn't in my nature to snap back at someone.

My place felt empty and cold without Liam sprawled out on my couch. After an hour of hanging out there, I was itching to leave. I went to the store, buying a stupidly large amount of food, enough to feed three grown men for a couple of weeks, and loaded it into the back of Rowe's car.

Once I got back in the driver's seat, I tried calling Liam. It went to voicemail, again. So then I tried Tori and got the same.

I swallowed thickly. Tori hadn't spoken a word to me since Heath's trial. I wasn't even sure I blamed her. The hurt and betrayal on her face when Liam had called her husband up to the stand, then accused him not only of having an affair but being a murderer, had gutted me. The moment the judge had dismissed Liam's accusations, Will had collected his wife from her seat beside me, and the two of them had walked out. Will had shot me a look of anger, Tori hadn't turned back at all.

I understood why they were mad. But I hadn't known what Liam was going to do any more than they had. And Tori was my best friend. I wasn't throwing a decade of friendship away without fighting for it. I'd get down on my hands and knees and grovel at her feet if I had to.

Tori's place was on the way to Liam's. Groveling started now.

With all the freezer items packed into cooler bags, I drove to Tori and Will's cute house in the suburbs of Providence. They were on the opposite side from my father and Liam, where sprawling mansions, hired help, and day drinking were the norm. Will and Tori's place was smaller but lovely. It was a cookie-cutter house, near identical to the others on their street. Their grass was always perfectly cut, not a weed in sight in their garden beds. The front door was a shiny sleek black that shone in the late afternoon light. I stopped Rowe's car in their driveway and tentatively picked my way across the little stone path that led to the front porch.

I shouldn't have been as nervous as I was. I normally flounced up their porch steps and walked in like I owned the place. I hadn't knocked in years. Why bother when I had a key? It was supposed to be for emergencies, but Will always just shook his head with a laugh every time he found me sitting on their couch or pouring a wine from their refrigerator. He'd tease me about the fact he might have been walking around naked, but we both knew that he never would have.

I tucked my key away in my purse now, though. After the way we'd left things, I couldn't just let myself in the way I normally would have. Things had changed. Whether that change was permanent remained to be seen.

I hoped with all my heart it wasn't. I already missed my best friend, and it had only been three days since I'd seen her.

With a trembling hand, I used the brass door knocker for the first time ever, then stood back and waited.

There were no footsteps from within, so I knocked again.

Still nothing. Maybe they weren't home. Their cars weren't in the driveway, but that wasn't unusual, since they normally parked in the garage.

The cry of a baby came from somewhere at the back of the house, and sadness spread through me. They were home. They just didn't want to talk to me.

I wasn't giving up that easily. I banged again, this time with my fist. "Tori! Please! I know you're in there. Can we just talk?"

I bit my lip at the silence from within.

"Please, Tori! I didn't know Liam was going to accuse Will like that. The judge was—"

The door flew open, and Will's angry face towered over me.

I took a step back.

"Are you seriously standing on my front porch, yelling so the whole street hears that your boyfriend accused me of—" He dropped his voice to a hiss. "Murder."

I shook my head as fast as I could. "No, I swear, I just came to say that I was sorry. I need to talk to Tori."

He looked at me like I'd grown another head. "No, Mae! She doesn't want to see you. Neither of us do."

That cut me right to my core. Tori and I never fought. Not so much as a mild disagreement. She always had my back, just like I always had hers. It was the sort of friendship that didn't come along often. I peered past him. Isaac had stopped crying, so I knew there was a good chance it was because Tori had picked him up to soothe him. That meant she could hear everything I was saying.

"Please, Tori," I called. "Please..."

She didn't come to the door.

Tears pricked the backs of my eyes as I stared up at Will. His expression softened, and he let out a long sigh.

"We're hurt and angry right now," he said in a more controlled manner than when he'd first opened the door. "You need to give us some time. What happened in that courtroom? Our whole church community heard about it, Mae. I know that doesn't mean much to you, but it's important to us. You embarrassed us, and now we're the center of stares and gossip. Tori's parents rang her in tears, and our priest came out to offer marriage counselling. It's mortifying."

I didn't think it was fair to blame that on me, when I couldn't control the judgmental nature of their church community, but I didn't say that. I didn't want to make the strain between us worse. Instead, I just said, "I'm sorry. Please ask Tori to call me when she's ready. I miss her and..."

Will stared at me. "You've changed."

I knew he was right. I wasn't the same woman I'd been before losing my sister. That Mae would have never even considered working at the prison, let alone busting someone out of one. The old Mae would have been too straight and vanilla to have two men inside her at once, but now that was on my mind regularly. I was different, and maybe some of the things I was doing went against their faith, but she was still my best friend. "I don't want to lose her."

He gave me a brief nod and then closed the door.

The lump in my throat grew while I trudged down their steps and back to the car. It was only a few minutes to Liam's place, but by the time I got there, tears rolled down my face. It wasn't just Tori and Will's rejection. It was a culmination of shock and grief and the pure terror of what we'd done. Will's words... You've changed. They played over and over again in my mind.

When had I become somebody who broke the law? I'd done it so many times lately, always justifying my reasons with the knowledge that Heath was innocent. But every time I did it, I felt a little of the old me slip away.

I couldn't get her back.

Just like I couldn't get Jayela back.

Or my father. My mother.

The tears blinded me. I took the elevator to Liam's penthouse apartment, blindly stabbing at the buttons and hoping I hit the right ones.

The doors opened onto his floor, and I threw myself at his door. "Liam," I yelled, voice cracking in the middle.

The door opened in an instant.

Shock punched through me at the sight of him. He was shirtless, gray sweatpants sitting low on his hips. His hair was a mess, as if he'd been in bed for days, but his eyes were red-rimmed with dark circles beneath them, telling me that even if he had been in bed, he hadn't been sleeping. An expensive-looking glass tumbler was clutched in one hand, a deep-brown liquid sloshing in the bottom.

His gaze searched me frantically. "What's wrong? Are you hurt? Is it Heath, or Rowe?"

I shook my head. Then shrugged because it was them. It was everything. Including him. "Tori won't speak to me," I told him.

He swallowed hard. "Because of what I did?"

I nodded.

"Fuck." He held his arms out to me, and I flew into them. They enclosed around me, but I stiffened inside his embrace.

It didn't feel right. He reeked of alcohol, so strong I was sure it seeped from his pores. "Are you drunk?"

He let go of me and turned away, padding barefoot to the kitchen island and putting his glass down heavily before refilling it from a half-empty decanter. "So?"

He was always happy, full of jokes and easygoing chill. This was like looking at an entirely different person.

His apartment was a mess. A stark difference to the last time I'd been here when it had been showroom clean and decluttered. Food packages and beer bottles littered the kitchen counter, and there were more on the coffee table in the living room. He took his drink there without offering me one. He sank onto one of the couches and stared at the huge screen that played a basketball game softly.

My stomach rolled as I followed him, sitting next to him carefully. "Liam."

He stared at the TV and took a sip without acknowledging me.

I picked up the TV remote and turned it off. He didn't even seem to notice. He just stared at it with unseeing eyes.

"Liam!"

"What?" he snapped.

I sat back. "You weren't at work the last few days, were you?"

He didn't say anything.

"You've just been sitting here getting drunk by yourself, for three days?"

He slammed his glass down hard on the wooden coffee table. "So what if I was? What does it matter?"

I fought to grab his hand, but he pulled away. "It matters because I'm worried about you!"

"Don't be. I'm not worth wasting your worries on."

I flew off the couch, kneeling on the floor in front of him. He sat back, trying to put space between us, but I pushed his knees wide, making a spot for myself between them. "Don't talk like that! Talk to me. Why didn't you come to us?"

He shook his head. "What is there to say? That I fucked up Heath's trial and got an innocent man sent to death row? That I beat the shit out of my best friend, so bad he ended up in the hospital?"

I shook my head. "Rowe's fine, he—"

"How about how I turned my back on every oath I've ever taken and broke numerous laws by agreeing to help Heath break out of jail?"

I sat back on my heels. "You regret it?"

He didn't answer. "Your best friend won't even speak to you because of something I did. And you know what? I can't blame her! I'd be fucking mad at me, too."

"They'll come around."

"They'll forgive you, in time. Yeah, probably. But they won't forgive me. How could they, after what I accused them of? I wouldn't! Heath and Rowe shouldn't forgive me either."

"There's nothing to forgive..."

He laughed bitterly. "There's everything to forgive. Just ask them. Maybe then you'll see the truth."

I shook my head, hating the pure tortured desperation in his voice. "This isn't about them. Or me. Liam, your mom..."

He got to his feet so hard the couch skidded back on the shiny white tiles beneath it. "Really? You want to talk about my mom? About how I was too embarrassed of her to involve her in my life for years? Or about how my grandfather—sorry, my father— raped her? Please, Mae, let's talk about that topic some more."

Tears rolled down my face. I was desperate to hold him. To curl my body around his and comfort him, but in that moment, he was the wild stallion no one could get near without being trampled.

He lowered his gaze to the floor. "Just go."

"I don't want to," I whispered.

His mouth drew into a grim line. "I don't want you here."

"You don't mean that."

"Dammit, Mae! I do! Leave!"

"No!"

He picked up his phone. He closed his eyes for the briefest of moments. "Leave. Or I'll call the cops and tell them where Heath is."

My mouth dropped open. "Are you serious?"

"As a heart attack."

"I don't believe you."

"Try me."

My heart tore down the middle. I knew that not one part of him wanted to do this. That he was drunk, and hurting, and lashing out at me because he had nobody else to yell at.

I walked slowly to stand in front of him and took the phone from his hand.

He let me.

Our gazes locked, and in his, all I could see was how very broken he was. My heart shattered into a million pieces for him. For us. For the fact he wouldn't let me in. "I'm walking away, only because you asked me to. But this isn't it, Liam. This isn't where it ends."

I backed off, giving him the space he needed. I walked backward to the door, picking up my purse that I'd dropped in the entranceway.

He watched me go, not making a move to stop me as I turned the door handle. Right before I closed it, I heard him whisper, "It has to be."

HEATH

*T*he scent of Mae's shampoo lingered even after she'd gotten in Rowe's car and disappeared down his long, gravel-lined drive. Rowe glanced over at me as I locked the door behind her.

"Well, now what?"

I tried to ignore how good he looked, even slumped in a cheap camping chair with a black eye. Something about him being the exact right height while I was standing and he was sitting... I shrugged. "You tired? You should probably rest."

"I've slept most of the last two days, and when I haven't been sleeping, I've been sitting on my ass watching TV. I am not tired. You want to go fishing?"

I gazed out the window. The sun was just starting its descent, changing from vibrant yellow to a more orange tone. In an hour, it would splash pinks and purples across the sky before night fell. It was the perfect time to go fishing. "You think that's a good idea?"

He shrugged. "The lake is right there. We're two hundred feet from the cabin if we have to hustle back.

Plenty of trees for cover. And we haven't seen a heli since that first one."

I was desperate to go farther than five feet outside. Before being locked up, I'd spent most of my time out in nature. Mostly working on rich people's lawns and gardens, but that was still better than being stuck in some office job where I never got to see the sky. The woods around Rowe's cabin just begged for hiking and fishing and camping. "You sold me. Let's go."

He grinned, and I followed him into the clearing. Despite his confidence, we both scanned the sky the moment we stepped off the porch, and I glanced around nervously, peering into the woods while Rowe took out rods and tackle from his storage shed.

He passed them back to me, a frown pulling between his eyebrows. "You okay?"

"Yeah, fine. It's good to be outside. I've missed it."

"Then why do you look like you're about to vomit?"

Rowe's cabin provided a false sense of security. I knew logically that I was no safer inside than I was out here. "I'm fine. Quit interrogating me and let's go."

Despite the day slipping away, the heat of noon remained. It settled over the lake, thick and muggy, while we found a spot secluded by thick trees and cast our lines out.

It was a picture-perfect-postcard sort of scene, but I couldn't relax. At even the tiniest of nibbles on my line, I jerked my rod, reeling it in before any fish even had a chance to latch on. Grumbling, I baited my hook again and cast it out with such force it sailed well past Rowe's.

He glanced at me but didn't say anything. I peered into the sky again, then down the lake, but there was no one in sight. Not a boat, not a person. Definitely no more police helicopters.

"This is supposed to be relaxing, you know."

"It's not."

He nudged me with his shoulder. "Just pretend you're not you for five minutes. You're just some guy who likes to go fishing with his buddy."

I shot him a look. "Is that what we are? Buddies?"

Rowe jiggled his line without turning in my direction. "Do you normally suck all your friends' dicks the way you did mine?"

Heat flushed through me at the memory of getting down on my knees in my solitary cell for Rowe. I welcomed it. It was a nice distraction from the stress that held my muscles captive. A little of my anxiety disintegrated. "No. I don't. Not once."

Rowe raised an eyebrow. "Never?"

I shook my head.

"I would have never guessed that...judging by your..." He pushed his tongue into his cheek so it bulged. "You know."

I sniggered. "Technique?"

He dissolved into laughter. "Yeah. You been practicing on cucumbers?"

"Shut up."

"Too small? Eggplants?"

I shoved him. "Don't fucking flatter yourself."

He stumbled a few steps, nearly dropping his rod, his grin ear to ear.

"I just gave you what I know I like. Not exactly rocket science. We got the same shit going on down there."

He quieted, and we both gazed out at the lake again.

"It was good, by the way."

"The blow job?"

"No, dumbass. Your artwork on the cell walls. Of course

the blow job." He shoved me with a laugh, the same way I'd shoved him.

Only I wasn't expecting it. I took a step sideways to right myself and put my foot down heavily, right on the edge of the bank.

There was no saving me.

My foot slipped off the edge, my ass crashed into the grass embankment, and I slid the rest of the way down the short drop into the waist-deep water.

Somehow, I managed to hold on to my rod.

Rowe stared at me with his mouth hanging open. Then he burst into laughter. "What the fuck just happened?"

I scowled at him. My shorts and underwear were soaked through, as was the bottom half of my shirt. "You shoved me in the fucking lake. What does it look like?"

"I barely touched you. If you'd wanted to go swimming, you should have just said the word."

I passed him my rod and clambered out while he laughed his ass off.

"Oh, stop with the face, you grump. Laughing like this is killing my ribs."

"Good. Hope it hurts." Water sluiced from my body as I dragged myself out. The water wasn't cold, but now my underwear and shorts were suctioned to me. It didn't help my mood. I tugged at the fabric, trying to readjust everything so I could catch a damn fish.

We stood in silence, watching the sun sink lower, until those pinks and purples appeared. But I was uncomfortable. I alternated between pulling at my wet clothes and peering around, making sure no one had gotten lost on a walking trail. I was convinced someone would stumble across us and report me to *America's Most Wanted* at any moment.

Rowe wound his line in and dropped it on the bank. "I'm done."

"We haven't caught anything."

"That wasn't the point."

"Then what was?" That wasn't how I rolled. When I went out fishing, I didn't come back empty-handed.

"Take your shorts off."

Heat flared low in my gut, and I nearly dropped my rod. "What for?"

"Because I brought you out here in the hopes of getting you to chill out, but it only seems to have succeeded in making you worse." He stepped in closer, and that connection between us flared to life once more.

What the fuck was that? It had always been there. Something so electric I could shock myself with it.

I put the rod down slowly. We stood near eye to eye, with him only an inch or so shorter than I was. His eyes were so impossibly brown, his unbrushed hair an identical shade and tousled from hanging around the house for the past few days.

"What are we doing?" I mumbled.

He inched closer. "Stress relief."

"Bullshit." It was more than that, and we both knew it.

"You want to put a label on it then?" He was so damn close. Close enough for our breaths to mingle.

"No," I huffed out.

"Good. Me neither."

Both of us stood there, breaths ragged while the sun went down. Both of us waiting for the other to make a move.

I dropped my gaze to his lips. All I could think about was how he'd tasted. My dick twitched.

He swallowed, his Adam's apple bobbing. "What do you want then?"

"Don't fucking ask me that."

"Already fucking did."

I groaned, giving in and pressing against him. My erection thickened, straining beneath my damp underwear. I wanted him on his knees. I wanted to slam my dick hard into his wet mouth and feel the suck and draw of his lips. I wanted him to feel the way I'd felt when I'd done it to him.

I pulled the drawstring on my shorts, loosening the waistband so I could shove the soggy material down my legs. Warm night air wafted around my damp thighs, doing nothing to help my growing erection. I let out a ragged breath as he lifted up my T-shirt, and then when he was taking too long, I fisted the back of it with one hand, whipping it off.

He stared at me, a challenge in his eyes. I couldn't wait to fuck the look right off his face. I moved in closer, so our lips barely brushed. I dragged my mouth along the stubble of his jaw, not caring that it scraped and poked at the sensitive skin of my lips and face.

Rowe's head lolled back, his groan clear on the night air. "Tell me what you want."

He asked for it. "I want to push you up against that tree and take you hard and fast from behind."

Rowe's hand dove into my underwear, circling his fingers around my erection and freeing it. He pumped me twice while I kissed his neck, sucking and biting, not caring if I left a mark. My boxers were shoved to the ground, and then my erection was between us. He worked me in long, slow strokes that instantly had precum beading at my tip. I ached to take him in the way I'd promised, ached to get inside him while I reached around and jerked his cock. But that couldn't happen here. Instead, I demanded the next best thing. "Rowe?"

"Mmm."

"Get on your knees."

He was on the ground in an instant, his hot, wet mouth going straight to my cock. It was better than I could have imagined, especially good after the cool lake water. My fingers went straight for his hair, like they had a mind of their own. I clamped down tight, way rougher than I normally was, but Rowe encouraged it, gripping my thighs, then my balls, squeezing tight and bobbing his head to take as much of me into his mouth as he could.

I dropped my head back on my shoulders and stared at the stars creeping through the budding darkness. "Fuck, that feels good."

He took everything I had to give, letting me thrust into his mouth without thought of being soft or gentle. My orgasm built low in my balls, teased thoroughly by Rowe's fingers and tongue.

When I couldn't hold it in anymore, I stared down at him. I jerked inside his mouth, deep spurts of hot cum sucked from my tip. He worked every last drop, taking it all until I was completely spent.

He wiped his mouth on the back of his hand as he stood. Then he kissed me, letting me taste myself on his tongue. His kisses were deep and drugging, and if I hadn't just been so thoroughly blown, I might have come again.

He pulled away and picked up the rods. "Should have told me that's all it took to get you relaxed. I could have done that back at the cabin."

He went to walk away, but I caught him by the wrist, spinning him back around and walking him backward until I had him pushed up at the tree I'd indicated earlier. I reached a hand between us, palming his erection over his shorts. "You didn't come."

The rumble of a car froze us both, but the car that jolted up the drive was Rowe's, Mae behind the wheel.

Rowe grinned at me. "Someone has to be able to get up for her. And judging by how much cum you just sent down my throat, it ain't gonna be you anytime soon."

The thought of Mae's sweet, soft curves, so different to Rowe's hard lines, twitched at my dick. "Wanna bet?"

"Wanna prove it?"

Fuck yeah, I did.

*H*eath and I were still messing around, joking and shoving each other out of the way in order to get to Mae first. She was just climbing out of my car when we got there, her long blonde braid falling down her back, a cropped white top showing off a sliver of her belly when she twisted at our shouts.

My dick, still semi-hard from everything Heath and I had been doing in the woods, kicked to attention once more at seeing her. I waited for her sunshine smile to spread across her face and light up her eyes.

It didn't come.

I stopped.

Heath glanced at me, confused, and then over at Mae. Instantly, he realized the same thing I had. He stopped dead as well.

"What's wrong?" he demanded.

She didn't try denying it. "It's Liam."

I fought down a wave of panic. They knew. The cops had worked out that Liam and Mae and I had helped Heath escape. I knew Liam wouldn't have said anything to implicate us, but if he'd been arrested, it was only a matter of time before they knew who else was involved. "We need to get Heath out. If he's caught—"

But Mae shook her head. "It's not that. I just went to Liam's apartment. He's there...but he's not. I think we have a big problem."

I hadn't been breathing. I sucked in a few deep breaths, and Mae filled Heath and me in while we took the groceries into the cabin. I made sure Mae had the lightest bags, and Heath and I split the rest between us so it only took one trip.

In the kitchen, Mae put her bags down on the countertop but made no move to put them away. "I went to Tori's place, but Will wouldn't let me speak to her. Then Liam was...not Liam. I've never seen him that drunk and angry."

Heath drew her to his chest, soothing the palm of his hand over her hair. All thoughts of anything sexual had flown out the window the moment we'd seen her expression. My erection had died, and now all that remained was the urge to hold her.

"I should go over there. He doesn't need to be feeling guilty about me. I'm fine." I picked up my phone and called Liam's number, but unsurprisingly, there was no answer.

"He doesn't need to feel guilty about me either," Heath agreed as I put the phone down. "I know he did his best. The judge had it out for me as much as the cops did. I was never going to get a fair trial. That's not on him."

"He probably knows that, deep down." Mae clutched Heath a little tighter. "But with his dad coming back...or his brother, I guess, and finding out what his grandfather did to his mother..." A tear dripped down her face. "He's strong, but no one is strong enough to endure that sort of family secret alone."

I took several cartons of milk from a reusable cooler bag

before folding it. "Give him some space tonight. I've got to go to work tomorrow morning anyway, and presumably so does he. I'll check in at his office on my way. If he's not there..."

"He'll be there." Heath did his best to sound reassuring, but it was clear he wasn't one-hundred-percent sure either.

He let go of Mae and gripped the edge of the countertop while she busied herself putting the milk into the refrigerator.

I couldn't stand the worry on her face. She didn't look reassured at all.

I couldn't have that. "If he's not there, I'll go to his apartment myself and drag him back here. Just give him tonight."

"You sure that's what he needs? I don't want him thinking we don't care."

I smiled softly at her. "Nobody could ever think that about you. You care about everybody and everything more than any person I've ever known. He'll probably call once he's sober and realizes what he's said."

She lifted one shoulder. "Maybe. I know I shouldn't but can I stay with you guys tonight?"

"As if you even need to ask."

The three of us slept on my mattress on the floor, both me and Heath tucked around Mae's smaller frame.

When I picked my phone up the next morning, I was convinced I'd find a message from Liam, full of hungover apologies, but my screen was blank. Mae seemed equally disappointed when she checked her own cell. Heath still slept deeply, one arm banded around Mae's middle, her back to his chest. My heart gave an uneven thump.

"What?" Mae whispered.

I forced a smile and leaned in to kiss her soft lips. "Nothing. Go back to sleep, it's still early." I smoothed the frown line from between her eyes. "Let me worry about Liam, okay?"

I showered quickly and dressed in a fresh uniform. Mae was asleep again, so I moved quietly around them, trying not to panic about the way feelings were creeping in when I looked at her.

And at him.

Despite her even breathing, telling me she was asleep, I brushed a kiss over her forehead.

"Where's mine?" Heath's sleepy voice held a hint of laughter.

I briefly considered kicking him. He was right at foot height. But I didn't want to disturb Mae. "See you later, asshole."

"I'll be here."

I left the cabin and made the drive back into Saint View. But I skirted the prison and drove to Liam's apartment in Providence. I'd been there a few times, mostly to watch sports, and I parked out front. The streets were quiet, the only people up and about were a couple of early commuters and a pair of joggers in designer active wear. The lobby of Liam's building was empty, the doorman seemingly off duty. I couldn't remember the door code from the last Super Bowl party we'd had, so I had no choice but to hold my finger to the little gray buzzer for the penthouse apartment.

I buzzed for a solid ten minutes before coming to the conclusion that he either wasn't ready to talk or he was still passed out from last night's drinking efforts.

"You're not getting out of it that easily, Banks," I muttered to myself. "If I have to drive into the city to your office, I will. I'll be back after shift."

A woman walking past with a baby in a stroller gave me a wide berth, and I couldn't blame her. I was standing in the middle of the road talking to myself. I slunk back to my car and took one last peek up at the penthouse windows. If Liam was watching me, I couldn't tell. But I had to get to work.

I stepped through the doors with nerves rioting around my belly. It was still too early for reception staff to be on, and I was grateful because it gave me a moment to get myself together. There'd be questions today. I'd already given my statement to the police while I was in the hospital, but I had no doubt that Tabor would want to interrogate me, and the other guards would no doubt want the gossip. I wasn't surprised when there was a note taped to my locker door that simply said 'come see me.' It was on prison letterhead, and I recognized the warden's blocky handwriting.

I stowed my gear in my locker, tapping Mae's as I walked past. She'd be back tonight to teach a class, but I'd be gone by then. A trickle of worry wandered down my spine over why the two of us had been scheduled on opposite shifts. It wasn't entirely uncommon, we'd worked opposite shifts before, but Tabor knew I preferred to be her guard.

I leaned on Tabor's open office door, and the man looked up from his pile of paperwork.

"You're early." He paused in his paper shuffling and sat back in his chair, indicating that I should take the chair opposite him.

"Not my favorite shift to work, but it's not in me to be late."

"Of course. You're nothing if not reliable."

I sat in the chair opposite him, his big desk between us overflowing with folders and office supplies. There was a hint of something in his voice that worried me. Suspicion, perhaps? Or maybe I was just being paranoid.

"That shiner's better. How's the ribs?"

"Fine, thanks. All better."

Tabor picked up a folder and handed it across the desk to me. "Says you. Your discharge paperwork from the hospital said light duties for at least a week."

I groaned. "How about we just ignore that? I'm fine, truly."

Tabor looked at me with that calculating gaze that made me think he was mulling over things he wasn't saying aloud, just biding his time for the right moment. Warning bells went off in the back of my mind, and instinct shouted that the man was smart. I needed to be careful around him.

Just as quickly as the expression had crossed his face, it was gone again, and he chuckled like we were old friends. Somehow, that made me even more paranoid.

"Not really wanting to open us up to a lawsuit because I didn't follow your doctor's orders. Sorry, Pritchard. You're riding a desk for a week. But don't worry, there's plenty to keep you busy in there." He pointed to the folder. "Paroles. And lots of them. They all need processing and the prisoners kicked out the doors. We're overcrowded, and need to make some room."

That I could get on board with. We had way too many men here. With the influx of prisoners after the riot, and the staff that had been fired and never fully replaced, we were operating at a guard-to-prisoner ratio well outside the accepted state rules. I tried to force a friendly smile, trying to keep the man on my side. "No problem. I've got it handled."

"I've got another man on light duties already in the processing office. Just buzz down to Gen Pop when you're ready to start."

"You got it." I stood to leave, but Tabor's voice called me back before I'd managed to escape.

"Pritchard, what happened last week... I've never seen anything like that happen in a prison, and I've worked in the system for twenty-five years." He cocked his head to one side as he eyed me. "I haven't been able to sleep for thinking about it. I owe you an apology. It shouldn't have happened, not under my watch. I intend to get to the bottom of how it did."

I froze on the inside. The last thing I wanted was him investigating what had happened any more thoroughly than the police were.

"If you need to talk about it, you know where I am, right? Anything you want to tell me, I'll be all ears."

That was when I knew for sure he suspected my involvement. The words could only have been construed as caring and concerned if you were deaf and didn't hear the thinly veiled accusations in his tone.

I forced a laugh. "Got a shrink for that. I'm good. Just want to get back to work."

"A man dedicated to his job. Good to see. On you go, then."

It took everything in me not to spin on my heel and sprint down the corridor. I forced myself to walk a normal pace toward the parole processing rooms and hoped the sweat trickling down my spine wasn't visible through my shirt.

It was a relief to put distance between me and Tabor, and by the time I got to the opposite end of the prison, I'd managed to normalize my breathing. I scanned my way into the office and grinned when I recognized the other man. Colt had his boots propped up on the desk, arms crossed over his chest, eyes closed as if he'd decided to take a nap while he waited for me.

He cracked one open when I entered and grinned. "Fancy meeting you here."

"I was about to say the same thing to you."

He stood, and I drew him in with one arm for a half hug. He thumped me on the back, and I winced at the jolt to my ribs. He stepped back and grimaced. "Shit. Sorry. I heard you got worked over pretty bad last week."

"Not as bad as you. How's the leg? We've missed you around here."

Colt had been injured badly by inmates during the riot. His leg had required surgery, and then physical therapy, so he'd been off work for weeks.

"Probably not going to be running a marathon on it anytime soon, but it's good enough for me to chase Lacey and Luna around, so that's all I'm really worried about."

"Luna's walking?"

Colt's grin spread ear to ear. "Yep. She's not even one yet, but she just got up one day last week and took three steps, and now there is no stopping her. Banjo's already teaching her how to run with a football." The pride rolled off him in waves when he spoke about his family,

I slapped him on the shoulder before we sat. "That's fantastic, man. I'm really glad to hear everything is going well for you guys." I turned away before my expression could give away how desperately I wished I could say the same for myself. I loved hearing about Colt's happy home life, but it always reminded me that things were not nearly as rosy for myself. I'd missed Ripley's first steps. He'd taken them at Norma's place, after I'd given her full custody of him. At the time it had been necessary for everyone involved, but now, I wished I could turn back the hands of time. Having him out at my cabin with Mae had only reminded me how much I missed that little boy. He was a part of me. He owned a piece of my heart and soul, and hearing about Colt's child only reminded me that mine wasn't with me.

I cleared my throat. "Did you see this pile of exits we have to do? Let's get on with it, huh?"

Colt nodded and made a call down to the offices of Gen Pop where the prisoners who were leaving today were waiting.

The next few hours were filled with paperwork and signatures and stern warnings to not step out of line or they'd be right back here. Of course, the prisoners all promised to be on their best behavior, assuring us they'd never be back. The sad thing was that we knew a lot of them would be.

The pile was dwindling, as was my interest, by the time our shift drew to a close. Colt yammered about college and sports while we waited for our last prisoners of the day to be brought up. I opened the final file and ran my finger along the neat black type that gave all of the prisoner's details, including their name, date of birth, and the crimes they'd committed to land them in here in the first place.

My blood ran cold.

"You okay? You look like you've seen a ghost."

I shook my head. "No, it's fine. This just must be a mistake."

"If you're talking about my release, it's no mistake." Zye slunk down into the chair opposite my desk and grinned his demented Cheshire cat impersonation. He folded his arms across his chest, his teeth shining, expression smug. "I'm getting out today."

"Over my dead body."

He leaned in, elbows on the desktop. "Now, now, Pritchard. As tempting as that invitation is, I don't plan on doing anything that might land me back in here. That would be a tragedy of epic proportions, wouldn't it? Because the thing is, while I was in here, my son's mother was murdered. Now he has no parents. Poor little baby. Isn't that terrible?"

The bile rose up my throat, thick and sickly, choking me from even replying.

Zye sat back on his chair again and tucked his hands behind his head like he didn't have a care in the world. "I can't wait to see the little guy. He is going to be so excited to see his daddy."

The thought of Ripley calling Zye daddy was almost too much. I gripped the desktop to keep myself from launching across the table and wiping the smug look off his face. My heart ached. Ripley could not be around Zye. He was just a boy who only a couple of weeks ago had fallen asleep with his skinny arms wrapped around my neck, safe and happy in my arms.

He'd ceased to exist if Zye got his hands on him.

Zye was dark to his very core. His jealousy and possessive nature was a danger to anyone who came in contact with him, but especially an impressionable kid who didn't have a father figure because I'd fucked up.

"He's never gonna call you daddy." I bit out the promise, words made of steel.

Zye chuckled. "You talk like you have any say in it. Thing is, you don't. It's my name on his birth certificate. It's my blood running through his veins. I'm getting out of here, and I'm taking my kid. I'm taking what's mine."

I pushed back my chair, shaking my head. "I'm not processing this. This is a mistake." Zye had never been charged with Rory's murder, but we both knew he'd done it.

"Rowe," Colt said quietly, leafing through Zye's paperwork. "This is all above board. He's been granted parole. We have to let him go. He's got a place at a halfway house and he'll have a parole officer up his ass twenty-four seven."

I knew Colt was trying to reassure me, but he didn't know Zye like I did. No parole officer was going to keep Zye from taking what he wanted. Not when it came to Rory and Ripley. Not when it came to me.

"No," I ground out. "No! It's not happening." I stormed from the room while Zye laughed. He'd got the better of me, and he was probably enjoying that power trip, but I wasn't hanging around here anymore.

I wasn't hanging around waiting for him to snatch Ripley in the middle of the night.

He wasn't taking my son.

My son.

13

LIAM

I was ready to rip the fucking buzzer out of the wall and throw it into the ocean, right along with my phone. After Mae had called a hundred times, and Rowe a few more, I'd had the sense to turn that off at least.

I shifted on the couch, trying to fit my too-big frame comfortably on the two-seater. Logically, I knew the couch beneath me was soft, but it grated at my skin like sandpaper. I'd tossed around on it for hours. Yet I did nothing to move to the bedroom and get some proper rest. The stomach-churning scent of alcohol wafted around me, either from the open bottle on the coffee table or just as likely, it was seeping out my pores.

Nothing like a good, old-fashioned bender to forget you shouldn't exist.

I'd never been a big drinker, but I'd been enjoying finding some oblivion in the bottom of a bottle. I liked the way I didn't have to think when alcohol was streaming through my system. The more I drank, the less I felt anything at all. Happiness, sadness, worry... None of it mattered. Being a flat line of nothing was nice. Easy.

But the incessant buzzing was impossible to sleep through, and I couldn't silence that the same way I'd silenced my phone. I dragged myself off the couch and peered through the window and down at the ground level, blinking in the harsh morning sunlight.

Rowe, in his guard uniform, glanced up, but I knew he couldn't see me. I was surprised he was here at all. Even from this distance, I could see the bruising around his eyes from where I'd hit him.

Guilt roared up, piercing through the waning alcohol barrier.

It never stayed away long. Guilt over hitting Rowe and then just leaving him in that cell with a concussion that could have killed him. Guilt over ruining Mae's friendships. Guilt over getting Heath's case wrong. Guilt that I existed at all because my grandfather was a piece of scum who attacked young girls.

That was the big thing. The stuff with Rowe and Heath and Mae I probably could have come back from, but not the rest. I'd first fallen for Mae while we were both sixteen. The same age my mother was when she'd been attacked. What if Mae and I had dated back then? I would have brought her to my house, introduced her to my grandfather... It would have just been history repeating itself all over. I'd idolized the man. I'd gone to Edgely Academy because he'd wanted it. I went to Yale because that's where he'd gone. I'd worked my ass off at the practice, desperately trying to impress the only father figure I knew.

Rage and disgust filled me every time I thought about how I'd been conceived. Every time I thought about it, my mother's face was replaced with Mae's, and the thought of anyone hurting her was excruciating. Yet my mother had managed to love me anyway. Did she see him when she looked at me? How could she not? I was a walking, talking reminder of everything she'd endured.

The buzzing finally stopped, but it still blared in the back of my head like a siren. It was never going to stop. Now that I knew, there was no going back to who I'd been before.

I drained the last of a bottle of rum, needing it for what I knew I had to do next. Sweat broke out on the back of my neck, but I pulled on a shirt anyway, letting it cling to my clammy skin. I found my shoes by the front door and took my keys from the hook.

In the hallway, I hit the button for the elevator and closed my eyes, counting backward in my head to try to calm the racing of my heart. The doors opened with an ear-splitting ping, and I winced at the noise, wondering how I'd never noticed how loud it was. The elevator began its descent to the lobby floor, and I stumbled at the sudden movement, crashing into the mirrored wall, banging my hip on the handrail. "Goddammit." I rubbed at the sore spot while my head swam. I couldn't drive like this. Work would be expecting me, but I didn't care about that either.

Out on the street, I tapped my pockets, searching for my phone, but came up empty-handed. I could have just gone back upstairs to call a cab, but I didn't. The long walk into Saint View was both a punishment and a chance to get my head on straight. It took two hours, but each step brought clarity. The fresh air combined with forcing my muscles to work pushed out most of the alcohol toxins, and by the time I stood in front of the house my brother and his banger friends were occupying, I knew exactly what I needed to do.

"Hayden!" I bellowed, hitting the front door with a fist. The last time I'd been here was with Mae. I'd been worried for her then, surrounded by the group of criminals my brother had fallen in with. But I felt no such fear for myself.

If this all went south, whatever they did to me would be no worse than what I wanted to do to myself.

The door opened, and my brother stood in the doorway. With his black baseball cap turned backward and low-slung jeans on his hips, it was the first time in years we'd dressed even remotely similar. His chest was covered in an array of colorful tattoos, most I'd never seen before.

"Well, this is unexpected. Where's the suit? You look like shit, brother."

I didn't argue. I knew I did.

"I need something."

He rested one shoulder on the doorjamb and crossed his arms over his chest. "I got no more info on Scythe or DeWitt. Told you everything I know last time you were here."

"It's not that." I pulled in a deep breath. Until I got here, I wasn't even sure I was really going to go through with it. But I had to. It was the only way to stop the black hole from opening up inside me and swallowing me whole.

"I need a gun."

14

MAE

"I fucking hate seeing you like this. I swear, I'm gonna rip Liam's balls off when he comes to his senses," Heath muttered.

I shook my head. "I'm fine. Like you said, he'll come around." I busied myself putting out a few bits and pieces I'd bought at the store to make Rowe's cabin feel more homey. A scent diffuser, a pot plant, and a big thick rug for the living area to start with.

Heath helped, shoving the camping chairs out of the way so I could unroll the rug.

"You're not fine. You love him, and he's hurting."

I did. I hated that he was shutting me out. But I'd tried and failed. I just hoped Rowe would have better luck at getting through to him.

The TV interrupted with a news bulletin, and Heath and I both tensed as the reporter stared down the lens of the camera. Heath's mug shot flashed up on the screen to her right. *"Days after the escape at Saint View Prison, convicted murderer, Heath Michaelson, remains on the run. He's thought to*

*be armed and dangerous. If spotted, the general public is warned
not to approach but to call the police immediately."*

"I'm armed and dangerous now? Great." He put his head
down, but not before I saw the flash of despair in his gaze.

I dropped the rug and let it unroll itself the rest of the
way while I stalked across the room to Heath's side. I
pressed my fingers to his arm. "This isn't forever. Something
will turn up. We just need one thing to go our way."

He moved out of my grasp. "It's fine."

"You're about as fine as I am."

He sighed and sat hard on the rug. He ran his fingers
through the soft woven fibers. "This is really nice by the way.
Good choice."

"You're changing the subject."

"You buy this with our conversation in mind?" He was
referring to when he and Rowe had promised to get naked
with me, if only we had somewhere to do it. He gazed up
from his spot on the floor and then held a hand out.

I threaded my fingers through his, and he tugged me
down to sit beside him. He leaned in and kissed the side of
my neck.

"I see what you're doing, Michaelson."

"You see nothing. Your eyes are closed."

I smiled beneath the touch of his lips to mine because
he was right. They had fluttered closed the moment he'd
touched me. I couldn't help it. My body was so incredibly
responsive to his. To all of them.

"Rowe isn't here..." The words came out as light and
feathery as my breath.

Heath kissed a trail across my collarbone, his stubbly
beard scratching over my skin. I dropped my head back,
giving him better access.

"Liam isn't either, but you snooze, you lose."

I cracked up laughing.

Heath looked up from undoing the top button of my shirt. "Don't need either of them to make you smile. Nothing is better than that, sweetheart." He brushed his thumb over my bottom lip. "Except making you scream."

His fingers worked the rest of my buttons free, and he gently pushed aside the material, exposing the lace of my bra. He sucked in a breath. "Do you know how often I thought about you while I was inside?"

I shook my head.

"Too often. I spent half my time hating myself for being so blind, back when we were friends."

"You were with someone else. It wasn't the right time."

"It wasn't," he agreed. "But then that night after the bar, before everything went to shit..."

"We were drunk."

"I still wanted you."

The night I'd seen him at the bar for the first time in years, when my old crush had lit up like an inferno, had been the start of everything. Both good and bad. "You don't regret it?" I asked quietly.

He glanced up from trailing his lips across the swell of my breasts. "Regret what?"

"Coming home with me that night. If you'd just walked away, let me go home alone, you wouldn't have been there when..." I still struggled to talk about it. "When Jayela died. None of this would have happened. You'd be off living your life somewhere, probably happy with a new girlfriend—"

"No. I wouldn't be. Because that night was it for me, too. You weren't the only one who felt the connection. It hit me like a fucking freight train. I couldn't have walked away. Not then. Not now. Especially not now, after everything you've done for me."

I let out a soft breath. "I don't want you to feel like you owe me anything. You don't."

He ran his nose down my cleavage. "I owe you an orgasm."

I laughed into his neck, inhaling the all-man smell of him. His scent soothed its way into my soul, putting a balm on my worries about Liam and Tori. He was here, and that was something. There were odds stacked against us, but he wasn't behind bars with a corrupt judge ready to walk him down death row herself.

"I did spring you from prison. That's gotta be good for at least one orgasm."

"You went above and beyond. Probably owe you at least three orgasms, huh?"

"Why lowball it?"

He undid my bra clasp and freed my breasts. They hung full and heavy, straining for his touch. He took greedy handfuls, pushing me back to the rug, the soft wool at my back as perfect for sex as I'd hoped it would be. My shoulders sank into the thick fabric, cradling me while Heath put his mouth to my nipple.

He dragged his teeth gently around it, sucking and licking me as he went. His fingers worked my other breast, teasing the nipple into a taut peak, and squeezing it in time with the draws of his mouth.

He stayed there so long, I squirmed beneath him, desperately fighting to widen my legs, but my skirt wouldn't allow it. "Heath," I moaned. I gave him a gentle shove, encouraging him to move lower to where I really wanted him, but the man would not be swayed. He kissed his way slowly across my belly, grabbing my hand when I tried to reach around him to lift my skirt.

"Stay still," he whispered. "I haven't had the chance to kiss every inch of you yet."

I stopped fighting him. He was right. We'd had that night in his cell, but that had been hot and fast and demanding. And then the night with Liam, but Heath clearly needed more than a physical release. He lowered my skirt, taking my panties with him and discarding them somewhere behind him. He mapped out my body with his fingers, his tongue, and after he pulled off his clothes, he marked me with his body. Skin to skin, he covered me, staring into my eyes, never looking away for even an instant.

"I've never wanted anyone the way I want you, Mae," he murmured.

"What about Rowe?"

He paused to gaze down at me, questions in his eyes.

I shook my head softly. "I'm just curious. I didn't mean it to come out sounding jealous."

"It didn't. I was just considering it myself."

"Have you guys talked about it?"

He snorted. "We don't really do that. But, Mae?"

"Mmm?"

His tongue paused against my skin. "I'd rather talk to you."

"About? Shopping list or the weather perhaps?"

"What I'm going to do to you."

My stomach clenched. "Oh."

"You blush when you're embarrassed, did you know that? You're pink all over right now." He kissed his way over my mound and, unashamed, I spread my legs for him.

He sucked in a breath. "Pink here, too. So fucking gorgeous."

I felt it. He ran his palms up my thighs, spreading me so

wide he could see every inch of me. My legs trembled in anticipation.

"Gonna suck you, sweetheart. Gonna suck and fuck you with my tongue so hard you beg me to stop. But I won't. I'm just gonna keep going until I've given you all three of those orgasms I owe you."

There was no playing in his voice. He was deadly serious.

His gaze met mine, and I gave him the nod of permission I knew he was waiting for.

He grinned, his mouth hovering over the spot I wanted him most.

I closed my eyes, bunched my fingers in the rug, and held on as he licked his way through my folds. My hips jerked right off the floor, pressing up toward his mouth wantonly, begging for more. He pushed me back down, pinning me to the floor, and did it again.

Something inside me lit up at being restrained, while he poured pleasure on me. As promised, his tongue worked my clit before plunging inside me. He ate my pussy like it was his favorite dessert, slowly and leisurely, savoring it, until he reached the bottom. Then he picked up the pace. He drove his tongue inside me, swapping to his fingers when my moans became more insistent. Pleasure swirled inside me, until it took over and exploded behind my eyes.

"Oh!" I yelled, not worrying about being quiet because there was nobody around. I clenched down hard around his fingers.

Heath abruptly turned me onto my stomach and slapped me on the ass. "Good girl."

I blinked in surprise, but the pleasure coursing from the minor sting only turned me on more. My pussy throbbed, and Heath's groan of approval made me sure he could tell.

"Facedown, ass up, sweetheart." He pulled my hips up, spreading my knees wide.

On the rug, I turned my face to one side, desperate for more.

Heath's palm massaged my ass cheek, rubbing over the spot where he'd made contact. "Even prettier when your ass is pink from my palm across it."

I clenched down on nothing and whimpered. I had no idea why that was so hot, but I wanted him to do it again. I'd heard other women talking about calling their men Daddy and always thought it ridiculous. But in that moment, the word scalded my tongue, begging to be yelled.

He used his thumbs to spread me wide and then dove between my legs once more.

I pressed back against his face, screaming out when his tongue flickered over the puckered star of my asshole. My eyes rolled back. I loved the way he felt there. It was so dirty, so hot, and I begged him not to stop.

"Not until you come," he promised. "Fuck, Mae. You're so wet. So sweet." He reared back and slapped my ass again.

"Yes!" I was so close to another orgasm and desperate to fall into it.

His thumb found my clit, two fingers slid into my pussy, and his tongue flickered over my ass. All three combined were too much and yet completely perfect. I yelped his name, grinding back on him while the orgasm rocketed through me once more. My thighs trembled, threatening to give out, but when they did, Heath followed me down, not letting up even when I was flat to the floor. I yelled again, nipples finding friction against the rug while the most ruggedly handsome man I'd ever seen devoured me.

I wanted him inside me. I wanted him everywhere.

He sprawled out beside me, propping himself on his

side, supporting his head with one hand. I turned my head toward him, watching his face while he trailed his fingertips all over my curves.

"What did you do the other half of the time?"

He paused to look at me. "Huh?"

"You said you spent half your time in prison hating yourself for not making a move on me earlier. What did you do the other half of the time?"

"Ate. Slept. Jacked off thinking about you."

I stole a glance down his body, over the tattoos on his chest and thighs. His erection jutted toward me, thick and hard. "Show me."

His eyes flared with heat. Slowly, he gripped his length and gave it a stroke. The head disappeared into his fist, only to reappear glistening with precum. He watched me as he touched himself, each stroke becoming a little faster until he was panting with need.

I raised my gaze to his eyes.

The heat there burned me. Scalded me from head to toe, then gathered in the depths of my core once more. With a feral groan, he pushed me onto my back, covering my body with his.

I wrapped my legs around his waist, inviting him home, and he sank in, eliciting an identical moan of ecstasy from both of us.

Watching me intently, he moved slowly between my thighs, his thick cock stretching my already sensitive center. He lowered his head to kiss me, and it was sweet and soft and everything we hadn't been before. My heart swelled. I knew him. I always had. He was the man I'd spent hours talking with about anything and nothing. He was the man who had occupied my thoughts and my heart ever since. He was the man I'd given up a life for, but found another in its place, a better one, one that involved him.

He gave me space to be me. To love who I wanted. And to be loved unconditionally in return.

"I love you," I whispered.

His big body paused, and he stared down at me as if he wasn't quite sure of the words I'd said. But then his lips crashed down on mine. Supported on his forearms, he gripped my head and kissed me until I was sure we were the sun, lighting up the sky. We exploded together, him deep within me, his tongue in my mouth and a full heart-and-soul connection that made this orgasm both the quietest but most earth-shattering of my life.

"I am so in love with you," he whispered back.

Tears pricked at the backs of my eyes. His words got inside me and wrapped around my heart. I couldn't stop them from spilling over. He kissed them away, his touch soft and gentle, his whispered words of love chasing them.

The front door swung open, cracking off the wall behind it. I squealed, and Heath pulled from my body, jumping to his feet, his dick still semi-hard and glistening with our lovemaking.

On instinct, I went to cover myself, but in the next instant, I registered Rowe's expression.

"What the fuck, man?" Heath asked, no shame in his nudity.

I scrambled to my feet, completely forgetting my own nudity, too. Rowe had seen me naked a bunch of times now, that didn't matter. Nor did the fact he'd just caught me and Heath in the middle of it.

All that mattered was the look on Rowe's face and the realization that we had a very big problem.

15
———

ROWE

"You go and get him and bring him here."

Mae paced the length of the small living room, her naked body wrapped only in a throw blanket I didn't recognize. It barely covered her pussy. The scent of sex caught in my nostrils, a deep longing to get in on the action myself flaring, but that was outweighed by the panic that had gripped me ever since I knew Zye was leaving the prison.

Ripley wasn't safe with him out of jail. Nobody I cared about was.

"I can't just go to Norma and take him from her," I protested.

Heath had pulled on a pair of shorts, but his torso was still bare. "Why not? He's your kid in every way that counts, Rowe. You might have let Norma take him while you couldn't, but she's an old woman. What good is she going to be if Zye turns up there? She'll have no chance. He needs to be here, where we can keep him safe."

"What if Norma won't give him to me? I'd be pulling him from the only home he knows."

Heath got in my face, his eyes blazing with an anger I hadn't anticipated. "You think Zye is gonna care about that? Go fucking get your son, Rowe!"

I blinked.

I was scared. Scared for Ripley. Scared for Mae. Scared for everyone I'd ever cared about. I didn't know how to be Ripley's father. All I knew was that I wanted to be. I always had. I'd just convinced myself I couldn't.

Mae's approach was gentler. She took my face between her hands and smiled softly at me, as if she could read my mind and knew every swirling, terrified thought running through it.

The truth of my worries came spilling out. "What if she does give him to me?" Because deep down, I knew she would. If I went there and told her Ripley's life was in danger, she'd give him to me in a heartbeat. Just like me, she always put Ripley first. "What if I'm not enough? What if I can't do it again?"

She brushed her sweet lips over mine. "Then we'll be here until you can. You aren't doing this alone anymore. You have me."

"And me," Heath huffed out.

Liam's absence hung heavy in the air, and I scrubbed my hands over my face. "Shit. I couldn't get back to Liam's place this afternoon. I found out about Zye and I came straight here without thinking about anything else."

Mae shook her head. "You don't need to worry about him right now. Go get Ripley. That's all you need to do."

The erratic beat of my heart slowed to a more normal rate, and I was glad for it, because the adrenaline and terror wasn't helping me think straight. I wrapped Mae in my arms, catching a glimpse of her naked body beneath the blanket when she put her arms around me. Later, when

Ripley was safe, I was going to thank her, multiple times, for her belief in me.

Heath squeezed my shoulder as I walked past, and then I was back on the road, driving back to Saint View to pick up my boy.

I'd always thought of him like that. It had killed me to give him up to Norma, but it would have killed him not to. He deserved the best, and after his mother's death, the best wasn't me. I was too lost to grief.

But I'd never stopped loving him. I checked in on him all the time, unable to stay away. My wallet was full of photos of him, the first ones from when he was a baby, the more recent ones from his fourth birthday party. He'd been so happy that day when he'd opened the huge present I'd brought with me. A miniature, battery-powered four-wheel drive decked out in a Spider-Man theme—his current favorite. I'd stayed long after his daycare friends had left, running alongside him as he drove the little car up and down Norma's street. His laughter had filled my head and my heart.

It was the best day I'd had in a very long time. Up there with the day that Mae had organized for me and him, when all we'd done was hang out at my cabin, but that had been enough, because we'd been together.

He may not have been my son by blood, but he was my son nonetheless.

And I wanted him back.

Norma's house was quiet when I pulled up, the lights all off inside. Ripley's swing set sat in one corner of the yard, a slight breeze blowing the seat gently. The grass was getting long. I'd need to come take care of that for her. That was always mine and Ripley's job. He followed me around with his little push-along mower, cute as hell. The house next door, the one I still owned, sat empty, waiting for my return. It was filled with memories of Rory, but for the first time, that didn't feel like an overwhelming burden. Maybe after Zye lost interest, we could come back here.

Or maybe that was just ridiculous. Liam had his apartment. Mae had hers. Heath was on the run; he couldn't just come back to suburbia.

What a clusterfuck the entire thing was.

Shoving all of that out of my head, I walked carefully up the steps of Norma's house and knocked quietly on the door. A light popped on in the front bedroom, and when the door crept open, it was with a double barrel shotgun pointing in my direction.

I blanched at it. "Jesus, Norma. It's me. Rowe."

"Oh. Come in. I'll put Old Betsy away in the safe. What the hell are you doing here at this time of the night? I'd already gone to bed! You trying to give an old woman a heart attack?"

I closed the door behind her and watched her lock the gun in a safe in her bedroom. I wasn't sure if it made me feel better or worse. "No, I'm sorry. But I do need to talk."

She eyed me, shrugging on a flowered robe from a hook in the closet and wrapping it tightly over her pajamas. "Well, then, out to the kitchen you go. If it's serious enough for a conversation in the middle of the night, then it requires milk and cookies."

A smile twitched at the corner of my mouth. "It's not even 9:00 p.m. And you've been living with a four-year-old too long when you start thinking all things can be solved with warm drinks and snacks."

She shot me a sidelong glare. "You'd be surprised at the things my cookies can fix." She pointed to the kitchen table.

I dragged out a familiar chair. I'd sat at this table many a time over the years. Both with Rory, and without. My heart still gave a pang, remembering her sitting beside me at this very table, her hand on my leg beneath it, while she introduced me to Norma for the first time.

I was surprised to find it was no longer a pang of longing. But more like a fond memory. One that made me smile but didn't feel like my insides were being torn apart.

She put a pot on the stove, filled it with milk, and then organized a tray of cookies. She set them down in front of me. "Ripley and I made them yesterday. I think he snuck some extra sugar in when I wasn't watching, but they're still good."

"Kid does have a sweet tooth. He's in bed?"

She nodded, taking the seat opposite mine. "He had a big day at daycare. He crashed as soon as I got him out of the bath. But enough small talk. Tell me what's going on."

I let out a wobbly breath, not sure how to broach the subject, but knowing Norma respected brutal honesty. "Zye's out of prison."

Her hand froze in the middle of reaching for a cookie. Then she shook her head. "No. He can't be. He still has years on his sentence."

"The prisons are all overcrowded. He got early release. He's out, Norma. I saw his parole paperwork this afternoon."

Her fingers trembled, and I took them in mine, rubbing her hand gently. She knew what he'd done and the danger he represented. I didn't need to explain any further. She stared around at the little house she'd owned for a lifetime. Rory had grown up here. Her childhood drawings were in frames in the hallway, right alongside Ripley's. "I need to leave," Norma stuttered. "I can't stay here. He knows this house. He'll come for Ripley, and I'll be damned if that animal is getting a hand on that boy."

The milk boiled and splashed over, but it didn't seem to register with Norma. I put her hand down on the table and stood to turn off the burner, moving the milk off the hot stove top but not bothering to pour either of us a mug. No amount of warm milk was going to make this better.

"I came to ask if you'd let me take him."

Her gaze snapped to mine, her eyes wide.

I swallowed down the nervous lump in my throat. "Please, Norma. I love him. I can protect him. I'll take him out to the cabin until Zye loses interest."

"And then you'll bring him home?"

I felt as if a steel band was wrapping around my heart. I knew I couldn't give him up twice. If I took him now and made a home for him in the cabin, tucked him in at night, prepared all his meals, and held him when he was hurt... It would kill me to give all that up again. But it wasn't my call to make. I stared down at the tabletop. "If that's what you want."

Norma's hand was like a rattlesnake. It shot out fast and gripped mine so tight her short, clean nails left indent marks in my skin. "Don't be stupid, boy. You know that's never what I wanted. Ripley is your son. My daughter chose you, and she chose damn well. You're a good man, Rowe Pritchard, and I hate that you seem to forget that."

I shook my head, unable to handle praise I didn't deserve. "I've done things—"

"None that change who you truly are. I see you. I know why Rory chose you. Ripley was always meant to be yours. I stepped in while you were hurting, but I'm not what he needs. Not on a day-to-day basis. I've prayed to the good Lord you'd come to see that, and now you have."

She smiled, and this time, it was filled with relief.

"This is the only home he remembers. I'm just his fun uncle-type figure. I don't know how to be a dad."

She patted the side of my face. "Silly boy. You already are one. You've proved it over and over again by sacrificing everything for him. You think he doesn't see it? He adores you. We both do. The home you give him will be the one he needs. You'll see."

I swallowed hard, fighting off the lump in my throat. I still wasn't sure I believed I deserved her admiration and trust, but when I closed my eyes, I heard Mae echoing the same thing, and Heath promising support.

Somewhere, I knew Rory was smiling.

"I need all his things. As much as I can fit in the car. I don't have anything at my place."

Norma nodded and pushed to her feet. "He doesn't have a lot, but you can take whatever you can find."

She followed me to Ripley's bedroom, and I pushed the door open quietly. He lay on his bed in Spider-Man pajamas, his arms and legs tangled around his sheets. Norma moved past me, and in the darkness, she started throwing things into a bag.

I couldn't stop staring at him. His dark eyelashes fanned out across his still baby-like cheeks. His blond hair was tousled and sticking up in every direction. The sweet bow of his lips, relaxed in sleep. I knelt at his side and gently shook him.

"He sleeps like the dead," Norma warned. "You could just pick him up and put him in the car."

"I don't want him to wake up and be scared because he's somewhere unfamiliar."

I shook him again and grinned when his little eyes fluttered open.

"Rowe?" He blinked in the darkness.

"Hey, buddy. Yeah, it's me. I was just wondering..." Wondering what? If he wanted to be my son again? I cleared my throat. "I was just wondering if you want to go on an adventure?"

"With you?" He sat up eagerly, rubbing at his eyes.

"Yeah, buddy. With me."

"Grandma, too?"

I glanced up at her. "Grandma can come, too, if she wants to?" My cabin only had two bedrooms, but we'd make do.

But Norma patted his head. "Grandma is too old for this adventure. This one is just for you and Rowe. Grandma will be just fine here with Old Betsy."

I nodded, respecting her wishes. I didn't think I would have wanted to uproot my entire life either. At least she had her gun.

She leaned down and gave Ripley a kiss before handing me an overstuffed bag of clothes and toys. "Take care of Rowe, okay, Rip? And I'll see you soon."

He flung his skinny little arms around her neck, and when she released him, he set shining eyes on me. "Let's go!"

He held his arms up for me to lift him, and I did.

In that moment, everything clicked into place. This wasn't like last time.

I was taking my boy home.

Norma shifted her car seat into my car, and once Ripley was strapped in, excited for his nighttime adventure, she turned serious eyes on me. "You keep that boy safe. Not a hair on his head gets harmed, you hear me? Or I'll be out at that cabin to beat you with my walking stick."

"You got it."

"He can't swim properly yet. He's close, but keep an eye on him by the lake."

"Of course."

Her bottom lip trembled. "Come back to visit as soon as it's safe, okay? Both of you."

I pulled her in for a hug, knowing that despite her conviction that Ripley should be with me, this was hard for her. She was giving up her last little daily reminder of Rory.

"I've got this," I told her.

And for the first time, I actually believed it.

16

LIAM

I'd never held a gun before. I'd never had any sort of urge to do so. In my line of work, I saw daily how guns ruined lives. Whether that be through gang violence, a case of mistaken identity, or a lover's quarrel that turned deadly. A gun never made any situation better.

Until now.

I sat in my car with the engine idling and the weapon in my lap.

Even when I looked out the window, staring up at the big house that had been a formative part of my teenage years, the cold metal reminded me it was there.

Taunting me.

Reminding me of what I was and how I came to be. My mother hadn't deserved that pain, and now it was mine. It weighed on me so heavily I could barely breathe.

I traced a finger over the trigger.

It would be so easy. A relief, really. A release of everything that currently held me captive. One quick pull and it would all be over.

And yet, I'd been sitting here for hours, frozen to the

spot, unable to move, and hating myself even more with every second that passed, because I was spineless.

"Just fucking do it!" I screamed at the empty car.

I couldn't.

I slammed the heel of my hand against the steering wheel over and over, swearing until my hand was bruised and I was all out of cuss words. In an angry flurry, I shoved the gun in the glove box and jerked the gearshift into drive.

The engine roared to life when I dropped my foot down hard on the accelerator, half my tires probably left on the road outside my grandparents' house.

I didn't have a destination in mind, but the longer I drove, the more I fell apart. Shreds of soul ripped off with every turn. The driving that had once comforted me now felt like as much of a farce as the rest of my life. My job had paid for this car. The job my grandfather—father—had forced me into. It all reeked of him and what he'd done. I was his clone after all. The little mini-me he'd always wanted.

As dark, and depraved, and dirty as he was.

I couldn't drive anymore. On autopilot, I headed to the one place I'd sworn to myself I wouldn't go back to.

Just for a moment.

A few hours.

One night.

Then I'd leave again. I just needed her one last time, before I ended it all.

My BMW bumped down the driveway of Rowe's cabin at a speed my mechanic would have had heart failure over. But I didn't care if I chipped and dented the bodywork. None of that mattered now. When I was done, the car could be incinerated for all I cared.

The headlights flashed through the darkness and then

lit up the little wood cabin in the middle of the clearing. The driveway curved and led me straight to the door. There were lights on inside, but no other cars.

I frowned. Where the hell were they all? Mae and Rowe should have both been home from work by now. And Heath couldn't leave at all.

Those thoughts were interrupted by the screen door flying open and Mae running down the steps.

Instantly, a weight lifted off me. Not all of it, but enough that I could draw in a full breath for the first time since I'd found out the truth.

Mae threw herself at me, and I stumbled back, shoved up against the car by the force of her hug. She tucked her face to my neck, and despite myself, I did the same to her. I drew in her familiar scent, feeling that same pang of love and longing for her that I felt every time she was near.

"I'm so glad you're home." Her voice was muffled by my clothes.

Home.

I placed a kiss on her head and let the word percolate. A huge part of me wanted to agree with her. My apartment wasn't a home. Merely somewhere I slept. There was nothing warm or friendly about it, and most of all, she wasn't there.

Heath leaned on the porch rail watching the two of us. When he caught me looking, he gave me a nod. "Good to have you back, Banks."

I couldn't even answer him. I was too wrapped up in the feel of Mae. "I'm sorry," I whispered in the darkness.

She shook her head, her loose blonde curls bouncing around her shoulders. "It's okay."

It wasn't. None of it was. She didn't deserve the way I'd spoken to her last night. Or the way I was going to leave her tomorrow. I was selfish, coming here at all, drawing on her strength because I didn't have the guts to go through with it.

God, she was beautiful, and holding her in my arms had always felt so incredibly right. I hoped Rowe and Heath felt the same way. I hoped they'd hold her, and tell her she was amazing, and protect her heart at all costs.

Mae stiffened and gazed up at me curiously. "Do you want to talk?"

I shook my head, brushing my lips over hers. "No. I just want you."

She kissed me back, an urgent press of her lips that seemed to say more than her words did. But then she moved away and picked up my hand, leading me toward the house. "Come inside. Rowe's not here, but Heath and I have been prettying the place up so it looks less like a bachelor pad."

I followed her inside, nodding and making small noises of approval at everything she showed me. But all I could think of was her. We made the full lap of the house, which didn't take long since it was essentially a living area with a kitchen, two bedrooms, and a bathroom. We found ourselves in the bedroom, Rowe's king-sized mattress on the floor made up with a pretty floral bedspread I'd seen in Mae's apartment. It was fluffy and smelled clean, and I just wanted to disappear beneath the covers with her and lose a few hours of the night until sleep took me.

Lights flashed through the bedroom window, though, and all three of us peered out.

"It's Rowe," Mae yelped. She dropped my hand and rushed through the cabin, throwing open the front door. Heath and I followed, but Mae stopped on the porch. "Did you get him?"

Rowe put a finger to his lips and went to the back seat, opening the door. He emerged with a blond-haired little boy

I knew instantly was Ripley. He'd come with his grandmother to a couple of our baseball games.

"Holy shit, are you adding kidnapping to your list of crimes?" I asked, lawyer brain kicking in.

Ripley woke for a moment, a startled expression on his face until he pulled back and realized it was Rowe holding him. Then he laid his head down on Rowe's shoulder and went straight back to sleep. Rowe smoothed his palm up and down the little boy's back, encouraging him to relax.

"Didn't they tell you?" Rowe asked me.

Heath went down to the car to grab something from the trunk. "He only just got here. We didn't get a chance."

My gaze bounced between the two of them and then finally back to Mae.

"He's just bringing our boy home," she said simply.

I widened my eyes at her, completely gobsmacked. "Our boy?"

Rowe smiled widely, and it was the smile of a proud papa handing out cigars in the hospital waiting room after his wife had delivered a healthy baby. He dropped a kiss on Mae's head as he moved past her. "Our boy," he agreed.

I watched him pass, shock still punching through my system. Rowe seemed...happy. I'd known him a few years now, and he'd never been one for smiling. He turned up for practice, did the job, and went home. If we socialized outside of work, he always let others fill the conversation, happy to sit back and just observe.

But he'd been different around Mae. That night we'd gone to the baseball game, and everything that had happened after, I'd seen a different side of him. And more of that, when he'd taken a beating for Heath.

Holding Ripley in his arms now, the man looked complete for the first time in years.

A hot spear of jealousy stabbed through me, sharp and painful.

He had the life I wanted. The life I'd been well on my way to claiming.

The life that had been ripped from me because nobody told me the truth.

I deserved none of it. Not if I wasn't man enough to step up and do what needed doing.

Heath and Mae had followed Rowe inside, and the three of them spoke in hushed murmurs, Mae suggesting they put Ripley down on the only mattress in the cabin, and Rowe explaining about a foldout sleeping mat and blankets Norma had given him. Mae's smile was soft as she raised a hand to brush a lock of hair off Ripley's forehead, and Heath placed an arm around her, watching over all of them protectively from his taller height.

I let the part of me that desperately wanted to join them win, even though the louder part of my brain told me to leave now and avoid hurting them anymore.

If I was stronger, I would have listened.

I closed the cabin door behind me at the same time Rowe partially closed the door to Ripley's new bedroom.

"When I woke up this morning, this was not how I expected the day to end," Rowe whispered. "I don't know whether to be terrified about Zye being out or just be fucking elated that Ripley's with me again."

The final piece of the puzzle clicked in my head. Nobody needed to explain it. If Zye was out, Ripley needed to be here where people could protect him. "Just be happy he's here. Good to see you smiling, brother."

"Feels good to smile. And to not have to kick your ass. You're lucky I got sidetracked with Ripley. Otherwise, I would have been at your place this afternoon, ready to drag you back here by your ear." He gave me a soft shove. "Don't fucking disappear like that, okay? You had us worried."

I knew he was trying to give me a pep talk, but it only made me feel worse. "Yeah, I know."

"Don't fucking do it again."

I didn't say anything, because I didn't want to break a promise.

No one seemed to notice.

"Let's have drinks," Mae said, pushing her way through her wall of men. "Maybe out by the fire? We need to celebrate. Heath is out, Liam's back, and Ripley is here."

"Can't all go outside," Heath pointed out. "We won't hear Ripley if he wakes up. Shame, it's beautiful out there tonight, and sitting around a fire with a couple of drinks sounds like heaven."

"I'll stay with him," I offered. "You guys should go and celebrate."

All three of them frowned at me. "We're not celebrating without you."

Rowe shoved me. "Trying to ditch your family already?"

I stopped in my tracks. Nobody else reacted, though. They all just went on like he hadn't even said anything.

"Family?" The word slipped out before I could stop it, and then I felt like an idiot. Embarrassment heated my cheeks.

Rowe laughed, his mood sky-high. "You think everything we've been through the last few days, hell, the last few months, makes us anything less than family?"

"And Ripley cements it," Mae added.

"You cement it," Heath said quietly to her, kissing her cheek.

He held up Mae's phone and flashed up an app. "Baby monitor app. One of you download it as well. We leave one phone in Ripley's room and take the other outside with us. They sync up and act like a monitor, so we'll hear if he wakes up. It's got video and everything."

Mae raised an eyebrow. "Impressive that you know of such a thing."

He shrugged. "There are apps for everything."

"Norma said he sleeps like the dead anyway. He probably won't even move. He was a dead weight by the time I laid him down. Grab the chairs from the living room. I'll go find us some wood."

"I bought drinks when I went to the store, too. Refrigerator is fully stocked. I'll get snacks."

Everybody bustled around me, doing what needed to be done, organizing a mini party for four in the yard, while I felt like I was sleepwalking. I went through the motions, trying to shake off the mood. When Mae offered me a drink, I bypassed beer and grabbed a can of Coke and a bottle of bourbon gratefully. Maybe that was all I needed. A drink to relax and blow out the cobwebs of my bender.

The cold liquid slid down my throat and gave me something to do with my hands. Heath gathered up all the chairs. I took a cooler of drinks from Mae, leaving her to carry the lighter snacks, and by the time we got outside, Rowe already had a small fire going in the firepit. The night was warm, the sky filled with more stars than I'd ever seen, the quiet whisper of a soft breeze through the surrounding trees. Heath produced a small Bluetooth speaker, and I passed over my phone, since it was the one not being used as a baby monitor.

"What songs you got on here? Anything good?"

I unlocked it for him with a shrug. "Depends what you're in the mood for."

I remembered something, and for what felt like the first time in days, I smiled. "Do the playlist right at the bottom."

He thumbed down the page and then looked up. "Seriously?"

I glanced at Mae. "Yeah, seriously."

"Teenage emo angst, coming right up."

Mae groaned, and I laughed, sitting next to her, taking another sip of my drink. But as the opening riffs of Paramore's "Misery Business" came through the speakers, she closed her eyes and started singing out the lyrics.

Rowe and Heath both stopped and stared at her, but I'd seen her do this before and knew how good she was. She didn't fit the part, with her innocent schoolteacher style, but Mae had a set of pipes on her that suited the grungy rock sound, and by the time she got to the chorus, she was belting out the words, like she'd only listened to this album yesterday.

God, I loved her. Her enthusiasm bled from her every pore. She found a release in music.

I found one in her.

The song ended, and she opened her eyes, immediately turning pink in the glow of the firelight when she realized we were all watching her.

She ran a hand self-consciously through her hair that had become tousled from her performance. "Right. Well, I guess the cat is out of the bag that I kind of like decade-old punk rock."

"You're good," Heath said, his gaze glued to her.

"Really fucking good." Rowe was staring at her with a mixture of surprise and desire.

I pointed at the phone in Heath's hand. "Put 'Fall Out Boy' on. She knows all the words to that, too."

She laughed, looking lighter and more carefree than I'd

seen her in weeks. She sang along to a few more songs, until Heath leaned over to me. "You knew she could sing?"

"Yeah."

"I envy that."

The alcohol was coursing through my system now, just enough to relax me. I laughed at him. "Hey, you wanna sing, get up there. I'll throw a bra at you."

He sniggered. "I meant I envy what the two of you have. You know stuff about her I don't."

I sobered a little. I did have the advantage of knowing Mae the longest. But knowing someone for a long time didn't necessarily mean anything when it came to loving someone. "I envy the connection you have with her. With both of them." The words were too raw, too honest, and I immediately wished I hadn't said them. They hurt.

But Heath stared at me like I'd said something committable. "What are you even talking about. She loves you, Liam. She was cut to shreds last night when you weren't here. The only reason she's like this now is because you're back." He jerked his head in Mae's direction, and I caught her gaze. She was on her feet, dancing and thrashing her head around with Rowe.

"All of that, is relief that you're okay."

Mae wiggled a finger in my direction, inviting me to come dance with her, but I shook my head. She pouted but went back to dancing. Rowe, sweat dripping from his temple, pulled his shirt off and moved his shoulders in time with beat, drink sloshing slightly in one hand.

Heath wasn't done with his pep talk. "And Rowe... He was the first one over at your place this morning. I have no doubt that he would have busted down your door this afternoon if the Ripley emergency hadn't come up. What he and I have is physical. I get you two don't share that, but what you do have is friendship." He nudged me with an elbow. "Things went to shit with your family. I get that. My family is fucked up, too. But what Rowe said about this? Us being a family? He's not the only one feeling it."

Heath leaned forward and grabbed another can from the cooler then shoved it into my hand. He grinned widely at me. "Now drink that and put something slow and romantic on so I can go grind up on my girl."

He left the phone with me, and I did as requested, switching to an Ed Sheeran song that changed the mood entirely.

Family.

I wanted it to be true so badly.

But a burning need for vengeance simmered in my gut, too hot to be ignored.

One night.

When the sun rose, I'd do what I had to do and let the cards fall where they may.

17

MAE

I closed my eyes and rolled my hips in time with the beat of the music. The rhythm pounded through me, aided by the two beers I'd downed. I had enough natural rhythm to sing, but it didn't really extend to dancing. But out here, with the night sky full of stars, a bonfire, and three sinfully good-looking men who all had their attention on me, I'd never cared less that I wasn't going to win any dance competitions.

All the anxieties of the last few days and weeks and months poured out through flinging my body around with Rowe and laughing until my face hurt.

He spun me around with his free hand, gazing at me with such complete and utter adoration that I almost couldn't breathe.

I fell into his chest, damp with sweat, despite the fact he'd shed his shirt. I ran my fingers over his abs, each ridge so perfect I wanted to lick him. He was beyond sexy when he was all glowering and grumpy, but this version of him—happy and carefree, if only for a night—was the hottest I'd seen him yet.

The song switched from punk rock to something low and slow, and the sultry voice curled through my body pleasantly. As did the way Rowe stared at me. His gaze rolled over my body, lingering on my lips, my breasts, and the sliver of skin between my top and my skirt.

A big body moved in behind me, and without glancing over my shoulder, I knew it was Heath. He pressed in close, his body melding to mine, picking up the rhythm Rowe and the music were setting. His fingers grazed my hip, holding me in place between the two of them.

"Welcome to the party." I leaned back against him, turning my face up to his for a kiss.

"You're too fucking sexy to sit on the sidelines." He wrapped an arm around me, steadying my body against his chest, and dropped his lips to mine.

It was sort of upside down, but I didn't care. The brand of his lips felt so good.

Rowe moved in even closer, his sweaty chest brushing over my breasts, my nipples beading beneath my clothes. The nearby fire crackled, letting off almost as much heat as the three of us created. A tingle took up at my core, and I had the sudden urge to start removing clothes. Whether that be from the heat of the night and the fire, or from the burn of being between two men I found irresistible.

There was something primal about being outside in the wilderness, with nobody else around for miles. It spoke to some basic part of myself that wanted her men, and wanted them now.

A tiny moan slipped from my mouth as I ground all over Rowe, hiking my skirt up so I could move better. Rowe slipped his leg between mine, and the sudden pressure against my clit was mind-blowing.

Heath groaned behind me, his fingers splayed out across

my belly, sliding high across my skin, beneath my shirt and up to my breasts. He took a handful, squeezing one gently, his erection growing behind me.

"Too many clothes on," he muttered.

With his fingers already inside my top, he pulled up, and I raised my hands so he could easily remove it. I'd worn a lacy white bra beneath, with no padding because my breasts were already plenty big enough on their own.

Rowe lowered his head and sucked my nipple through the sheer lace. The combination of his mouth and the texture of the lace was heaven. I plunged my fingers into his hair, shamelessly holding him in place while I fell back against Heath.

He made short work of the clasp on my bra, and then Rowe was sliding it down my shoulders, exposing my breasts to the night air.

I'd never felt more sexy or free.

I glanced over at Liam, who still sat on the other side of the fire. He held a bourbon in one hand, but his legs were spread wide, erection straining behind his sweatpants. He made no move to get up and join us, and I didn't invite him again, knowing that this was what got him turned on.

I wanted to be naked for him.

With the next beat of the song, still pressed between Rowe and Heath, I slipped my fingers into the elastic of my skirt and pushed it down over my ass and thighs. By the time it neared my knees, it fell away by itself. I'd already kicked off my flip-flops and danced barefoot on the soft green grass.

Leaving me in a tiny white lace thong.

Liam's eyes flared. He took an unsteady sip of his drink and dropped one hand to his crotch. He massaged his erection through the fabric, the outline of his dick growing the more he touched it.

I rewarded him by taking off my panties.

Heath's hand was on my clit in an instant, his palm sitting over my mound so his fingertip could rub the little bundle of nerves.

I immediately lost the rhythm of the music and instead moved to the rhythm he controlled. I leaned against him, resting the back of my head on his chest and drawing one hand up to hold on to his neck. His other hand took an indecent grope of my breast, Rowe's mouth still working the other.

My nipples sang out in pleasure, both tortured and teased in different ways, both so incredibly good. Tremors of pleasure spread through my body, heading south to my core. I ached to have them inside me. All of them. I was so empty and needy it was making me desperate.

I glanced over at Liam again.

His gaze was trained on me but flickering between the places the other two men touched me. One hand fisted the arm of the camp chair, the other locked tight on his pants.

He was holding back. Torturing himself with the sight of me naked between two huge men but refusing to touch himself.

I wanted to break him down. I wanted him to fall apart with me.

"Rowe," I moaned.

"What do you need, baby?" His lips trailed up from my nipple, across my chest to my neck. He sucked hard on the sensitive spot below my ear before his tongue flickered over it. I would have collapsed in a puddle if Heath wasn't supporting me.

"Fuck me," I begged him, desperate to be filled.

"Not yet."

I nearly cried at his refusal, but then his fingers were joining Heath's, but dipping lower, slicking through the heat between my thighs. I was so wet; he met no resistance when two fingers were pushed up inside me.

I rocked on my heels, moving in the way that got pressure on my G-spot. I went harder and faster, grinding against them, all while watching Liam.

He couldn't hold out. He lifted his ass, pushing his sweatpants and underwear down his legs. Sitting back down, he spread his legs wide, fisting his cock almost viciously, squeezing his balls with the other. He jerked himself in the same tempo that Rowe's fingers thrust into me.

I wanted to kiss him. I wanted to walk over there and take the pain he was trying so hard to hide.

I saw it.

I saw him.

With a groan he yanked up his T-shirt, holding it with his chin, so his hands were free. He jerked himself hard and fast, his gaze never leaving mine. He let out a shudder of pleasure, a full-body tremor that sang of intense pleasure.

"Come with him," Heath murmured in my ear.

Pleasure coiled deep within me, Rowe's fingers fucking me hard and fast while Heath worked my clit until a shout of ecstasy bubbled up and exploded.

Hot, white spurts of cum shot from Liam's tip, coating his fist and landing on his abs.

Rowe and Heath forced me over the edge at the same time.

I came so hard the night stars and the lights behind my eyes became one, pleasure taking over until nothing else remained.

I was almost sure I blanked out for a moment, because I barely remembered getting down on my knees, shoving Rowe's shorts and underwear off and taking his cock deep in my mouth, rewarding him for the talent he'd shown me with his fingers.

He didn't hold back.

He grabbed my head, fingers tight in my hair, and shallowly fucked my mouth hard and fast.

I loved it. I wanted more. His taste was all man, all him. My own arousal soaked the inside of my thighs, a perfect reminder of the way I wanted him to feel.

I made encouraging noises, gripping his perfect ass with my hands and urging him to go deeper.

I had the tip of him hitting the back of my throat and his shout of pleasure. "Fuck, Mae! I'll come if you keep doing that, and I don't want to come down your throat."

I let him thrust deep into my mouth a few more times before I pulled off and stared up at him. "Where do you want to come?"

My voice was deep and throaty, not me, and all sex goddess.

They brought that out in me. This woman who wanted more than just vanilla sex. I wanted whipped cream and chocolate sauce. I wanted every freaking topping. I wanted the lot.

Rowe groaned. "You don't want to know, baby."

Heath slapped me on my ass. "He wants you here."

I moaned at the thought of it.

Heath knelt behind me. "Suck his dick. Get him harder than he's ever been. Don't let him come."

I did as I was told, loving when he talked like that. I took Rowe in my mouth again, this time going a little slower, knowing I couldn't make him come. Not yet.

Heath's face pressed between my legs, and I cried out when he opened his mouth over my still throbbing pussy.

"You taste so sweet, Mae. So fucking sweet. I could eat you out all day long."

He tortured me with his mouth, while I did the same to Rowe. I supported myself with one hand on the grass, the other wrapped around the base of Rowe's cock, alternating between gasping and moaning with my mouth full as Heath drove me straight toward another orgasm.

"I want it," I begged. "Heath, please."

His thick cock was inside my pussy a moment later. He pounded me hard, each thrust pushing me forward so Rowe's dick slid a little more down my throat.

I'd never felt higher. I was so lost to sensation; I didn't think I could feel anything more than I already did. The sex was hot, and hard, and yet at the same time, it held a quality of worship. That even when I was turning them on, sucking their dicks and welcoming them into my body, that it was all still about me. They fucked me harder because my body craved it. Their fingers stroked every inch of my skin because I cried out for more.

I spiraled into a mind-blowing orgasm, my body full of two men, with the knowledge the third watched. I reached for my clit, supporting myself on one hand while I added to the sweet torture.

Heath saw me out through my orgasm. I clenched down on him, over and over, and behind me, he cursed, fighting to hold on.

Why, I didn't know.

Until when I was finally sated, he pulled out, coming all over my back and ass. The hot liquid seared me, and I dropped down onto my forearms, still weak from my orgasm and the force of his.

Rowe took up Heath's spot behind me. His dick nudged against my asshole, slick with his arousal as well as Heath's.

I was instantly ready for him, mewling out my need. My fingers found my clit again, working it up slowly in anticipation of having Rowe inside me.

"Do you want this?" he asked quietly. "We don't have to if it's too much."

I wanted it so bad.

"Please," I begged. My nipples rested on the soft grass, my ass up in the air. I'd been taken like this a few times now, and my body remembered how good it felt. Without any deliberate thought, I ground back against him, pressing my ass down on the tip of his dick.

He hissed out a groan, his entire body locking up.

I had no such problems. I just wanted him inside me. I ground back slowly, adjusting to the thickness of him. He was the biggest of the three, though neither Heath nor Liam were far behind, all three of them nothing to complain about in the dick department. Heath had primed me well, and now Rowe reaped the benefits.

He hissed out a curse, fully seated inside me, before he slowly began to move.

"Yes!" I encouraged. "God, yes!"

It just got better and better every time I did it.

Rowe seemed to realize he didn't need to be as careful with me as he'd thought. He picked up the pace, cautiously waiting for me to stop him, but he found nothing but encouragement from me. I rubbed my clit, occasionally dipping two fingers into my pussy when the need became too great. The arm I supported myself on trembled but held, though I knew I'd be aching tomorrow.

I didn't care.

I kept up the torture, teasing myself while Rowe rode my ass.

It was sweet and sexy and mind-blowing. My third orgasm barreled down on me too quick, but there was no stopping it.

"Harder," I moaned.

I wanted him to feel as good as I did. I wanted him to come with me.

He listened.

He slammed hard into my body, five deep thrusts all he could handle after I'd near drained him with my mouth, but that was all we both needed. A gush of arousal coated my fingers as Rowe spilled himself inside my ass. I fell over the edge with a shout that probably could have been heard for miles. But nobody would have mistaken it for anything other than a cry of ecstasy. The third orgasm just built on the first two, a culmination of tingles, and tremors, and shakes that had my arm giving way and my core pulsing.

Rowe slipped from my body, holding me up so I didn't completely face-plant on the ground.

Heath picked himself up off the ground. I hadn't even noticed him lie out beside us, but now he crawled over and kissed me. From across the campfire, Liam stood, too.

He hadn't touched me, but it didn't matter. The connection was still there. All three of us covered in the effects of hot sex, none of us giving a shit. Liam held a hand out, and I took it, helping me up from the ground.

I'd be stiff and sore tomorrow. There was no doubt about that. But for tonight, I was the happiest woman on Earth.

We left our clothes where they were, and I followed Liam back to our home, happier than I'd been in a long time.

I led Mae to the tiny cabin bathroom and got the water running in the shower. It took a minute for it to get warm, and I filled that time drinking in her swollen lips, her heavy breasts, and the sweet throbbing slit between her legs. I brushed a leaf from her hair, both of us watching as it fell to the floor. Heath's and Rowe's cum shined on her skin, evidence of amazing sex.

I leaned in and kissed her softly. "I've never seen anything more beautiful than you right now."

I loved her. I loved her so fucking much. And watching her with Heath and Rowe had only cemented it further. The three of us together could bring her more pleasure than any one of us alone. And that was all I ached to do. All I could think about was giving her everything I could. Because she deserved it all, and more.

She deserved the best version of me.

There was only one way I could get him back.

But first, I needed to care for my girl.

I checked the warmth of the water, and finding it perfect,

I let her in. I wasn't sure where Heath and Rowe were, but they were giving me this time with her, and I appreciated it. I needed to wash her, touch her, remind myself of every curve of her body. Not wanting it to lead to sex, just to reassure myself she had everything she needed before I left.

The warm water cascaded over her, and she turned her face up to the spray, letting it run over her body in waves. Her nipples were still dark and hard, swollen from having Rowe's mouth and Heath's fingers on them. I had no idea how long we'd been out there for, but it felt like hours. The night outside was deep and dark.

I followed her into the shower even though there was barely room for both of us. She picked up a bottle of bodywash, but I took it from her hands. I squirted a generous amount across her tits, enjoying the way her eyes flared. They became hooded with desire as I cleaned her, massaging the soap over her nipples and cleavage. I roamed lower, removing the traces of the other men from her stomach, and then, turning her around, I did the same to her back. Her ass was so bitable, perfectly round in my hands. I slicked soap all over her cheeks, while she leaned against the glass shower door, tits pressed against it. She widened her stance a little, an unspoken invitation for me to move lower.

But I let the spray wash off the soap and twisted her back to face me. She gave me a happy, sated smile. "Still need cleaning in one more spot."

I sucked in a breath when she took my hand and guided it to her snatch. I let her push my hand around, gliding my fingertips through her folds.

"I didn't mean for this to turn into sex," I murmured. "I just wanted to take care of you."

She moved my hand more insistently. "You are."

I touched her clit, and my dick hardened when she panted out my name. She was close to orgasm already, so oversensitive that it took nothing for me to draw her in and kiss her deep.

She hooked one leg around my waist, opening herself up to me and lining the tip of my dick up with her entrance. Quietly, I sank home, my eyes closing when I fell into her deep warmth.

The hot water rained down on my back, likely in danger of running cold, but we took our time, gliding together, finding our connection once more.

"I love you. I wish you'd talk to me." Her voice sounded far away, soft and fairylike, barely more than a whisper of her thoughts.

I wanted to. But I didn't know how. Every time I tried, the words tangled up my tongue. So I just kissed her instead, stealing the words and pushing my hips against hers. We made love slow and sweet in between kisses and I love yous and tiny moans of pleasure. Her orgasm wasn't the kind we'd elicited from her body by the fire outside. It was gentler. The kind where she dug her fingernails into my back and promised to never let me go.

When I came, it was with the knowledge that it might be the last time.

I hoped it wouldn't be. But after tomorrow, after I grew the balls to do what was right, it wouldn't be up to me.

When we finally emerged from the shower, both of us wrapped in towels, we found Rowe and Heath already in bed, their hair wet. The sheet pulled up over but low enough that it was clear they were both naked beneath. The sheet barely covered their junk. They'd been watching something on Rowe's phone but they stopped when we entered. Their gazes flew right to Mae, and Heath patted the spot between them.

Mae dropped the towel, shameless, and wriggled beneath the sheet, in the space they'd left for her. "Why is your hair all wet?"

"Took a shower in the lake since you two were hogging all the hot water."

"Ew. There's fish and stuff in there."

"They didn't seem to mind. They got a nice long look at Rowe's huge cock. I'm sure that made up for disturbing their peace."

Rowe rolled his eyes. "I'm not that big."

I sniggered. "The fish probably thought it was a giant eel and swam off terrified for their lives."

Mae giggled and then yawned.

It was contagious. A sleepy feeling crashed over me, too. I flicked the bedroom light off and kicked Rowe over until I had a sliver of the only mattress in the house.

"We need a bigger bed," Rowe grumbled. "King-size ain't cuttin' it with you two around."

"If your giant cock wasn't taking up so much room, we'd probably be all right."

Heath snorted on his laughter, joining Mae's giggles, and Rowe grumbled good-naturedly. All four of us settled down, Rowe and Heath snuggling Mae tight between them.

Rowe glanced over his shoulder at me. "Glad to see your shitty sense of humor has returned. Even if my penis is the butt of your jokes."

He was asleep before I could come up with a witty reply about penises in butts.

I waited for sleep to take me, too.

It didn't come.

Instead, I found myself waiting for the sun, growing increasingly agitated with every minute that passed.

When the first light of dawn finally crept over the horizon, I left with it.

19

MAE

I woke, hot and sweaty in the middle of a Heath-Rowe sandwich. I lay on my belly, one leg and arm over Heath's muscular frame. The other was stretched uncomfortably behind me, resting dangerously close to Rowe's morning erection.

I ached from head to toe, especially between my thighs, but it was the pleasant throb of a night of great sex, and I wouldn't have swapped it for the world. I circled Rowe's cock with my fingers right as a little voice yelled out in panic from the next room.

All three of us flew into action, Rowe jerking out of my grasp and stumbling for the door, desperate to get to his son. He crashed right into a wall in his half-dazed state, which was probably just as well because it woke him up enough to realize he was still naked.

"It's okay, Rip. I'm coming!"

Heath was already throwing a pair of shorts at him when Ripley's cry started up in earnest.

Rowe's expression crumpled in dismay, and he looked at me in panic.

I kept my voice calm. "It's not personal. He just woke up somewhere new and he's scared. Go. He'll be fine as soon as he sees you."

Rowe nodded and ran for the other room. I pulled a sheet up around me and Heath and I peeked out the door, watching as Rowe tripped on Ripley's bag of things. "Hey, buddy!"

It didn't stop him from crashing into the floor.

I winced. Heath laughed.

So did Ripley. He stopped crying instantly, his giggles as sweet as spun sugar. "You fell."

Rowe laughed, too, crawling across the floor to Ripley's foldout bed. "I didn't. I just wanted to be down here on the floor with you."

"Pfft. Totally fell!" Heath called.

Ripley looked our way with interest. His eyes lit up when he saw me.

"Mae!" He scrambled to his feet and flung himself at me.

I knelt just in time to catch him, Heath grabbing my sheet when it threatened to fall.

"Hey, sweetie. I'm so happy to see you. Are you ready to have a day of fun?"

"Yeah!"

I couldn't help it. I knew I was overstepping but I kissed his soft cheek and then sent him back to Rowe. "Go back to your dad so I can get dressed."

As soon as the sentence was out of my mouth, I clapped a hand over it, realizing what I'd said. Ripley didn't call Rowe Dad. And it was already so much that he was here, he didn't need me confusing him any further.

I widened my eyes at Rowe and mouthed, "Sorry!"

But if Ripley had noticed, he didn't comment on it.

Rowe worried his bottom lip, but his expression slowly

evened out as Ripley carried on as normal, running in excited circles around his new bedroom.

I closed the door quietly, and Heath and I got dressed. We met Rowe and Ripley in the kitchen fifteen minutes later. Rowe had already started making breakfast for everyone, and Ripley played with a bunch of flowers that sat in a glass in the center of the kitchen table.

I sat and smiled warmly at him. "What have you got there? Those are pretty. How did you pick them so fast?"

"I didn't. I like this one. It's orange."

"It is! Clever boy," I praised.

Rowe glanced over his shoulder at us. "Flowers were there when we came out. Liam must have picked them this morning before he left."

My heart sank. "He left again?"

Ripley looked up at me with his big eyes. "Does that make you sad? Do you need a hug?"

Oh, my heart. This child was the sweetest. "I always need a Ripley hug."

I held my arms out and let him scramble onto my lap. I squeezed him for a quick moment, careful to let him determine how long the hug went on for. But when he didn't let go, I hugged him tighter. I was so grateful I'd had the chance to spend time with him and Rowe before all this happened, so that now I could be a source of comfort for him.

Rowe poked at some eggs he had cooking on the stove top. "He's probably just gone to work. He was better last night."

Ripley grew tired of the hug and clambered back to his own seat.

I shrugged in response to Rowe's question. "Do you think? I thought something still felt off with him."

Rowe shook his head. "Seemed normal to me."

I nodded thoughtfully, tucking that away. It made me feel better. In the shower last night, I'd still gotten the sense that Liam was struggling, but Rowe's conviction helped those nervous feelings settle.

Heath wandered into the kitchen, and Ripley stared up at him, eyes wide. "Whoa. You're big."

Heath leaned down so he was closer to Ripley's height. "You'll be this big one day, too." He stuck his hand out for Ripley to shake. "I'm Heath. Nice to meet you."

Ripley giggled and clamped his tiny hand in Heath's tattooed one. "Nice to meet you, too, mister. I like your drawings."

He traced over the lines on Heath's arm while I melted inside at the exchange. Heath had an easy way with him, and Ripley seemed to have taken an instant liking to him, too.

Rowe glanced over at them occasionally, humming something under his breath. I could barely believe the change in him. Rowe, humming? Unheard of.

The aroma coming from the food Rowe had sizzling on the stove top had my mouth watering, and we all shoved down huge platefuls when he placed them in front of us.

The bacon was crisp. The eggs fluffy. I eyed him with another forkful hovering over my lips. "You've been living on takeout all this time when you can cook?"

His gaze followed my fork as I put it to my lips. "Didn't seem worthwhile when it was just me."

My heart squeezed, and I looked over at Ripley. "It's not just you anymore."

"No, it's not." He ruffled Ripley's hair. "If we're gonna get this guy as big as Heath, we're going to have to have lots of fruits and vegetables."

Ripley wrinkled his nose at the idea.

"And chocolate for dessert," Rowe tacked on. "Of course."

Ripley brightened at that.

I stifled a smile. "You like chocolate, buddy?"

Ripley launched into a list of his favorites, and I could practically see Rowe's brain ticking over, trying to remember them all.

"My best friend Tori loves Oreos, too. She actually named her cat Oreo because he's black and white."

Ripley's eyes went huge. "Cats are my favorite animals! Can I see him?"

My heart sank. Because just days ago, I would have been able to say, yes, sure, let's go there now. Sadness dropped over me like a veil. I wanted to take Ripley to my best friend's place. He might not be legally mine, but I'd promised to be there for him and for Rowe, and so for as long as Rowe wanted me in their lives, I was going to be here.

I had so much love to give a child. I'd always known I was meant to be a mother. It had made my doctor's prognosis at sixteen nearly impossible to bear. It had been the whole reason I'd gone into teaching. I needed something to fill the void I couldn't fill with a child of my own.

And now here I was, with a little boy who needed that love. A chance for me to be the mother I'd always dreamed of.

But no best friend to share it with.

I took my phone quietly from the countertop and walked out onto the front porch. I could feel Heath and Rowe pick up on my mood, their gazes firmly burning my back, but they didn't ask me what was wrong or try to stop me.

I sat on the porch swing, now much more comfortable with a few throw pillows, and called Tori's number.

"Hi, you've reached Tori. I can't come to the phone right now, so leave a message and I'll get back to you. God bless."

"It's me. Again. I just...something's happened. It's pretty big, and you're the person I want to share it with. I know you're angry at me right now, but please, Tor." I sucked in a deep breath as tears pricked the backs of my eyes. But I wasn't going to let them fall. I was stronger than this. She might be mad, but us taking custody of Ripley was huge. I knew my best friend. Once she got over being mad at me, she'd then be mad at herself for not being here to celebrate Ripley being with us. "I'm not taking no for an answer. We're not ending a decade-old friendship without even talking about it. I'm coming over there right now. See you in ten."

I instantly felt better, lighter, for having decided to be proactive. I'd go all *Romeo and Juliet* on her if I had to, throwing pebbles at her window until she came outside and talked to me.

I stuck my head back inside the door, but Rowe and Heath were right on the other side.

Rowe jingled his keys in my face. "Off you go."

I grinned at them. "Eavesdroppers much?"

"It was Heath's idea. He's a massive gossip." Rowe sniggered.

Heath rolled his eyes but pressed a kiss to my forehead. "Was just making sure you were okay. Go get your friend back."

I grabbed the keys from Rowe, brushing my lips over his quickly, and called goodbye to Ripley who was still scarfing down bacon at the kitchen table.

The need for good coffee ached in my veins, but I refused to stop. I drove straight to Tori and Will's place, pulling into their driveway and storming the path to their front door. I wouldn't be swayed by Will this time. If Tori didn't want to see me, she'd have to tell me to my face.

I needed a clear head to think through all the suspects in Jayela's murder. We were well and truly at the point of desperation, and so every one of them needed to be considered again. Johnson, the asshole cop. My father's mistress and her family. Or had we missed the mark completely? We needed to go back through all of Jayela's old cases and rule out anyone she'd ever investigated or put behind bars. Because I wasn't losing what I had. Heath wasn't going back to jail. And I couldn't think straight if I was constantly reciting my apology to Tori over and over in my head and wishing I could just call her and talk the way we always had.

"Tori!" I banged on the door, hoping the baby wasn't asleep. "I'm not leaving until we've talked!"

A neighbor opened her front door and tutted at me, but I ignored her and kept on banging and peering through the window until it became abundantly clear that nobody was home.

Then I realized what day it was, and the time, and that Tori would be at her church meeting. Embarrassment flushed my cheeks as I slunk away, but the determination was still there beneath it. This needed to be sorted and it needed to be sorted today.

Though church wasn't my thing, I'd been there plenty of times. Not only for Jayela's funeral, but for Tori's son's baptism and the handful of times I'd tagged along with Will and Tori because I wanted to see what they found in the place. There was an appeal in just trusting a higher being, in turning over all your problems to someone else, and trusting that it all happened for a reason.

But at the end of the day, I hadn't found the comfort there that I was seeking.

I'd found that in the arms of three men instead.

I didn't imagine my current lifestyle and the nights of wild sex would go over too well with Tori's priest and the other church leaders.

Tori hadn't judged me when I'd said it wasn't for me, though. She'd just nodded and said she understood when I'd told her I wasn't coming back.

That was one of the best things about us. We didn't judge each other. We had our own separate interests, and morals and beliefs, but that never interfered with us.

In the church parking lot, I spotted Will's car instantly and parked beside it. The little white church in the middle of Providence was one of the oldest in the area and beautifully maintained thanks to the affluent churchgoers who gave generously each Sunday. On a weekend, this parking lot would be full of older couples and families in their Sunday best. But this morning it was quiet, only a handful of cars for the weekday morning meeting.

I got out of my car, right as the church doors opened. A small group of people exited, smiling and chatting while they slowly made their way to their vehicles. My gaze bounced over each person who left the building, waiting for Tori's face to appear. I spotted Will holding Isaac while he chatted with the priest, but the door closed behind the two of them. I leaned back on my car, and when Will met my gaze, I raised an eyebrow at him.

He turned back to the priest who was locking the church doors and bid him farewell before making his way down the stairs, jostling the baby on his hip.

I smiled brightly at Isaac, and he gave me a gummy grin,

reaching for me with chubby hands. "Hey, baby boy." I glanced at Will. "May I?"

"Of course. You're his godmother. He obviously wants to go to you."

Will passed Isaac over, and I instinctively put my lips to his head, inhaling his sweet baby scent. He normally smelled of a mixture of baby lotion and Tori's perfume. But the soft flowery scent of her was missing from him today.

"Where's your mommy today, sweet boy?"

Will sighed, reaching for his son again. "She's not here."

I gave Isaac up without argument even though he squawked at being taken away from my hair. "Where is she then? I tried your house, but she's not there either, and then I remembered she's always here on Wednesday mornings."

"She's sick."

I frowned. I was doubtful Tori was sick enough to sleep through the ruckus I'd made at her house earlier. She'd have to have been practically comatose. But if she was unwell, and she'd taken something, it was possible she might have crashed harder than normal. "Poor thing. Is it the flu? I'll come back to the house with you then. I'll stop and get some chicken soup at that place she likes, and maybe some flowers. Fresh ones always make her happy."

Will unlocked his car and leaned in, tucking Isaac into his rear-facing car seat. When he emerged baby free, he avoided looking me in the eye. "You can't. She can't have visitors."

A prickle of unease danced across the back of my neck. "What do you mean she can't have visitors? Is it something contagious?"

Will shook his head. "No."

"Then what?" The prickle of unease turned into a full-blown warning siren. "What's going on?"

He shot me a sharp look and then another at the priest who was standing on the step watching the two of us bicker with interest. I felt like flipping the old busybody the bird, but I knew Tori wouldn't have appreciated that.

Will yanked my arm. "We're making a scene. Get in and I'll tell you."

I slid into the passenger seat, and Will got behind the steering wheel but made no move to turn the car on.

He stared at me over the center console.

I waited for answers.

"She's in the hospital."

I reared back, fear spiking through me in a rush that came out in a tumble of questions. "What for? Is she okay? Which hospital?"

But Will shook his head again. "It's not a regular hospital. They don't have visiting hours."

None of this made any sense. She was fine last week. "What kind of public hospital doesn't have visiting hours?"

Will glanced at the back seat, like Isaac could understand us, and lowered his voice. "It's not a public hospital. It's a private institution for people with mental conditions."

"What on earth for? What is this place? Like a rehab or like you had her committed?" I screeched it so loud Isaac let out a worried cry.

Will reached a hand back to his son, patting him around the seat belt. "Keep your voice down. We don't need the entire congregation knowing our business, Mae. I'm only telling you because you're her best friend." He shook his head. "I didn't have her committed. She voluntarily checked in on the weekend."

My brain mentally sorted through every conversation and interaction I'd had with my best friend over the last few months. I couldn't come up with anything that warranted a stay in an institution. But I'd been so wrapped up in myself, and Jayela's murder and getting Heath out of jail that I knew I hadn't been a very good friend. A lump rose in my throat at the thought she might have needed me and I hadn't been there for her because I was too distracted. "Why? Is it post-partum depression or something?"

Will scrubbed his hands over his face. When he turned back to me, his eyes were huge and full of pain.

I grabbed his hand, holding it tight.

"There's things she's done. They're..." He swallowed hard. "Depraved."

"What the hell? Depraved? Nothing can be that bad. Will, tell me!"

"God, I can't do this." He stared down at his trembling hands. His voice dropped to a whisper. "It all came to a head after Heath's trial. I asked why Liam would think I was having an affair, and we got in an argument, she admitted things. Fuck, Mae, so many things..." He swiped angrily at a tear that spilled down his cheek.

I stared at him wide-eyed, partially because he'd cursed and Will never cursed. Not in all the years I'd known him, not even the day he fell while we were hiking and broke his arm. And partially because I couldn't think of a single thing about Tori that would cause this level of anguish. I'd never seen Will so torn up in all the years I'd known him.

But then he gave it to me.

He laid it right out on the line, in black and white so there was no mistaking it.

"I think Tori killed Jayela."

*S*aint Paul of God Private Hospital wasn't anything fancy from the outside. It wasn't all that far from our place in the woods, but if I hadn't been searching for it, with careful directions from Will, I never would have known it was there. There were no signs posted on the road in that indicated a health facility, and it was tucked away behind the Saint Paul church, hidden from view of the public. Without Will's instructions to drive past the main entrance, I would have assumed I was in the wrong place and turned around.

It was an ugly rectangular building, but the grass outside was neatly tended. I didn't care about any of it. My lungs ached from forgetting to breathe, and my shoulders were knotted with stress. I parked crookedly at the front of the building and stormed inside, though my legs felt like giving out with every step.

Will's accusation was a rush of noise in my head that hadn't cleared with the drive over.

"I promised Tori when I checked her in that she would be the one to tell you. She knew you'd come looking eventually. Please don't go to the police. Not until you've spoken to her."

Will had plugged the address into the map app on my phone, and I'd driven straight here. I hadn't wanted to hear any more from him anyway. Whatever Tori had done, I needed to hear it from her, with my own ears. As much as I wanted to uncover the truth about who'd murdered my sister, no part of me believed it was Tori, so going to the police wasn't even on my radar.

She'd have to tell me herself if it were true. And even then, I'd ask for proof.

The doors to the center opened automatically, and a waft of hospital disinfectant hit me square in the face. The large room was stark, mostly bare white walls, though a vase of fresh flowers did add some washed-out color to the reception desk.

The woman behind it glanced up when I approached, her lips pressing into a line. Her face was free of makeup, and her ID tag hung around her neck on a string, resting on her scrubs-covered chest. "Can I help you?"

"I need to see Tori Dudgeon, please."

"And you are?"

"Her best friend. Mae Donovan."

The woman clucked her tongue and ran the tip of her pen lightly down a sheet of paper with a list of names and rooms and other symbols and letters I didn't understand. I strained over the desk, trying to see Tori's name, but the woman gave me the stink eye and pulled her clipboard away. "This is confidential information."

I fought to keep my tone polite. "I just want to see my friend." As an afterthought, I added on, "Please."

The woman found Tori's name and ran a finger across it, then shook her head. "Sorry. She isn't allowed visitors at this point in her treatment."

"Excuse me? Says who?"

The woman put her clipboard down on her desk and leveled me with a no-nonsense look. "Her doctors."

Anger rose inside me, and I fought to tamp down on it. What kind of treatment program didn't allow a woman to see her family and friends? Nothing felt right about this. "Who made them judge, jury, and executioner? Just tell her I'm here. She'll want to see me."

"Mrs. Dudgeon herself agreed to this treatment plan when she was admitted—"

"I don't care!" I yelled, losing my battle with my patience. This place gave me the creeps. I stormed around her desk to the door behind and yanked on the handle. It did nothing, remaining firmly locked. A noise of frustration took hold of my throat, but it was better than yelling again.

"Ma'am, if you'd like to fill out a form, you can make a request to her doctors for an exemption—"

I whirled on her. "And how long will that take to be approved?"

"It depends. It could be up to ten business days."

I blinked at her.

The woman stared back and me, and with a sigh, like she'd done this way too many times, she picked up the phone from her desk. Cradling it between her ear and shoulder, she punched in a number. "Security, you're needed at reception, please."

I glared at her.

She held up the form she'd been talking about, and I snatched it from her fingers as I stormed out.

"Have a lovely day," the woman called sarcastically.

On the outside, I stared up at the second story, wondering if one of those rooms belonged to Tori. No matter what she'd done, I hated the idea of her stuck behind those walls.

"I'll be back," I promised her, form clutched in my fingers. Whatever was going on here wasn't aboveboard. Of that, I was sure. She might have been mad at me, and Will might have accused her of something horrific, but whatever the truth was, she was still my best friend. And until somebody gave me some proof or she confessed herself, I refused to believe it.

Only problem was, a nagging voice in the back of my mind reminded me that Tori had been the last person to see Jayela alive.

20

HEATH

"So, looks like it's a guys' day, huh? What should we do?" Rowe tossed a ball to Ripley, who missed it and had to chase after it.

He came back holding the ball in one hand and threw it at me. I caught it easily and gave an exaggerated stagger backward. "Whoa. Boy has an arm on him. You a pitcher?"

Ripley was all cheesy grins. Fuckin' kid was cute as hell. I gently lobbed it back, which he missed again but happily chased after while chattering about how his granny said he could play Little League next year, and how Rowe was gonna come and watch every weekend.

I raised an eyebrow. "Yeah? Maybe that's what we should do today then? What do you say, Rowe? Get some baseball practice in?"

Ripley cheered. He'd been a happy little dude all morning, excited to be around Rowe, but he seemed to like me, too. The way he'd thrown himself at Mae this morning had cracked my heart open wide.

I'd wanted kids for years. A whole fuckin' tribe of 'em.

Rowe caught the ball when Ripley threw it to him and

tucked it in his pocket. "Come on then. There's baseball gear in the shed, I'm pretty sure. Let's go see."

Ripley ran ahead toward the end of the clearing, and I walked behind with Rowe. Without Ripley's constant chatter, the smile fell from my face.

"You okay?" Rowe peered over at me.

"Yeah, just something Liam said last night is getting to me. Or maybe it was something he didn't say. I dunno."

"What did he say?"

I lifted one shoulder. "I can't pinpoint something specific. I just think this whole thing with his mom and his grandfather is getting to him. I think he kinda idolized his grandfather, and now..."

"Mae was worried this morning, too—"

"She was?"

"Yeah, but I thought he seemed okay." Rowe's gaze focused on Ripley again, but he raised one shoulder in a shrug.

I shoved my hands in my pockets. "You didn't see the way he stared at you when you brought Ripley in. Or when you called us family."

Rowe's forehead furrowed. "Too much? I was just feeling it last night, you know? Having everyone here..."

"Yeah, I know. I was feeling it, too."

Something passed between us, and this time it was something more than a physical thing.

I cleared my throat and looked away. "Did you see him before he left this morning?"

"Nope."

"Me neither. Something isn't sitting right. He was too quiet last night. It almost felt like..." I wasn't even sure I wanted to finish that thought.

"Like what?"

I shrugged, but the idea wouldn't leave me alone. "Like a goodbye."

Rowe passed me his phone, worry etching into the lines of his forehead. "Call him."

I nodded and made the call, but it went to voicemail. On a hunch, I searched the number for Liam's work and got his receptionist. We talked for a moment while she answered my questions, and I thanked her for her time. I hung up while Rowe rifled through the shed, but he paused when I leaned on the doorway.

"You get a hold of him?"

"His receptionist said he hasn't been in all week. Not last week, either. They have a big case, and everyone is frantic because he's not there."

"That's not like him."

"I know."

Mulling that over, Rowe searched a shelf for a baseball mitt. My gaze flittered around the dim space, bouncing over dirty sports gear, an old car seat that Rowe must have used when Ripley was a baby, lawn mowing equipment, and finally settling on a dirt bike. "That thing run?"

Rowe paused, casting an eye over it. "Yeah, should. Rode it not all that long ago when my car was at the mechanic's."

Hope lit up inside me like a firework. "It's licensed?"

Rowe shook his head. "No."

"Damn, it's not?"

He sighed. "No, it is, but I could read the expression on your face. Ride it round here all you want. But you aren't taking it out on the road."

I pointed at the helmet hanging over the handlebars. "Full-face helmet. Perfect disguise."

"The perfect disguise is the one you don't need at all cos

you keep your ass where it belongs. And that's here, just in case you needed a refresher."

But the urge to assure myself that Liam was just having an off day wouldn't let up, and the thought of getting out on a road, with a bike beneath me was so tempting. I craved that sort of freedom. "I've basically swapped one jail for another, Rowe. It's a ten-minute spin around the block to check on Liam and I'll be back."

"I can check on Liam."

"You've got a kid here, and Mae took your car."

"Mae will kill you."

"I'll make it up to her."

I was practically vibrating with excitement. God, I'd missed riding. It was a straight shot from here to Providence. I wouldn't go anywhere near Saint View, where the cops liked to hang out. They never did random patrols in the ritzier suburbs. I'd get to Liam's place and back before anybody even noticed I was gone.

He rolled his eyes. "I can already tell nothing I say is going to stop you, so just go. Keys are in the ignition. Take my phone so we can at least find you later if we need to."

I closed my eyes for the briefest of moments and let myself feel the happiness.

Then leaned in and kissed him.

I realized what I was doing as soon as my lips touched his. I jerked back so quick the chance of whiplash was real.

We both glanced at Ripley and found him watching us with big eyes.

Fuck. I'd just put Rowe in the most awkward position.

I coughed. "Sorry." I made for the bike, but Rowe's fingers wrapped around my wrist, jerking me back.

"I'm not." His voice was deep and husky, and he pressed his lips to mine again.

Instant heat surged through me, a combination of Rowe's lips against mine and the thought I'd soon have the rumble of a bike beneath me. He opened for me, accepting the quick flick of my tongue against his. It was just enough to engulf me in desire before he pulled away.

Ripley grinned. "Rowe, do you love Heath?"

The two of us froze.

But Ripley's little voice filled the void. "Grandma told me that boys can love whoever they want to love. And that girls can love whoever they want to love. And you can love a dog. And a cat. And rats, too, but I don't like them. Toby at school says..."

Heat prickled at the back of my neck, and the shed was suddenly too small for both Rowe and me to be in. Avoiding eye contact with Rowe, I ruffled Ripley's hair on my way to the bike. "Cover your ears. This might be loud."

I threw a leg over the dirt bike and pushed down hard on the kick start. The engine lit up with a roar that echoed around the shed, and Ripley clasped his hands over the sides of his head like mufflers. His smile was ear to ear.

I made him a promise before I left. "I'm gonna take you for a ride when I get back, okay?"

I was pretty sure he heard me because his feet started up an excited little dance on the spot. I was still grinning when I tugged the helmet on, fastening the clip beneath my chin. Rowe watched from the doorway, keeping an eye on Ripley. I rode past slowly, too close to him, but he didn't move. I let my hand brush his on the way out.

The sparks between us crackled with electricity.

"Be careful," he yelled.

"Always." I flipped the visor down, and then I was flying through the clearing, heading for the private road that would take me back to civilization.

The dirt bike was a zippy thing. It didn't have the same growl of the road bikes I'd owned throughout the years, but it was quick and perfectly suited for the ruts and dirt. Most importantly, it did provide that feeling of freedom that had been sorely missing in my life for too long.

When I hit the main road, I opened the bike up and whipped along toward Providence. I would have preferred to take the scenic route, along the road that would eventually run beside the coast, but that meant going through Saint View. I was smart enough not to do that right now, because attracting the attention of the cops could only end in a chase. I didn't want that. I wanted my girl on the seat behind me, her arms wrapped around my middle, her tits pressed to my back while she held me tight. I wanted her cheek resting between my shoulder blades and her squeals of excitement over riding with me as loud as when I rode her.

Last night had been the singular most mind-blowing night of my life. Having Mae between me and Rowe, knowing Liam looked on, watching us make every inch of Mae's body tremble. I'd never known sex like that. It filled my head with ideas and promises of more.

I had no idea how to make this life a permanent thing. One without the threat of cops finding me and hauling me back to jail. But I wanted it. And I was willing to fight for it.

That started with getting Liam back on track. Rowe had Ripley to think about, Mae had Tori problems. They both loved Liam, but he was my family now, too. He'd gone out on a limb for me with my trial. He'd stepped up and belted the shit out of Rowe when I couldn't, even though it had hurt him to do it. He'd broken every oath he'd ever taken, for me.

I owed him more than checking in on him when he was hurting.

I bypassed the security gate at his building by taking the dirt bike up on the sidewalk. In his parking garage, his BMW was very noticeably missing from his parking spot. I already knew he wasn't at work. My mind churned over the words he'd said last night and the way he'd acted.

It suddenly hit me that it had all felt like a final goodbye.

Dread crept up the back of my neck. I realized that everything he'd been last night, had been me once upon a time. Things I'd done playing over in my head, tormenting me, never leaving me alone, until darkness had tried to control everything I was.

I yanked out Rowe's phone and called Liam over and over again. "Dammit, Liam!" I yelled into the empty garage. "Answer your fucking phone!"

The insults echoed around me then lapsed into silence. Something urgent and insistent in the back of my mind knew I had to find him. I should have seen it earlier. I'd been caught up in Mae and Rowe and distracted by Ripley. I should have realized...

All of Liam's problems centered around his grandfather.

His biological father.

The man who'd attacked his own son's girlfriend, raped her, and gotten her pregnant.

Grateful I had Rowe's phone, I did a quick internet search and easily found Liam's grandparents' address. My search also brought up multiple articles about his grandfather's law work, his retirement, and charities his wife, Isadora, supported. I was already deep in the most affluent part of Providence. Liam's grandparents' place was only two blocks away.

I shoved my helmet back on and twisted the accelerator, leaving a plume of white smoke behind me.

I might be wrong, I told myself silently as I passed mansions in a blur. Liam might not be here at all. He might be at the gym, taking out his frustrations on a boxing bag. Or maybe he'd gone to his mother's place. For all I knew, he was having a fucking cup of tea with her over their little kitchen table.

I hoped one of those were true. I'd never set foot in a church in all my life, and yet I prayed for that to be the case.

But I knew what I would have done in his situation. I knew how that darkness pulled you in and made you think listening to it was the only way out.

I turned onto Liam's grandparents' street and knew instantly which house was theirs.

Liam's car was parked silently outside.

A rising sense of dread urged me on, and I hit the accelerator harder instead of slowing down.

Something was wrong. I felt it in my gut.

I rode the bike straight up over their perfectly manicured lawn, leaving a dirty tire trail behind me. I threw the bike down at their front steps and pounded on the door with one hand while I yanked off the helmet with the other. "Come on. Come on."

The door eventually opened, and an older woman stood behind it, her clothes too expensive, her hair too neat to be the hired help. "Can I help you?" Her blue eyes were sharp, taking me in carefully but without judgment.

"I'm a friend of your grandson. Is he here? I need to speak to him. It's very urgent."

She opened the door a little wider. "Liam? Well, yes, he's in the den with his grandfather."

I didn't wait for her to invite me in. I stepped over the threshold, forcing her back. "Where is that, please?"

She pointed down a corridor, and I had to hold myself back so I didn't run. But I sure as fuck didn't dawdle, waiting for the older woman to catch up either.

Halfway down the hallway, the shouting led me to the den.

"You're a liar." Liam's shout was hoarse with the accusation.

I hesitated, knowing he needed to say his piece.

"Your mother is the liar. That cheap whore could never tell the truth about anything."

I bristled at the slur. Liam's mother had been nothing but sweet to us. And she'd kept my identity a secret.

The woman, Isadora, cleared her throat uncomfortably. "It seems it isn't a good time—"

Liam's roar of anger and frustration bellowed back to us, cutting his grandmother off midsentence.

I blinked at the ferocity of it. It set off every alarm bell in my head and confirmed for me that I'd been right. Liam wasn't in the headspace to have this conversation rationally. Maybe he never would be, but I wasn't letting him do this without backup. He needed someone in his corner, and fuck if that wasn't going to be me. I threw open the door.

Isadora gasped behind me.

Liam's gaze didn't turn my way for a second.

He was fully focused on the gun held to his grandfather's temple.

The older man sat behind a beautifully carved mahogany desk. I imagined he'd made many a deal from that position, leaning back in his padded chair, powerful and experienced in his job. He was the sort of person who would have had a cigar in one hand, a whiskey on ice in the other, while he commanded an entire room.

Right now, he was none of that. He was a frail, terrified old man, whose sins had finally caught up with him. He sat trembling on his seat, his hands raised, not daring to look at his son.

"Don't you ever, *ever* speak about her like that. You don't even deserve to say her name after what you did."

"Liam? What is this?" Isadora asked, trying to edge around me. "Where did you get a gun?"

For the first time, Liam seemed to notice that there were other people in the room. He swung the gun in our direction, and I stepped in front of Isadora, not willing to have her hurt.

Liam barely registered me. But he turned the gun back on his grandfather who had been too frozen to move. "Did you know?" he yelled at his grandmother without looking at her. "Did you know what your husband did?"

She stifled a sob. "We love you, Liam. Why are you doing this?"

He let out a bitter laugh, but behind it was the agony of a broken man. "She doesn't deny it. Of course you fucking knew. You knew everything that happened in this house. Every party I ever threw. Every girl I ever snuck in. I used to think you had spies. Is that how you found out what he'd done?"

"Your mother was a very promiscuous young woman. She—"

Liam slammed the gun down on the desk.

An earsplitting shot echoed through the room.

Isadora screamed.

My ears rang.

Liam stared down at the gun like he had no idea what it was.

I moved in quick. "Liam. Give it to me."

His fingers went limp. Relief fueled me as I took control of the gun, putting on the safety and shoving it into the back of my jeans.

Liam's gaze transferred to the bullet hole in the plaster wall.

His grandfather stared at it, too, and then at me. There was a flash of recognition in his eyes, and then confusion, like he was trying to place me.

And that's when I knew the entire thing was about to come crumbling down on top of us.

Shit. I'd taken my helmet off and shown my face. Exactly what I'd promised Rowe I wouldn't do. I hadn't even thought about it, I'd been so intent on getting to Liam.

But I couldn't care about that right now. I grabbed the back of Liam's shirt and hauled him out of the den. Isadora reached a hand out to her grandson.

"Isadora!" his grandfather snapped.

Her hand fell limply at her side, and she stepped away, letting us leave. I shoved Liam through the house like I was his bodyguard. His grandparents' expensive things flashed by in a blur, until we were out on the porch again.

"What are you doing here?" he mumbled.

But the man was clearly in shock. He was as limp as a rag doll, only on his feet because of the grip I had on him. I bypassed my bike entirely and shoved him up against his car. It was only then that I hissed, "What the fuck were you doing? Are you fucking insane? Are you trying to go to jail?"

I shoved my hands into the pocket of his sweatpants, the same ones he'd worn yesterday, and yanked out his keys. He practically fell into the passenger seat, but by the time I'd rounded the car to get in behind the wheel, he was staring at the front door again like he was ready for a second go.

I slammed my hand down on the lock button, threw the car in reverse, and hit the accelerator so hard the tires let out a squeal of protest.

Rowe's bike was left stranded on the manicured lawn, the handlebars squashing delicate flowers. Under the circumstances, I had no other choice. Putting distance between Liam and his grandfather was the number one priority.

My heart rate slowed the farther we got out of Providence. On autopilot, I drove us into Saint View, the streets there familiar and comforting. With no destination in mind, I waited for Liam to say something.

"I need to go back."

I sighed. "Not what I wanted you to say, bro. You aren't going back there. Not today. Not ever."

"I have to."

I jerked the steering wheel, pulling us over by the Saint View end of the beach. Down on the sand, happy families played in the shallow water, enjoying the last days of summer. Farther out in the water, surfers attempted to catch waves, though it really wasn't the right time of day for it and the swell was puny.

They all went on about their business, no idea that the man sitting beside me had just nearly killed his grandfather.

I stared out at the waves. They just kept rolling in, no matter what was going on around them. "Not letting you do that."

Liam's fist smashed against the glove box.

I flinched at the sudden movement, but it was the release of aggression Liam had been looking for. "He raped her, Heath! That's the only fucking reason I'm alive. He was an old man, who took advantage of a sixteen-year-old girl and ruined her goddamn life. He left her to rot in Saint View, took away the only support she had, and only came back for me when he realized I was just like him. So what do I do with that? If I don't kill him, then the only other person left to kill is myself. And trust me, I already fucking thought about that. I thought about it for an entire day yesterday, and I didn't have the guts to do that either."

He stared straight out over the beach, a tear rolling down his cheek.

His words hit me hard, and suddenly I was back there, drowning in those old feelings and memories I'd fought so hard to bury. My throat was thick with an emotion I didn't want to remember. "I know how you feel."

"No. You don't."

I swiveled to stare at him. "I do. You think I don't want to put a bullet through that old bastard's head for what he did to your mother? For what he's done to you? I do. And damn, if I didn't know exactly how you feel right now, then I probably would let you walk back in there and finish the job you started."

The silence drew out, both of us breathing hard.

"Let me go," he whispered.

I grabbed Liam's chin and forced him to face me. "I'm not letting you because it doesn't fix anything!"

I didn't want to say the words. I didn't want to let the memories out, but I knew I had no choice. The only way to make him understand that pain was to show him.

I let my guard drop.

I let the past back in.

Every deep, dark, depraved memory that I had tucked away, buried deep just so I could function... They all came flooding back. "I was fourteen when I first held a gun on my dad."

Liam didn't say anything, but he stilled enough I knew I had his attention. I let my hand fall away, knowing he was listening.

It was just as well, because I was sure I couldn't tell the story with him looking at me. "He wasn't like your grandfather. Yours hid his evil. Mine never bothered." I rubbed absently at my arm, the one where a looping tattoo of patterns and dark ink hid scars that had long healed, physically, if not emotionally. "He used to like putting his cigarettes out on me. I had an armful of scars before I even started high school and an ongoing threat that he'd do a whole lot worse if I showed anyone."

"You never said anything. I knew you had a sealed record, but most kids who grow up in Saint View do."

I shrugged. "No point bringing up the past until you try and go making the same mistakes I did."

Liam didn't say anything.

I sucked in a breath. "The burns were the least of my worries, really. After a while, I almost didn't feel them because everything else hurt so bad. He liked to rape my mother, too. Hold her down while she kicked and screamed and fought him. He never cared whether me or my brothers and sister were in the room or not. That was him through and through. Only ever cared about himself and what he wanted."

"Fuck."

I nodded. "The first time I pulled a gun on him had gone pretty much exactly like how you just went with your old man. Only I didn't even have the guts to pull the trigger. I just stood there, with it limp in my hand, shaking like a fucking leaf cos I was so terrified."

It all played back in my head, clear as they day it had happened. The darkness billowed around me like a storm cloud, fighting to engulf me. "He took the gun out of my hand and pushed it right between my eyes and told me if I ever touched his gun again, I'd be dead before I could blink. The pistol-whip to the side of my head knocked me out, and I came to in the exact same spot hours later with my little sister standing over me."

"Did your mother get you out?"

I snorted on my laughter. "When I woke up, my mother was sitting on the couch smoking like nothing had even happened. Doubt she even checked for a pulse."

Liam slumped back in his seat. "That's messed up. They still together?"

"No. The next time I did it, I didn't freeze."

Liam sucked in a breath. "For real?"

I could see my father's dead body lying at my feet as clear as the day it had happened. "I was a minor. And I had clear signs of abuse. Everybody knew my old man was a violent, abusive fuck. When they saw the condition of my mother and my siblings, nobody fought too hard for me to go down for it."

"Fucking hell."

"So I do know. I know that place you're at. I know exactly what it's like to feel worthless and helpless and to have to live with a man who thinks nothing of destroying the people he's supposed to love." I stared Liam right in the eyes. "But I also know what it feels like to be the person who takes another life. There's no coming back from that. None. Even if they deserve it, even if the world is better without them in it. It changes you. You don't ever forget. And the darkness creeps up until it consumes you or you find a way to bury it. I don't want to have to watch you do that. It's too hard. It doesn't make that feeling of wanting to die go away. There's no relief in it. It only makes it worse."

Liam leaned forward, resting his arms on his knees, a sob breaking free. And with it came all the pain and hurt he'd been bottling up. I didn't try to stop him. Just clapped a hand to the back of his neck so he knew I was there. His shoulders shook silently until I was battling back tears myself.

After a minute, his sobs became hiccups, and then eventually he sat straight. He blew out a long breath that lifted hair off his forehead. He turned to me and let out a half laugh. "Fucking hell. I held a gun to my grandfather's head."

I grinned and shrugged. "Eh. The old prick deserved it."

Liam burst into laughter, the kind that was half embarrassed and half relief. His eyes were red-rimmed, which accentuated the dark circles beneath. "I don't know how to deal with any of this."

"You go home to your family." I glanced over at him. "Home to Mae."

I was relieved when he nodded. I turned the car back on and got us back on the road to Rowe's cabin. "Ain't neither of us spending the rest of our lives in jail."

But with Liam's grandfather recognizing me, and my prints all over Rowe's bike, left at the scene of a crime, I doubted that was true.

21

ROWE

he sun was getting low, and though I kept a wide smile on my face for Ripley's sake, I kept staring down the drive, waiting for the others to return.

All of them should have been back by now. And yet not one car, nor my dirt bike, had appeared. I was also an idiot because I'd sent Heath off with my phone. There was a land-line here, but I hadn't thought to write down anybody's number before he'd left. I definitely didn't know any of them by heart, except my own, and Heath wasn't answering it.

I dragged my gaze away from the drive and let it glide back to where Ripley had been playing with some sticks in the dirt. I frowned when he wasn't there, the sticks lying abandoned on the grass. I stood, quickly scanning the rest of the clearing. "Ripley!"

Nothing.

My heartbeat became a pound, and I jogged down the porch steps, running to the end of the clearing and peering into the woods. "Ripley!" I fought to keep the panic out of my voice. "If you want to play hide-and-seek, you need to come out first so I can count to ten."

Why the hell had I taken my eyes off him? He couldn't swim that well yet. I staggered toward the lake, fear rushing my body. If he'd wandered down there...

"Hi, Rowe!"

I spun around, relief washing over me at Ripley's voice. He waved from some long grass by the shed, and I ran over to him, scooping him up into my arms. "Hey, buddy. You scared me for a second there. What were you doing?"

He paused, then said, "Nothing."

He had the distinctly guilty look of a kid who'd gotten his hand caught in a cookie jar, but I was so relieved I didn't even care. I squeezed him tighter. "How about a piggyback up to the house? I think there's a shower with your name on it."

"Okay."

I slung him over my shoulder and let him hang upside down. He giggled. "Byeeeeeee."

"Bye dirt, and leaves, and stinky little boy!" I jostled him so he bounced around. Laughing, I got him into the bathroom and lathered him up with soap until voices sounded on the porch. I left him filling up a cup to splash it against the glass walls and stuck my head out into the hall. Mae, Rowe, and Liam all traipsed in the door.

"Where have you guys been? It's been hours."

"Long story," Mae replied.

"Even longer for us," Heath said. He squinted at me. "Might have lost your bike, by the way. Sorry."

I widened my eyes at him. "How the hell did that happen?"

Heath glanced at Liam, who looked so emotionally drained he couldn't even stand. He'd slumped into a camping chair with the air of a man who needed to sleep for a week. "I'll get it back."

"Family meeting when we get home tonight, I think." Mae glanced between all of us.

I frowned. "Are we going somewhere?"

She scraped her long blonde hair up in her fingers and fitted an elastic band to hold her ponytail. "You and I have gotta go to work before we lose our jobs."

I shook my head. "I'm not leaving Ripley—"

"He'll be with me," Heath said. "Go."

There was no hesitation in leaving Ripley with Heath. I knew he'd protect Ripley just as fiercely as I would. And even though Liam was like death warmed over, he'd be here, too. Ripley would be in good hands. I just didn't want to let the real world back in.

I got Ripley out of the shower and wrapped him in a towel while I explained to him that I needed to go to work.

Heath was waiting in the hall and reached for Ripley with a grin. "Let's get dressed then you can help me cook dinner."

Ripley went to him without hesitation. "Can you teach me how to ride that motorbike?"

They disappeared into his new bedroom, and I went into mine. Mae was already in there, getting ready for work. I closed the door quietly behind me and leaned back on it, watching her pull off her shirt and skirt in front of the full-length mirror on the closet door. When she was down to her underwear, I stepped in close behind her, wrapping my arms around her middle and resting my chin on her shoulder.

"You want to talk about it?" I asked her in the mirror.

She sighed heavily. "Will thinks Tori killed Jayela."

"What the hell? That's insane. She's like a mouse."

"I know. It's ridiculous. Her size wouldn't have stopped her slitting Jayela's throat while she slept, though."

"What are you going to do?"

"Nothing until I talk to her." Tension lines creased her forehead, and her posture went rigid.

I pressed my lips to her bare shoulder. "You're stressed. If we're five minutes late, nobody will notice."

She raised one eyebrow, her expression softening slightly. "Five minutes? When have you even been just five minutes?"

"You think I can't get you off in five minutes?"

She laughed. "Not what I meant. I meant sex between us is more like a marathon than a sprint. In a good way. Women don't want a five-minute fuck." She tilted her head to one side with a grin. "Not all the time, anyway."

I nuzzled into her neck, unable to resist the urge to place open-mouthed kisses there. I sucked at her skin, tasting the faint saltiness of her being out in the summer heat all day. "You want a five-minute fuck now, Mae?"

I held her to me, one hand flat on her stomach, the other taking a handful of her ass and squeezing. More kisses to her neck had her relaxing back against me, and the thought of getting to work on time vanished.

She twisted her head so I could claim her lips. She devoured mine, hard and fast, tongue seeking entrance. But I pulled back, nudging her to face the mirror again as I slid my fingers lower into her panties.

"Rowe..."

"You want me to stop?"

Her moans said otherwise. "Five minutes."

"I'll have you coming around my fingers in three."

She lifted one hand to grab the back of my neck, massaging it lightly and stroking the hair at the nape.

I pushed my fingers low, tugging her panties down a touch to reveal her mound and her sweet pink clit beneath it. I pinched it between two fingers, eliciting a gasp from her, before finding her wet and needy, ready for my fingers. My dick strained against her ass, but this wasn't about me. This was about getting her off fast and hard and dirty.

"Watch me," I demanded in her ear.

She opened her eyes, her gaze meeting mine in the reflection. With one hand plunging into her core, I used the other to work her tits. Her hips ground in time with the rhythm of my hand, and I took one breast from her bra cup, watching in the mirror as her perfect pink nipple popped free, only to be immediately engulfed between my eager fingertips.

By now, I knew exactly what she liked. Hard tweaks of her nipple, followed by softer caresses of her breasts and stomach. Slow rubs of her clit and quick but steady thrusts of my fingers. I loved how wet she got for me, and I was desperate to get on my knees in front of her, but her thighs were already trembling, and I'd promised to get her there quick, not drag it out and torture her like I really wanted to.

"Rowe," she panted, clutching my hair.

Fuck, that felt good. It prickled at my scalp, sending heat right through my body that demanded I free my erection, push her up against the mirror, and take her from behind.

But I wanted her to watch herself come more.

"Don't close your eyes or I'll stop."

Her eyes were half-mast, heavy with desire. She rolled her hips, getting my fingers exactly where she liked it most. We worked together, the perfect team, building her orgasm until my fingers were dripping with her.

I flicked her little bud of pleasure with my thumb, and her breaths changed to frantic gasps of breath.

"Rowe!" she cried. "Yes!"

I bit down on her shoulder, and her cries grew louder. I

clapped a hand over her mouth, muffling the noise. From outside the door, loud music started up, and I almost laughed, knowing it was Heath or Liam, attempting to muffle Mae's cries, either for Ripley's sake, or possibly to stop themselves from busting in here and joining us.

One more hard squeeze of her nipple, one more thrust, one more kiss, and she came. Her eyes widened, connecting our gazes in the mirror once more. She watched herself fall apart, my fingers deep inside her snatch.

Nothing had ever been more beautiful. Her cheeks flushed pink. Her worries completely evaporated from the planes of her face.

My family was here, their voices floating down the hall, and she was the one who'd given them to me.

Gratitude swelled inside me. This had all become difficult and messy and yet at the same time it was beautiful.

She was ours.

Mine.

I pressed my lips to her temple and breathed in her scent, smothered now by the smell of her arousal.

All of it perfect.

"I love you," I whispered.

I froze, meaning the words with every ounce of my being, but in saying them, I'd laid myself wide open for the first time since Rory's death. That was fucking terrifying. I forced myself to swallow, trying to wet the sudden dryness in my throat.

She stared at me in the mirror, surprise flashing across her features. Then she turned in my arms. She gazed up at me with her huge brown eyes. "I love you, too. You and Ripley. I love you both. I have for a long time."

I stared at her, wondering how the hell we'd gotten here. A sudden need for her overwhelmed me. A desperate urge to show her physically as well as verbally how much I loved her. Work be damned. I was making love to my woman.

Desperate for her, I shoved her panties down her legs and hoisted her into my arms. She instantly wound her legs around my waist, her arms around my neck, and I kissed her hard and deep as I walked her back against a wall. Using my body to hold her in place, I grappled with my shorts, shoving them down just far enough that I could free my erection and sink inside her cunt.

We both shouted at the intrusion, her slick heat engulfing me so sweetly. I slammed into her body while she cried out my name. I kissed her over and over again.

"Say it again," she moaned.

"I love you, Mae." I ground into her body. "I love you so fucking much."

"I'm going to come!"

So was I. I slammed home once more, my pubic bone grinding against her clit.

We came together, an explosion of feeling and sensation, and for the first time in years, I came wrapped inside the body and heart of a woman I loved.

"I love you," I whispered once more.

She unraveled herself from me, and I set her down on her feet again.

She was a mess, half falling out of her bra, my cum glistening between her thighs. And yet she'd never been as sexy.

I suddenly realized she was probably sore from last night and that I'd just made it worse. "Shit, Mae. Are you okay? I didn't mean to take you so roughly, especially after last night."

But she shook her head and pressed up on her toes to kiss me. "I asked for a five-minute fuck."

"That was a lot more than five minutes."

"We're very late for work," she agreed.

"Probably going to get fired."

In that moment, so high on each other, I wasn't sure either of us cared.

---

*L*iam and Ripley sat at the kitchen table eating steak and fries, their meals mostly untouched because the two of them were too busy singing along with the radio that blared around the cabin. Heath scooped fries onto his own plate but paused when Mae and I reappeared, freshly showered and dressed.

He raised one eyebrow in our direction, but there was heat in his eyes, too. Like he'd really wanted to join us but had held himself back.

Liam put his microphone fork down and chuckled at us. "Heath, you can turn the radio down now. They're done."

Heath hit the volume button a few times, and Mae blushed pink again, but I didn't drop my arm from around her shoulders. I couldn't stop touching her. We really did need to go to work, though. I kissed Ripley's head and said I'd see him in the morning.

His bottom lip trembled. "I miss Grandma."

I swept him up in a tight hug. "I know you do, kiddo. We'll get her to come out here for a visit, what do you think?"

He nodded and then scrambled to get back down to his fries. Liam challenged him to a fry sword fight, and he was smiling again as we walked to the door.

Heath's horny-as-fuck gaze followed us.

I smirked at him and closed the door.

I suspected I'd pay for that later, but it would be in a good way. My dick twitched just thinking about it, and not wanting another hard-on, I forced my thoughts away from Heath and the promises in his eyes.

I got behind the wheel of my car, and Mae got in the passenger seat. "We should pick my car up after work."

I shot her a glance. "You giving up on making your neighbors think you still live there?"

She shrugged. "I just can't bring myself to stay in my apartment alone when all of you are out here. The police don't seem interested in talking to me, so I don't know why I'm bothering."

"Good. Because I don't want you sleeping alone either."

"Settled then."

I twisted the key in the ignition, then glanced down at the dash and groaned at the red fuel light that flickered on.

Mae cringed. "Oops. I forgot about that. Didn't have time to stop for gas. Lucky you love me, right?" She peered over my shoulder. "We have enough to get to work, don't we?"

"Doubtful. Tank isn't that big. We're late anyway. Might as well get gas now rather than after shift."

Mae reached across the center console and rested a hand on my thigh, dangerously close to my groin.

I shot her a warning look.

She grinned. "What?"

"Don't 'what' me. I see what you're doing."

"We just had sex ten minutes ago. I'm not doing anything."

I guided the car down the road that led from my property. "Innocent as Snow White until you're screaming my name with a pussy full of my cock, aren't you?"

Her eyes bulged, and I laughed at her expression. I loved when my dirty talk caught her by surprise.

On a high, I drove to the closest gas station on the edge of Saint View. Both of our spirits were high, fueled by great sex, good music, and the little touches that neither of us seemed to be able to quit. Mae's hand never left my thigh, but she cranked up the stereo and sang along at the top of her lungs. I parked the car by the gas pump and got out, laughing when I could still hear her singing outside the car with all the doors closed. I wouldn't tell her. I didn't want her to stop.

I rounded the car and grabbed the nozzle, inserting it into the gas tank. Movement caught my eye across the paved lot. I dismissed it instantly, realizing it was just someone walking back to the car parked on the other side of mine. I smiled in his direction, in the mood to be friendly because happiness was pouring out of my every pore in a way I'd never known before.

At the flash of his blue eyes, every ounce of happiness faded.

Zye pulled back his hood and strolled over to me like he didn't have a care in the world. I shot a worried glance toward Mae, and Zye laughed.

"Don't worry. She didn't see me. She's too busy having a concert for one in there."

That was good. I didn't want her noticing him. I didn't want her anywhere near him. The last time she'd been this close to him, she'd Tasered him with the stun gun phone case I'd brought her. We couldn't do that here, surrounded by fuel. I hit the lock doors button on my key fob.

Zye leaned against my car, watching me pump gas. "You think that's gonna save her from me if I really wanted to get to her?"

I didn't answer. He'd burst my bubble with his appearance so thoroughly it had disintegrated into nothingness.

"Where's Ripley?"

I squeezed the nozzle tighter. "At his home, I would assume."

Zye clucked his tongue. "See, Pritchard. I went to my dear old mother-in-law's place—"

"She's not your mother-in-law. You and Rory were never married."

He chuckled. "No. You stole that opportunity from me, didn't you? Made sure you had your clutches tight in her. Did you have to drag her down that aisle? Did you ever wonder if she was thinking about me when she said those I dos?"

I rolled my eyes and leaned in, my voice just as low and deadly as I knew his could get. "No. Not for a second. Because she hated everything about you, Zye. From the tip of your head to the very depth of the black hole that is your soul."

Something flickered in his gaze, and a part of me roared in victory.

But he covered it quickly. He slapped his hand against the roof of my car. "Norma says Ripley is with her sister in Texas for the summer. Playin' with his cousins."

I kept my face schooled in nonchalance. "Lucky kid. Norma's sister has a big ranch with horses, and her grand-kids are Ripley's age. He's probably having the time of his life."

"Yeah, I don't believe that for a second." Zye looked me up and down, inching in closer, getting up in my face, chest to chest. "I want my son back, Pritchard. I know you have him."

I shoved him off me. "You don't know shit, Zye. How about you walk your ass back to your parole officer before I call him and tell him you're drunk or high or, I dunno, disrupting my fucking peace."

We were drawing the looks of people around us.

Mae cracked her window and casually as hell called, "I already called the cops. They'll be here in five. Feel free to hang around to say hi."

Zye glanced in her direction, a slow smile spreading across his face. But it was me he spoke to. "Ripley's back in twenty-four hours, or people start getting hurt. Don't test me, Pritchard. You know exactly what I'm capable of. I took someone you loved once before. I'm not afraid to do it again."

22

MAE

I was distracted and jumpy for my entire class. Rowe sat at the back of my room, ass on the edge of his seat, his gaze darting to meet mine every few minutes.

How had we gotten to the point where we were safer inside the prison than out of it? I scrubbed a hand over my face and tried to pay attention to what my class was doing. For once, though, they were mostly well-behaved. The interest had died off, and now I was left with the men who really wanted to be here.

I found my gaze wandering to Vincent's empty seat. Rowe had delivered some work to the psych department for him, but I hated that he couldn't come to class anymore. Despite the fact he was almost certainly a complete psychopath, who could kill without remorse, I saw the good in him. His desire to learn needed to be nurtured. I had no real idea of his past, but I knew he couldn't possibly have had the greatest upbringing, and that broke my heart. What if he'd once been a little boy like Ripley who'd just needed someone to take an interest in him?

He was bright. He'd likely finished the stack of papers

Rowe had left for him. Determined to show the man that someone gave a shit, despite his crimes, I opened my desk drawer and found a fresh manilla folder and filled it with worksheets. I studied each one carefully, debating whether there were enough instructions that he could understand the work without me being there to teach it. Some I added handwritten notes to with additional explanations I thought he might need.

Rowe wandered down to see what I was doing, side-eyeing the prisoners working at their desks as he went. He watched me write Vincent's name on the front and frowned at me. "What's this?"

I passed him over the folder. "More work for Vincent. Can you ask if he can return the last lot I gave him? I want to mark them and write him some notes."

The corner of Rowe's mouth flickered. "You care too much."

I shook my head. "Other people don't care enough."

He rubbed at the stubble on his jaw. "You're probably right. It's quiet in here tonight, and your shift is just about done anyway. Want to finish five minutes early and swing past psych to deliver it yourself? They probably won't let you see him, but you could ask the nurses there how he's doing."

I beamed at him. A few weeks ago he would have flat-out refused my request. But he was mellowing and seeing that everything wasn't always so black and white. No person was all good. No person was all bad.

Except maybe Zye.

He hadn't shown a redeeming quality yet, but Vincent was different. He might be ruthless, but he cared about me enough to save my life and protect me during the prison riot. The least I could do in return was pass on some photo-copied algebra.

I dismissed the men, answered a last question from one as he left the room, and then locked my classroom behind me. We took the same route as the men, but when they turned off to go to Gen Pop, Rowe and I kept walking. We moved past the cafeteria, and I couldn't help remembering the way Vincent had stabbed another prisoner in the eye the last time I'd been in there. I shuddered at the memory, and though I was still determined to get the work to him, it did remind me that Vincent wasn't the hero I occasionally let myself think he was.

At the double doors marked Psych Ward, I clutched my folder a little tighter to my chest. Of all the places in the prison, this one scared me the most. The unpredictable nature of the men behind the doors was terrifying. But I reminded myself they weren't just free to walk around, and that we'd merely be speaking with the nurses or guards on duty.

And I really did want to know how Vincent was.

Rowe held his ID tag up to the scanner. But instead of beeping and turning green, it turned red.

I pointed at the red light. "Did they remove your clearance?"

"I don't think so. They would have told me." He tried the swipe card again, but the same thing happened. He peered through a glass panel on the door and then rapped his knuckles across it.

A man came to the door, his green hospital scrubs identifying him as a nurse rather than a guard. He was big and burly, though, so he could have passed for either. He squinted through the window at us, and both Rowe and I flashed our ID badges. The man disappeared from behind the glass, but a speaker panel by the lock flared to life.

"Sorry, Officer. I can't admit you."

The doors were so heavy, we wouldn't have heard a word he'd said without the intercom.

Rowe pressed a finger to the button on our side. "What's going on? We just have some schoolwork for a patient."

The man's voice came again. "Psych is currently under full lockdown. I can't open these doors at all, unfortunately."

Rowe gave the man a nod of understanding, and we watched him through the glass as he walked away. "Sorry, babe. Gonna have to come back another day."

I tucked the files under my arm, disappointed. "What happened?"

"No idea, but it isn't unusual in psych. If someone loses it, they lockdown for the safety of all patients."

I worried my bottom lip with my teeth. "I hope Vincent is okay."

"Leave the work with me. I'll try again tomorrow while you're at the women's prison." He slipped the file out from beneath my arm and tucked it under his own. "Ready to go get your car? I'm due a break. I'll drive you over to pick it up before I come back to finish my shift."

I nodded distractedly, Vincent on my mind. But when we got to the staff locker rooms, the ringing of my phone distracted me. I hurried to my locker and pulled it out in the same moment it stopped ringing.

"Dammit," I muttered.

Rowe peered over my shoulder. "Probably just Liam or Heath calling to say they miss me."

I sniggered at him. "Unlikely. If they were calling you this many times it would be with dick jokes."

He groaned good-naturedly. "Don't start that shit again."

"Most people would be happy to hear about their giant schlong."

"Most people don't mind smoke being blown up their asses. I do. And when men as well hung as Liam and Heath start making dick comments, you know they're full of shit."

The room was completely empty, as it almost always was at this time, so I took the chance to cheekily pat him on the crotch. "I happen to like your giant eggplant, for the record."

"Keep patting it like that and I'm gonna show you how much it likes you, too."

I elbowed him away right as the phone started ringing again. I flashed it up at Rowe so he could see the screen. "Private Number. All the missed calls were. I don't think this is about your penis."

Rowe snorted. "Answer it and ask."

I giggled as I answered the call and pressed the cell to my ear. "Mae Donovan."

A woman cleared her voice on the other end. "Uh. Hello, Mae. My name is Angela."

I squinted toward the open door. The name sounded familiar…

"We haven't met but—"

I suddenly realized exactly who it was. "You're my father's mistress." The words were completely flat.

She paused on the other end. "That's not what I'd call myself, but I guess essentially, yes."

"What would you call yourself then?"

"His partner."

Anger licked at my blood. "His partner." It sounded more like an accusation from my lips. "Lady, I'm his daughter and I've never even met you."

Rowe put a hand on my arm. "Hey. Just remember, she's not your dad. As angry as you are for what he did, and for the lies and secrets he kept from you, she isn't him."

He was right. I knew nothing about this woman. At the very least, I could give her the courtesy I would any other stranger. "I'm sorry. That was unfair and rude of me. I just didn't expect a call from you."

"I never expected to talk to you either. Your father made it pretty clear you were off-limits. But I've had the police at my house, and I just wanted you to hear it from me, that my family and I had nothing to do with your sister's death."

"So my father doesn't owe you years of child support?"

"He does. But I certainly wouldn't kill a young woman to get it. I hope you know that."

I didn't answer because I didn't know that for sure. But it did seem a little far-fetched.

She cleared her throat. "Your father and I had our differences, Mae. Many of them. He wasn't always good to me, and I wasn't always good to him. But we were a family. Even if you didn't know about us."

I swallowed hard because that stung to hear. Jayela and I had been a family, but my father had never really been a part of it.

Angela sighed. "I'm sorry, that probably hurt you. That wasn't my intention with this phone call."

"Then what was?" Tears pricked the backs of my eyes, and I had no idea why. I didn't care one iota about my father. I hadn't done a single thing to organize his funeral, and for all I cared, they could bury him in a cardboard box somewhere. His years of neglect weren't suddenly moot because he wasn't breathing.

"I wanted your permission to organize a service for him. I know he wasn't always a great father to you—"

"He wasn't a father to me at all."

The woman paused. "He regretted that. But you..."

"Look just like my mother. I know."

"I'd like to bury him. For all his faults, he was still the man I love. I need to put him to rest."

I twisted the combination on my locker, needing something to do with my hands. "So, what do you want from me? Money?"

"No. Just your permission."

I steeled my spine. "Knock yourself out."

"Thank you," she said quietly. "May I send you the details? I know it would mean a lot to him if you attended."

I opened my mouth to refuse, but then she filled the silence quickly. "If not for him, come to meet your half-siblings."

I sucked in a breath, my stomach flipping over.

Rowe looked at me questioningly, and I shook my head. I couldn't even explain the turmoil coursing through me at that suggestion. I wanted to yell no and cheer yes all at the same time, and that was incredibly confusing.

I ended up just saying nothing.

"You don't have to decide right now. The service will be done before the end of the week, I hope. I'll text you the details and maybe you'll come."

I had no words. This woman was nothing like the villain I'd imagined in my head. She was going out of her way to be kind to me, even when I'd done nothing to deserve it.

"Maybe," I managed to squeak out.

I could hear the smile in Angela's voice. "Good. I know I never got to meet you personally, but your dad did talk about you and Jayela a lot. I feel like I know the two of you almost as well as I know my own children."

I shook my head. I didn't want to hear that my father

talked about me to his other family. Even if that were true, it was all too little too late.

"You might not be my blood, Mae. But you are my children's. That means something to me. I hope you'll come. I'd like to meet you in person."

She didn't wait for me to say yes or no. She just hung up.

While the part of me that felt orphaned, suddenly felt a little less lonely.

23

LIAM

*T*he elevator doors pinged open, and my assistant glanced over, mid conversation via a headset with a microphone that hovered at her lips. Her eyes widened when she saw it was me. "Gotta go, Mario. The prodigal son has returned."

I chuckled and leaned on the desk in front of her. She'd been my assistant ever since I finished college. Well, the office assistant. We all shared her, but I knew I was her favorite.

She pressed a button on her headset, cancelling the call. "You're back."

"Why do you make it sound like an accusation?"

She ignored me. "Were you whistling when you walked in?"

I blinked. "I don't know. Was I?"

"It sounded like whistling."

I shrugged. "Guess I was then."

Slowly, a smiled crept across her face. "You really are back."

"In the flesh."

She shook her head. "That's not what I meant. When you came in that one day last week after the Michaelson trial, you were here...but not really here. And then you disappeared altogether."

The vise that had let up on my chest threatened to squeeze again, but I refused to let it. I didn't want to go back there, where I'd been when Heath had pulled me from my grandfather's house. Our talk on the beach had really put things in perspective, as had a few days out in the woods with Mae and Ripley and Rowe.

Ripley called me Li-yam, his tongue not quite wrapping around the letters properly. I didn't know why, but that one little thing had gotten inside my heart and taken up root. There was an easy relaxation at the cabin. One where it was just the four of us—or four and a half if you counted Ripley—against the world. I'd tucked him into bed last night and sat on the end of his foldout mattress and told him a story about a family who lived in a bubble. I'd been making it up as I went along, not really thinking about it, but in hindsight, it was the story of us.

Something about being around them, isolated and in nature, had helped heal the worst of my broken bits. Not fully. Some wounds would never heal completely, and I knew the things my grandfather had done would sit as a chip on my shoulder for the rest of my life, one I'd constantly need to watch to make sure it didn't eat away at me.

But I was happier, if not completely happy.

My mind had turned back to proving Heath's innocence.

The elevator doors behind me binged open again, and the smile slid off Elise's face. "Back again, Officers?" She shot a worried glance in my direction.

I schooled my face into something pleasant and polite before I turned around.

I recognized the two men in uniform instantly. Johnson and Stewart had been the officers who'd beaten a confession out of Heath the morning after Jayela's murder. Johnson crossed his arms above his beer gut that strained at his button-down shirt.

His eyes narrowed on me. "Just the man we've been looking for."

I acted like I didn't have a care in the world. "Oh yeah? About a case? Which one?"

The younger guy spoke up from beside his colleague. "Where have you been the last few days, Mr. Banks?"

First rule of lying was to stick as closely to the truth as possible. "At my apartment, mostly."

"Doing what?"

"Getting drunk, to tell the truth. I needed a break."

Johnson cocked his head to one side, studying me. "Stressed?"

"Always. Comes with the job."

"Not stressed because your client is still on the run?"

I raised an eyebrow. "Why would I be stressed about that? It wasn't me who lost him. And it's not me who can't find him now. That's your job. I'll be stressed about him when he becomes my problem again. But until you find him, that's not my department."

Johnson rammed his lips together in a scowl. "You got anyone who can back up your story?"

Fuck this guy. I knew exactly what he'd done to Heath. I wanted to throw my fist straight into his smarmy face. So many of our problems had started with him and his negligence. It was nothing new, the police department in Providence had been poorly led for decades, their chief just recently landing himself in jail. But the apple didn't fall far from the tree. He'd trained his men in his own image. The handful of good ones, like Boston and Jayela, either didn't last or moved on to other precincts when they realized who they were working with.

"My girlfriend can confirm if you really need my alibi."

"She got a name?" Johnson's voice was barely above a sneer.

"Do you think I made her up?"

Pink spots of annoyance flared on Johnsons already ruddy cheeks. "Answer the question, smartass."

Elise inhaled sharply.

I didn't look in her direction, instead keeping my gaze firmly and steadily on the officers. "Mae."

"Mae Donovan? Jayela Donovan's sister?"

I almost rolled my eyes. He clearly knew exactly who I was dating. "Yes."

He clucked his tongue, the sound loud in the otherwise silent room. "I saw her at Michaelson's trial. Seemed pretty cut up when he was declared guilty. Odd reaction, I thought."

"Not when she knows you beat that confession out of his mouth and that the person who actually killed her sister is still walking around because of your incompetence." The words dripped fake sugar. I straightened to my full height, an inch or two taller than the cop, and stared down at him. "If you wanted her to look appropriately pleased by a judge's decision, perhaps you should have done your job properly in the first place instead of taking out your petty jealousy on Jayela's ex-boyfriend."

He stepped in, an attempt to intimidate. But I wasn't

budging. Anger and hate for the man buzzed around my system. After what Heath had done for me the other day, I was going to have his back more than ever now. He was so much more than just a client I was defending.

My gaze locked with Johnson's, neither of us willing to back down.

But I was well-practiced in this. If you couldn't handle direct eye contact, even when it made you uncomfortable, you had no place being a criminal lawyer.

And I was a fucking excellent lawyer.

I'd made a mistake with Heath's trial, but I'd fix it. Starting now.

Johnson was the first to look away. Just like I knew he would be. Because inside his bravado, the man was a spineless coward who got off on using his badge as power.

I saw through his bullshit.

He huffed out a breath, his dislike for me clear behind his watery blue eyes. "I'll be having words with your girlfriend."

"Unless I'm under investigation for something, no, you won't. I've already been more than accommodating with you. If you're accusing me of something, speak up now, Officer. Because I'd *love* to hear it."

He had nothing, and we both knew it. He could suspect me of helping Heath all he wanted. But if there was any proof of it, I'd already be behind bars.

He took a few steps backward, but his gaze didn't leave mine. It said everything his words weren't.

I know you're involved. I'm watching you.

When the doors closed, my heart raced.

"Liam?"

I spun around to Elise, trying to control my blood pressure. "Mmm?"

"Johnson may not be the smartest man, but he's a mean old coot and stubborn to boot. You're in his crosshairs." She paused, eyeing me critically. "Wherever you're hiding Heath, I hope it's good."

24

MAE

*C*asting an eye over the three pages of paperwork, all filled with tiny type and dozens of questions, I stabbed my pen onto the page. It left an ugly black ink stain. "This is ridiculous."

Heath, sitting on the other side of the picnic table in a plastic chair that looked ready to collapse under his bulk, glanced over from watching Ripley play at the back of the clearing. "What's that?"

I picked up the paper and flashed the front page at him. "Paperwork from the hospital Tori's being held prisoner in."

He raised an eyebrow. "She's not being held prisoner. She checked herself in."

"Yeah, well, they won't let me see her without filling in this stupid form that requires angel's blood and the tears of a leprechaun."

He plucked the paperwork from my hand. He studied it for a moment, his eyebrows inching together with every line he read. "Why do they want to know *your* religion for? What's that got to do with anything?"

I shook my head. "What about the essay I need to write

on the topics I want to discuss with the patient? And the declaration that I won't speak of anything else besides those listed topics? What if I want to discuss how heavy my last period was? Do they want me to write that down, too?"

Heath chuckled and went to say something, but the rumble of a car on the drive stopped us both.

Heath jumped to his feet and shouted for Ripley. "Shit, where is he? I only took my eyes off him for a second to read that form. He keeps going down the back of the clearing where I can't see him."

I shoved him toward the door. "Go inside. I'll find him."

I ran down the steps, though there was no squeak of the front door opening which told me Heath wasn't going inside. I shot a glare over my shoulder because we weren't expecting Rowe or Liam home anytime soon. "Go, Heath! If that's the cops—"

"And if it's Zye come for Ripley, I don't want him to find the two of you out here, served up for him on a silver platter."

I blanched at the thought. "Ripley!" I shouted again.

He popped up from the back of the clearing at the same time the car came into view.

I let out a double sigh of relief at both Ripley's appearance and at the fact the car was Liam's.

Ripley ran over, and I picked him up, shoving down my fear and putting on a happy face for him. "Hey, sweetie. Look who's home early from work."

"Li-yam!"

He struggled to get down and ran to the driver's side door as Liam opened it. Ripley chatted Liam's ear off about the baseball game he'd watched with Heath on TV that morning, and Liam hoisted him up onto his shoulders to meet me and Heath at the picnic table.

We smiled at Ripley, but it was clear from Liam's expression that this trip home in the middle of the day wasn't for pleasure.

I swallowed down nerves, fighting to keep my leg from twitching beneath the table. "What's going on?"

Liam shifted Ripley on his back. "Why don't you go play, bud?"

"No! I'm staying with you!"

"Of course you are," Liam agreed. "Silly me."

But he looked at me and Heath. "I had a visit to my office this morning. From some uh...pigs?"

Ripley struggled to get off Liam's back at that news, and Liam set his feet down on a chair, holding his hands while Ripley jumped up and down on it. "There were pigs at your office? Were they pink? Did they snort? Did you bring one home? Mae, can I have a pig?"

I wasn't sure whether to laugh or be horrified. It was clear Liam meant the cops had been there, but Ripley always made things seem a little brighter.

"Uh, I don't know about that, Rip," Liam interrupted before I could answer. "These pigs were really mean ones. Old and fat."

Ripley's face fell. "Oh. Do they have names?"

Liam nodded. "They do. One was named Johnson, the other was named Stewart."

Heath stiffened at my back. "They were looking for..."

Ripley's big-eyed gaze bounced around the three of us. "They lost something?"

Liam nodded. "Yeah, they lost their...um..."

"Rooster?" I supplied.

Heath raised one eyebrow, then shrugged, like he didn't mind being the rooster in this analogy.

Liam sniggered. "Yeah, they were looking for their rooster." He picked Ripley up again and tossed him into the air, catching him easily as he fell back toward the earth. "But you know what I told those mean old pigs, Rip? I told them that they could go back to their pigpen, because they're never gonna find the rooster by hanging around my office."

Liam's meaning was clear enough. The cops had come. They were putting on the pressure. We needed to be more careful than ever.

We needed to find the person who truly had killed Jayela so we could clear Heath's name and stop hiding.

Ripley nodded in agreement. "Those pigs do not belong in offices. They belong in the mud."

For those two pigs in particular, I couldn't agree more.

I dropped the request form at Tori's hospital on the way to work, and after my shift, there was a text message waiting for me on my phone. It was from an unknown number, but the moment I read the message, I knew who it was from. It wasn't the hospital, like I'd been hoping for.

It was the details of my father's memorial. Sent to me by the woman who probably should have been my stepmother, if my father hadn't been a cold-hearted bastard who kept everybody at arm's length.

As Rowe always did, he walked me to my car after my shift, before going back inside to finish his. He worked a mishmash of day and night shifts, but always tried to make sure he was there when I was. He opened my door for me. "Are you going to go?"

I tossed my purse onto the passenger seat but didn't get in. "I think so."

Rowe shoved his hands into his pocket while he studied me. "Huh. I didn't think you would."

I understood where he was coming from. He'd been there the night my father had died. He'd heard my stories of how he'd treated me growing up. He knew there was no love lost between the two of us. "Surprises me, too. But Angela..." I shrugged. "She's not what I expected. And her kids..."

"Are your siblings."

I blew out a breath. "Exactly. She seems to want me there. It's tomorrow. She apologized for the short notice, but she says I'll be welcome."

"I'll come, too. For moral support. Liam will as well, for sure. Heath would if he could."

I leaned in against his chest, clutching my fingers in the shirt of his uniform and breathing him in. "I know."

He pressed his lips to my forehead. "It'll be good. You can share shitty father stories with them."

My laugh was stifled by his chest. "I guess so."

"Go home and get some sleep."

I tried, but sleep didn't come. I was still awake when Rowe came home hours later and slipped into bed behind Heath. We had more room now, after bringing in an extra mattress, but we were still all on the floor. I didn't mind when it meant I got to have all three of them with me. We'd work out something more permanent eventually, something prettier and less like camping, but for now, just being with them was enough.

The sun rose, and Ripley burst in, jumping straight onto Rowe's back. Despite the fact Rowe had only been asleep a couple of hours, he immediately tossed Ripley to the mattress and started tickling him.

I closed my eyes, enjoying his little boy laughter, and

sighed contentedly when he grew tired of wrestling with the boys and came looking to me for morning cuddles.

I hated the thought that someone out there had the power to take him away from us. There was nothing about the child I didn't like, even when he was tired or grumpy at me for making him come inside for a shower.

He'd stolen my heart in a different but no less powerful way than Rowe, Heath, and Liam.

"Love you, Rip," I murmured to him.

He beamed at me, then wrinkled his nose. "Your breath smells like poop."

All adults in the room burst into laughter, and I found the ticklish spot on his ribs. "Thanks, kiddo. I love your honesty." I scrambled to my feet and locked myself in the bathroom for some girl time that included brushing my teeth. Twice.

By the time I came out, dressed in a long navy summer dress, the guys had all gotten themselves dressed, too. I was used to seeing Liam in a suit, and that always did it for me, but Rowe took my breath away.

"Quit staring at him like that," Heath said in my ear. "Or neither of you are going to make it out the door."

Liam moved in on my other side, placing a soft kiss beneath my ear. "That sounds like more fun than a funeral. I vote we do that."

I swatted them both away. "Stop tempting me, because I would rather do almost anything than go to this funeral." I gave Rowe and Liam stern looks. "I need the two of you to make me go, not entice me to stay."

They grumbled their agreement, and Heath and Ripley walked us out to the steps of the cabin. Heath paused while we piled into the car. "Watch out for each other... Just in case Z—" He glanced down at Ripley by his side. "You know who might show up."

"I sicced his parole officer on him when I went to warn Norma, so he's on a short leash."

Heath relaxed a little at that, and he and Ripley waved us off.

Liam drove us to the church in Providence. The same one where I'd said goodbye to my sister only a few months ago, her body buried in the graveyard at the back.

I squeezed my eyes shut and clutched my purse. I needed to visit her grave, but it was hard. It only reminded me that the person who'd murdered her had gotten away with it.

She would have hated that. I could practically hear her voice growing louder as we walked toward the church, screaming at me to do more. To fight. To find the truth.

Heads turned as we walked in, none of them familiar. I realized I didn't know the people in my father's life. Angela had been the right person to organize this service. I wouldn't have known where to start. It was clearer than ever that she and her children really had been his second family. She wasn't just some woman he'd screwed when it was late at night and he was feeling lonely. She knew his friends. His work colleagues.

I knew nobody.

Liam gripped my hand tightly, and Rowe put his to the small of my back. They guided me into a seat at the back of the room, and I sank onto the hard wooden pew gratefully. At the front of the room, the wood of my father's casket gleamed in the morning sunlight flooding through the church windows. They'd placed it perfectly, so it looked as if it sat in a beam of light sent straight from Heaven itself.

I fought the urge to rush up there and shove it into the darkness where it belonged.

The priest stood to the right, his hands folded in front of him. He wasn't the same priest I remembered from Jayela's funeral, or the one I'd seen outside the church the day I'd confronted Will there. This one couldn't have been much older than me. His gaze met mine, and he nodded slightly, like he knew who I was.

Liam leaned forward, resting his elbows on his knees and squinting a little. "Does that priest have a tattoo on the back of his hand?"

Like he'd heard us, the priest tugged at the sleeve of his robe.

I dropped my voice to a whisper, something Liam seemed incapable of doing. "He might, judging by the way he just pulled his sleeve down. Also, are you ever not loud? Pretty sure he heard you."

Liam shrugged. "I'm just curious. Not often you see a priest with a tattoo."

Rowe sniggered quietly. "You're such a gossip. It's the lawyer in you. You gotta know everybody's business."

Liam straightened against the backrest, at least attempting to whisper. "I'd deny that, but it's true, so whatcha gonna do?" He shrugged with a grin.

I picked up his hand, remembering that this was about the same spot he'd sat in the day of Jayela's funeral. "I'm kinda glad you got in my business last time we were here."

"You and me both." He leaned in and brushed his lips over mine. When I didn't stop him, he took both sides of my face in his hands and kissed me properly.

I kissed him back. In fact, I encouraged it. I opened my lips and pressed my tongue into his mouth. It was partially a fuck you to my father and partially a thank you to whatever higher being had brought me this man who I loved with everything I had.

There was a throat clearing from behind us, and Liam and I broke apart. I turned, expecting to be told off by some asshole friend of my father's.

But instead, there was a smiling face I recognized. "Will! What are you doing here?"

Isaac gurgled happily on his lap, aiming a gummy smile at me.

I reached out and touched his soft cheek, smiling at my godson and wishing I had Ripley here so they could meet.

"I hope it's okay. I'm here all the time, and I saw your father's name listed on the funeral services for the week. I know you'd prefer Tori, but since she's not well, I thought I'd come and be her stand-in."

Tears welled. I knew he was probably still mad at me and at Liam for what we'd put him through during Heath's trial. Maybe he hadn't fully forgiven us, but he was here to support me anyway.

That spoke a lot to the sort of friend he was. He and I weren't really huggers, but I squeezed his arm, and when I said thank you, I meant it with every part of my heart.

My family wasn't the people I was born to. It was the people I'd chosen to do life with. Will and Tori were part of that. I missed my best friend so desperately. "Have you spoken to her?"

Will shook his head. "I've tried. They keep making me fill in paperwork, and then nothing comes of it. When I've chased it up, I've been told she either doesn't want to talk or her doctors don't feel she's strong enough for contact with the outside world yet."

"What the hell kind of program are they running there?"

He screwed his face up and glanced down at the baby.

"Aunty Mae didn't just say that in the middle of a church, did she?"

Rowe chuckled. "Aunty Mae probably needs to start a swear jar if she doesn't want to end up there herself."

I elbowed him roughly. "That's rich coming from you. You drop F-bombs like they're going out of fashion."

The church doors closed behind us before we could talk anymore, and the priest got up behind the pulpit to begin the service, but I didn't really hear what he was talking about. Will disappeared halfway through the service when Isaac started crying, but it was Tori on my mind.

Angela got up and gave a eulogy. It was neither glowing nor hateful. It portrayed a man who'd loved and lost and been damaged by that. She spoke of me and my sister, as well as her own children. She reminisced over years together and the life they'd shared. She didn't make it sound like they'd been the Brady Bunch, but she didn't paint him to be the evil ogre like I would have.

The casket was carried out by pallbearers I didn't know, and we sat quietly, waiting for the rows at the front to leave behind it.

A younger woman walked beside Angela, their arms linked. Her gaze met mine, and my breath stopped.

The woman was so much Jayela. Everything from her skin coloring to her eyes to her height and the shape of her body. It was like watching a younger version of my sister walk past me.

I'd been warned by my father's hired help that I had a half sister who looked more like Jayela than I ever would. And yet the surprise of seeing her in the flesh still hit me like a cold shower.

Liam followed my gaze. "Wow. That's uncanny."

Rowe and I both nodded. They waited on my cue, and

eventually, when almost everybody had filed out of the church, I pushed to my feet. My men flanked me, escorting me out.

"You okay?" Rowe asked softly.

I didn't know how to answer that. "I honestly don't know."

We stepped outside into the brightness of another beautiful summer day and walked slowly down the steps. It was all too much. Seeing my half sister, who looked so much like the one I'd had to bury. And the tiny of part of me that mourned. Even though I'd hated my father, I had never thought I'd be attending his funeral so soon. "Let's just go." I moved toward the car, completely and utterly overwhelmed by the morning.

"You sure?" Rowe stared down at me with his big dark eyes that seared my soul. "We'll be right here with you if you want to stay."

"And we'll also be right behind you if you want to leave," Liam tacked on.

"I just want to get out of here. I can't do this today."

Liam took his keys from his pocket. "You got it. One getaway driver coming right up." He paused, his lips curving up slightly. "I've had practice and everything. I'm practically a pro by now, huh?"

The three of us weaved through the crowd, slipping between groups of people chatting quietly, and the good-looking young priest deep in conversation with Angela. She didn't notice me leaving, which was a relief. I didn't want her trying to pull me back in and introducing me around.

"Mae?"

I stopped.

The woman really was so much like Jayela it hurt my heart.

"Are you leaving?"

All I could do was nod. I didn't trust myself to speak.

The woman glanced over to where her mother was, surrounded by people. "I get it. Funerals suck."

"We buried my sister here," I confessed to her without thinking. "And you..."

"Oh." She stared down at her hands. "Yeah, I realize I look like her. I could never really see it, but Jayela said she looked very similar at my age."

My heart thumped. "You met her?"

"Just a couple of times."

There was so much Jayela had never told me. I knew she was probably just trying to protect me. She always was the big sister who would have burned down the world if it tried to hurt me. But keeping something this big from me...just like with her pregnancy...it all just made me think she'd thought me too weak to stand on my own two feet. I hadn't needed her taping me in bubble wrap.

I just needed her by my side.

The young woman cleared her throat. "I'm Annabelle by the way."

"It's nice to meet you, Annabelle."

"I know the others are curious about you. I have three brothers...I mean, we do."

I swallowed hard. "I've never had a brother."

"I never really got to have a sister. I'd like one, though."

I could feel Angela's gaze on us, and a rush of guilt swamped me. These people lived in one of the poorest neighborhoods in Saint View. At one point, I'd considered them suspects in Jayela's murder. And yet here they were, asking me to be a part of their family, at least in some small way.

"I'd like that, too. We could exchange numbers. If you'd

like?"

Annabelle took out her phone, and I saved her contact details in mine. She tucked hers back in her purse, her expression happier than it had been when she'd first approached. But then her smile slipped. "I'm sorry about Jayela. I wish I'd gotten to know her better. I saw her, the night she died, and if I'd known what was going to happen, I would have said so many things...different things."

"You saw Jayela the night she died?" Liam asked.

Annabelle nodded. "Outside the Watersmith Hotel. I was with some friends, so I didn't stop to talk long when we spotted each other. I wish now I had."

Liam untangled his hand from the bone-bruising grip I had on it. I had to shake my fingers out, releasing the pressure of clamping down on him so hard. As far as we'd been aware, on the night of Jayela's death, she'd left me at the bar, dropped Tori home, and then gone to work, before returning to our apartment late.

Nowhere had we known about her stopping in at a hotel on the night she'd died. I stared up at Liam. "There was no record of a hotel on her credit card, was there?"

He shook his head. "Not that night. There were a handful of other credit card charges made at hotels, which is why we'd thought she was having an affair with Will."

"Will, as in William?" Annabelle asked.

I nodded dumbly.

"So...she wasn't gay?"

I blinked. "Jayela? No."

"Oh, sorry. I just assumed. That night I saw her, she was with a woman."

I stared at her. "Short? Long brown hair— Wait." I scrolled through my phone and found a photo of Tori. "Is this her?"

Annabelle leaned and peered at it. She nodded slowly. "It was a while ago, and it was dark, but yes, pretty sure that's her."

"What made you think they were together?" Liam asked. "Romantically, I mean."

Annabelle shook her head slowly. "Just a vibe. Well, a vibe and the fact they were going into a hotel in the same area she lived in. That's not exactly common unless you're booty calling."

Will's insane accusations rang around my head, louder and more potent with this new information. There was no way Tori could have killed Jayela. How? She was tiny, and Jayela was strong and well-trained. She couldn't have gotten the upper hand in an argument or fight. Not to mention the fact that Tori was deeply religious and completely in love with her husband. The idea of her cheating, and with a woman?

I could barely stay on my feet.

"I think it's time to leave." Rowe stepped in, putting an arm around me in support.

Annabelle nodded and went to walk away but then hesitated before stepping in to give me a brief hug. It was over before I could even return it. "I'm sorry. I didn't mean to out her. I would never do that to someone intentionally. Even after their death."

"It's okay. Thank you."

She walked away quickly, joining her mother, who gazed at me with a worried look on her face. "Are you okay?" she mouthed at me.

I nodded and turned, letting Rowe and Liam lead me back to the car.

Silence surrounded us once we were all inside.

It was Liam who broke it. "Mae...we need to go to the

police. If Tori and Jayela were in a romantic relationship, this changes everything—"

"No!"

Liam bit his lip.

I lowered my voice. "No. We already threw Will and Tori in the middle of this shitshow once, and we were wrong."

"You mean I was wrong. You had nothing to do with the things I accused Will of."

Rowe shook his head. "That doesn't matter now. But for the record, babe? I'm with Liam. We need to report this."

But again I shook my head. "So Johnson and Stewart can fuck it up again? Or just completely blow us off like they did every other time we tried to get them to see things our way?"

"I see your point, but this is new evidence that might get Heath's case opened again."

They were only seeing one side. "And it might ruin Tori's life. If it's true that she and Jayela were in a relationship, and that gets out? Her family will disown her, Rowe. They're devout Catholics. Divorce is a sin in their eyes and barely tolerated. Cheating? And with a woman? They'd crucify her. Her entire identity is wrapped up in that church and in being a wife and mother. I'm not just going to throw all that out there and make it public knowledge. Not until I've talked to her."

Liam pressed his lips together. "Have you heard from the hospital about visiting her yet?"

"No. But when I submitted my form, they said she was in 'deep treatment' for another three days, and then the doctors would consider my request."

"First thing Monday, we go down there then."

I nodded. I needed answers.

Even with all the evidence stacking up against her, I needed to hear my best friend say she'd killed my sister.

25

ROWE

*L*iam and I had an entire conversation just in worried glances in the rearview mirror. His gaze darted over at Mae, huddled in the passenger seat, then up into the rearview mirror to meet mine. His was full of *'What do we do?'* questions, and my answering looks were all *'I have no idea.'*

So we just drove toward home like yet another bomb hadn't just been dropped on us. But hope rose in my chest. I didn't want it to be Tori or for Mae to lose her best friend. But I didn't want Heath on the run for the rest of our lives either.

Now that I'd told Mae how I felt about her, there was no going back. This wasn't a fling for me. And I knew it wasn't for Liam either.

My gut instinct told me Heath was all-in, too, even if he did keep his cards close to his chest.

My phone rang, interrupting the uncomfortable silence in the car. "Speak of the devil," I muttered. But then said louder, "It's the cabin landline. Must be Heath."

We'd programmed our phone numbers into the old

phone that sat in the corner gathering dust because nobody ever used it. We'd kept promising to get Heath a burner cell because the landline battery died constantly but it was enough to get a call out in an emergency.

Which I really hoped this wasn't.

I answered the call, willing myself to remain calm even though I knew Heath wouldn't just call for a chat because he got bored. Sure enough, when I answered the phone, Ripley's cries were loud in the background. Fear wrapped its way around my heart, squeezing it so it thumped too quickly. "Heath? Is he okay? What's wrong with him?"

"Quit stressing. He's fine, physically."

A little of the fear eased up. Parenting came with a bucketload of stress I'd managed to forget over the last few years while he'd lived with Norma. Though I was better equipped to deal with it now that I wasn't drowning in grief. "What's going on then?"

"He misses his grandma. He wants to talk to her, but we didn't program Norma's number into the phone."

"Oh." I breathed out slowly. Outside, the houses flashed by. We weren't actually far from Norma's house in Saint View. "Put him on. I'll talk to him."

Ripley's tears grew louder as Heath passed him the phone.

"Rowe?" he asked between sobs and hiccups.

The tone of my voice changed instantly. "Hey, buddy. You missing your granny today?"

There was a pause, and then Heath's voice, farther away, added, "He's nodding."

"That's okay, Rip. I miss her, too. I'll be home in fifteen minutes, and then we can call her on my phone. You remember how we did that the other day, and you could see her on the screen?"

But his sobs only grew louder. "My Spider-Man toy is at her house, and I haven't got any of her oatmeal cookies and I haven't got any of her hugs."

I scrubbed a hand over my face, my heart ripping in half at the pure anguish in his voice.

Heath got back on the phone. "He's really upset. I don't know what set him off. One minute he was fine, the next minute he was bawling."

"It's okay. He's been through a lot. It's understandable he'd be missing her. We've distracted him pretty well ever since we got him, but this was bound to happen." I paused and looked to Liam. "We're not far from Norma's place. Can you stop in there for a moment? I need to pick up some of Ripley's things and maybe organize for her to come out and visit. He needs her."

"Of course. On it." Liam changed lanes, gunning for the looming Saint View exit we were about to pass.

"Tell him we're en route to pick up Spider-Man, and hopefully Granny, too."

Heath let out a breath. "Good. I hate seeing the kid like this. It's breaking my heart."

He actually sounded like he was in physical pain, and though I hated that Ripley was upset, the fact that it made Heath upset, too, only cemented the feelings I had for him.

It drove home the fact that I wanted Heath in my life, in more than just a platonic way, as well as Mae.

I hung up without saying any of that, though, and waited until we parked out in front of Norma's house. Ripley's swing set still sat in the corner of the yard, but his toys were no longer scattered about, all of them picked up neatly and placed in a large bucket on the porch. I peered into it, searching for the telltale blue and red Spider-Man colors, but none of the toys there matched what I was looking for. I picked out a couple of other things, though, and with one arm full of balls and bats, I knocked on the door. "Norma! It's just me!"

The door swung open beneath the force of my knocks. The interior was dim, but I took a step inside. "Norma?"

There was no answer. I wasn't entirely comfortable just walking into the older woman's house, but I did know her well enough that it wasn't completely weird either. I stuck my head into the living room and then the kitchen. A quick check of the backyard told me she wasn't there either. Determining she must have gone out, I ducked into Ripley's bedroom, and there, in the corner of the room was the Spider-Man figurine he'd been coveting. "Gotcha." I retrieved the toy from the floor and then took a few more shirts and T-shirts from his chest of drawers. We'd bought him some more, adding to the few things we'd grabbed the night we'd picked him up, but I thought some familiar clothes might help ease his homesickness.

Laden down with his things, I went to leave, but Norma's bedroom was the front room of the house, the last door I had to pass before going back outside. I hesitated, not wanting to intrude on her privacy, but if she was inside just taking a nap, I didn't want her to worry when she woke up and realized more of Ripley's things were gone.

I knocked softly. "Norma?"

It was completely silent from the other side. No sounds of snoring, though I had no idea whether the woman snored or not. I twisted the handle and peeked around the corner.

I immediately wished I hadn't.

Norma's body was slumped on the floor by the gun safe, her limbs at an unnatural angle. "Norma!"

I dropped to my knees beside her, books and toys scattering in the process. I rolled her to her back and pressed my fingers to her throat.

But there was no point.

The moment I saw her face, I knew she was gone. Her skin was still faintly warm, but her eyes were fixed and staring, and the strangulation marks around her pale neck were telling.

My stomach churned, and I stumbled back, hitting the door. It closed behind me with a click, enclosing me in the room with a woman who was very much dead. I slid down it to the floor, my heart pounding, sweat breaking out across my forehead. I pulled my phone from my pocket and punched in a number.

"Hello?"

Heath's voice was a balm to the ache in my heart, but fear wasn't far behind, chasing away the shock. "It's me. Norma's dead. Get Ripley inside. Don't take your eyes off him for a second."

Heath swore softly. But then his voice came down the line strong. "I've got him. He's right here next to me watching a movie. You do what you need to do there, with the cops or whatever."

I hesitated, desperately wanting to be there with my son.

Because now, after this, I was the only person he had left.

Like he could read my mind, Heath said quietly, "I've got him, Rowe. I've got both of you."

I knew exactly what he meant. He had my back.

He always had.

Every time there was drama, there was Heath, dependable and strong.

Emotion clogged my throat while I stared down at

Norma's body, until I wasn't sure if it was for Heath or because Zye had taken another person I cared about.

"Rowe, what's taking so long..." Liam's voice called from the porch. "Is Norma coming with us?"

I squeezed my eyes shut so I didn't have to see her body. "I'll be home soon," I said to Heath, then hung up. I got to my feet and opened the bedroom door, finding Liam and Mae standing there.

I could tell the moment they saw her body.

Liam's eyes widened.

Mae gasped, drawing a hand up to her mouth. "What happened?" And then her eyes widened. She grabbed my arm. "Ripley. We need to go."

"We can't." Liam ran his hand through his hair and closed his eyes for a moment. "We have to call the police. If we leave the scene of a crime... We can't draw any more attention to ourselves."

I gaped at him. "Standing here with a dead body isn't drawing attention?"

He grimaced. "I admit, it's not ideal. But what's the alternative? We leave her here for flies and maggots? Is that really how you want to play it?"

The thought twisted my stomach. "She's a good woman. Was. She doesn't deserve this. Fuck! This is all my fault." I balled my fingers into fists, desperately wanting to punch something.

Mae put her fingers around mine, her hands warm where mine were suddenly cold. "None of this is your fault. It wasn't you who brought Zye into Norma's life. And it wasn't you who chose to end it."

It didn't matter, when all of it still equaled Norma being gone. "I should have brought her to the cabin with us. I knew she wasn't safe here."

"You tried, remember? She wouldn't have it."

I turned desperate eyes on them. "We need to get back there. Zye won't be just going back to his halfway house and turning up for parole checks like a good little prisoner. Not after doing this. He's going to be searching for Ripley."

The two of them stared at me.

Mae's fingers trembled. "He's right."

Liam tugged at the collar of his shirt, looking like it was suddenly strangling him. "Shit." He glanced back toward Norma, then tossed me the keys. "Go. I'll stay here with her and talk to the police. I'll say I was the one who found her."

I hesitated. "You've got no reason to be here, though."

"I'll say I was meeting a potential client. We've all got alibis. We were at the funeral, there's dozens of people who can ID us."

I could see it all fitting together in his head, and as each piece slotted in, his nods became more insistent. "Go, Rowe. If Norma gave up where Ripley was before she died, Zye could already be out there, and Heath and Ripley are in very real danger."

---

*W*ith Liam's words ringing in my ears, I pushed his car as fast as I dared, getting us out of Saint View and back on the road to the cabin.

Mae gazed out the window. "This is just the day that keeps on giving, isn't it?"

She wasn't wrong. But I could barely breathe for all the adrenaline crashing my system. Liam's car took a beating on the dirt road, kicking up stones that bounced off the under-carriage and the paint. Mae steadied herself with one hand on the door, the other on the center console, but didn't say a word about my reckless driving. I knew she was as desperate to get back to Ripley and Heath as I was.

Finally, the little cabin came into view.

There was nothing amiss that I could tell. It was exactly the same as when I'd left it this morning. Normally Heath and Ripley would have appeared on the front porch, or from somewhere on the edge of the woods, ready to greet us. But not today. The house was deathly still.

A bad feeling spread through me. "Stay in the car."

"Not a chance." She had the door open and her seat belt off before I'd even fully stopped the vehicle.

I sprinted after her, catching her easily on the front porch, and we thundered up the stairs together.

Heath and Ripley peered up from the floor, *Finding Nemo* playing on the TV.

"Hi, Rowe! Hi, Mae! You're back. Did you bring my Spider-Man? Can I call Grandma now?"

I glanced at Heath who just shook his head lightly. "I've been checking the windows but nothing."

"Nothing at all?"

"Zip."

Ripley tugged at my shirt, his sapphire-blue eyes staring up at me. Fuck, his eyes were so like Zye's. Maybe snatching him wasn't Zye's game. What if he'd taken Norma out and then filed for custody through the courts? Without her as a viable family member with a stable home, a court might decide Zye could have custody of him. I had no legal claim.

I just desperately wanted him to be mine.

In my heart, he already was. His mother and grandmother had both been taken from him way too young. I wasn't leaving him without a fight. I scooped him up from the floor and rested his butt on my forearm. "We can't call Granny right now."

"Why not? You said we could!" His eyes watered.

My heart fucking broke. "I know I did, bud. I'm sorry, I thought you could, but she's…"

I couldn't say it. I couldn't tell a four-year-old that I'd let his biological father take another of the women from his life.

Mae stepped in, wrapping an arm around both of us. "She's not feeling well right now, sweetie."

I gazed up at the ceiling, not wanting Ripley to see my expression. How the hell were we going to tell him?

"Oh." His shoulders slumped, but then he tapped me on the side of the face. "Did you get my Spider-Man toy?"

I nodded. "I did. Here." I set him down and pulled the figurine from my pocket before handing it over to him.

He snatched it from my fingers with a whoop of delight and took off, flying it around the room. "Yes! I've been waiting for this one! I can't wait to show my friend!"

I slumped down into one of the camping chairs, mentally exhausted to the point I wasn't sure my legs would even obey my demands to hold me. "Remember, Rip. We talked about this. You can't go back to daycare just yet. I promise you, as soon as I can, I'll get you back with your friend."

Ripley flew the Spider-Man toy in my direction. "That's okay. I'll just show my friend in the woods."

All three of us stopped and stared at him.

I suddenly wasn't so tired.

"Rip?" Heath asked quietly. "What do you mean your friend in the woods?"

"You know, the man? He talks to me sometimes when I'm playing."

My blood ran cold. "What man, Ripley? Where?"

He ran over to the window and pointed to the back of the clearing. "We play down there, behind the trees."

"Was he here today?"

Ripley nodded his little head. "Yep. I talked to him just before. He's real nice. He said I can come stay with him whenever I want to."

Mae stifled a cry.

I glanced over at Heath. He looked as panicked as I felt.

"I haven't seen anyone," he murmured. "But he does keep disappearing down the back there... *Fuck*!"

Ripley jumped at the harsh word, and Heath was quick to pick him up, reassuring him it was okay and that he and I just had something to do. But the worry between the three of us spilled over, and Ripley's bottom lip quivered as Heath passed him over to Mae.

She held him tight to her chest, and her expression turned to one of fierce determination.

I knew in that moment she'd go to the ends of the earth to protect him.

He was her son now, too.

I hugged them both but pressed my lips to Mae's ears so only she'd hear. "Close the blinds and lock the doors. There's a G. U. N in the safe."

She turned wide eyes on me.

"Do you know how to use one?" I asked.

"Jayela showed me a few times. We went to the shooting range. But where are you going?"

I smiled tightly at my son, hoping he wouldn't see how forced it was. "I'm going to go find Ripley's friend."

26

HEATH

*W*e waited on the porch until Mae locked the door, the sound of the deadbolt sliding into place only giving me mild reassurance. "You sure about this? Are you really going to use that thing if Zye is out there somewhere, and it comes down to it?"

Rowe's fingers clenched around the hunting knife he used to gut fish. His eyes flashed. "All I know is that he's not taking anyone else I love. I can't just sit by and wait for him to come to us."

I couldn't disagree with him. The little cabin suddenly didn't feel safe, and I was desperate to make it feel like home again. If Zye was out there, I needed to know about it. "One of us patrols the clearing, never losing sight of the cabin. The other can go deeper in, starting with that end of the yard where Ripley always plays. You know how to track?"

Rowe shook his head.

"You stay in the clearing then. I'll see what I can find going in a bit deeper."

Rowe looked like he wanted to argue, the stress pouring off him. His face had paled to an unhealthy white color.

I wasn't entirely sure he wasn't going to pass out. "You good?"

He nodded. "Go."

Fighting my reluctance to leave any of them behind, I stomped across the grass to the spot where Ripley had said he'd last seen his 'friend.' There was a dip in the ground, and the grass was longer here, and it was easy to see how I'd lost track of him a couple of times. If I'd sat in the grass, you likely wouldn't have seen me from the house.

Which meant we wouldn't have seen Zye down here, either.

I wandered around, toeing at a pile of sticks. Nearby, others were sticking out of a dirt mound, and a couple of matchbox cars lay discarded in the grass. All signs of a little boy having a great time, but nothing more than that. Some of the grass was trampled, but Ripley had been down here a lot, so I would have expected that. There was no way of telling if the grass was flat because of kid-sized feet or adult ones.

I wandered farther into the woods, scanning my surroundings, hand hovering over Liam's gun that I'd never given back to him. I'd had it locked in the cabin gun safe, beside Rowe's rifle. "Come out, come out, you psychopath."

My muscles wound tight, anxious and on edge, expecting Zye to jump out of the bushes and rush me at any minute. I moved cautiously through the trees, branches scraping at my skin now that I was off the beaten paths. I looked for footprints or other signs a man had been here, but the undergrowth was thick, and I wasn't an expert in tracking by any means. I'd learned a little while on camping trips in my early twenties, and that was better than nothing, but in these conditions, the minimal skills I had didn't help much. I went with the lay of the land for the most part, but when I was a few hundred feet out, I started working my way in a circle, stalking back around the clearing, checking for any signs of a disturbance.

There was nothing.

With each passing minute, my tension seeped away. The birds sang overhead, and the only other things around were the mosquitos feasting on my skin because I hadn't put on bug spray before I came out.

I'd done a full, wide circle around the house, finishing back at the river, when the cracking noise of someone stepping on a stick froze me to the spot.

I hadn't been moving.

I pulled Liam's gun from the waistband of my jeans, thrusting it out in front of me as I spun in a silent circle.

The footsteps grew closer, and I held my breath, desperately trying to see through the thick undergrowth.

A flash of dark hair alerted me to the man's whereabouts.

"Take another step and you'll wish you hadn't."

The man stopped, then Rowe's voice came back to me. "Wanna not shoot me, please?"

I dropped my aim, my breath coming out in a whoosh.

Rowe appeared fully from behind the bushes, and I scowled at him. "I could have put a bullet through your brain, you dickhead. What are you doing out here? You were supposed to stay in the clearing! We can't leave Mae and Ripley—"

"Liam's back. He's with them."

The wind went out of my argument. "Oh."

"Yeah, oh. You seriously think I'd leave them unprotected?"

I didn't bother answering. He was right. I knew he wouldn't have. I just hadn't been thinking clearly in the moment. "I've done a full circle around the clearing. There's nothing here."

Rowe glanced around us, though all there was to see were trees. "We keep looking then. Keep patrolling until we find something."

There was no arguing with him. He was in full-blown parent panic mode, and I didn't blame him. The thought that Ripley might have been anywhere near Zye without us even realizing it was paralyzing.

I beat myself up as I walked, berating myself over and over for the mistakes I'd made. The guilt rode my ass. "I'm sorry."

Rowe shoved aside a low-hanging branch. "For what?"

"I should have realized earlier. I'm the one here all the time. Most of the time it's me watching him. I should have noticed that something was going on."

"It's not on you. I've spent plenty of time out in the clearing with him and never had any reason to suspect there was anybody out here but us."

We went on in silence, making more and more laps of the woods around the house, each time widening our search circle, until the sun got low and darkness began to fall.

Still, Rowe marched on like a soldier, his pace never slowing.

"Rowe."

"We're not going in."

"It's getting dark."

"We're not going in."

"We haven't eaten in hours. And we're low on water. We can't just traipse through the woods all night. That doesn't make any sense."

"Go in, then. I'm going to keep looking."

Irritation crept up the back of my neck. "Rowe, come on. Be sensible. Ripley is probably getting ready for bed and is going to be wondering where you are if you aren't there to tuck him in."

"He's got Mae and Liam and you. He'll be okay for tonight. Go. I'll be fine."

He trudged off, leaving me behind.

"For fuck's sake. Stubborn asshole." I rushed to catch up with him. We wandered around the woods for another hour until we neared Rowe's dock. There was barely any light left in the sky when I let my irritation get the better of me. "That's it. We're done."

"No."

"Yes."

I shoved him toward the house, and he spun and glared at me. Dark shadows passed over his face from the trees moving in the slight breeze. But his anger was clear even in the darkness. "I told you, I'm not going in."

I threw my hands up in the air. "You do realize we've been walking for hours, right? And there's nothing here. Nothing, Rowe. Not one sign of another human being in these woods, except for the five of us."

"I can't shake the thought he's here somewhere, just waiting for me to give in."

"If he was here, he's not now. And honestly, the more I think about it, the more I think Ripley's friend is of the imaginary variety."

"He's not a liar."

I glared at him. "I never said that. Kids make up their own friends all the time, especially when they've suffered a trauma."

Rowe's fingers clenched into fists. "So now I've traumatized him by bringing him out here?"

"Oh, for fuck's sake. Is that seriously how you're going to take what I said?"

"You said it!"

"The kid's mother died. He might have been too little to remember her but he still knows that the other kids at school have a mother and he doesn't. He still has that loss."

"And that's my fault, too, isn't it? I didn't protect her."

"You know that's not true. If Zye had been out here in the woods, talking to Ripley, why wouldn't he have just taken him?"

"Maybe he wanted to get to know him, build a trust between them so when he does take him, he won't be scared."

I laughed at the absurdity. "Are you hearing yourself? That's what you'd do, if you were planning on kidnapping a child. Because you're a decent fucking human being. Zye isn't! If he'd been out here, he would have slapped a hand over Ripley's mouth and carried him off without a second thought to the kid's well-being. He's not here, Rowe! He never was! Now would you please come the fuck inside with me?"

Rowe and I glared at each other, chests rising and falling in unison.

And suddenly we were back in that supply closet in the prison, too close to each other, our breaths mingling, everything we wanted forbidden.

Except nothing was forbidden anymore.

His gaze dropped to my lips, and that was all the invitation I needed.

I grabbed the back of his neck and hauled him in, smashing my mouth down on his.

He groaned at the contact, immediately opening, his tongue seeking mine. Need, hot and heavy, rose deep within me, and like he knew, he fumbled for my zipper, frantically trying to get my fly down while yanking my shirt up. I helped by fisting the back of it and pulling away from him just long enough to get it over my head, before we were back at each other's lips, desperately kissing away every bad thing that had happened today.

The need didn't ease up when Rowe freed my dick from my underwear and stroked me until I was thick and hard in his hand. Our tongues moved together, until I was so turned on, I was thrusting into his hand just to find some relief.

I kissed his lips, his jaw, his neck. I dragged his shirt off, tossing it to the ground somewhere in the dark. "Fuck, I want you," I murmured.

He groaned in answer, pumping my dick harder.

I pulled away before he could make me come and pushed my hand down into his shorts. His cock was hard and perfect. I wrapped my hand around him, taking out all the frustration, fear, and now desire on his shaft. I worked him until the head of him turned slick with precum, and he was rolling his hips in time with the movements of my hand.

"Fuck, Heath. I'm going to come if you keep doing that."

I pressed my lips to his bare shoulder, watching his abs flex while he fucked my hand. "Good." I bit down on his shoulder, way harder than I would have if he'd been a woman.

His groan of satisfaction nearly had me orgasming. His hot spurts of white liquid covered my hand, and I jerked him until he was completely dry.

I ached to fuck him. But we stood there in the quiet night while he came down from his release. Slowly, he raised his gaze to me, the fire that burned there now only one of passion. All the anger gone, and only a desire for me, and the way I made him feel, left.

He wrapped his hand around mine, still covered with his cum, and guided it to my dick. I hissed as I gripped myself, my fingers slick with Rowe's jizz. God, it felt good. Wet and warm, and when he took over, I closed my eyes and gave in to the sensation. I needed more. I wanted to do things with him I'd never had the desire to do with other men. And every time he looked at me, I was sure he could tell.

Instead of saying what I really wanted, I bit out other words against his lips. "Need to kiss you."

Our lips met again, and there was less smashing of lips and teeth and more falling into each other. He kept my erection hard with expert flicks of his wrist, while I walked him backward, kissing him until his shoulders hit the tree.

The need to own him, dominate him, rose sharp and swift, and I channeled it into the kiss. But all too soon it overpowered the limp chokehold I had on it.

I gave in.

I grabbed Rowe's wrist, taking it away from my cock, and used it as leverage to spin him around and push him chest first into the tree. He gripped the bark with both hands, his face turned to one side to watch me over his shoulder. His breath came in short, excited pants that had precum leaking from my tip again.

"Tell me to stop," I groaned, pressing my dick to his ass.

He didn't say anything.

I ground on his entrance, the tip of my cock nudging, testing him. "Fuck, Rowe! Tell me to fucking stop or I'm taking you here, in the middle of the woods, like some savage who can't control himself."

"Then fucking kiss me while you do it. Cos I'm not saying no."

Goddammit.

He gripped the tree and drove back against my erection,

the head of me nudging inside. I froze, both at how tight he was and because I didn't want to hurt him.

His groan echoed in the darkness.

For half a second, I thought it was because of pain, but then he dropped one hand to his cock, fisting himself, his dick hard once more while I pushed all the way in.

It was almost unbearably tight, and I had to stop to fight off the urge to come right there. I wanted this to be as good for him as it was for me. So I forced myself to go slow. I pulled out, then pushed back in, inch by inch, letting him get used to the feel. He craned his head back, searching for my lips, and I met his tenderly. Our mouths moved just as slow as my hips, leisurely plunges of tongues while one hand gripped his side. Rowe's fingers around his cock and balls picked up the pace as he fell into the chemistry between us. We thrust in unison, him into his hand, me into his body. When he increased the speed, so did I. He ground back on me, taking everything I had, the way he kissed a silent beg for more.

I dragged myself away from his lips, steadying myself behind him while my head spun. Desperate with need, I gave in to sensation, pistoning behind him, grinding into him until I couldn't hold on anymore.

"I need to come," I moaned into his shoulder.

His hips pushed back, encouraging me. His grip on his erection never let up, and he set a pace I couldn't come back from. I didn't want to. I slammed home into the tightness of his ass, letting go and exploding into an orgasm with a shout I couldn't contain.

Rowe's knees trembled when he found his own release for the second time, spilling harmlessly over his hand and onto the ground while I came buried deep inside him, hot and mind-blowing and with feelings welling and storming around me.

I collapsed onto him, leaning on him heavily, holding him up while we both came down from our highs. Our chests rose and fell together, mine pressed to his back, the heat between us turning sweaty and warm. I needed a shower, but I didn't care. My dick slipped from between us, completely and utterly spent, and reluctantly, I broke the connection. "Can we go home now?" I asked again, finding my pants around my ankles and pulling them up while he did the same.

He turned and watched me fasten the fly on my pants. His eyes were full of expression that matched how I was feeling, but neither of us voiced it.

I swallowed down the urge and waited for him to reply.

"We can go home."

27

MAE

I was exhausted when I left the cabin on Monday morning. Dark circles lined my eyes, and the giant travel mug of coffee Liam had made for me really wasn't putting a dent in the bone-weariness that dominated my limbs.

It had been a long and tense weekend. Though the men's searches hadn't shown any sign of Ripley's friend being a real person, and we'd put it down to kids' games, I couldn't shake the anxiousness. It was only now I realized that it was Tori and the anticipation of seeing her that had me feeling that way.

The coffee probably wouldn't help my nerves, but I sipped the steaming liquid anyway, because it warmed me from the inside.

The Saint Paul of God Private Hospital appeared at the end of the drive and was no less sterile and intimidating than the first time I'd been here. Behind those doors lay answers, and today, I wasn't leaving until I had them.

On unsure feet, I stepped into the reception area, relieved when it wasn't the same nurse on duty as last time.

This one listened to my request politely and then searched something on a computer. She smiled at me above her black glasses. "Okay, yes. Mrs. Dudgeon was cleared for your visit. You'll need to sign this paperwork before you go in."

She passed over a sheet of paper, and I scanned an eye over it quickly before looking at her. "I have to seriously sign a declaration saying I won't discuss anything other than the approved topics?"

She nodded calmly. "I know it seems a lot, but the patients here are fragile. Too much information or upsetting topics from the real world can be detrimental to their recovery."

Worry trickled down my spine, but I signed my name on the line and waited for her to file the paperwork. I gripped the desktop, knowing that the things I needed to hear from Tori weren't ever going to be on some approved chat list. I was fairly sure '*Discuss the way you murdered my sister in cold blood*' wasn't going to be a topic that got approved by the staff here.

My fingers shook around the coffee cup that had become some sort of safety blanket. The remaining liquid inside had turned cold, but clutching it gave me something to do with my hands. My nail polish was chipped and scratched from a weekend of stressing about everything from a murderous psychopath in the woods, to whether my best friend was truly the woman I'd known since we were teenagers.

I was led into a small, sterile room with an ugly painting on one wall and two single hard plastic chairs that faced each other across a rectangular table. A limp potted plant sat in the corner, offering a little color to brighten the dull beige walls.

"Take a seat," the nurse told me. "I'll let her know you're here."

I was suddenly sure I was going to vomit; I was so nervous. I told myself I was being ridiculous, that this was just the same as me turning up at her house, not even knocking and just walking in to plop down on her couch. She'd come in any minute now and find me sitting here and sink down beside me so we could catch up on everything we'd missed.

The woman who walked in was barely recognizable as the friend I'd once known. There was no stopping it, my mouth dropped open, and a gasp slipped from between my lips.

She'd lost weight. On her petite frame, already slim from the rigors of taking care of a young baby, the few pounds she'd dropped had hollowed out her cheeks, and the collarbones jutted out alarmingly.

Her hair was combed, but it was lackluster, all its usual shine dulled. A man followed her in, bringing a chair with him. Her doctor, judging by the white coat.

I grabbed her hand as soon as she sat and squeezed it.

Her answering grip was stronger than she seemed.

My gaze darted to hers, and the fire behind her eyes startled me. But that was the moment I knew.

Even though her appearance had changed, even though she'd been mad at me when she'd come in here, she was still my best friend. All her spark and fire were still there, just locked down by this place and by these people.

Fuck that list of approved topics.

I glared at the doctor, sitting by the door, all my usual politeness evaporating at seeing the condition of my friend. "Can we have some privacy, please?"

He shook his white, middle-aged, bald head. "I'm sorry, no. There are no unsupervised visits allowed in the center."

I gaped at him. "So you're just going to sit there and listen to everything we say?"

"That is the procedure Mrs. Dudgeon agreed to when she checked in."

I ground my molars. I didn't like or trust the man as far as I could throw him.

But Tori squeezed my fingers. "I'm so happy to see you."

I breathed out a sigh of relief. "I tried to come last week, but they wouldn't let me in. I had to fill out a whole host of paperwork and wait to have my visit approved." I shot a dirty look at the doctor, who wrote something on his notepad.

I wanted to rip it out of his hands and tear it up.

"Have you seen Isaac? Is he okay?" Tori's voice was barely above a whisper, but the room was so small, there was no doubt the doctor would have heard.

"I saw him on Friday, at my father's funeral—"

The doctor cleared his throat. "Please, no talk of death. That wasn't an approved subject."

I stared at the man, who gazed back at me calmly.

He gave me the creeps. I wanted to wrap Tori up and take her home with me. "What is this place?"

"We're a treatment facility for mental health issues."

If looks could have killed, the doctor would have been dead on the spot. "She can speak for herself." I turned back to my friend, worry and warning signs flashing all around me. "Are you okay?" I asked her.

"She's doing as well as can be expected for the depth of her sins."

Tori closed her eyes.

And the sick feeling rose from deep in my belly. I

narrowed my eyes at the man. "Where did you go to medical school?"

"Surley School of Medicine."

"And they taught you how to treat sins there?"

"They taught me how to treat many a condition there, Miss Donovan."

Tori's gaze lowered to the tabletop. A tear dripped onto the back of her hand, but she made no move to wipe it away. The resignation in her posture made me realize that there was no point in continuing this. I couldn't get a word in with the doctor around. I'd be inquiring about his credentials and the school I'd never heard of the minute I got home.

But I couldn't just leave Tori like this either. Not until I'd spoken to her properly. "Tor..."

She lifted her gaze, and that same fire burned behind the tears. "Thanks for coming. But I'm tired. I don't think I'm ready for this."

My stomach lurched, and I jumped to my feet, grabbing hold of her hand when she stood. "Wait, no!"

I blinked in surprise and glanced down at her hand when I felt the piece of paper she'd pressed against my palm. She pulled me in quickly, forcing my gaze away while she hugged me. "I'll see you when I get out, okay?"

Over her shoulder, the doctor glared at us. "Tori," he snapped. "You were warned of the rules."

Tori stepped back, letting go of my hand, but not before I'd wrapped my fingers around the note. Alarm coursed through me, and I itched to open the message.

She walked backward, her gaze never leaving mine, until she reached the doctor by the door. "There's a bathroom just before reception, if you need to use it before you leave," she said quietly. "I know you have a long drive, and after a coffee that size..." She pointed to my coffee cup and forced a laugh that didn't meet her eyes.

I didn't have a long drive at all. Even if Tori thought I was going back to my place on the edge of Providence, that was still only fifteen minutes. My gaze met hers as she was escorted from the room.

The desperation there gutted me. Not waiting for an escort, I stormed down the hallway, Tori's note burning against my palm.

The bathroom door closed behind me, and I quickly checked the stalls to see if I there were any feet sticking out from beneath them.

There wasn't.

I unfolded the tiny note that said one word.

Wait.

My heart pounded. At footsteps in the hall, I locked myself inside a stall, sitting on the closed toilet seat.

The door opened several times, staff or patients coming and going, occupying the stalls beside mine, flushing when they were done, and then leaving. Time ticked on, and I fingered the edge of the note, wondering if *wait* didn't mean 'wait in the bathroom.'

I replayed our conversation, but the more I thought it over, the more I was convinced that there was no other place she'd been trying to tell me to go.

I couldn't sit here all day, though. At some point, somebody would notice. I hadn't signed out of the facility. If somebody was checking it, they'd realize I was still here.

I was ready to give up when the door opened again. "Mae!"

Her voice was a hiss of a whisper, but it calmed the ache in my chest because she sounded like her. Strong. Fiery. The girl I'd known half my life. I jumped off the toilet and unlocked the stall door.

We stared at each other for a moment, and then she flew into my arms. Her hug was tight, and I held her desperately, battling back tears. "Oh, thank God. I wasn't sure if I'd misunderstood your message or—"

She shook her head. "They escorted me back to my room and though they don't lock us in them, I wanted to be sure he wasn't hanging around."

I gaped at her. "What the hell is going on? What is this place?"

She slumped back against the door and locked it. Suddenly tears filled her eyes, and all her strength at getting herself in here vanished.

I gathered her in my arms and held her, smoothing out her hair. "Hey, shh. It's okay. Whatever's going on, it's okay."

"I...I've done something."

I stiffened at the words I didn't want to hear, my stomach all but plummeting through the floor. I dropped my arms from around her and swallowed down the sob that threatened to break free.

It was true then.

We stared at each other. Neither of us coming out and saying it. Eventually, though, the silence forced my hand. I couldn't stand it. "You killed Jayela."

My heart broke to even say it to her out loud. It was impossible to believe. Tori had barely aged in all the years I'd known her. She still had the slimmed-out, wrinkle-free, baby face of the girl I'd met on the first day of high school. We'd joked in the past about how often she got dirty looks from people who likely thought she was some knocked-up teen mom, not a married woman of twenty-seven.

This wasn't the face of my sister's killer. It couldn't be.

Tori's eyes widened. "Killed...Jayela? What the hell?"

The relief that coursed through me was so instant and complete that it was like rainbows and butterflies descending.

Because the other thing that came along with knowing someone for as long as Tori and I had known each other?

I knew when she was lying.

And that complete and utter confusion? That hadn't been a lie.

I threw myself at her again, wrapping my arms around her tight, a heavy weight lifting off me. "I knew it wasn't true. That's why I wouldn't go to the police."

Her eyes went wide. "The police? Why on earth would you think I murdered Jayela?"

"Because your husband told me you did."

"Will said that?" she choked out.

I swallowed hard but nodded, because it was the truth.

Her face crumpled. "I didn't kill her. But, Mae..." Her tears dripped down her cheeks. "I was...we were...in a relationship." She hiccupped on a laugh. "That's not even fair of me to say because how can you have two relationships at once? I'm married."

"You're gay."

"Why don't you look more shocked?"

"My half sister saw you and Jayela outside a hotel the night she died."

Her face twisted in anguish. "So it's out there for the world to know then? That I'm a cheating whore, and that I like women."

I blew out a long breath. "You aren't a whore. Don't say that. And the fact you like women—"

"Is why I'm here."

My heart broke for her, for the pain etched into her

being. But then the anger coursed in. At this place. These people who called themselves Christians. "This is a conversion camp? Are any of these people actually real doctors?"

She lifted one shoulder. "Maybe a few. They treat depression and anxiety and a range of other things...but yeah. I'm here because of my relationship with Jayela."

"Oh, Tor. Why didn't you tell me? Why didn't either of you tell me?"

"Tell you I was cheating on my husband every time he went to work? How sometimes Jayela would come over while Isaac was asleep and make me come in my marital bed because Will never had? Or how we met up at hotels sometimes, like I was a hooker she'd picked up on the street?"

I blanched at the harshness in her words, at the anger of them, and at the hate she had for herself.

"Did Will force you to come here?"

She shook her head. "No. I committed myself voluntarily. I promised him I'd get better." Her face filled with desperation. "I want to stop. I need to want my husband. I'm *married.* I took vows in front of God and family."

I gripped her shoulders, terrified of the pain pouring from her. Scared of the self-loathing she'd inflicted on herself. I shook her hard. "Stop it. You married a man straight out of high school when you barely knew yourself."

"I knew," she said softly. "Even back then, I was never attracted to men."

My shoulders slumped. "You've gone through all this alone."

She swiped at a tear on her cheek. "I was too ashamed to tell you."

"I never would have judged. And I would have kept your

secret, both of you, if that's what you wanted. You could have told me."

She shook her head. "I asked her not to. I was scared that if we told even one person, then it would landslide into more and more people, until eventually she would be pressuring me to leave Will and come out." She sniffed miserably. "I couldn't do that. My family would have disowned me. Will would try to keep Isaac from me. That's why I checked in here. I need to get rid of it."

I sighed and hugged her once more. "You know it doesn't work like that."

She pulled back miserably. "Will is so disgusted in me that apparently he thinks I'm morally on par with murderers. I can't believe he seriously thought me capable of something like that, but others will, too, if they find out. It's all the same to them. If you don't fall in line with everything they believe then you're going to Hell." She laughed bitterly. "So what other choice do I have? My church, my family, my whole community are old-school conservative. If I can't get rid of it, I can't be a part of any of that."

"You can't just get rid of a part of yourself, Tori. You're twenty-seven. Are you really going to live another fifty years with a man you aren't in love with? One who thought you capable of taking a life?"

Anger at Will resurfaced. At times, his strict beliefs and values had bothered me, but at the end of the day, he and Tori were grown adults who could make their own choices. They'd never tried to push their religion on me, and I'd never tried to convince them there were other ways of thinking.

We worked because we respected each other. Because they were happy, and so was I and we could coexist like that.

I couldn't coexist with a man who let his wife feel like

she was scum for who she was. I couldn't coexist with beliefs that Tori should be excommunicated from everything she knew just because of who she was attracted to.

She straightened her shoulders. "It's my choice to be here. I need to do this, Mae. I need to at least try. Maybe I'm not gay and it was just her I couldn't resist."

I could hear the lie in her voice. "I want you to come home with me. If Will and your family won't accept you, I always will. No matter what."

"You say that now, but—"

"There is no buts! I've had enough proof to accuse you of killing Jayela for days now, and yet I didn't go to the police. That's how much I believe in you. In your heart. I don't want you to change! I don't want a watered-down version of you because you're so miserable you can barely function. You're as much my sister as she was. I can't lose you both."

We both broke down in tears, holding each other in the small bathroom. It was minutes before she pulled back. "I need to try, okay? I'll get my phone back somehow and I'll answer it next time you call. Or I'll call you. But I need to stay here."

In my heart, I knew she was right. It wouldn't work, but she needed to feel like she'd given it everything she could. She needed to take that shot at having the life she'd always thought she'd have.

All I could do was nod and say, "I'll be here when you're ready."

28

MAE

I didn't go home after seeing Tori. I needed some time and space to breathe, so I went straight to work and sat in my empty classroom, half putting together work for the next few weeks and half thinking about my best friend.

Sadness crept over me, for her and for Jayela. For the fact they hadn't been able to tell anyone about their relationship. Tori had only ever gotten to grieve as Jayela's friend. Not as her partner. She needed that time. Maybe being at the center would at least give her that.

I tried to fix my face into something neutral as the men all filed into class. But none of them paid me any attention. There was an excitement around them, and they yelled over the top of each other, all buzzing over something.

I glanced at Martine, my guard for the evening, but she didn't seem interested. She read a book at the back of the classroom like she didn't have a care in the world.

I clapped my hands together, calling for the men to settle, but it had little effect. Martine eventually took pity on me, put two fingers in her mouth, and let out an ear-piercing whistle by blowing around them. "Your teacher is trying to speak. So sit down and shut up."

They grumbled, but they did settle into their usual spots.

I wandered to the center of the classroom, but the hum of chatter remained. "Okay. Something has happened obviously. One of you has two minutes to fill me in on what's going on. We'll discuss it as a class for five, and then we're going to put it to bed until you're outside my classroom. Capiche?"

"Capiche," they replied as one.

I pointed to a big man in the front row who'd seemed to be the most animated during their discussion. His name was Markus, and he was terrifying to look at, but despite his appearance, he was a bit of a teddy bear.

He sat back on his chair now, his eyes animated.

I almost laughed. These men loved nothing more than fresh prison gossip. I couldn't blame them, really. There wasn't much else to do in here. "Okay, tell me what the gossip is."

"Psych Ward lost a prisoner."

I squinted. "They lost one? How do you lose a prisoner, exactly?"

The class erupted with theories on what was going on behind the locked doors, but I waved at them all to shut up and let Markus continue.

"Happened a few days back, apparently. He's just gone. Poof! Disappeared. I reckon one of the officers killed him and they're covering it up."

Psych Ward had been oddly locked down, even to staff, last week when Rowe and I had tried to drop off work for Vincent. "I highly doubt one of the officers killed an inmate and then tried to cover it up by saying they lost him, Markus."

He raised one shoulder. "Stranger things have happened."

He wasn't wrong there. There was a lot that happened in this prison behind closed doors. I was proof of that.

I glanced around at the other men, all patiently waiting for their turns. The corner of my lip lifted into a smile. I'd trained them well. This was actually a func-tioning class these days, full of students who respected me and the rules. The proof of that was in the way Martine practically took a nap in the back corner now. Rowe still wouldn't have been as relaxed, but he was personally involved.

Pride washed over me as I picked a few more men to tell the gossip they'd heard. I'd promised a five-minute discus-sion, so that's what we were going to get. Little did they know, that things like this actually taught arguing skills, so while they thought they were just gossiping, I guided the conversation so they argued two sides.

I pointed to an inmate in the back row. "What else might have happened? If you were a lawyer, debating this case, what evidence could you bring forward?"

"He might have escaped."

But then one of the other guys scoffed, "Without any sign of it? You saw what happened when Michaelson escaped. We went into lockdown, there were police heli-copters, reporters. A prisoner escapes just a couple of weeks later, and there's no word about it? Nuh. No chance. It would have been all over the news. They killed him for sure."

"He could be hiding somewhere!" another prisoner shouted.

"For an entire week? How many places to hide are there

in Psych? Isn't it all bare white walls and no furniture in case they try to hang themselves?"

"Maybe he did off himself and the new warden just doesn't want that on his shiny record?"

I listened to them in amusement, knowing that the truth was probably much more boring. There was no chance that someone had escaped or been killed without all the staff hearing about it. And Rowe would have told me if he'd heard anything. Rumors that grew bigger and more ridiculous as they were passed from one person to the next were a real problem in prisons. A department being closed for cleaning easily became 'someone was murdered in there and they're covering it up.'

The clock on the wall hit the five-minute mark, and I called it. "Right. Conspiracy theory time is done. Time to do some exam prep."

They groaned but got out their books. We only had weeks until some of these guys could take their exams, and I was damn determined to make sure they all passed. Prison gossip wasn't going to get them anywhere on the outside. It might have been a fun distraction, but the real world was out there waiting for them, and nobody out there cared if one psych prisoner was hypothetically missing.

---

*R*owe, Liam, and Heath were all in the living room when I got back to the cabin. Rowe and Heath sat in the camping chairs, Liam was sprawled out on the rug, all three of them watching an old *Lethal Weapon* movie. They all looked over when I dumped my purse on the floor just inside the door, movie forgotten.

"How did it go with Tori this morning?"

I dropped down on the rug with Liam, and he immediately put his arm out for me to use his biceps as a pillow. I snuggled into the familiar, comforting smell of his clothes and his skin, his white business shirt half unbuttoned, his tie long lost after he'd returned from the office.

"She didn't do it."

I eyed Heath as I said it, but he didn't argue. That somehow made me feel worse. "I'm sorry, I know—"

"I didn't want it to be her, Mae. It sucks we still don't know who it was, but I'm glad it's not her."

I nodded, grateful they believed and trusted in my judgment. "Kinda puts us back at square one, though, doesn't it?"

Liam pressed his lips to my forehead. "Been here before. We can do it again."

"No sign of Ripley's possibly imaginary friend today?"

Rowe's camp chair creaked beneath his weight. "No, but I followed him around like a shadow, so if Zye was out there somewhere, he wouldn't have been able to get near him."

"We can't do that forever, you know." I tried to lighten the moment by smiling at him. "You don't want to be known as the helicopter parent at daycare, do you? I've heard they're terribly unpopular with the other moms."

He grumbled. "If I ever let him go back to daycare, that is. Right now, I want to quit my job and just be his full-time bodyguard. The police called me today, officially informing me of Norma's death. I did my best to act surprised, but I don't know how good my acting skills are."

"You did fine," Heath assured him. The two of them had their camping chairs as close together as they could. Any closer and someone would have had to sit in the other's lap.

"Did you tell Ripley about Norma yet?" I asked Rowe.

He let out a sigh that felt laced with both sorrow and

defeat. "I don't know how. It's too fucking cruel. I don't want to be the person who tells him."

I swallowed hard. "I can do it."

But Rowe shook his head. "I know it needs to be me."

"We'll do it together," Liam interrupted. "All of us. He needs to know that even though Norma is gone, he isn't alone."

"I agree. We'll do it first thing in the morning."

Rowe looked like he'd rather eat sand, but he nodded reluctantly. "Fucking hell. What a day. What a week."

Liam rolled to his side. "Let's not worry about it until the morning. We're all here right now. Rip is safe. I'm so fucking exhausted. I just want to watch this movie and forget every bad thing that's happened lately."

"Agreed." Heath leaned back and stretched his long legs out. "We deal with it in the morning. Tonight, let's just watch this and eat bad food and drink a few beers."

I couldn't think of anything more perfect. I twisted so I was on my side facing the TV instead of Rowe and Heath. My head was nicely cushioned by Liam's arm, his other wrapped tight around my waist, while he spooned me from behind.

Heath got up and went to the kitchen, and a moment later, the telltale sounds of popping corn floated back.

Liam sniffed the air before calling, "Don't be stingy on the butter."

Heath came back with two big bowls heaped with buttery popcorn. He placed one in front of Liam and me, then took the other to the chairs for him and Rowe to share.

Liam wolfed down our bowl, practically inhaling it like he hadn't been fed in a month. I picked at a few pieces, but I wasn't really hungry. I was content just to lie there snuggled with him.

When Rowe got up to get beers, Liam took one, but when I tried to move off him so he could sit up to drink it, he hauled me back down. "Don't move. I can drink it around you."

I settled back down, and we watched the movie. Liam finished his beer, putting the empty bottle on the hardwood floor to the side of the rug. We watched quietly, his steady breaths regulating my own until I was more relaxed than I'd been all day. Liam's fingers found the bottom of my top, inching it up and untucking it from the waistband of my skirt until he had a sliver of bare belly to stroke. His touch was featherlight but still sent quivers rippling across my skin.

In the dim light cast by the television, his lips lowered to my cheek, placing silent kisses along the side of my face turned up to him.

His fingers slipped inside my skirt, quickly finding my panties and sliding beneath those, too.

I stilled.

"Watch the movie," he whispered in my ear.

Rowe and Heath were right behind us, doing exactly that. I had no idea whether they'd noticed what Liam was doing or not.

But I didn't stop him. As directed, I kept my eyes trained on the screen.

He found my clit, keeping his touch light and teasing at first. He stroked in tiny circles around and over it, barely moving his wrist. I lost focus on the movie, letting my body fall back against his and my eyes close, just enjoying the touch of my man and the feelings he could bring out in me so easily.

The movie continued, the actor's voices distant in the

background while Liam's fingers worked my clit until I was wet and aching for more.

He didn't disappoint. Silently, his hand wandered lower, fingers pushing between my folds to gather my arousal, coating his fingers in it. I let out a tiny gasp.

If Rowe and Heath heard it, they didn't comment.

My pussy throbbed, and the need to spread my legs wide so he could spear into me and get all the angles I desperately wanted rose swift and fast. But there was another part of me that was thrilled by what he was doing. It was like sitting in the back row of a movie theatre and making out while everybody else was engrossed in the screen.

His lips brushed along my jaw, his tongue rasping over my ear, while his erection grew behind me. He ground against my ass so subtly that to anyone else, he might have just been adjusting himself on the floor because it had started feeling hard.

I knew the moment we'd been busted.

Liam plunged a finger up inside my core, and it was all I could do not to cry out his name. He hit my G-spot perfectly, and the noise I muffled was barely better than a dirty groan of need.

Heath chuckled. "If you two think you're being subtle, you're not."

I glanced over my and Liam's shoulders, my gaze meeting Heath's. His mouth was twisted in a smirk, but the hard-on behind his shorts was a dead giveaway for the fact he wasn't minding watching.

Liam laughed against my neck. "Oops." His tongue darted out to lick me while he dragged the fabric of my skirt and panties over my hip bone. The gap between my skirt and top widened beneath his hands, my top riding up to expose my belly and bra, and I raised my hips so he could push my skirt off all the way.

He had me bare from the waist down, his fingers buried deep in my pussy, with my nipples hard. I wanted to remove my bra and get naked with him, but Liam had other ideas that all centered around getting me off. Still on our sides, he maneuvered my top leg up and back so it rested over his. This opened me up to him, creating room between my thighs for his fingers to plunder. I moaned as the need for him grew, and when he stopped to undo his fly, I frantically took up the job of working my clit myself.

Liam's erection, free from his pants, slid between my legs from behind.

He put his hand over mine, controlling the speed and pressure we put on my clit. I let him guide, setting the pace he wanted. He was so in tune with me, I couldn't have done any better myself. If anything, I would have gone too hard and fast, desperate to come, but he slowed things down, making me take my time.

My orgasm would be better for it. I knew it, but I still blew out hot, hard, impatient breaths.

Liam gave me what I wanted. His cock slid inside me, stretching me deliciously. Neither of us let up on my clit, but he took his time filling me, then withdrawing, sometimes sliding in shallowly, sometimes diving deep. He held me tight in place until I was squirming against him, desperate to come.

Rowe groaned, and then he was on his knees in front of me, his camp chair hitting the floor behind us in his haste to get on the rug with us. But it was Liam's gaze he met. "Don't let her come yet."

I whimpered.

He flipped the cups of my bra down, my breasts spilling

out over the top. He grabbed greedy handfuls of my flesh, cupping, groping, his finger and thumb squeezing my nipples hard so that sharp spears of pleasure joined the ones emanating from between my thighs.

He worked my breasts, but his gaze was fixed on my slit, full with Liam's cock. Rowe's gaze grew deeper and darker while he watched Liam fuck me. He brushed my and Liam's hands away from my clit so he could see better.

Heat flushed my body. Then his head lowered, and he flicked my clit with his tongue.

I moaned so loud, Liam clapped a hand over my mouth. But none of us stopped. Rowe's tongue was relentless, and the orgasm building inside me became a tornado, wild and furious and impossible to avoid. It ripped through my body, swirling up pleasure I couldn't describe. I yelled against Liam's hand as the orgasm destroyed me, and I clamped down on his cock, sending him into the swirling abyss right along with me. He pulsed inside me, spilling into my body while I writhed between his dick and Rowe's tongue.

Liam's erection eventually faded, and the two of us stilled for a moment. But Rowe didn't stop. He continued licking at my clit, slowly but surely, building me up once more.

I couldn't come again. Not yet. I pushed Rowe away, onto his back, and straddled my legs over him. I knew my pussy was slick with Liam's cum. I shoved Rowe's shirt up, exposing his lower abs and the fly on his shorts. I yanked it down, impatient and needy once more, taking his boxer briefs with me. His dick sprang free. He was big and hard, and it was tempting to go down on him, the way he'd been going down on me.

But the ache inside me was real. I impaled myself on his

erection, taking all of him in one deep plunge that had us both crying out.

I cringed at how loud I was, but then Heath was behind me, wrapping a hand over my lips while he whispered in my ear, "Ride him, sweetheart. I'll worry about your mouth."

I jerked my head away, and he let me go.

"Your dick," I panted, rocking my hips over Rowe's. "Not your hand. I want your dick in my mouth."

All three men groaned so loudly, I widened my eyes at them, a reminder of who slept in the room just down a short hall. Ripley could walk out at any minute, but none of us were stopping now. He hadn't woken up one night since he'd been here, so I prayed he wouldn't start tonight when I was being railed by two men with the third naked and watching on. Heath stood, pulling off his shirt and pants quicker than I'd ever seen anyone get naked. I bounced on Rowe's dick while I waited, him as interested in Heath getting undressed as I was. Rowe grabbed my tits again, when Heath's dick appeared at my mouth.

I opened for him and was rewarded with the head of his thick cock. It was a welcome distraction from everything Rowe's body was making me feel. I didn't want to come again, not too soon. I wanted them both to feel as good as I did.

Rowe's hands glided over my sides, down over the curves of my hips and dug in there, guiding my movements while I concentrated on sucking Heath off. He gathered up my long hair, twisted it into a ponytail that he secured in place by wrapping the long lengths around his fist. My scalp prickled with awareness, and I moaned around his length.

"Fuck, Mae," he bit out. "That feels so good." His gaze raked over me, slow and steady, burning a trail across my skin.

I knew what he was seeing. Full breasts bouncing as I rode Rowe's dick. A flush across my sweaty, pink-tinged skin. Eyes at half-mast, looking up at him while he thrust into my mouth. I found his balls, heavy between his legs, and licked my way down his dick and over his sac. I drew them into my mouth one at a time, pumping his dick with my hand while I made him moan. His fingers tightened in my hair, clenching and releasing the same way I did on both his and Rowe's erections.

He yanked out of my mouth, his chest rising and falling so fast, the smattering of hair across his tattooed chest damp with sweat. I pouted at him, and he shook his head at me. "Can't keep fucking your mouth when I need to ride your ass, sweetheart. You look too fucking gorgeous to come down your throat."

I whined at the promise.

Heath moved behind me, getting on his knees and gently pushing me down so I was chest to chest with Rowe.

Rowe raised up and kissed me deep, his tongue tasting and owning my mouth.

Heath's palm slapped across my bared ass cheek.

I groaned into Rowe's mouth, the sting so good I wanted Heath to do it more. But then his wet cock was at my ass, pressing its way inside, and there was no hanging on anymore. Rowe held my head while I screamed out my pleasure, the second orgasm hitting me in my already sensitive places like a sledgehammer.

I was so full of both men. I'd never felt anything like it, and the orgasm was second to none. It shattered through my body, wrapping its way around every muscle, every nerve ending. Rowe pounded up into me, using my clenching pussy until he came with a deep groan of his own.

Heath moved slower, taking his time, his broad palm

smoothing down my spine before smacking my ass again. He did it over and over, each slap stringing out my orgasm until I was sure I might go blind.

Heath was the perfect mix of rhythm and strength. He pushed inside me the last few times before the last time became too much. His fingers dug into my flesh, and his big body shuddered over me when he came.

I was so spent I couldn't move. All I could do was receive everything he had to give, with the knowledge I'd gotten all three of them off.

Liam's fingers found mine, and he brought them to his lips. Wearily, I lifted my head to face him, and he rolled over, drawing my head down to his for a kiss. "There is nothing like seeing you come like that, Mae. Nothing." His kisses turned soft and sweet, and he didn't seem to care in the least that two other men were still inside my body.

Rowe's lips found my shoulder. Heath's the back of my neck. All three kissed me like I was something sacred. Something worth worshipping.

They proved it again, washing the products of great sex from my body, before tucking me into bed.

I fell into the deepest sleep imaginable, one where all that mattered was the men I loved.

All three of them.

29

HEATH

*R*ipley woke up with the sun, like he always did, which meant the four of us were up early, too. Ripley was distinctly more energetic than we were, but once we were all fueled by coffee, his energy was contagious. Liam ran around the house with him while Mae made breakfast. I found myself sitting in front of Ripley's cartoons, the only one actually watching them while he tore through rooms, playing a chasing game with Liam.

"Not in the kitchen!" Mae called when they zoomed past, a little too close to where she was cooking pancakes. "Someone is gonna get burned!"

I wandered in her direction, lured in partially by the scent of food, partially by the fact that all she wore was a long sleep shirt. She poured the mixture into a pan and watched as it took on the circle shape.

I ran a hand up her bare leg, stopping when I got to the hem of her shirt to keep it PG for the little eyes that roamed around the house. "How are you feeling this morning?" I kept my question low and private, just between the two of us. "Last night was a lot."

She smiled down at the pancake beginning to bubble. "Feeling like I want to do it again. And again. Probably for the rest of my life."

My heart soared. I didn't know how I'd been lucky enough to be chosen by this woman. By all of them, really. I'd gone from a sad, lonely bachelor, to an immediate family. Of course, the whole "Convicted death row murderer" thing was a hitch in the plans, but I'd lain awake last night, listening to the three of them breathe around me, knowing Ripley was just across the hall, and questioned whether if given the chance for a do-over, would I take it?

And instantly, the answer was no. Not if it meant that this wasn't where I ended up. If I had to go back to spending nights on my couch by myself, cranking up the volume to drown out the crackheads next door, and eating ramen because cooking for one was barely worth the effort, then no. I didn't want it.

Because here in this cabin with four other people, I'd found where I was meant to be.

Liam and Ripley zoomed past again, and then there was a grunt from the bedroom, as presumably, Ripley threw himself on top of Rowe, who was still in bed.

I went in and picked Ripley up. "Let your da—Rowe—sleep." I glanced down at his mess of dark hair spread out across a pillow. "He had a big night. Used up lots of energy that he needs to restore because Mae says he has to do it again tonight."

He cracked one eye open. "She did?" The hope in his voice made me laugh. Ripley ran off again, losing interest in Rowe because he wasn't moving fast enough. I held a hand out to him. "Come on. Get up. Your son is tearing the house to pieces. We need to get him outside."

He groaned but took my hand and let me pull him to his

feet. It wasn't our usual shtick—we were much more explosive passion than tender caresses—but I stepped in and brushed my lips over his.

He paused, gaze flickering over my face curiously, before he kissed me back. "What was that for?"

I shrugged. "Can't I fucking kiss you?"

"You can. You just normally don't. Not like this."

I lifted a shoulder. "Shut up about it or I won't do it again."

He sniggered and reached a hand up over his head, stretching. Something crashed from out in the kitchen, and we both cringed at Mae's yelp and Liam and Ripley's instant apologies.

"I think our breakfast just hit the decks." Unfortunate, because those pancakes had looked amazing. "Maybe we should take Ripley outside before we lose any more food to the kitchen floor."

"Take Liam with you, too. He's just as bad!" Mae called crossly from the kitchen.

Rowe and I made our way into the kitchen just in time to see Liam sweep Mae off her feet and kiss the scowl off her face. She was breathless when he put her down, smiling at her impishly. "I'll see myself out. I just wanted to do that first." He pecked her on the cheek and then scooped Ripley up and ran for the front door, flinging it open with Ripley hanging over his shoulder, laughing hysterically.

We still needed to tell him about Norma, but none of us brought it up. I wasn't going to piss on his parade when he was this happy. It could wait.

We ate at the picnic table outside, and then Ripley wanted to go swimming, so we all got changed and headed down to the dock. With a little floatation device strapped to his back, he threw himself into the water, no fear and full of confidence he wouldn't sink. Rowe followed right after him, Liam cannonballing in behind them. Mae settled herself on a low chair on the bank, her swimsuit hugging her curves and a long flowing cover-up over her arms but really not covering anything else.

For which I was extremely grateful.

She was hot in anything she wore, but the black one-piece swimsuit showed off her tits, and I was thinking about how easy it would be to pop them free of the silky material if I could just get her into the water and away from the others. "Want to swim?"

"You look like you want to do more than just swim."

"Water is dark. It hides a multitude of sins."

She stood, dropping the cover-up, and I pulled my shirt off, so all I wore was swim trunks. Her gaze flickered over my abs for a moment before she took off, running for the water and throwing herself off the edge.

I went right along with her, diving in the deep end with her in more ways than one.

The day passed in a happy blur of swimming, sunbaking, grilling burgers for lunch, and just being together. I didn't want to think about brainstorming new suspects in Jayela's case, plus I knew Liam's office was inquiring into that. It was a downer always in the back of my mind but easily pushed aside on a day as beautiful as this. No one wanted to go inside. We ran back and forth to the cabin, eventually taking everything we needed down by the water.

Night was starting to push the sun down when Mae finally called it. Ripley was nearly asleep on her lap, and she glanced over at us. "I think it's time to head back. He needs a shower before he falls asleep."

I didn't want to move. I was warm and comfortable lying on a blanket on the bank, the last rays of sun sinking into my skin. Rowe lay beside me, sunglasses on, though I suspected he'd fallen asleep not long ago, content in knowing that one of us would always be watching Ripley if he wasn't. But Mae was right. We couldn't lie out here all night. The mosquitos would eat us alive. I stood and grabbed the edge of the blanket, yanking it hard so Rowe rolled right off it. Ripley and Mae both giggled at Rowe's grunt and subsequent lifting of glasses to glare at me.

"Wake up. Time to go home."

I gathered up an armload of things, then went on ahead while they packed up the last of the food. Back in the clearing, I dumped chairs and fishing poles into the shed and took the blanket with me toward the house.

A glint of silver on the picnic table stopped me, and I frowned at the knife lying there. "Super safe to leave a hunting knife just sitting in reach of a four-year-old, guys," I mumbled, picking it up and returning it to the shed. I put it up high on a shelf where Rip couldn't reach it. The entire shed needed reorganizing really. None of it was set up for an inquisitive child who might wander in. At the very least, we needed to get a lock for it. The fact he couldn't reach the handle yet really wasn't enough. If a kid wanted to get into something bad enough, they'd find a way.

I was halfway back to the house when a scream ripped through the open air.

I froze.

Liam was the opposite. He banged his way out onto the porch and stared at me with huge eyes. "Was that—?"

My heart started again. "Mae."

A million thoughts tumbled through my head.

"Heath! Move! What if it's the cops? You can't be here!"

He might have been right. Mae's scream might have

been a warning that we'd been found and I needed to disappear into the woods.

But what if it wasn't that?

Even if it meant going to jail, I was going back to them.

"Get a gun." I pushed my legs harder than I ever had before, sprinting down the path.

Everything around me became a blur in my hurry to get to them. "Mae!" Where the fuck were they?

I got to the dock, then froze at the scene playing out in horrifying detail in front of me.

When I'd returned to the house, I'd left Rowe, Mae, and Ripley by the water.

An extra person stood among them now.

Rowe and Zye were locked in a silent battle, no more than fifty feet separating them.

Zye had one hand clamped down on Ripley's shoulder.

The other held a shining silver gun. He held it barely out of Ripley's line of view and pointed right at the back of his head. He didn't look in my direction, but there was no doubt he'd noticed my arrival.

"Well, hey, Michaelson. Fancy meeting you out here in the woods? It's like a class reunion now, all of us here together. You, me, Teach, and Pritchard. Shall we get drunk and reminisce about the good old days in Gen Pop?"

None of us said a word. All I could focus on was the gun pointing at the back of Ripley's head.

Behind me, Liam skidded to a stop, taking in the scene.

He pulled his gun, aiming it at Zye. "Let him go."

Zye gave a lazy glance in Liam's direction. "What is this? Were you guys having a party? I'm going to assume my invitation got lost in the mail, and not that you didn't want me here."

"Nobody has ever wanted you anywhere, Zye." Rowe's

eyes flashed. He took a step forward, but Zye moved the gun closer to Ripley's head.

"Now, now. Stay where you are. I'm having some time with my son. Aren't we, Ripley? Some father-son bonding is what we need."

Liam's voice was strangled from behind me. "I said let him go."

Zye clamped down on Ripley's shoulder. "How good a shot are you, lawyer? Confident enough you'll hit me and not him?"

Ripley let out a wail of pain.

It cut through me like glass. I staggered forward but froze when Zye glared at me. "Don't even fucking try me, Michaelson. You know exactly what I'm capable of."

I wished like anything I hadn't left that knife behind in the shed. Cursed everything for not putting it in my pocket instead.

Zye knew perfectly well that he had the upper hand. "Right, so here's how we're going to play it. I can either walk out of here with Ripley, nice and calm and nobody has to get hurt. Or, I can turn the four of you into the cops. Heath goes back to prison, and the three of you join him for aiding and abetting a convicted murderer. And Ripley ends up with me anyway, since I'm his last living biological relative."

My stomach rolled at both options, nausea rising in my gut.

Zye's grin spread ear to ear, twisted and menacing, not meeting his eyes. Shadows fell across his face in the darkening evening, sharpening his cheekbones and glinting off the barrel of his gun. "Well, what's it to be? Time's a ticking, boys. Ripley and I have places to be."

None of us said a word.

Zye had us, and he knew it. He knelt to Ripley's height, twisting him around so he faced him.

Ripley's cries grew louder, faced with a man he didn't know who held him too tightly. He struggled to get to Rowe, terror clear in his wide eyes, the tears streaking down his face and a cut-off cry that ripped from his throat. "Daddy!"

Rowe's knees buckled at the word. My heart clenched, and a sob ripped from Mae's throat.

Zye frowned. "I'm your daddy, son."

Ripley wasn't having any of it. He twisted and turned in Zye's clutches, arms out toward Rowe, his high-pitched screams reverberating around in the silence. "Daddy! Daddy!"

Rowe choked on an agonized cry. "Please, Zye. Let him go. We'll give you whatever you want—"

I searched for an opportunity to get Ripley away. There had to be something, but I'd never thought Zye stupid. He knew exactly what he was doing. None of us could get to Ripley without risking Zye opening fire. I didn't care about myself, but Zye was just as likely to pull that trigger with the gun aiming at Ripley or Mae.

I couldn't have that.

Zye snarled in Rowe's direction, pulling Ripley back tight against him, pinning his arms. His laugh was bloodcurdling. "What I want? Hey, kid? You like guns?"

Zye shoved the gun in Ripley's face.

The little boy blinked, his eyes crossing when he tried to see the gun pointed an inch off his forehead.

He stopped crying.

Agony speared through me at the realization of what was going down. It punched through the shock, sharp and fast. I was going to have to stand here and watch Zye take him. After everything we'd done to keep him safe, it was all going to come down to this one moment, where there wasn't a thing we could do. Zye held all the power with that gun held to Ripley's head.

He seemed encouraged by Ripley's silence. "Of course you like guns. All little boys like guns, don't they? Well, where we're going, there'll be all sorts of guns for you to play with. I'll teach you everything I know about them. How to clean one. How to shoot one..." He chuckled as he looked over at Rowe. "I'll teach you how to point one right at a person's head and watch their brains fly out the back of their skull. Sound good?"

Ripley didn't make a sound.

Neither did the figure moving in the shadows.

I saw him in my peripheral vision at the last second, but it wasn't long enough to make a sound.

Zye turned, sensing the same thing I had, but it was too late.

Vincent's knife was already deep in his neck.

Blood spurted from his mouth, spraying over Ripley's face. Ripley screamed, and I lunged forward in unison with Rowe, Mae, and Liam.

But Vincent had Ripley up in his arms before any of us could reach him, gently wiping off the blood with the sleeve of his black shirt.

Zye slumped over on the grass, knife still buried deep in his flesh, blood trickling from the wound.

But I couldn't worry about him bleeding out at our feet. Ripley had his arms tight around Vincent's neck, and that didn't help the thumping of my heart.

Vincent was just as psychotic as Zye. But he and I had a connection. And however the hell he'd gotten out of prison, he'd come here. That had to have something to do with me.

Or Mae.

That thought instilled as much fear as Ripley in Vincent's arms. Subtly, I put myself between Mae and Vincent, blocking her from his sight.

"Vincent." I stepped toward him cautiously, like I was approaching a bull that might gore me—or the little boy in his arms—at any moment. "He's scared. Can you give him to me?"

Vincent nodded, moving toward me. "Of course." He patted Ripley on the back, but his gaze remained on me. "I'm sorry for all the blood. That wasn't how I intended to do it, but then he started talking about guns, and teaching Ripley to..." He shook his head. "That's how I grew up. I don't want that for him."

I breathed a sigh of relief when they reached me, and Vincent tried to hand him over.

But Ripley's arms tightened around Vincent's neck. "Don't leave again! Stay here with us. My dad and Heath and Liam and Mae will let you! Heath is hiding, too. You can hide together. You don't have to go again!"

Rowe, Liam, and Mae all looked as shocked as I felt, all of us staring at the unlikely pairing.

Vincent tried to pry Ripley's arms from around his neck. "I promise, I'll come back another day."

Ripley's friend.

We'd thought it was Zye. And then we'd dismissed it entirely. "You're the man he's been talking about?"

"I dropped by a few times to check on you and Miss Donovan. Didn't you get my housewarming gifts?"

"Housewarming gifts?"

He nodded. "I left some flowers in the kitchen for Mae, and a knife for you, Heath. I didn't want to intrude on your family time. But Ripley and I got to talking whenever I dropped by. We're friends now."

I wasn't sure how I felt about that. Not exactly good, but I also knew that while Vincent might be a little unhinged, he protected those he cared about.

We weren't all that different in that respect.

I managed to get Ripley from his arms and immediately passed him to Rowe and Mae. The two of them wrapped him between them, forming a shield around him. Rowe clutching his son to his chest with Mae sobbing into the back of Ripley's T-shirt.

I swiveled back to Vincent. "How the hell did you even get out? I didn't see anything on the news."

He lifted one shoulder. "Wasn't hard from the psych ward. That place desperately needs an upgrade of security."

Mae spoke up. "The men in class were talking about them losing a patient. I didn't believe them..."

It was Rowe who came up with a theory. "Tabor would have covered it up. He would have already been mortified over Heath getting out. The entire system would be under review if he had two prison breaks to his name."

There was a ripple of agreement from all of us.

With that decided, our gazes strayed to Zye on the ground. Mae blanched, like she'd only just remembered he was there. Rowe turned away so Ripley wouldn't see.

But Ripley wouldn't be swayed. He kept looking to Vincent. "Please come with us? I want to show you my Spider-Man toy."

But Vincent shook his head. "I've got to go, little friend. And it's past your bedtime."

Rowe hesitated, then held a hand out to Vincent.

Vincent looked down at it with interest, then took it to shake.

"Thank you," Rowe said quietly.

Vincent seemed pleased by that, but then his expression

dropped. "Unfortunately, I'm not just here for a social visit. I came to get Heath."

"What do you mean?" Mae asked.

"I heard Zye on the phone on the way in. He has a friend calling in your location in..." He checked the time on a phone he pulled from his pocket. "About five minutes."

I stared at him.

Vincent misunderstood my silence for confusion and spelled it out for me. "He was never going to just walk away, even if you had given him Ripley. The cops will be here in fifteen minutes, Heath. You need to get out of here."

I stared down at Zye's body. And then at the shocked faces of my family. I couldn't. I turned back to Vincent. "I can't leave with a body here a few hundred feet from the house."

Vincent frowned, but his tone remained calm and patient as always. "Of course not. But I haven't needed longer than fifteen minutes to clear a murder scene since I was twelve."

"Twelve?" I choked out. Who the hell was this man? What kind of family had a child killing at twelve?

One who liked to.

I shuddered.

"I'll take care of this." Vincent gave me a stern look. "Go. You can't end up back in prison. You'll have a lethal injection in your arm in under a week if you do."

He paused, waiting for me to move.

My feet felt like they were made of lead.

"Go, Heath!"

I blinked, stumbling back, away from Vincent and the body of the life taken. Then Liam was at my back, shoving me toward the house, all of us running, me still barefoot and in slightly damp swim trunks from a day of fun that now felt like a lifetime away.

Liam sprinted ahead, faster than all of us thanks to his baseball fitness. By the time we reached the clearing, Ripley still clutched to Rowe's chest, Liam was back outside with car keys in his hand. He threw them at me and put the gun against my palm. "Go." He shoved me frantically toward the car. "Go, Heath!"

I glanced around at them. I couldn't leave. Not like this. Not without time to say goodbye. Where the hell was I gonna go? I had nobody else. "I can't."

Mae stepped in front of me, her gaze burning with fire. "You have to. You can't stay. As soon as it's safe, we'll be together again."

The words ripped at my heart. Because when would that be? It could be weeks if the cops decided to put surveillance on them. What if they fingerprinted the cabin? They'd know I was there and that they were closer to finding me than ever. They wouldn't just ease off the gas if they had a lead like that.

I stared down into Mae's eyes, eyes that had become so familiar. Was I really going to leave her? How the hell was I going to wake up every day, knowing she wasn't beside me?

I didn't want to live a life without her.

Her eyes filled with tears, and like she could read my mind, she lifted up on her toes, putting her lips to mine. I gripped the side of her face with one hand, hauling her in with the other and crushing her to me, while I kissed her mouth for the last time.

"If they find you, they'll shoot on sight." Liam's voice was strained.

I could feel an invisible clock counting down. It whispered a threat with every tick of the second hand, and I knew that out there somewhere in the darkness, the police were closing in. I glanced at Rowe.

His face said everything his mouth wasn't. I hauled him in, pressing my lips to his before pulling Mae in tight, circling her with one arm. "I love you," I whispered against the top of her head.

"I love you, too," she whispered back, but then she was pushing me toward Liam's car, tears streaming down her face, and I had no choice but to go.

"Ditch the car somewhere when you can. Once they get here, they're gonna put two and two together pretty quick." Liam was the voice of strength and reason. He clapped a hand on my shoulder as I nodded, a mutual understanding and respect between us, and then he slammed the door.

In the silence of the car, all that was left was the beating of my heart and the rushing of blood in my ears. I gunned the engine and put my foot down on the accelerator. I forced my eyes to stay on the road, knowing it was bumpy and unpredictable in the daylight and worse at night.

Looking into the rearview mirror would help no one.

But I did it anyway.

I watched the figures get smaller, the four of them huddled around each other while I drove away.

"Dammit!" I pounded the steering wheel, fighting off the lump in my throat.

A new determination finally bore down on me. I put my foot down harder, screeching around the last bend of the driveway. The road to freedom lay beyond, I just had to take it.

Barely tapping the brakes at the top, I spun out onto the road in a squeal of tires suddenly finding grip on the asphalt road. The engine roared, and a thrill of adrenaline shot through me, a battle cry of victory bursting from my lungs.

I could lay low somewhere for a few days. A few weeks if I had to. I could let this all blow over, and once it did, I'd get them back.

I just had to be patient. It would all work out if I stuck to the plan.

The flashing of police lights lit up the dark night sky.

The road was completely blocked with half a dozen cars parked side by side. Fear erupted at the sight of the officers, their guns all pointed directly at me while they sheltered behind their open doors.

I jumped on the brakes, shoving the gearshift into reverse. Panic shook my fingers, and I put my hand on the passenger seat, twisting to glance over my shoulder.

My foot fell away from the accelerator.

More blue and red lights closed in from behind, and I knew if I looked to the left or the right, I'd find more.

This wasn't how this was supposed to go. We were supposed to find out who'd murdered Jayela and clear my name.

We were supposed to get our happily ever after.

And now we'd get none of it.

30

MAE

*T*he four of us stood in the darkness after the taillights of Liam's car disappeared. The roar of the engine filtered back until it faded into nothingness and all that was left was the night.

"We need to get Ripley inside," Rowe murmured.

I nodded numbly. "I know."

We trudged inside. Liam went to the kitchen, claiming he was going to make tea, while Rowe and I squeezed into the bathroom with Ripley. Rowe got the shower started, while I stripped Ripley's clothes, wiping at his face as I went. He stared at me silently, his big blue eyes blank, his face streaked with Zye's dried blood.

I wanted to let my tears fall, but I couldn't. I couldn't fall apart when he needed me. "Hey, sweetie. I know some really scary things happened tonight, but it's all okay now. The bad man is gone and —"

"Is Heath a bad man?"

I shook my head, those tears threatening to fall. "No. He's not. Heath is the best kind of man. The very best. Just like your daddy. Just like you're going to be one day."

"The shower is ready," Rowe interrupted quietly.

I nodded and led Ripley over. I got down on my hands and knees, not caring that the water splashed back at me while I lathered up his hair with shampoo and washed off all traces of the trauma he'd witnessed.

He was going to live with that for the rest of his life. The guilt sat heavy on my shoulders, even though logic tried to reason that it was Zye at fault here and not us.

Guilt spoke loudly, though, and was hard to ignore.

Rowe began pulling off clothes, too, and when I looked up at him, he had Ripley's clothes clutched in his hands. "We need to burn these."

I swallowed and nodded. Ripley's clothes were covered in blood, as were Rowe's from where it had transferred when he'd picked him up. "We should probably burn mine and Liam's, too. Just in case."

I ducked into the bedroom quickly to get changed even though I couldn't see any blood on the clothes I'd been wearing. Liam and Rowe took care of the clothes and the fire while I dressed Ripley in the snuggliest pajamas he had, then lay down with him on his bed. His fingers twisted in the lengths of my hair, seeking comfort. I curled my body around his little one and waited for his breathing to even out into the deeper pulls of sleep.

The scent of smoke from the fire drifted in the open window, and slowly my panic eased. In the darkness, a calm settled over me. One that told me I was exactly where I needed to be. And that this little boy needed me as much as I needed him.

In the whisper of the breeze outside, I felt Rory's blessing. I felt her handing over the reins, and her soft smile as she gifted me her child.

My child.

The one I would never have been able to birth but who I already loved like I had.

"I'll look after him," I whispered to the darkness. "I'll take care of both of them." It was a promise to the woman who had loved them first.

I would love them last.

I didn't move until Rowe and Liam appeared in the doorway.

Liam squeezed my foot from the end of Ripley's bed. "Hey, you need to get up."

I retracted my arm from beneath Ripley's head and pushed up off his mattress. Liam and Rowe flanked my sides, and the three of us walked into the darkened living room together.

Through the windows that overlooked the clearing, red and blue lights flashed silently.

The yard was full of police, more cars than I'd ever seen before. Officers swarmed about everywhere.

Two of them mounted the porch steps, their boots heavy on the brittle wood we'd talked about replacing. Their knock was loud and sharp.

None of us moved.

There was nowhere to go.

Nothing left to do.

Standing between them, I picked up Rowe's and Liam's hands and held them tight.

"It's open," Rowe said in a voice so quiet I was almost sure the officers wouldn't hear it.

But they did. The door opened hard and fast, and then they were standing in front of us. I narrowed my eyes when I recognized Johnson.

There was pure, sick amusement in his. "Mae Donovan,

Liam Banks, and Rowe Pritchard. You're under arrest for aiding and abetting a known criminal..."

His voice faded out as blood rushed in my ears, drowning everything else.

They'd caught him then. He hadn't made it out. Heath was either lying dead somewhere, with a police bullet in his chest, or he'd meet the same fate via lethal injection.

And now we'd go down, too.

Johnson grabbed me, his fingers biting around my upper arms. But the pain shocked me into action. I struggled with him, jerking my arm, trying to fight him off. "No! Stop! Our son is here!"

Rowe stopped and stared at me, but then Johnson's partner was slapping cuffs on his wrists. The cold metal encircled my own, too tight, instantly cutting into the skin.

"Don't say anything," Liam directed, cuffs on his own wrists. "Not one word."

"My son!" Rowe roared. "There's no one else here. We can't just leave him!"

"An officer will stay with him until Child Protective Services arrives to take him into foster care."

"Foster care!" Rowe turned panicked eyes on me.

I shook my head frantically, watching the entire thing spiral out of control. "No. Johnson, please. You knew my sister. *Please.* She wouldn't have wanted this. Let me make a call. I'll find someone to take him. Don't put him in the system."

His eyes were cold. "Yes, I knew her. What a disgrace you are to her name. You're kidding yourself if you think she would have wanted you whoring around with the man convicted of killing her." He spat the words in my face. "You people disgust me."

I recoiled but there was little I could do to wipe the spit from my face with my hands cuffed behind my back.

"Please," I begged the other officer. "He's only four."

He looked bored by the entire thing. "You'll get your one phone call at the station."

"No!" Rowe yelled again. "You can't!"

Johnson shoved him into the wall of the cabin. "You want to keep going? I'll add resisting arrest to your list of charges. Now fucking move."

There wasn't anything we could do. Johnson and his partner shoved us out the door. I tripped on the bottom step and fell face-first into the ground. Without my hands to break my fall, the unforgiving dirt and grass was like hitting stone. Blood dripped from my lips, and I was unceremoniously yanked up by the shoulders and shoved into a police car.

Separated from the other two.

Around my tears, I made the mistake of looking back at the house. Ripley was held back in the doorway by a uniformed officer.

Even with the windows rolled up, all I could hear was Ripley's screams of terror as he called for me with a single word.

"Mommy!"

I'd only seen the inside of Providence Police Station once before, when I'd taken my first graders on a field trip. But we'd been escorted straight into an education room, well away from the main entrance, where my sister and Boston had given a talk about stranger danger and personal safety.

I'd sat at the back of the room grinning at the two of them, proud as heck of my sister. I'd never visited her at work, because I was busy working, too, and most of the time she was out on patrol anyway. She'd never liked sitting behind a desk, so there'd been no reason for me to come here other than that one day.

She'd hate that I was here now in handcuffs, sitting on a hard plastic chair in a holding cell, with red marks around my wrists from the cuffs I'd had on.

I shared my cell with another woman who snored loudly from a bench on the other side. I suspected she was actually passed out, because she hadn't even flinched when Johnson had thrown open the door and pushed me inside.

Anxious nerves rioted around my stomach, but none of them were for me. They had a combination of names printed across their fluttery wings. I battled worries for all of my guys, but Heath's and Ripley's were the ones that took up the most space.

I couldn't bear the thought of Ripley scared and alone.

Couldn't even think about Heath lying dead in Liam's car or on the side of the road. How far had he gotten? Had he tried to run, or had he surrendered quietly? Was he alive or dead?

I had to believe he was alive somewhere, either in a cell here at the station, or back at the prison.

Footsteps that stopped outside our door had me looking up, but I groaned when it was Johnson again. "What?" I bit out. "I told you, I'm not saying a word without a lawyer. So unless you have one..."

Johnson's beady eyes filled with hate. "Your sister would be ashamed of you, you know? For what you've done."

I snorted. "Rich coming from you, when you were the one who beat her ex into confessing to a crime he didn't commit. You think she'd be proud you fucked up the investigation into her death so royally that her killer has been allowed to roam the streets, while the man she once loved rots in prison?" My hate for the man bubbled over. "You know what? It doesn't matter that Jayela would hate you for what you did. You should hate yourself."

"You little bitch."

I shook my head. "You disgust me. Where's my lawyer?"

"Get up and call one yourself. You have five minutes."

He stepped aside, letting me out into a bigger room where a phone was attached to the wall. But a lawyer was the last person I cared about calling. I knew Liam would handle that anyway. He probably already had someone from his firm—the very best someone—on their way.

I needed to take care of Ripley.

I called the one number I knew by heart because I'd been calling it for a decade and prayed she'd answer the unknown number calling her in the middle of the night.

"Hello?"

I slumped in relief against the wall and turned away so Johnson wouldn't see my face crumple. "Tor, I need you."

She instantly sounded more awake. "What is it?"

"I've been arrested. So has Rowe, Liam, and Heath."

"What? What on earth did you—"

"Don't say anything else. They'll be recording this call."

"What do I need to do?"

I let out a relieved breath. "I know you're still at the clinic, and I know you want to be there—"

"I've already got my shoes on and my purse in my hand, Mae. Whatever you need, I'm there."

I loved this woman so hard. I couldn't believe that I'd entertained the thought she might have killed Jayela even for a second. I'd spend the rest of my life making up for that lapse in judgment. "Rowe's son, Ripley. He's at our cabin. I need you to go get him. They're threatening to put him in foster care if there's nobody to take care of him tonight. He's already been through too much. I need to know he's safe."

"Don't think about it again. Give me the address."

I rattled it off, but my stomach was in knots. "Don't let them take him, Tor. We can't lose him. He called me Mommy tonight…"

A sob came down the line. "Oh, sweetheart. Really? I know how much that must have meant to you."

I nodded miserably. "I just want my little boy."

There was a new resolve in Tori's voice. "Don't worry about me. I'll rain down Hell and highwater on anyone who tries to take him. We'll both be there when you get bail."

I knew she would. Tori was like a dog with a bone when she wanted something. She'd convinced the police to let her and Will into a murder scene when I'd needed her. She might have been tiny, but so were chihuahuas. And everybody knew how crazy they were.

I couldn't have loved her more.

She paused. "You are going to get bail, right?"

"I really hope so."

31

MAE

*L*iam looked as bleary-eyed as I felt by the time his colleagues got our bail sorted out. My lawyer, Linda, had walked in like she owned the place and run circles all around the cops. I'd never seen a woman so determined, and frankly, pissed off. Not at me, she assured. But she was the senior partner at Liam's law firm, and she wasn't having one of her colleagues, or his family, sitting in a jail cell until they'd had a fair trial.

Whoever had been assigned to Liam's case had been equally skilled because both of us found ourselves standing outside the police station, waiting for an Uber to come pick up our sorry asses.

We'd been promised that Rowe wouldn't be far behind, but it was still a relief to see him walk down the station steps. I flew into his arms, and he caught me tight. "Where's Ripley? Have you heard anything?"

"I sent Tori," I assured him. "I don't know if she was able to convince them to leave Ripley with her, but I'm willing to bet she's camped outside his foster placement if they didn't."

Rowe swallowed hard. "And Heath?"

We both looked in Liam's direction.

"He's alive." His lips pulled into a grim line. "Gave himself up before they could warrant opening fire. He's back in solitary, waiting for his turn on death row. Likely right at the very top, though Linda didn't say that in as many words. But what she did say wasn't good."

Rowe grimaced. "Tell us."

Liam put his phone in his pocket. "They've gone through all of Jayela's old cases and ruled out everyone involved with them."

My mouth dropped open. "What? All of them? That has to be hundreds of people."

"Every single one. I had them look into anyone Jayela had arrested, their gang affiliations, their families...there's nothing."

Panic gripped my chest like a vise. "What do we do?"

Nobody had an answer for that.

The Uber pulled up, but I was too numb to move. Rowe put his hand to the small of my back. "We need to get home to Ripley."

I nodded. It was all we could do in the moment.

The Uber ride felt decades long, with the chatty driver asking questions that nobody answered and making jokes nobody laughed at. The man eventually gave up, and the rest of the ride was silent.

I semi expected our house to be cordoned off with police tape, but it wasn't. All the cars from last night were gone, and the only evidence they'd ever been there at all was the flattened grass.

And the fact I was one man down.

My gaze strayed to the path that led down to the dock. Had the police gone down there? Since they had Heath and we were all there, basically just waiting to be arrested, I hoped they hadn't felt the need to poke around.

Though something told me that when Vincent cleaned a crime scene, he did it thoroughly.

Tori's car was parked by the front door, and the moment the driver stopped, all three of us scrambled to get out. Rowe was halfway up the steps when the front door opened, and Tori appeared in the doorway.

Our little blond boy, still in the snuggly pajamas I'd dressed him in last night, held tight to her hand.

"See, buddy?" she said with the brightest of smiles. "I told you they'd be home any minute now."

Rowe stumbled up the last few steps and fell to the floor at Ripley's feet, pulling him onto his lap. Ripley wrapped his arms around Rowe's head, and Rowe buried his face in his son's neck, his shoulders shaking with emotion. "Thank God," he mumbled over and over.

I hugged Tori hard, hating that I could feel her bones when I did. "Thank you."

She stepped back and nodded.

Ripley wriggled in Rowe's grasp, his arms reached out to me. "Mommy."

Rowe jerked back in surprise, and Liam blinked as well. Obviously neither of them had heard him call me that last night.

But I had.

And now I wrapped him in my arms and relished the sound of the word on his sweet mouth. "Hey, my boy. How're you doing? I'm sorry about last night."

"I was scared."

I clutched him tighter. "You know what? So was I. But we're all together now, and that is never going to happen again, okay? Liam is going to make sure of it."

Liam leaned in and ruffled his hair affectionately. "It's a promise, Rip."

"Tori said we could have pancakes with chocolate on them for breakfast."

I raised one eyebrow. "Did she? Let's go make them then, huh?"

He smiled, and I was relieved to see it. I carried him inside, and all five of us made the pancakes together, heaping in cocoa powder and chocolate chips and then serving them up with ice cream and gooey syrup. We carried our plates to the outside picnic table, placing them all down in the center of the circle and then taking up the seats around it. Tori sat next to Liam, with Rowe on her other side, Ripley and me opposite her. Ripley kept staring up at me with big eyes and asking questions, his butt scooted so close to me our thighs touched.

Every time I looked at Tori, her grin was wide.

The hollowed-out version of her I'd spoken to in the clinic was gone, and my best friend was back.

"Motherhood suits you," she commented casually.

"I think so, too."

My heart swelled every time Ripley did anything. Ate all his pancakes? Pride flushed through me. Used his manners? Another rush. It didn't even matter that I wasn't the one who'd taught them to him. He was mine. I wanted the world, and especially my best friend, to love him like I did.

At the sound of an engine on the driveway, all five of us glanced up. A tremor of fear pulsed through me, and Rowe looked down at Ripley.

"Hey, buddy, why don't you take your pancakes inside and watch cartoons. You can turn the TV up as loud as you want."

Ripley scurried off with the grin of a kid who'd just been

told he was allowed to do something naughty. I watched until he disappeared into the house and then turned back to the engine sound growing closer. "Who is it?"

Rowe's fingers gripped the tabletop. "Nobody panic. At least we know it's not Zye. It's probably a delivery driver."

I prayed with all my heart that he was right.

We all breathed a sigh of relief when I recognized the black sedan. "Oh. It's just Will."

Liam and Rowe both went back to their pancakes, but Tori had completely frozen.

I reached across the table and squeezed the hand she'd left hanging in midair. "Tor? You okay?"

She shook her head. "What's he doing here? Did you call him?"

I frowned and glanced over my shoulder at the car bumping over the track through the clearing. "No. Didn't you message him?"

I would have assumed that had been the first thing she'd done once she'd left the hospital. Though things obviously weren't good with them. He'd accused her of something horrible. She'd cheated. Theirs wasn't exactly the rosiest of relationships right now, both of them at fault in different ways.

Will's car came to a screeching halt in the driveway, haphazardly parked on an angle. His door opened, and from inside the car, Isaac's cries were heartbreaking.

Tori's face crumpled at the sound.

But they seemed to have no effect on Will. He stumbled out of the car, his gaze glued on Tori.

"Hey, Will..." Rowe's voice died off at the expression on the other man's face.

Something was very wrong. Will's normal, reserved but friendly demeanor, was nowhere to be found. An icy coolness emanated from him that I'd never seen before. Isaac's screams from the back seat intensified, but Will acted like he didn't even hear them.

The fact he was completely ignoring his obviously distressed child set off alarm bells in my head.

Tori put a hand on Rowe's shoulder, using it as leverage to stand. "Is Isaac okay? He—"

Will's gaze narrowed on the spot Tori touched Rowe. "What the hell is going on here?"

I blinked at the harshness of the question. And at the fact he'd dropped the word hell so casually. It was barely a curse for most, but one that Will took very seriously. I'd never heard the man utter even a whisper of the word.

Tori stopped in her tracks, too, her mouth open. "Don't talk like that. That's not you."

But he wasn't done. He stalked the distance between the car and where Tori stood and glared down at her. "I got a call from Saint Paul of God this morning saying you were missing, so I'm out of my mind with worry, but of course, you're here. I should have known."

Rowe, Liam, and I all glanced at each other awkwardly. I wasn't sure if we should stay where we were while they argued or if we should try to get up and leave them to have some privacy.

But it was my fault Will was angry. I didn't want him taking it out on Tori. "Blame me. I had an emergency last night that I needed her for."

His angry gaze turned on me. "An emergency? Is that what you're calling it now? This lifestyle you've chosen where you sleep around with half a dozen men? Just call it what it is, Mae. It's an orgy." He spat the word out like it offended him to even think it.

Liam pushed to his feet, a possessive growl in the back of his throat. "Watch your mouth."

But I was angrier than Liam. I got off my seat quicker than he did and put my hand on his shoulder. I could fight my own battles. "While I sleep around? How dare you? Don't come at me with your narrow views, especially not in my own home. If you don't like what I'm doing here, that's fine. Nobody asked you to come out here."

He glared at me. "You didn't leave me much choice when you lured my wife into your sick game."

My mouth dropped open. He made me sound like a complete predator. "Lured? She's not a kid at the park taking candy from a stranger, Will. I didn't *lure* her anywhere."

He ignored me, storming around me and over to Tori. "This is over. Get in the car. I'm taking you back to the hospital." He wrapped his hand around her upper arm and yanked her.

She stumbled a step toward him, shock in her eyes. "Ow, Will! No, stop! You're hurting me."

He whirled on her. "Get. In. The car!"

Rowe was on him in seconds, putting himself between Tori and Will, breaking the grip Will had on her arm. The two men went chest to chest as Rowe shoved him back. "What the fuck, man? Get your hands off her."

"Oh, here he is," Will drawled sarcastically. "Tori's savior and protector, jumping in again to save the day just like you did during the riot. How many weeks will I have to hear about how fucking wonderful you are? How you saved her life? Are you fucking her, too?" He turned to Liam. "How about you?" But his last question was directed at Tori. "You going to tell me all about that as well, wife?"

I ran to Tori's side, wrapping an arm around her while

silent tears fell down her cheeks. Her voice broke. "Why are you doing this?"

Her words fell on deaf ears. Will didn't even give Liam time to say anything before he hurled his accusations at me. "And you, too, I suppose." He let out a bitter laugh. "Are you all fucking my wife behind my back?"

"Will!" Tori's shout was full of pain. "Stop it! I'm not sleeping with anyone!"

But Will wasn't even close to done. His eyes were wide, and sweat beaded across his forehead. Dark circles lined his bloodshot eyes. "You're such a liar. What about Jayela?"

"We talked about that. I made a mistake."

"One you promised you would never do again and yet look at you and Mae now. All wrapped up in each other, her hands all over you." His eyes blazed. "She's just like her sister. You both make me sick. I can't even stand to look at you."

"He's drunk," Rowe said beneath his breath. "Fucking hell. It's barely eight in the morning."

Will laughed bitterly, obviously hearing Rowe's comment. "Can you blame me? I'm at home, raising our son to be a man of God while his mother is out here acting like a whore! Did you drop your clothes for him the minute my back was turned, Tori? Did you get down on your slut knees and suck his cock the way you never would for me?"

I was so shocked I couldn't even get a word out. I felt like I was staring at a stranger. And yet, Will had always been so reserved. So shoved into the box his parents, his church, and community created for him. He'd been raised so strictly, rules and values and morals all shoved down his throat at every opportunity.

When you bottled all that up and shook it around, was it any real surprise if it exploded once the top was off?

Liam and Rowe seemed to be in stunned silence as well.

It was only Tori who had control over her tongue. "How dare you? I'm your wife!" She seethed. "You drove here drunk with our child in the back? What were you thinking!" She tried to get around him to Isaac still crying in car, but he blocked her every attempt.

Will tugged at his hair, his fingers raking through the dark strands. "I don't even know you anymore. You're not the woman I married. The Tori I knew believed in God and faith and marriage."

"I still do!"

"And yet here you are, surrounded by other men. What do I have to do, Tori? Do I have to soil myself by allowing other people into our bedroom just to satisfy you? I thought this would end when Jayela was out of the picture. I took care of that so that you could come back to me. But it's never going to end, is it? Nothing I do is ever going to be good enough. Because it's not them, it's you!"

My heart stalled.

"What do you mean, 'with Jayela out of the picture'?" Tori asked quietly.

But Will kept going like she hadn't spoken. "You deceived me. You promised me a wife who would love, honor, and obey, and yet all you are is a filthy slut. It should have been you. It should have been your throat I slit and you who I watched bleed out on the bed. But I wanted to believe it was Jayela who had the Devil in her, not you. But oh, wasn't I wrong. It was you all along. You did this. All of this."

The world spun around me. If Liam hadn't stepped in behind me, wrapping an arm around me and moving me behind the shield he and Rowe made standing side by side, I would have toppled over.

Tori flew at him, pummeling her fists on his chest. "No!"

The agonized cry ripped from her chest over and over. "No!" Her pain turned to sobs as she slumped against him. "How could you? How could you, Will? I loved her."

He pried her off him, shoving her away like she was tainted and dirty. "I did it for you! So you wouldn't be tempted. So you'd be the woman I married again!"

Tori glanced down at Will's hand and stepped back. Her gaze fixed on whatever he held, and her postured stiffened. Her voice went calm and her sobs abruptly stopped. "Will. Look at me. I'm still her."

His laugh was bitter. "You'll just keep doing it."

"No, I swear. That's why I checked into the hospital. I'm trying to change. I don't want to be like this. I never loved her. I don't know what I was saying. You're right. You're always right."

He shook his head sadly. "But once a whore, always a whore, right?" He leaned down and sneered at her. "There is no saving you."

And then I saw it. The silver glinting in his palm.

My warning yell was too late.

He sank the blade deep into Tori's belly.

The world moved in slow motion. In a blur, Tori clutched her stomach and stared down at the blood gushing from the wound.

Rowe and Liam both sprang into action, rushing Will and tackling him to the ground. He hit the ground hard but fought the entire time while Rowe and Liam kept him down.

It all happened through a fog, like a dream I couldn't control. I stood there in the middle of the chaos, my brain fighting through shock to make sense of any of it.

Tori turned to stare at me, her eyes wide and terrified. "Mae."

The world came back in a burst of color and noise. Tori

slumped to her knees, and I realized the ringing in my ears was my screams. I rushed to her, dropping down beside her. "Call an ambulance! She's been stabbed!"

I got her down on her back, the knife I hadn't seen until it was too late still sticking out of her abdomen. "What do I do? What do I do?"

The basic first-aid training I had didn't cover stab wounds.

"The ambulance is on its way, but they're coming from Providence." Rowe appeared beside me, pressing his hands around the wound on Tori's belly.

Her scream of pain forced a sob from my throat. "You're hurting her!"

"I've got to try to stop the bleeding. Take my phone. Call Perry. Her place isn't far. If she hasn't left for work yet, she might get here quicker."

I stabbed at Rowe's phone, finding Perry's number. It rang in my ear while I spun in a circle, desperately looking for help that wasn't there.

Liam had Will facedown in the dirt, his hands pinned behind his back by Liam's bodyweight. But Will had stopped fighting, his gaze pinned on Tori. "Oh God. Tori. I'm sorry. I didn't mean it!"

"Shut up!" I screamed at him. "You don't get to say that to her now!" I wanted to kick and punch and bite and tear the man limb from limb for everything he'd done. He'd taken my sister, the man I loved, and now he was trying to take my best friend as well.

"Rowe? What's up? You need a ride to work?"

"Perry! It's me. I need help. Tori's been stabbed."

"What?" But that was the only moment of confusion Perry had before her nurse's training kicked right in. "I'm getting in my car. Where are you? Have you called an ambulance?"

"We're at Rowe's cabin on Old South Road. We've called an ambulance, but there's so much blood..."

"Mae, listen to me. You need to get pressure on it. Put the phone down."

"Rowe's here. He's already doing it." My tears streamed down my face. "Perry. Hurry." I dropped to the ground without waiting to hear her reply so I could pick up Tori's hand.

It was covered in blood.

I stared down at her pale face, clutching her fingers between mine.

She gazed up at me with wide, terrified eyes. "You'll take Isaac, right? If I..."

I blanched. "No! You're not dying. Not here, not today. Isaac needs you. I need you! So you fight, you hear me. This isn't how this ends. Because you and me? We're soul mates, too. We're growing old and wrinkly together, and watching our boys grow and become best friends, too. I'm not doing that without you."

She closed her eyes and smiled softly. "That sounds nice."

The strength in her grip faded. Rowe looked as helpless as I felt. The blood was everywhere, coating his hands, Tori's clothes, the ground.

I didn't even notice Perry arrive until she was pushing me aside. She gazed down at Tori and brushed a sweaty piece of hair from her forehead. "Fancy seeing you again. And in another life-or-death situation. We need to stop meeting like this."

Tori gave a painful laugh. "At least there's no flames this time."

"Amen to that, sister. Amen."

She moved around Tori with a medical bag of equipment, taking out gauze and other things I couldn't identify. Locating a pair of gloves, she snapped them on, then nodded to Rowe to let her take over.

He stepped back, right as the first wail of ambulance sirens reached us. He stormed over to where Will still lay on the ground with Liam on his back. Tears streamed down Will's face while he sobbed for his wife, but Rowe showed no remorse. He wiped Tori's blood down the center of Will's face then grabbed his jaw in a bone-breaking hold. "If I didn't want to see you spend the rest of your sorry life in jail, I'd kill you myself."

He pushed his face away roughly and stood, wiping the rest of the blood off on his pants. Then he stormed to the back of Will's car, yanked open the rear door, and reached in. He emerged a moment later with Isaac cradled in his arms, fast asleep after crying himself into exhaustion.

Rowe didn't look at Will when Will called out for Isaac. And Liam yanked his arm painfully to shut him up. Rowe squeezed my hand as he moved toward the house. "I need to check on Ripley. Go on to the hospital with her. I've got them both."

God, I loved him.

The ambulance finally arrived in the clearing, two cop cars close behind. Liam took the chance to lean down and hiss in Will's ear, "You ever want that God of yours to forgive your sins? You better confess everything. You'd better get up on that stand and tell the world how you let an innocent man be sentenced to death row for a life you took. I don't know much about religion, but I do know enough that you don't get forgiveness unless you confess."

Damn, I loved him, too.

He pushed off Will's back with unforgiving force that likely wrenched Will's shoulder at best, dislocated it at worst. He let out a scream of pain that I was sure nobody felt sympathy for.

The police rushed in to arrest him, among the flurry of medics who descended on the scene. Liam stood at my side, his palm on the small of my back while they worked on Tori, and after a moment, got her onto a stretcher.

"Is she going to be okay?" I begged, running alongside them. "Please. She has a baby."

"We're doing the best we can. Are you family?"

I nodded without hesitation.

"Get in."

I scrambled into the back of the ambulance with them, Liam's worried face the last thing I saw before the doors closed.

And then we were racing to the hospital, while a team of medics tried to save Tori from suffering the same fate my sister had.

32

LIAM

*R*owe lay on the rug with Isaac propped up in a sitting position, pillows pilfered from our bedroom spread out behind him in case he toppled over. Ripley lay beside him, busily showing the baby all of his toys and explaining in his little voice why each one was amazing.

Rowe glanced over at me and left the two boys playing on the floor to join me by the door.

"Is Rip okay?" I scanned over him, searching for signs he'd seen the whole thing go down outside, but he seemed happy and excited to have a baby to play with.

"I don't think he noticed anything. He had the TV blaring when I got in here." Rowe scraped a hand through his hair. "I hope not anyway. Last night was traumatic enough to leave him needing therapy for the rest of his life."

"Him and me both. We need to get some formula for Isaac. There's a baby bag in the car, but the cops won't let me have it. It's part of a crime scene, so they won't even give me a diaper."

Rowe pointed toward the kitchen counter. "I already

started making a list of everything we'd need for him until Tori is out of the hospital."

I nodded. "We can get it on the way to the prison."

A smile flickered at the edge of Rowe's mouth. "You mean..."

A smile spread across my own. "I mean, I'm going to tell Heath he's getting out. You want to come?"

Happiness lit up Rowe's eyes. "Hell yes, I want to come." He jogged back over to Ripley and crouched to his height. "You want to go get Heath?"

"See Heath," I corrected. "There's still going to be a court hearing. But that'll be a piece of cake."

Ripley's cheer was so loud it startled the baby into a cry. Ripley cringed. "Sorry, baby Isaac." He dropped his voice to a whisper. "Can we see Vincent, too?"

Rowe glanced at me, and I shrugged. I had no idea how to answer that any more than he did. Rowe scratched at his head. "Ah, maybe not today, buddy. I'm not too sure where Vincent is right now."

"He said he'd come back and visit me."

Rowe nodded. "But if he does, you make sure you tell me, okay? No more secrets."

Ripley nodded solemnly.

Rowe hugged him and then sent him off to find some clothes to wear for the day. Rowe and I both had to give the police a statement before we were allowed to leave, and by then, Isaac was fully fed up with the water we'd been holding him off with.

We picked up some formula and bottles and got him going with one of those, and then finally we were on our way to the prison.

Rowe and I had checked our phones about a thousand times, and yet there was still no word from Mae. In the commotion, she'd left her phone at home, so we just had to wait until she got in contact. There was no point calling the hospital and bothering the nurses. Mae would call as soon as they told her anything.

I glanced back at Isaac in the old car seat that had once been Ripley's, which had been stored away in the shed. "I don't know how I went from no kids to two all of a sudden."

Beside me in the passenger seat, Rowe nodded. "As much as I want a whole tribe of kids, I hope we get to give Isaac back to his mom."

All I could think about was the copious amount of blood Tori had lost. "I do, too."

"You want kids?" Rowe asked, flashing his badge to the security guard at the prison gates.

I nodded. "Badly. But I want Mae more." I grinned at him. "So you'll just have to share Ripley with me."

He settled back, looking relaxed for the first time in forty-eight hours. "I don't think Ripley would have it any other way, would you, buddy? And you're better at baseball than me, anyway. You'll be a much better Little League coach."

Something deep inside me wanted that so bad. I reached back and high-fived Ripley who chatted animatedly about how many runs he was going to score until I finished parking the car in the staff parking lot.

Inside, Rowe went to talk to the officer on duty while I stayed back, holding Isaac with one hand and Ripley with the other. A contentment settled over me. Neither were mine, but it didn't matter. I already loved Ripley, and holding Isaac in my arms, knowing he needed me right now, I realized how easy it would be to love another child. When this was all over, and Heath was home, I'd talk to Mae about adopting.

I already knew she'd be as eager as I was.

I suspected Heath and Rowe would be on board as well.

Rowe came back with a frown on his face. "They won't let us see him. He's still in solitary and not allowed visitors. I tried telling them you were his lawyer, but they know you're off his case." He bit his lip. "What if Will didn't confess to the cops? Is our word enough?"

I rolled my eyes, though I shouldn't have expected anything less. "He'll have confessed. I've seen enough men break down like that. Once the wall tumbles, so does the whole story. Here, take Isaac. Let me make some calls."

I off-loaded the baby into Rowe's arms and fell back into lawyer mode. It took four phone calls, and twenty minutes where Ripley grew restless and began walking along the chairs of the waiting room, before I eventually went to the officer on the desk. "Can we see Heath Michaelson now, please?"

The officer sighed. "I told Pritchard. Michaelson can't—"

"Check again."

He grumbled, but he did it, clicking at something with his mouse. One eyebrow crept up. "Apparently Michaelson is now eligible for visitors."

I gave the man a wink. "Thought so."

I gave Rowe the thumbs-up, and the look on his face was priceless. I mulled it over for a moment as we walked toward the visiting room, then elbowed him. "You love him."

I'd said it in a teasing, singsong way, expecting Rowe to shove me back and tell me to shut up. But he didn't. He went quiet instead.

I widened my eyes but didn't say anything.

The guard on duty in the visiting room was one Rowe knew, and the two of them talked while I got the boys settled at a table.

"Li-yam?"

"Yeah, buddy?"

"What is this place?"

I debated over how to answer that. And then decided that truth was the best solution. "A prison."

Ripley's mouth made a little O. "Isn't prison for bad people?"

I nodded. "Yes. But sometimes good people get put in here by mistake. That's what happened to Heath."

Ripley's bottom lip stuck out. "I want him to come home."

"We do, too. And he will, we just have to be patient." There was something else I needed to warn him about, but goddamn, this was so much harder with a kid. I didn't want to disappoint him. "You know how at daycare you have rules? There's some here, too."

"No running on the concrete?"

I smiled. "Actually, you are allowed to run on the concrete. But here, the rule is, no hugging."

His blond eyebrows drew together. "Why not?"

I sighed. "The guards said no."

"Oh." His little face was so crestfallen it broke my heart.

The doors at the end of the room buzzed, and we all turned in that direction, Rowe pausing his conversation with the other guard.

The doors opened, and Heath walked out.

Rowe stepped forward, staring at him. He took another step and then another until his steps became a half jog. They collided, and Rowe hugged him tight.

I glanced over at the guard, expecting a reprimand. He turned the other way.

Heath hugged him back, and then Ripley took off up the aisle, throwing himself into Heath's arms. Heath hoisted him up and high-fived him. His expression was a mixture of overwhelmed and bewilderment when he nodded at me. "What's going on? How did you swing this?"

I grinned. "You're getting out. Will confessed to Jayela's murder."

Heath looked as if Rowe had punched him in the gut. "Will? Tori's Will?"

"One and only."

"Holy shit." Then he cringed, glancing at Ripley. "Holy stuff, I mean. Not shit. Don't say shit."

I snorted and motioned them over. Heath gazed down at Isaac asleep in my arms as he came to sit at the table with me. "Why are you carrying a baby like it's a purse? And where's Mae?"

Rowe settled down on the picnic bench next to Heath, across from me. "With the baby's mother. Tori was...hurt earlier."

None of us wanted to say anything more in front of Ripley. Heath immediately understood. "Is it bad?"

I gazed down at Isaac. "Could be. Hoping it's not. Still waiting to hear."

Heath nodded gravely. "Will, though..."

"Yeah."

"Damn."

There was a moment of silence where we all reflected on exactly how messed up the whole thing was.

"But he really confessed?"

I blew out a relieved breath. "In front of all of us. I just called my boss, and she got confirmation he confessed to the police as well. They've arrested him."

Heath leaned heavily on the table like he wasn't entirely sure he was going to be able to remain conscious. "So it's over? I can leave?"

Rowe leaned into him. "Liam said not right away, but in a day or two, you'll be a free man."

I bit my lip. "Uh, about that...I might have been a bit hasty."

They both stared at me.

"Are you serious?" Rowe spat out. "Will confessed!"

"And Heath broke out of prison. That in itself is a chargeable arrest."

Heath gaped at me. "They had me on death row for a crime I didn't commit!"

I held my one free hand up and waved at them. "Keep it down. Sleeping baby. I know all that. I don't want you to worry. Linda is the head partner at the firm. She's already agreed to represent you."

"Is she good?"

"She taught me everything I know."

Rowe groaned dramatically, but it was around a grin. "Great, so we're doomed."

I flipped him the bird and then cringed at Ripley. "Also don't do that."

I turned back to Heath. "Seriously. I don't want you stressing about it. Go back to your cell, chill out, read a book, bide your time. We'll see you in court."

Heath seemed anything but assured. "We've done this before..."

"Not with a fair judge, we haven't. And after this freaking debacle, you'd better believe they're going to put their best people on the case."

Heath nodded slowly.

I grinned at him. "Trust me?"

Heath snorted. "Barely. You got me death row."

Well, that was insulting. "Hey. That judge got you death row. I was right. Wasn't it me who accused Will at the trial?"

"You had his motives all wrong, and the jury didn't believe you, but yeah, sure, if you want to claim that as a win, go ahead." Rowe's laughter echoed around the empty room. It was a giddy sound, one that we were all feeling.

I grinned back.

They could rib me all they wanted.

Heath was coming home.

And I had a family.

I didn't leave the hospital for two days. Tori's surgery lasted hours, while I sat in a sterile room, waiting for a doctor to come and tell me whether she'd lived or died.

When the doctor finally emerged from the operating theatre, the words that came out of her mouth barely registered. *"Alive, but it will be touch and go. She may not wake up."*

It was the news I'd hoped for and dreaded all in one sentence. I'd sat my ass back down on the chair and waited some more. Hours, and then the day slid by, and at some point, a kind nurse had taken pity on me and found a clean pair of scrubs for me to change into. I'd already refused to listen to their suggestions to go home and get some rest. I didn't want it. I knew that Rowe and Liam had Heath's back, but Tori had no one. I wasn't leaving my best friend. Not when she needed me more than ever.

They moved her to a private room on the morning of Heath's court case.

She still hadn't woken up. The same nurse who'd

brought my clean clothes now came to get me and take me to Tori's room.

"She's hooked up to a lot of monitors and she lost a lot of blood. Don't be scared that she doesn't look very healthy."

I nodded, and the woman let me walk in alone.

Tori was almost child-sized in the huge bed covered with white linen. Her dark hair hung in stringy clumps around her face, her arms resting on top of the covers.

She was too still. Her chest rose and fell, but it didn't seem like enough. The color had drained from her cheeks, replaced by a sickly white. She'd already been so underweight, this couldn't help. I picked up her hand and squeezed it tight between mine. "Hey, Tor."

She slept on. The doctors had promised me that she wasn't sedated and could wake up at any time.

Or she may never.

I desperately needed her to. "Tor? I really need you to wake up, okay? Isaac is safe with the guys, but he needs you. I do, too."

I studied her face for any sign of change, but there was nothing.

Exhausted, I lay my head down on the bed next to her arm. I needed to close my eyes, just for a minute. But I wasn't going to stop trying to convince her to come back until sleep dragged me under. "You might be thinking about going to Jayela right now. I know you miss her. And I'm sorry I didn't understand how much. I wish you guys had told me. I understand why you didn't...but, Tor? I need you more than she does. So if she's standing at the gates to Heaven right now, can you tell her I love her but she has to wait?"

"She tried to bribe me with Pop-Tarts and candy, but I told her I'd have to take an IOU."

I jerked up, not entirely sure the scratchy voice belonged to Tori, even though it came from right there in the bed.

Her big eyes followed my movement, and a tiny smile lifted the corner of her mouth. "You look like you just saw a ghost."

I burst into something that was half tears and half laughter and tried to hug her. She laughed, too, but then groaned. "Oh my God, that hurts so bad. No hugs. Can we get a refill of the drugs, please?"

I pulled away laughing, while tears streamed down my face, and grabbed the buzzer that alerted the nurse. "We'll get you all the drugs you want."

The nurse came in, a huge smile appearing when she saw Tori was awake. She put her hand on my shoulder. "And that's why I fought for you to get in here. Sometimes, they just need to know someone still needs them earthside."

I stood and hugged her, since I couldn't hug Tori, and then stepped back and let the nurse do her checks. A doctor was called, and soon the little room was so full of people I was pushed to the edge.

"Hey, she's awake?"

I glanced over, surprised when I saw Perry's mop of familiar auburn curls. "What are you doing here?"

She shrugged, pink spots appearing on her cheeks. She held up a little bouquet of flowers. "I was worried. I wanted to check on her and bring something to brighten her room, but this is obviously not a good time. I can come back."

I glanced at the clock on the wall. There was two hours until Heath's trial. "Actually, it's great timing. Because I have to leave. Will you stay with her? I don't want her to be alone, but Heath's court case is today."

"Of course. I can stay as long as she wants me around."

I kissed her on the cheek. "Thank you. For everything."

She waved me off. "I've got my fingers crossed for Heath today."

"Me, too."

Excitement built as I hurried down the stairs and out to the front of the hospital where there was a taxi. I could have called one of the guys to come pick me up, but this would be quicker. I didn't even have my purse, but I could pay when I got back to the cabin.

I sat in the back seat, impatient for the miles to fly by. This had to be it.

The driver pulled up outside the cabin behind Liam's and Rowe's cars. "Just wait, someone will be back to pay you."

The driver nodded, and I thanked him before getting out.

Inside the cabin, a flurry of activity all stopped when I walked in.

"Mommy!" Ripley yelled, racing down the hallway, arms outstretched.

Oh, how my heart had missed him. "Hey, sweetie."

Rowe and Liam both appeared from the bedroom in suits, Isaac in Liam's arms.

I nearly swooned at the sight of them.

Or maybe that was just the exhaustion talking.

But either way, they looked damn good. Liam with a baby did all sorts of wonderful things to my insides.

"You're home," Liam yelped. "Tori..."

"Is awake and talking. I left her with Perry."

They both breathed a sigh of relief, and Liam gazed down at Isaac. "Hear that, little man? Your mommy is nearly all better."

Rowe went to pay the taxi driver, while Liam set Isaac down in a rocker I hadn't seen before. He dropped a kiss below my ear as he passed, pausing only long enough to whisper, "I want one."

Warmth spilled through me. Because I did, too. Once upon a time, with another man, in another life, those words might have made me feel inferior. But Liam knew me. And I knew him. And when he said I want one, he didn't mean he wanted me to carry his child. He knew I couldn't. When Liam said I want one, he meant he wanted a child with me. No matter whose genes that baby was made of.

I turned into him, kissing the stubble on his cheek. "Me, too."

He grinned cheekily at me, like we were naughty kids, hatching a plot, even though Rowe had come back in and heard every word. He just shook his head with a smile that said he was up for it, too. "Go get ready. Nobody is having any more babies until we give back the one we currently have, and we get Heath out of jail."

I practically skipped down the hall to quickly shower and dress, and then we were all piling into Liam's car, me squished between the two baby seats. "Gonna need a bigger car," I complained.

"Gonna need a bigger house," Rowe commented idly.

"I'd sell my place." Liam spun his hand around the steering wheel. "If we wanted to get something bigger."

My gaze bounced between them, eyes wide. "We, as in all of us?"

He glanced over his shoulder at me, a puzzled expression on his handsome face. "Yeah, of course."

I settled back between the baby seats, silently stoked with this revelation.

We dropped the kids off at the house of one of Liam and Rowe's baseball teammates. I hadn't met either of them, but I trusted that Liam and Rowe knew them well enough to leave Ripley with them. They had a little girl around his age, and within a minute the two of them had run off out to the backyard where apparently there was a clubhouse.

It was only a short ride from there to the courthouse, and I was fine until I stepped inside the doors and remembered the last time I was here.

I gripped Liam's hand. "He's going to get out, right?"

Liam nodded. "I'm confident."

I stared up at him, but he refused to meet my gaze. Confident wasn't a definite yes, and that set my fingers trembling. But I planted myself in the front row, the same seats we'd occupied at his last case. Only this time, Liam sat beside me, unable to be Heath's lawyer when we had pending charges against us as well.

Linda, Liam's boss, already sat behind the desk in front of us, waiting for Heath to arrive. She sat with her back ramrod straight, not looking left or right, her entire focus centered on the judge's seat.

Rowe leaned across me and whispered to Liam, "Please tell me we didn't get the same judge as last time?"

Liam wiped his palms on his pants. "No. We got Judge Cardinal."

I didn't like the way he suddenly looked nervous. "Should we be worried?"

"He's known for being sharp-tongued and direct to the point. I don't know whether that will work in our favor or not."

"Fuck." Rowe slumped back against his seat. "I can't take this. I feel like I'm going to have a stroke from the anticipation."

I knew what he meant.

I just wanted this over with.

The door at the back of the courtroom opened, and

Heath was led in. He sought us out with his eyes, but if he was happy, sad, or terrified, I had no idea. His expression was completely blank.

I was all three on his behalf. I clutched Rowe's and Liam's hands as the judge took his seat and the proceedings began.

Things moved much faster than last time, and it was mostly Linda explaining the case to the court. There were a few witnesses called forward, but the judge never gave anything away. He watched and listened without his attention wandering for a moment, his mouth pulled into a grim line.

By the time he was ready to give his verdict, I'd twisted my hands so badly they were pink and sore.

He banged his gavel and folded his arms across his chest, his attention fixed solely on Heath and no one else. "Mr. Michaelson. It's clear to me you've suffered some terrible injustices at the hands of our police department. On behalf of the entire community, I feel we owe you an apology."

My heart fluttered, and I gripped Liam and Rowe tighter.

The judge stroked a hand over his graying beard. "Clearly, the murder charges are dropped. All that we're left with is the fact you managed to escape from a maximum-security prison. That holds a ten-year sentence."

"I'm aware, Your Honor," Heath replied respectfully.

He sighed heavily. "Despite the circumstances that led to you being incarcerated in the first place, the fact is, you did commit a crime by breaking out. And for that, I regretfully, find you guilty."

My stomach sank. "What? No!"

Rowe couldn't be silenced either. His shout of anger and frustration mingled with mine until the judge closed his eyes and motioned for us to sit down. When we didn't, he banged his gavel and barked the order more sternly.

Linda glared and hissed at us. "Sit down and shut up!"

But I didn't listen until Heath turned around. His sad eyes pleaded with us to stop.

They hit me right in the gut. This wasn't fair. None of it was fair. But because he'd silently asked us to, we sat in unison.

"As I was trying to say..." Judge Cardinal glared at us again. "I find you guilty of the charges brought against you today. And I am ready to pass sentencing on those charges now."

Rowe dropped his head into his hands.

The vise around my chest was so tight I could barely breathe.

"Heath Michaelson, on the charge of escaping a federal prison, I find you guilty. I sentence you to a term of two months, three weeks, and three days." He lifted his arm and peered at his watch. "And seven minutes."

The judge leveled Heath with a look. "If you haven't already worked it out, or for your cheer squad in the back there, that's time already served. You're a free man, Mr. Michaelson."

Tears appeared and rolled down my face as Heath spun around, staring at us with wide eyes. And then I was running into his arms. The hip-height barrier created a wall between us, but Heath lifted me over it, sweeping me into his arms, his forehead pressed to mine. "I'm free," he whispered.

I touched my lips to his, my grin so wide it hurt. "I love you."

"Not even close to as much as I love you."

Rowe got his turn for a hug that was so hard it was like

boulders crashing against each other. Rowe turned his lips to Heath's ear, murmuring something too low for me to hear. Heath jerked back, looking at him in surprise, then crashed his mouth to Rowe's. Liam's hug came last, and it was full of a different sort of love. One that said we did it, we're here, and that this was all finally over.

The judge cleared his throat, and we all stopped. He had some papers clutched in his hand, and he peered down as he read from them. "The three of you are Mae Donovan, Rowe Pritchard, and Liam Banks. Is that correct?"

We all paused to nod. "Yes, Your Honor."

"I've just been reading over the charges brought against you for aiding and abetting a wanted fugitive." He peered over the top of his glasses. "You truly believed in this man so much that you not only helped him escape a prison, but then kept him hidden for weeks?"

I didn't dare say anything, Linda's warning to keep my mouth shut still ringing in my ears.

"Yes, Your Honor. We did believe in his innocence that thoroughly. We were also the ones to bring forward the real killer." Liam addressed the judge as confidently as he did when he was defending a client. Even though this time, it was his own hide on the line.

"I see." The man shuffled his papers, tapping them on the desk so they all fell into a neat pile. "I'll be recommending these cases be dismissed. I don't see any point wasting the court's time when the three of you were the only ones who seemed to see sense in this case. I'll also be requesting legal action to be taken against certain individuals within the police and judicial services." He stood, straightening his robe. "To all of you, I apologize for what you've gone through."

I swallowed hard so I could reply. "Thank you."

He nodded, then smiled. "Well, go on. Go enjoy your lives."

I intended to do just that. I stared at the three men I loved more than anything in this world and put my hands out to them. Then the four of us walked out of the court.

Free.

EPILOGUE
MAE

"I can't believe that just happened." Liam laughed to himself. "I've never seen anything like it."

Rowe had run his hands through his hair so many times it stuck up at odd angles. "I still don't believe we actually just walked out of that courtroom, and now there's nothing hanging over us. No psychopath trying to take our child. No pending charges, murder or otherwise. No prisons—"

"Except the one we work in."

Rowe shrugged. "Gotta pay the bills somehow. But do you know how much better I'll feel going there knowing that Heath isn't sitting in our cabin just waiting for the cops to show up?"

"Vincent still might," I added cautiously.

None of us had seen him since that night. Rowe and Liam had gone looking for evidence of the murder that had taken place and had come back claiming that they couldn't find anything even remotely amiss. It was like it had never even happened. If I hadn't seen it with my own two eyes, I would have thought I dreamed it.

Heath beamed at me, and I shifted on the back seat so

we were closer. I'd always thought him beautiful, but there had been a sadness in him. I was sure I'd never seen him truly happy.

Until today.

He picked up my hand, slowly bringing it to his mouth. While Rowe and Liam chattered out their relief in the front seats, Heath kissed my fingertips, my knuckles, and then my palms. Every touch was featherlight, and yet each one told me exactly how much he loved me. "Thank you."

I leaned back into the comfortable leather of the seat. "You should be thanking Linda. Or that judge. But I don't think he'd appreciate this sort of thank you as much as I do."

Heath smiled against my hand. "Thank you for not giving up. I don't know why you believed me. But I'm glad you did."

I drew my hand to his cheeks. "Because I know you."

That was all I needed to say. I knew him. I knew that he was good, no matter what the evidence said. I knew he never would have hurt Jayela, even if he had been mad at her. Just like I knew he'd never hurt me.

"Do you think she knows?" he murmured.

I knew what he meant. "I have no doubt. I've felt her presence so many times since this all happened. Each time it urged me on to find the truth. "

"And now?"

I smiled. "She's quiet. She's at peace."

He closed his eyes briefly, and I knew he was thinking of the version of Jayela he'd once loved. "I want that for her."

I did, too. And now she had it.

There were other things I wanted for myself, though. Things of a much more tangible nature. I leaned forward, sticking my head between the two front seats. "Can Steve and Alora have the kids for a bit longer?"

"I thought the case would go a lot longer than it did, so I organized for them to have them all day. We have hours to spare." Liam glanced over his shoulder at me. "Whatever shall we do with them?"

I wriggled my eyebrows suggestively. "I have a few ideas."

Heath's gaze turned heated. "Does one of them involved you taking your panties off right now?"

It hadn't, but heat instantly surged through me. "We aren't even home yet."

"I've been back in prison for days, and I just found out I'm never going to have to go back there. Mae, when we get home, I don't even want to think about having to take your clothes off. I want you ready for me by the time we pull in the driveway."

My breath hitched. Liam and Rowe went still in the front seat, but my gaze was trained on Heath.

I would have given him anything he wanted in that moment.

I drew my skirt up to my knees and then slipped my fingers beneath the soft fabric. At my hips, I tucked my fingers in the sides of my panties and lifted my ass so I could draw them down my legs.

They hadn't seen anything, my skirt had covered it all, but Heath put a hand out, a silent demand for me to turn over my underwear to him.

I did so, squeezing my thighs together, while he ran his fingers over the silky lace of my panties. "You're wet already."

I nodded. I always was, whenever they were around. I

was a constant state of low simmering need that was always ready for them, just like they were always ready for me.

My core throbbed at the thought of getting back to our cabin.

I already knew what would happen once we got there, and I was breathless in anticipation. I wriggled on the seat, trying to get some relief.

"Fuck, Mae," Rowe groaned. "I can practically smell how hot you are right now." He cupped his dick, rubbing it through his pants.

If he could, then so could I. The fabric of my skirt was so thin and floaty. I put my hand between my legs, spreading them wider so I could touch myself through it. I found my clit and applied pressure to it, in just the way I liked.

A low growl started up in the back of Heath's throat, but he made no move to take over. His eyes held promises that I was probably not even going to make it inside the front door before he was inside me.

I could give him a show until then, though. I leaned back on the seat, adjusting my posture slightly so I had better access. I slowly drew my skirt up so it settled around my hips, flashing all of them how naked I was beneath. I pushed my fingers between my folds, gathering arousal on my fingers and pushing them up inside me.

It wasn't even close to as good as when they did it, but it took the edge off, and I enjoyed the power I wielded over them in that moment. I closed my eyes and let myself do what came naturally, gradually building the desire into a budding orgasm.

We got back to the cabin with my fingers still deep inside my slit, my head thrown back, and my hips rolling with need. I barely even noticed Liam stop the car, or Heath get out and slam his way around to my side, throwing open the door.

For a moment, he just watched me. My legs trembled with need, and I pumped into my body faster, trying to find a friction point I couldn't quite reach.

Heath's growl became a roar. He unclipped my seat belt, grabbed my legs, and twisted them so I faced him standing outside. He yanked me forward so my ass was on the edge of the seat, and then he parted my knees to stand between them.

I hiked my skirt up for him as I lay back across the seats, knowing he needed me, hot and hard and fast.

Exactly how I needed him

"Your pussy is so fucking sweet. Look at you, always ready for me."

He yanked down the fly on his suit, taking out his thick cock. His fingers dug into my thighs and he drove inside me.

It was all I needed to fall over the edge after working myself up on the way home. I clamped down on him while he pounded into me, his hips unrelenting until my orgasm subsided. He lay his body over mine, kissing me deep, his tongue plunging into my mouth, owning mine while he gathered me to his chest. I wrapped my legs around him, holding him inside me while I rode out the last of my orgasm tremors on his still-hard erection.

He managed to get me out of the car without smashing either of our heads and carried me up the stairs to the cabin, his cock still deep inside me. "You didn't come," I murmured, as he lay me out on the bed.

"Not yet. I will, but not yet."

The other two had followed us in, both their gazes hot and needy. Liam had his shirt already half undone, and I stood, letting my skirt fall back in place. I helped him undress while Heath pushed Rowe up against a wall.

Liam ran his fingers through the back of my hair, then tugged sharply on the strands, tilting my head back so he could take my mouth while I undid the half a dozen tiny buttons on his shirt.

His shirt fell away, showing off the perfectly sculpted abs I couldn't get enough of, but had to abandon all too quickly in order to get his belt undone. His suit pants dropped to the floor followed by his underwear. My top was abandoned soon after, my skirt shoved off my hips. Liam kissed a hungry path across my collarbone while Heath ground against Rowe, the two of them kissing deeply, having a reunion of their own.

They were so hot together. Heath's tattoos moved, his muscles flexing and bunching. They were almost savage in the way they needed each other, and it was so raw and primal, it was impossible not to watch.

It was only made better by the man getting me naked at the same time. Liam's fingers found the clasp on my bra and dragged the straps off my shoulders, leaving me as naked as he was. I stared up into his eyes. We'd started all this, the two of us together. At times when I wondered why all of this had happened, I then looked at Liam and I knew. Without Heath's wrongful imprisonment, I would have never reconnected with Liam. And I would have never taken that job in the prison. I would have never found my true calling as a teacher, and I wouldn't have ever met Rowe.

It had been hard, but it had all happened for a reason.

And now we got to reap the benefits.

I dropped to the floor, taking Liam's cock in my mouth.

His fingers tightened on the back of my head, and he groaned, leaning back against a wall for support.

He was thick and hard. Not as big as Rowe, but then nobody but porn stars were. Liam was perfectly sized for my hand and mouth to work in unison. And he knew exactly what he was doing. He let me set the pace at first, but once I started making moany little noises, turned on from what we were doing, his hips took over. He thrust into my mouth, letting it hit the back of my throat. My scalp prickled deliciously, and he seemed to know exactly how much pressure to apply to make it feel good, rather than hurt.

I closed my eyes, feeling sexy and confident in the knowledge of how wanted I was.

How loved.

Liam worshipped me, even when I was the one on my knees bringing him to orgasm.

I was so lost in the power I held that I didn't notice Rowe slide between my legs. He lay flat on his back behind me, his face between my thighs.

"Widen your legs and sit on my face. I need to taste you."

Liam groaned and pulled from my mouth.

I didn't want to stop sucking him. He got down on his knees, and I leaned forward, resting my hands on the rug so I was on all fours. Rowe forced his shoulders between my legs, and they were so broad, they opened me right up so my pussy was right over his face.

"I said sit, Mae. Not fucking hover."

I hesitated. I was never going to be a tiny stick of a woman. My thighs had cellulite. As did my ass. My tummy had rolls. I'd suffocate the man if I truly sat on him.

Liam chuckled like he could read my mind. "Trust me, he wants to fucking die buried in your pussy. There'd be no better way to go."

Rowe proved it by banding one thick, muscled arm around my thigh and yanking me down. My wet pussy collided with his open mouth, and the moan I let out was entirely indecent and worthy of an adult film.

I smothered my cries of pleasure by taking Liam into my mouth again. I sucked and swallowed, loving the way he gave up and fucked my mouth without the fear of hurting me. My moans grew louder with Rowe's talented tongue delving deep between my folds, spearing me with his tongue before pulling back to lap at my clit. The little bundle of nerves sent pleasure flying through my entire body, until my hips rocked over his face and he pressed two fingers up inside for me to ride.

Rowe's groans met my own, and from the way he moved beneath me, I knew he had Heath working him toward an orgasm, while he built me up to mine. I pulled off Liam's dick for a moment to glance over my shoulder at what Heath and Rowe were doing and nearly came on the spot. Heath had Rowe's hips jacked up, legs wrapped around his waist. Heath drove his erection into Rowe's body, all while pumping Rowe's dick with his free hand. When I looked up at Liam, his gaze was trained on them, too, and his precum hit the back of my throat, salty and teasing at the main event.

"Jesus Christ," he murmured. "Say 'I' if you're on the verge of having your mind blown."

I would have laughed if Rowe hadn't chosen that moment to add a third finger into my core, stretching me so good the orgasm I'd been battling back had no choice but to come barreling forward. I screamed out as my second orgasm hit me, twice as hard as the first. I ground down on Rowe's face, no longer self-conscious.

Liam's eyes flared, and he fucked my mouth harder and faster while I yelled around him. His hot cum came in a spurt, a satisfying explosion that told me I'd pleased my man. I swallowed, staring up at him, knowing it turned him on.

He pulled from my mouth the moment he was done, but my orgasm lasted longer. Rowe guided me through the entire thing, until my legs trembled too much and I collapsed to the side.

Heath and Rowe together were a thing of beauty. There was no shame in their joining. No hiding. Heath's abs flexed as he drove into Rowe's ass, his hand keeping the same time on Rowe's cock. Rowe threw his head back, his eyes closed, back arching, his fingers digging into the rug at his back. "Fuck!" he yelled.

His cum spurted all over his lower abs, and then higher across his chest when Heath didn't stop jerking him. Heath roared out his own orgasm, coming deep in Rowe's body, his last few thrusts powerful and raw.

We hadn't even made it to the bed.

All four of us sprawled in various positions on the floor, our labored breaths mingling.

"Anybody got a smoke?" Liam asked. "I could use one right now."

"You don't smoke." Rowe's arm was slung over his eyes, his chest and abs glistening with cum.

"Doesn't matter. Still feels like the thing to do."

I knew what he meant. The relaxation that coursed through my body was like nothing else. I imagined the rich swirl of tobacco might be quite nice right now. If I didn't value the health of my lungs, that was. Which I did, so I was content to just lie there and watch them instead.

At some point, Rowe and Heath disappeared into the bathroom, the shower starting up again. Liam and I found our way to the big bed we'd created on the floor, that was really more of a love nest. I found him beneath the sheet again, working him 'til he was hard and then letting him cover my body with his. When Rowe and Heath returned, fresh and clean, they took turns as well, making love to me one at a time, kissing me constantly, whispering how beautiful I was and how loved.

I had more orgasms than I could count. More I love yous than any one woman should be entitled to in a lifetime, let alone in one afternoon. I reconnected with each of them and reminded them all that they were so very loved in return.

I would never get enough of the three of them.

It was a good thing they were mine.

---

*S*teve and Alora, Rowe and Liam's baseball friends, called Liam's phone as the evening began to approach. All four of us were still lying around, naked in bed, and Liam reached over and grabbed it, looking at the screen. He smiled, flashing it at us. "The real world and parenthood is calling. Time to wrap this gang bang up."

Rowe kicked him hard enough to shove him off the edge of the mattress and onto the floor. He slumped onto the rug while I giggled at their antics. Heath had his head resting on my belly, and I stroked my fingers through his hair, enjoying his blissed-out expression He'd been all frowns and hard lines for too long.

Liam read the message from his spot on the floor. "Oh, this is interesting. Steve said Ripley and Ivy are begging for a sleepover. They're saying they'll keep Isaac for the night as well if we want. Alora has baby fever and isn't ready to give him up."

Rowe glanced at me. "You good with that, Mama?"

A thrill ran through me as I nodded. I knew Rowe wouldn't leave the kids anywhere that wasn't safe for them and I loved the idea that Ripley had made a friend. A real one his age...not just the escaped convict with a penchant for murder who roamed our woods at will. As much as I'd come to care for Vincent, and to realize he was no danger to my family, I didn't want him to be Ripley's only friend. We'd be able to send him back to daycare now, so having him away from us for a little bit was good practice, both for him and me. "That sounds amazing. Tell them yes, Liam."

Liam fired off a text and then dive-bombed back onto the bed, half landing on me. A twinge of pain shot through me.

Liam must have seen my expression. "Shit, I'm sorry. Are you okay?"

I kissed the worry off his face. "I'm fine. Let's get up and have a nice dinner, though. We've been in bed all afternoon. I need to eat before we come back here again."

They all agreed, and lazily we all got up and pulled on clothes.

The guys insisted on making me dinner, so I sat outside on the porch swing with a book, nestled amongst the bright-colored cushions I'd bought. I swung in the evening breeze, losing myself in the romance of the story. My core still tingled from the complete and thorough workout it'd had this afternoon. I was a little sore. My thigh muscles ached, probably from being wrapped around men all afternoon, but when the low grumbling of pain kicked up deep in my belly, I groaned. My periods were so irregular, but those cramps were always a telltale sign. I sighed and got up to check my underwear. No signs of Aunt Flo arriving yet, but I put on a pad because I knew it was coming.

We ate dinner outside and then hung out around the

bonfire again. There was none of the sexual antics that had happened last time we did this, though. By the time it got truly dark, my stomach cramps had intensified, and I felt like shit.

Rowe paused on his way to the cabin to get another round of beers from the refrigerator. I declined his offer, but he stooped, studying my face in the firelight. "Are you okay?"

I forced a smile. "I'm fine." I wasn't going to be the one who ruined our party.

He brushed a strand of hair behind my ear and tipped my chin up with two fingers beneath it. "No, you're not. What's wrong?"

I screwed up my face. "Girl stuff."

I hadn't had a period in months, which was pretty typical with my polycystic ovaries. But it meant the guys had been spared the drama.

"Oh." He stood back. "What can I do? I can get you chocolate? Painkillers?"

I held my hands out to him and let him pull me up off my chair. "I think I'm just going to go to bed early, but both of those would be good if you want to bring them in to me."

Liam and Heath both watched on, worry etched into their faces.

"I'll come to bed with you." Heath had instantly gone into full-blown protector mode, which I loved, but unfortunately, he couldn't protect me from this.

I shook my head. "Don't be silly. It's barely eight, and you just got out of prison. Stay. Have fun. All of you. I'll be fine. This is nothing new."

None of them looked convinced, but Heath and Liam sat back down while Rowe walked me to the house. I got myself settled in bed, while he rummaged around the kitchen for painkillers and chocolate. He brought me both, along with a glass of water.

I swallowed the pain relief but left the chocolate, suddenly too exhausted for it now that I was in my comfy bed. He hovered in the doorway, but I waved him away. "Go!"

He trudged off, but when the cabin door opened, the sound of Liam's and Heath's laughter floated back in, and I was glad they were all out there celebrating.

My body just had shitty timing.

I tried to close my eyes and sleep, but the pains never eased. The pain moved, becoming more acute on my right-hand side, but that wasn't uncommon either. Often one side hurt more than the other, and I knew I just had to ride it out.

Sometime around midnight, the door crashed open, and the three of them tumbled back inside. Even curled up on my side in agony, the sound of their drunken laughter made me happy.

They were trying to be quiet but doing a piss-poor job of it. Somebody opened the bedroom door, and the light from the hallway spilled over me.

All three of them froze.

"What the fuck, Mae!" Heath dropped down onto the mattress beside me.

I groaned as the mattress bounced, sending shooting pain through my body once more. "I'm fine," I repeated, though by now, my protests were weak.

Liam already had his phone out. "I'm calling an ambulance. You are not fine."

Something inside me warned to stay quiet. Because I wasn't fine. The pain was intense to the point I could barely breathe.

Liam barked the address and then my details into the

phone, suddenly sounding completely sober. "She's in a lot of abdominal pain. She thought it was just period pain, but we think it's something more."

He paused to listen for a moment, then looked at me. "Where is the worst of the pain?"

I was too breathless to answer.

"On her right," Rowe piped up. "That's the side she's holding."

All I could do was nod limply.

"They want to know if you still have your appendix?"

I moaned. "Yes. Goddammit. Is that what this is?"

Liam grimaced. "That's what they're thinking."

Heath paced the length of the bedroom, shooting terrified glances at me. I wanted to comfort him, but I couldn't. All I could do was clutch my side and hope the ambulance had the good drugs.

Liam disappeared soon after, and Rowe wiped sweat from my brow. "I shouldn't have left you. I'm so sorry."

"Not your fault," I managed to get out.

But it didn't ease the worry on his face any. Heath was pale by the time the ambulance wail sounded from the clearing, and then Heath and Rowe were both moving aside so the paramedics, led by Liam, could get to me.

The man and woman both introduced themselves, but I couldn't retain either of their names. They moved me to a gurney, and I yelled at the pain.

"Definitely looks like an inflamed or possibly burst appendix, but we'll get her to the hospital and get her checked out. Is one of you her partner?"

"Me," all three answered in unison.

Even with the pain, it was a laughable moment.

The paramedic raised her eyebrows then looked down at me. "Lucky girl."

If I hadn't been in agony, I would have high-fived her.

She turned to the guys. "Only one of you can come in the ambulance. I'll leave it to the three of you to decide who, but we need to go quick. I don't want her appendix bursting before we get there."

"Liam, you go," Heath decided. "I'm sober enough to drive me and Rowe. We'll be right behind you."

Liam ran alongside the gurney as they wheeled me out and put me in the back of the waiting ambulance. He climbed in and sat on the seat beside my head and leaned down so he was eye level with me. He gave me a shaky smile. "At least Ripley wasn't here this time."

Thank God. The poor kid had already been traumatized enough. He didn't need to see me like this. Another stab of pain took the ability to speak, and worry coursed through me. Would I even know if my appendix had burst?

Liam held my hand all the way to the hospital, murmuring encouraging things to me and brushing back my hair from my sweaty forehead. At the hospital, he fielded as many questions as he could from the staff, all while refusing to leave my side.

A nice-looking male doctor appeared in my line of view and smiled at me. "Hey, Mae. I'm Dr. Obidsen. Think I could have a peek at your belly?"

I groaned but forced myself to move my hands out of his way.

Liam's face twisted in pain as I yelped at the doctor's touch. He stepped back, snapping off his gloves and tossed them into the trash can in the corner of the examination room. "Okay, that definitely presents like an inflamed appendix, but your partner said you had some ovary issues that you were also concerned about earlier in the evening, and I want to rule out an ectopic pregnancy, so what we'll do is get an ultrasound real quick and go from there. Sound good?"

Anything sounded better than pain right now. I nodded my consent.

A portable ultrasound machine was rolled in and my belly slathered in slimy blue goop.

The doctor looked at me apologetically. "Sorry, this is going to hurt if those drugs haven't kicked in yet, but I'll be quick."

God, I just wanted the pain to stop. Even the light touch of the gel hurt.

I closed my eyes and let Liam soothe me with his fingers massaging my palm. It did help distract me a little, and I fought to keep my attention on the patterns he was making.

The doctor glided the wand over my stomach, clicking a few things with his mouse and taking measurements. I already knew what he was going to say before he said it. The polycystic ovaries didn't hurt in the same way this did. This was definitely something new.

"Congrats, Mae. That's a lovely case of appendicitis you have there."

I groaned, though it was expected.

Liam squeezed my hand. "So what happens now? You take it out?"

"Yep, and ASAP, because that thing is ready to bust at any minute. I'm surprised you lasted at home as long as you did. They hurt."

"You don't say," I groaned.

The doctor grinned. "Don't worry, though, it's just a little laparoscopic surgery. It won't hurt you or the baby."

I froze. "The what?"

Liam's fingers gripped mine tighter.

The doctor glanced over at us in surprise. "You didn't know?"

"I can't have kids."

The doctor winked at me. "The fetus in your belly says otherwise. Good surprise or bad?"

A whole host of emotions crashed down over me, complete and all-consuming shock being the major one. I forgot the pain. All I could think about was the fact I was pregnant.

The tears that streamed down my face weren't pain related. They were pure joy.

"Good," Liam answered, his voice choked with all the emotion I was feeling. I glanced over at him and reveled in his expression. "So fucking good."

He pressed his lips to mine. "I love you both. Whether it's mine or one of the others. It doesn't matter." He grinned at the doctor. "I'm gonna be a dad!"

He said it loud enough for someone in another cubicle to yell out, "Congrats!"

The doctor chuckled, but he was already flicking off the brakes of the gurney and wheeling me away toward surgery.

The entire way I cradled my belly. No longer because of the pain, but because of the little miracle growing inside me.

"Wakey-wakey, sleepyhead."

The lights were too bright. I closed my eyes again. The next time I tried, they didn't seem quite as bad, and I managed to leave them open. It took me a minute to work out where I was, though, until Tori's familiar face came into focus.

She grinned at me, practically bouncing on her hospital

bed in excitement. "I love that you love me so much you wanted matching belly scars. We're roomies!"

My head clouded with confusion, until it all came flooding back, the pain of last night, the ambulance, and the...

I widened my eyes and clutched my stomach. "Was I in a pain-induced hallucination last night or did a doctor really tell me I was pregnant?"

She grinned and flicked her head toward the door. "Pretty sure you didn't dream it. There's three very excited daddies out there in the hall, waiting for you to wake up."

"They're here?"

She shook her head with a laugh. "You came to in the recovery room, and they brought you here, but you were asleep again by the time they let the guys in. They haven't left, though. They've been hanging around like a bad smell...oh look, they're back."

She made a 'come in' gesture to the window in the door, and when it opened, she grinned. "Baby mama is awake."

The three of them crowded in. Heath went straight for my mouth, kissing me hard, his eyes bright with a mixture of concern and excitement. "Are you okay?"

I nodded. "Liam told you?"

Rowe grinned. "As if he could have kept that quiet."

I glanced between him and Heath. "How are you feeling about it... It's a lot..."

Heath kissed me again. "Best fucking news of my life."

I couldn't stop my smile.

Liam perched at the foot of the bed, watching as Rowe moved in and kissed my forehead twice. "One for you, and one for the baby," he explained. "I'd have kissed your belly, but that might be a no-go area for a few days."

I looked to Liam. "Did their heads explode when you told them?"

He grinned. "I thought Heath was gonna bust down the surgery doors to get to you."

"I did contemplate it for a minute," Heath admitted. He shook his head in amazement, staring at my belly buried beneath the sheets. "I still can't believe it."

I couldn't either.

This was what I'd dreamed of for my entire life. In my dreams, it had only been one man sitting beside me, but how lucky was this child? To have three of the best men I'd ever met.

"Rowe immediately claimed dibs on the 'Dad' title, since that's what Ripley calls him. I'm claiming Da, and we've decided that since Heath is ancient, he gets Pops."

Tori giggled.

Heath shoved Liam in the shoulder. "I'm two years older than Rowe. Fuck off. The kid is not calling me Pops."

Their laughter echoed around me. Steve and Alora brought the boys to the hospital, and with Ripley's arms tight around my neck, my three men surrounding me, and the tiny miracle baby in my belly, there was nowhere else I'd rather be.

One day when we told the story of how we came to be, it would be full of prisons, murders, and violence. But the ending was this. Love, peace, and the family we'd all dreamed of.

It was mine.

It was ours.

And we were going to live it every day.

Free.

The End

Want to know who the baby daddy is? Need more of Vincent? Want to see who Tori's new partner is? It's all in the bonus epilogue! Get it free from the bonus material section of my website. www.ellethorpe.com

Or read on for a sneak peek of other Saint View series.

WANT MORE SAINT VIEW?

kindle
AVAILABLE

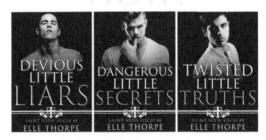

COMPLETE!

REVERSE HAREM . BULLY ROMANCE

There's a new Saint View series coming in 2022. But in the meantime, have you read the original?

You've already met Lacey, Colt, Banjo, and Rafe in this

series, but their happily ever after was full of murder, mystery, sexual tension, and hot nights between the sheets.

Read on for a sneak peek or download book 1 from Amazon/Kindle Unlimited.

LACEY

I was about to be arrested.

That was my first thought when a flash of movement outside the window caught my attention.

Extreme overreaction?

Perhaps.

But when you'd illegally let yourself into your school on a Sunday, these were the worries that plagued a girl.

Acting on instinct, I hurled myself off the piano stool and onto the floor, scuttling to the windows overlooking the quad. Maybe they hadn't seen me yet. The late afternoon sun was sinking, and perhaps, if I was lucky, the glare would temporarily blind them. I could make my escape out one of the back doors. There was an exit in the administration hall. Others in the math and history wings. Of course, not one anywhere near the music rooms. Helpful.

Ever so carefully, I lifted to peer out the window, and yelped at the face on the other side. I ducked down again, though there was no chance he hadn't seen me, what with his nose an inch from the glass.

I was totally busted. But at least it wasn't the police.

Lawson's laughter on the other side of the window made me realize how ridiculous I was being. I stood, embarrassment heating my face.

"You want to let me in?" he yelled.

I squeezed my eyes closed but nodded. "I'll meet you at the door."

Scrambling down the hall, I tried to come up with a plausible story that would result in the least amount of trouble. I still had nothing by the time I pulled open the heavy, ancient oak doors of Providence School for Girls.

My uncle stood on the other side, boxes of his work balanced precariously in his arms. He shifted beneath their weight, sending a USB stick and a pile of papers sliding off the top. They fluttered down around our ankles.

I knelt hastily, tucking the USB stick into my pocket and gathering up the runaway pages. I glanced up at his familiar face. "Before you say anything, just remember, I'm your favorite niece."

"You're my only niece," he grumbled, but there was still a hint of laughter in his voice.

I put the papers back on top, then took the box from him, lightening his load. "Which means you won't have me arrested?"

He kicked the doors closed behind him. "Well, that depends on how quickly you start explaining why you're at school on a Sunday night, instead of at Meredith's, which is where you said you were going. How did you even get in here without tripping the alarm? If you broke a window, I won't be impressed." He walked toward his office.

I hurried to keep up. "No, no. All windows are intact. I used the code."

"What? How do you even know it?"

I snorted, then remembered I was probably about to be

grounded until I turned eighteen. Which, admittedly, was only a couple of weeks away. But still. I tried to force my expression into something more suitably chastised. "Sorry. But you've been driving me to school and unlocking that door in front of me for the past three years. The code is my birthday. Just like all your passwords."

That resulted in a withering look, but I knew he wasn't really angry at me. We wove through the administration offices until we reached Lawson's, his gold-plated Principal nameplate on the door. He unlocked it, and we both dumped our boxes on the table.

Then he turned to me, folding his arms across his chest, giving me his best principal's glare. "How long have you been sneaking in here for?"

No point lying about it now. "Months."

His mouth dropped open. "To do what? Please don't say drugs. If you say drugs, I swear, I'm going to take you down to that police station myself."

I sniggered. "No. Something much worse."

"Sex? Booze? What could be worse?" He narrowed his eyes, but they crinkled at the corners. He was trying not to laugh. "Are you running some sort of illegal cock fighting ring out of the gym?"

I raised an eyebrow. "No, but wow. Thanks for the ideas. If college doesn't work out for me, I'll be sure to consider those options. I've just been practicing in the music rooms. All alone. No sex, drugs, or farmyard animals of any kind."

My uncle frowned and grumbled. I'd won him over. He knew how important music was to me. "So. No police?"

His expression morphed into fatherly affection. He put his arm around my shoulders and kissed the top of my head. "What do you think? I'm hardly going to call the police when I'd be the one to pay your bail. I've got work to do. Go on, go do your thing. But set your alarm and meet me back here in two hours. You know how you lose track of time when you play."

I breathed a sigh of relief. He so rarely lost his temper, and almost never at me. I couldn't have stood it if he were angry. I kissed his stubbled cheek. "Love you..."

Not for the first time, the word 'Dad' formed on my lips. But at the last moment, I swallowed it down. Instead, I gave him a grateful wave and hurried back to the music rooms.

When I got there, I shut the door behind me and made a beeline for the piano, running my palm over its gleaming black surface. This was my happy place. And it filled something inside me in a way that nothing else did.

Pulling my phone from my pocket, I set the alarm so I wouldn't be late.

Then I pressed my fingers to the keys and closed my eyes, the first lilting notes lifting to the air. Time ceased to exist until a blaring alarm cut through my bubble.

I lost focus, hit the wrong key, and the entire song unraveled. "Dammit!" I slammed the keys hard.

I glanced at my phone and silenced the obnoxious beeping. In the blink of an eye, two hours had passed, and the real world came rushing back in. The sun had set, leaving me in near darkness, and I hadn't even noticed. Patting the top of the piano like it was a dog who'd just completed a new trick, I murmured, "Until next time."

In the corridor, I stopped dead as I caught a whiff of something unpleasant. "What the hell..." I murmured, wrinkling my nose. I took a few more steps, then froze.

Smoke.

I peered into the darkness, trying to remain calm while my brain scrambled to find logical conclusions. It was nearing the end of summer. People could be having barbecues nearby, and the smoke might have just blown in on the breeze. Or perhaps a wildfire had started. The smoke alarms weren't going off. Nor were the sprinklers. I picked up the pace, heading for the admin offices. The entire time, I scrabbled with my thoughts, fighting against the obvious. Pushing myself to believe those excuses, because what was right in front of my eyes was too scary to comprehend. I rounded a corner and stopped dead.

There was no denying it anymore.

The building was filling with thick, acrid smoke.

Something instinctual pushed me forward, and my feet went with it, instead of listening to the panicked voice in my head screaming to turn and run in the opposite direction. I fumbled for my phone, pulled it out, and dialed nine-one-one. Smoke invaded my chest and eyes. I coughed, trying to clear it while fear clawed its way up my spine.

"Fire!" I gasped when the operator answered. "Providence School for Girls." Racking coughs took over. I hung up, but the farther I got, the thicker the smoke became, until it didn't matter if I spoke or not. I held my arm over my mouth and nose, trying to keep it out, but it was a losing battle. My lungs protested, but I moved on, my pace increasing until I was running. I skidded around the corner, bashing my hipbone on the wall. The darkness was disorienting. The visibility next to nothing. I couldn't see farther than a few steps ahead of me.

"Lawson!" I yelled, immediately regretting it when smoke filled my mouth and nose. It got thicker with every step. I coughed again and ran my hands over the wall where I thought the light switch should be. I came up empty, my nails scratching over nothing but drywall.

I spun around, confused now at exactly where I was. I needed to get to my uncle. I knew, that if there was a fire, he would have come for me. Called me. He knew where I was. And there was only one way to get there. We couldn't have missed each other. I pushed my legs harder, not certain that I was even heading in the right direction, but I had to try.

Suddenly, the room around me opened up, and I nearly wept with relief as I recognized the foyer. But there was no time for that.

I'd found the source of the smoke.

Flames licked the walls.

"Lawson!" I yelled again, tasting ash. Panic surged, adrenaline kicking in and powering my movements. My brain short-circuited, whether from lack of air or fear, I didn't know. The one thing I was certain of was that I couldn't lose another parent. I couldn't add my uncle to the broken part of me that had existed ever since my birth parents' disappearance. He was the only father I really remembered. And he wouldn't have left without me. I knew that without a doubt. He wouldn't have left me there to die.

Which meant he was still inside.

I ran in a crouch toward the flames. They grew with every second that passed. "Laws—" I couldn't even get his name out this time before the lack of air stole my voice. I held my breath and rushed toward his office, throwing open doors as I went and dodging the deadly heat.

I skidded to a stop at the glass window of the principal's office. A scream curled up my throat but came out silently.

Lawson's still form lay facedown on the floorboards.

Flames billowed up around him, higher in here than anywhere else. They crawled across the ceiling, like slithering beasts of orange fury. I bashed on the window so hard it should have broken, desperately yelping my uncle's name between racking bouts of coughing.

Overhead, a beam cracked.

Sparks flew and I flinched away. I tried again, lunging for the door, but the heat drove me back. Tears streamed down my face. "Help," I croaked.

I couldn't save him alone. He was right there, the flames getting ever closer, and I couldn't reach him. I stumbled back the way I'd come, dropping to my knees and crawling when my feet wouldn't take another step. My eyes stung. My gaze flitted around the smoke-filled room, but my head grew cloudy.

With a sudden certainty, I realized we were both going to die.

There was no way out.

I closed my eyes. At least the last thing I'd done was something I loved. I remembered the way it felt to have my fingers flying over the piano keys, the song soaring, not only in my ears but in my heart. When the flames took me, that's where I'd be in my head. In the place I was happiest. The only place I had true peace.

Something grabbed me.

Not something, someone.

I dragged myself back into the present. There was somebody else here. Someone who could help. Hope surged within me.

"My uncle," I choked out.

Startled by hands on my bare skin, and my body being lifted from the floor, I tried to force my stinging eyes open. But my vision was so blurred I couldn't make out a face. I turned into the person's chest, and my gaze focused instead on the thing closest to me. Letters floated across my vision, a mere inch from my nose.

The man—it had to be a man, his body had none of the softer curves of a woman—didn't say anything, but gripped me tighter while he moved through the crumbling building.

Heat seared at my legs, my arms, my face. I couldn't do a thing but fist my fingers into the material of his shirt and hold on. The embroidered feel of the letters scratched, in contrast with the softness of the fabric.

He muttered something that sounded like, "Hold on, Lacey."

A thought floated through my head, but it was too hard to grasp. I wanted to chase it, grab it, and force it to make sense. But I was too tired. I watched it go, disappearing into a smoke tendril.

My body jolted against his with each step. I wanted him to run. I wanted him to get me out of this place, but it all just seemed impossible now. Everything hurt. My lungs screamed in pain. It was too hard to hold on. My grip on his shirt loosened.

"Lacey!" he yelled, but his voice was far away.

I closed my eyes and let the darkness take me.

Get Devious Little Liars on Amazon/Kindle Unlimited.

ALSO BY ELLE THORPE

Saint View Prison series (Reverse harem, romantic suspense.)

*Locked Up Liars (Saint View Prison, #1)

*Solitary Sinners (Saint View Prison, #2)

*Fatal Felons (Saint View Prison, #3)

Saint View High series (Reverse harem, romantic suspense. Complete series)

*Devious Little Liars (Saint View High, #1)

*Dangerous Little Secrets (Saint View High, #2)

*Twisted Little Truths (Saint View High, #3)

Saint View Strip series (Male/Female romantic suspense)

*Evil Enemy - Boston and Eve's story coming in 2022

Dirty Cowboy series (Male/Female small town cowboys. Complete series)

*Talk Dirty, Cowboy (Dirty Cowboy, #1)

*Ride Dirty, Cowboy (Dirty Cowboy, #2)

*Sexy Dirty Cowboy (Dirty Cowboy, #3)

*25 Reasons to Hate Christmas and Cowboys (a Dirty Cowboy bonus novella, set before Talk Dirty, Cowboy but can be read as a standalone, holiday romance)

Buck Cowboys series (Spin off from the Dirty Cowboy series)

*Buck Cowboys (Buck Cowboys, #1)

*Buck You! (Buck Cowboys, #2)

*Book 3 coming in 2022!

The Only You series (Contemporary Romance, series complete)

*Only the Positive (Only You, #1) - Reese and Low.

*Only the Perfect (Only You, #2) - Jamison.

*Only the Truth - (Only You, bonus novella) - Bree.

*Only the Negatives (Only You, #3) - Gemma.

*Only the Beginning (Only You, #4) - Bianca and Riley.

*Only You boxset

*Only the Lies. Free when you join Elle's reader newsletter below.

Add your email address here to be the first to know when new books are available!

www.ellethorpe.com/newsletter

Join Elle Thorpe's readers group on Facebook!

www.facebook.com/groups/ellethorpesdramallamas

ACKNOWLEDGMENTS

Wow. Another trilogy down. What a ride that was. A big thank you to all my readers. Whether you've been here for eighteen books or just these three, I'm glad you found me. If you want to hang out some more, make sure you join my Facebook readers group. I love getting to know you all.

Thank you to my family - Jira, Thomas, Flick, and Heidi. I wrote 2 out of 3 of these books while in lockdown, which made a frustrating time even more difficult. But I do all of this for you four. Thanks for putting up with my long hours, average dinners, and I'm sorry I was a sucky homeschool teacher. It's much better when mum gets to work while you're at school, huh?

Thank you to my author besties, Jo and Zoe. And to my awesome editors, Emmy and Karen. Thank you Wander and Jeff for the awesome cover image.

Huge shoutout to Dana, Louise, and Sam for beta reading this one. Your feedback and enthusiasm is always appreciated

And finally, lots of love to my Promo and ARC team. I love you guys. Thank you for jumping on board with whatever I throw at you.

Love, Elle xxx

ABOUT THE AUTHOR

USA Today bestselling author, Elle Thorpe, lives on the sunny east coast of Australia. When she's not writing stories full of kissing, she's a wife and mummy to three tiny humans. She's also official ball thrower to one slobbery dog named Rollo. Yes, she named a female dog after a dirty hot character on Vikings. Don't judge her. Elle is a complete and utter fangirl at heart, obsessing over The Walking Dead and Outlander to an unhealthy degree. But she wouldn't change a thing.

You can find her on Facebook or Instagram(@ellethorpe-books or hit the links below!) or at her website www.ellethorpe.com. If you love Elle's work, please consider joining her Facebook fan group, Elle Thorpe's Drama Llamas or joining her newsletter here. www.ellethorpe.com/newsletter

facebook.com/ellethorpebooks

instagram.com/ellethorpebooks

goodreads.com/ellethorpe

pinterest.com/ellethorpebooks

Made in United States
North Haven, CT
14 August 2022

22704825R00211